Hanuspx

rvazquez_md

_jalyn_curtis

TheDellverator3132

the_skunk

?100pppcyc9p

bluebird

stinkysmellery

_jalyn_curtis

TheDeliverator3132

Lou_Harding

qc476rbtwe?

_bluebird

stinkysmellery

rebeccalsteiner2s

xxe243xug

Lou_Harding

qc476rbtwe?

Lackiechan

_thestetson

> praise for *rekt*

"Alex Gonzalez fearlessly plumbs the depths of our present and future online hell and the result is a visionary book that is at once pensive, rollicking, and truly, bone-deep unsettling. rekt is an absolute stunner."

> —**Paul Tremblay**, *New York Times* bestselling author of *Horror Movie* and *A Head Full of Ghosts*

"The best horror debut in years. As dark as 3 a.m. despair, Alex Gonzalez's *rekt* is the depraved, bleeding edge of the genre, combining the intimate, personal dread of Paul Tremblay with the merciless grotesquerie of Eric LaRocca. Like the novel's main character, you won't be able to look away."

> —**Christopher Golden**, *New York Times* bestselling author of *Road of Bones* and *The House of Last Resort*

"*rekt* goes past the 'dark web' and into online corners that pose a threat to life and sanity. Oddly enough, it also makes me want to visit these corners. A great exploration of the dangers and seductions of the internet."

> —**Poppy Z. Brite**, author of *Exquisite Corpse*

"There are two versions of you: Before you read Alex Gonzalez's *rekt* and after you read it. In fact, this is not a mere book. It's a fucking experience to survive, to be endured. Like Danielewski's *House of Leaves* and Palahniuk's *Haunted*, *rekt* feels like a spiritual successor to those masterpieces with the frightening ability to actually harm the reader—to eviscerate them with such a singular style, such masterful prose, and such utter mercilessness. This is a bleak, vicious, and harrowing examination of grief, internet lore, and one young man's descent into the depths of depravity. Gonzalez's debut is one of the most shocking and cold-blooded novels I've ever read."

—**Eric LaRocca**, Bram Stoker Award–nominated and Splatterpunk Award–winning author of *Things Have Gotten Worse Since We Last Spoke*

"*rekt* is a nihilistic annihilation of the senses, a David Fincher–directed *Faces of Death* for the digital age, a novocaine *120 Gigabytes of Sodom* by a debut de Sade that leaves the reader uncomfortably numb. This book takes just as much from you as you take from it. Alex Gonzalez left me utterly gutted."

—**Clay McLeod Chapman**, author of *What Kind of Mother* and *Ghost Eaters*

> rekt

> Alex Gonzalez

EREWHON

an imprint of Kensington Publishing Corp.

erewhonbooks.com

Content notice: Graphic violence and death, anti-Latinx racial slurs, homophobic slurs, ableist slurs, murder, body horror, self-harm, alcoholism, sexual predatory behavior, child abuse, torture and physical assault, and mentions of rape (non-graphic).

EREWHON BOOKS are published by:
Kensington Publishing Corp.
900 Third Avenue
New York, NY 10022
erewhonbooks.com

All Kensington titles, imprints, and distributed lines are available at special quantity discounts for bulk purchases for sales promotions, premiums, fundraising, educational, or institutional use.

Special book excerpts or customized printings can also be created to fit specific needs. For details, write or phone the office of the Kensington sales manager: Kensington Publishing Corp., 900 Third Avenue, New York, NY 10022, attn: Sales Department; phone 1-800-221-2647.

Erewhon and the Erewhon logo Reg. US Pat. & TM Off.

This is a work of fiction. All of the characters, organizations, and events portrayed in this novel are either products of the author's imagination or are used fictitiously.

ISBN 978-1-64566-159-7 (hardcover)

First Erewhon hardcover printing: April 2025

10 9 8 7 6 5 4 3 2 1

Printed in the United States of America

Library of Congress Control Number: 2024943940

Electronic edition: ISBN 978-1-64566-163-4 (ebook)

Edited by Diana Pho
Interior design by Leah Marsh
Interior images courtesy of finist_4/Adobe Stock (Wax Man); Erstudiostok/iStockPhoto (profile picture); creative/Adobe Stock (blood spatter); Abigail Kowalczyk/The Noun Project (anonymous profile picture); Amy Myoung/The Noun Project (Florida); Numero Uno/The Noun Project (thumbs up); Kang Firman/The Noun Project (quill); Rohman haris/The Noun Project (share icon); Caesar Rizky Kurmiawan/The Noun Project (comment icon)

For Uncle Mike

rekt /ɹɛkt/
an online spelling of "wrecked"
usually describing someone being hurt or defeated
or even killed in a snuff film

I don't weep.
Do you?

> Be me, 10
> At sleepover
> watching clips

I was ten years old when I first saw somebody die. I was sitting on a bed with Lucas and Austin, and I was pale and queasy. A Middle Eastern guy with a well-shaped beard took a giant bread knife to the neck of some poor bastard. He sawed left and right, and the video quality was so poor that you didn't see the spray of blood cross the air, you only saw it pool on the ground like it was coming from below, rising up to flood the place.

When the video ended and the screen went black the three of us stared at our own reflections. I felt like a ghost. I went to get snacks downstairs, and when I came back Lucas was queuing up another. I think it was called Split Face. After that we watched another with a man and a jar, although I don't think he died in it. After that we watched one where a girl slept belly-down in her bed. A guy in a balaclava came in and hit her in the back of the head with a silver hammer. She started shaking and spazzing right there, her heels kicking and bunching up the blankets. People off camera laughed. Then the guy took off his pants and got on top of her. The video was called Russian Rodeo.

At school we talked about it like secrets, whispering behind the white backs of shuffling nuns.

At reconciliation, huddled in the chapel, we all promised not to tell the priests about it.

I kept my mouth shut and looked out through stained glass.

> Be me, 11

I saw him through the window and heard him crying and begging for help and I took off my glasses and ran to my room and hid under the bed. The whole bed. Not just the blankets. And my room was so close to the garage I kinda heard it all and he knew I saw him and I think over time everyone knew I saw him and everyone knew I pretty much could have opened the door to save him. The crying got really bad and I knew right then to never cry alone like he was doing right there in the garage where, again, I pretty much could have saved him.

That video goes on forever.

There is no need for confession.

Everyone already knows.

A lot happens in this story so bear with me.

> Be me, 26
> About to end it all
> Feels good, man

Blood Mountain sits at the northern border of
Georgia and is the introduction to the Appalachian Trail. In
reality, it's a foothill with ambition, and I had driven down
from New York with one goal in mind. I dropped the trunk
of my Isuzu Amigo and took out the sawed-off shotgun that
Izzy had given me. It was greasy and heavier than I remembered even though I had just used it a few hours earlier. Now
it felt foreign in my hands, an awkward object that was trying
to slip away and leave me for dead. When Izzy gave me the
gun back outside of Horseshoe Beach he told me, grinning
through his ski mask, "You gotta get up close and personal
with this guy." *Guy* referring to the gun and not who I'd be
using it on—a mystery even still as I crouched in the bushes
and climbed up the hillside.

It was dusk and the trees were dying at crooked angles,
their branches shedding leaves in the wind. In the day, when
I scoped the place out, I understood why they called it Blood
Mountain. The reddish clay blended with the autumn foli-
age and gave the land the aesthetic of an abattoir. The dew
reflected the various shades of brown, orange, rust, and red
and put a mist into the air like somewhere around the bend

a woodchipper coughed up gore and human vapor. I hadn't been sleeping well for months (years, really) and the stale coffee in my stomach gave me the shakes. You get on your fifth cup, and it doesn't really make you any more awake. You just become tired and jittery. I felt the gas station creamer curdle in the acid of my belly. I felt my lips crack in the cold wind. There was a moment where I considered putting both barrels of the sawed-off under my chin and spreading my brain all over the fallen logs and flora of the land. Blood Mountain? Don't mind if I do. But you see those movies where the hero says something like, "I've come too far to stop now," and I kind of related.

The truth is, though, I had been passive for too long. For years I let what lay on that hill torment and torture me and bend me into the worst possible version of myself. I had become a living and breathing goblin because of what lay just a few miles up ahead. Have I come too far to stop now? No, no. I've put this off for too long. Back when I was still in school, the notion of kicking down a shed door and blasting at anyone inside would've made my skin crawl, but now I was approaching thirty, and everything I loved was gone. College me was a putz. He had been through nothing.

Yet, perhaps, I always knew it had to end this way. Even back when Becca was breaking up with me at Beef O'Brady's, and I got drunk and watched the Rays lose another game. Back when I stalked dive bars and clubs around Tallahassee. Back when Lucas knocked me out and I clocked my head against his desk. Back when I met Jay. Back when I met Alexa. Back when I saw more blood and guts and carnage than most people could ever stomach. Back when I cried every day because I didn't know what else to do. Back when I drank my weight in whisky and chain-smoked and used my carpet as an ashtray, eyes glued to my laptop, watching neon yellow flash before my eyes, showing me suicides, disembowelments, mass shootings, and everything in between. And maybe, possibly, way far back to when Ellery died, and we put her in the ground. Jay had studied the coordinates and circled the place on the map. It was high up there. A shack, really, humming with the energy of computer processors and whirring fans. Thick cables like tendons reached underground and stretched into the rock of the hills. This was one of many Betting Rooms outside of Tallahassee. You see, there were Rooms all over the country. The world probably. I guess I could've made it easier on myself and found one in Miami. Could've driven down to South Beach and unloaded my gun wearing flip-flops. See someone turn to me in a swivel chair, their mouth drop open in surprise as pellets rip the skin off their face and their skull blows apart in shards, all while Pitbull thumps in the background. But I went to Atlanta instead. Because this is the one the Skunk said.

I took out a pack of Marlboro Reds and lit one. I left the Amigo somewhere down the hill. For a second, I wondered if I had locked it behind me, but it didn't really matter. There was a fifty-fifty chance I wasn't coming back down. And what if I did? What part of me would be in working order? I vaguely remembered the video I had seen years ago of me getting shot out of a doorway by a pump shotgun. That could be the very winner of all of this. I imagined myself trying to start the car while I bled from my stomach, my hands slipping all over the wheel, the gear shift, everything going slick and crimson under the cloudy moon. Some hikers find my gray corpse in the morning, mouth agape, slumped against the window. Blood Mountain? Don't mind if I do. Or what if

I came back in a worse mental state than I already was in? I bust open the door and it's just an unmanned terminal running numbers and data, digits flickering across the screen in patterns and columns that mean nothing to anyone. Some Harlan Ellison nightmare: a computer with a chip on its shoulder. Or what if it was just another dude? They always seem to just be dudes.

Something cracked and fell in the woods. I turned with the gun. A pair of eyes glinted in the moonlight and then turned and trotted deeper into the trees. My threadbare hoodie was losing against the wind. I held the gun by the barrel and started climbing up the hill, like an animal on all fours. I could see the lights on inside. I could feel evil emanating from it like a downstream current. I could feel it vibrate with chaos. Enough was enough.

> Be Me, 21
> Grieving
> Extremely online

Ellery passed away when we were twenty-one.
It was a car accident. I never saw the body, but when the casket was lowered into the ground I felt something in me fall. Like a book closing or an anchor hitting bottom. A dark wet seed was planted into soil, and I let it germinate into a root system that filled my veins. We had been in love the way children were, growing closer and more entwined as the years passed. She filled my cracks, and I moved and bent into her corners. For us, there were no other options. We'd wanted to be together since we looked at each other in high school all those years ago. Her sitting with her friends at a bright-red octagon. Me walking with chicken strips and French fries to my table, my dork friends showing each other videos on YouTube, laughing and fucking around. I asked her out a couple months later in between classes. She kissed me a few weeks after that.

The funeral was in November in Tampa, and it was rainy and muggy. My parents came, but they kept their distance. Both of my dad's folks were gone. Two out of three of his sisters were dead. He was a hairy, stocky Latino that wore a lot of rings, and loss was commonplace for him. He didn't cry, but my mother did. She was tall and dark brown. Toward the end, he broke from her side and approached me and looked at me with a strange and accusatory glare. "This has to stop," he said. "No más." To this day I'm unsure what he meant although I have an idea.

My parents and Ellery's parents knew each other but never really clicked. My parents were straightforward and honest and said their opinion. Her parents were more of the passive-aggressive wealthy Caucasian type. They'd invite you over for dinner, and if they didn't like you, they'd make you sit there and feel unwelcome without ever saying so. It was a small and quiet suffocation, something only the particularly privileged could pull off. There was a time when Ellery and I humped quietly in her bedroom and her mom came home early. She climbed up the stairs and stopped right before the door, sensing our sin. She walked away and Ellery and I stared at each other, listening to her recede down the stairs. I tried not to laugh, and she put her soft white palm against my mouth. I pulled out and came into a condom. I didn't speak a word for three consecutive meals.

The casket was pearly white, and the ceremony was by the books. To that point I had only been to one other funeral: my uncle who had a heart attack in my garage clutching a twelve-pack of Coors. That messed me up pretty bad, and I spent a lot of my teen years writing Creepypastas about it online. It was a strange way to cope, but I thought that by fictionalizing it, I was putting it away. Crafting the story to my specifications so it existed more as *canon* than *reality*, which, I think if you spent a lot of time online, you started to form an effective distinction between. But when Ellery died, I didn't have the same energy.

Ellery's mother, Claire, pulled me aside after the soil was tossed into the pit. "You were so good to her," she said. Claire was in her later fifties and had short, feathery hair. She was athletic and was in a running club with a bunch of racists, although she wasn't racist herself, at least not by my measure (not calling me a spic and being okay with me dating her white daughter). She brought me in close and started crying. Her breath was warm and her arms were tight around my back. I could feel the slickness of her tears on my neck. The way she pinched my shoulders kept my feet planted. I did the best I could to keep my composure, but every time Ellery cried, I turned to jelly like the flip of a switch, and this wasn't much different. Her mom was letting it out, and I felt my jaw tense up and my eyes grow misty. My cheeks felt heavy.

"She was good to me too," I said. I kept my voice low to keep it from cracking.

"She was good to all of us," said Bill, Ellery's father. "Claire, get off him. Let him breathe." He pulled her off me and then took her spot, patting my back. "We were ready to have you in the family. You know that, right?"

"I know, Mr. Waters. Bill. Sorry."

"You two were together since you were kids. Christ. You were already like a son-in-law to me. I'm telling you this, so you're not surprised if I call you. Okay? Just to check in."

"Thank you," I said. His face was ruddy and his lips were chapped. He had small glasses that sat on his gin-blossom nose—a small and spreading pinkness revealing that he had taken to the bottle. And who could blame him? After I heard about Ellery, I nearly drank my weight in Cutty Sark because some asshole on a forum told me it was a real sad guy's scotch. I was twenty-one years old, and I didn't know how to cope like a man. I couldn't go crying to my father who dawdled around pretending that his heart wasn't already callused over. And I couldn't go to my mother either. She had a real icy quality when it came to death. Had been that way ever since Uncle Ted. So what else could you do?

Bill never pulled away from me. He just started crying heavier and louder than Claire had, but then Claire came over too, not to be outdone. The two of them held on to me like I was their buoy and, finally, I gave in. I felt my knees grow weak and I clawed into their backs like we were climaxing. I cried so hard eyelashes fell off. God Almighty. Ellery was my everything.

>>>

At Florida State University, if you underwent something tragic you were allowed a few free sessions at the Wellness Center to get yourself together. I was in no rush to get my ass off the ratty couch in my apartment, but the knowledge of those sessions rolled around in my head, refusing to be forgotten, like when an app on your phone keeps reminding you to check in and get your fill. Some professors graciously froze my grades until the new year, but most were pretty cagey about it. I was an undergrad for data analysis, and long stretches of staring at my laptop, reading grids and spreadsheets wasn't exactly helping my mind relax, but eventually the new year came and the grading started again and I still hadn't done a single thing to help myself. I accepted the Wellness Center's offer. I heard there was group therapy for the grieving held on Thursday nights, and when I grabbed my bike and pedaled down the road, it took every fiber of my being not to bank left into the liquor store and say hi to the Pakistani behind the counter.

"A flask of Cutty," I'd say.

"Things will improve, my friend," he'd say.

"Sure," I'd say back.

The group session seemed like the better option, and at the very least, I didn't know what people would say.

The place was down a few halls to the right behind this door and the other, a labyrinth of vacuumed carpets and frigid A/C. This was in February, I think. In Florida it never really dipped too low, and most buildings didn't adjust their temperature settings. They figured it'd be hot again in a few weeks. When I entered, I had to zip up my hoodie. The harsh fluorescent lights bounced off my glasses. I got that nervous feeling in my stomach like when you're about to go on stage and present something. The idea of talking about Ellery's death made me want to vomit. I felt my cheeks fill with saliva. I couldn't keep a grip on my phone.

Once inside it was pretty anticlimactic. Most things are when you take a step back and look at the bigger spread. It's not like I was numb or any melodramatic feeling like that, but when something really tragic happens your emotional level spikes and anything after that seems manageable. I suppose that's a blessing. If I encountered anything that spiked higher than Ellery's death, I don't know what I'd do. I'd pull my hair out and run into traffic, probably. I'd pluck out my own eyes and swallow them. Seize right there on the gold-and-garnet carpet, my heels knocking against book bags and foam shaking out of my mouth.

I sat in a circle with a few other students, and we all listened to the counselor talk to us in a soft, pleasing tone. She wore a big red sweater with our school's Seminole mascot. She had large eyes and big, black framed glasses that seemed to double the thickness of her eyebrows. She looked at me and sized me up. She said I didn't have to share if I didn't want to, and I said I was fine enough with listening. I sat with my arms crossed. I took off my glasses and hooked them into my hoodie. The people's faces blurred, and I liked that. I always took off my glasses when I was a kid because it made me feel invisible. Like if I couldn't see them, they couldn't see me, couldn't know what I was feeling.

When I put my glasses back on someone else was talking. She had tan skin and long hair. Filipina, I guessed. She plucked at her bracelets when she talked and kept rearranging herself on the plastic fold-out chair. "I knew that he was sick," she said. "And honestly, sometimes I get mad at myself for crying all the time. Like I knew he was dying when I met him. But what the fuck, right? I still loved him. I can't help who I fall in love with. Right?"

Various people murmured their agreement. We made eye contact, and I looked away first. She seemed familiar, but I couldn't place her.

"And, you know, it's not like he was always in the hospital," she continued. "We had good memories and good times. My friends always ask if I really expected to be with him forever and I never know what to say to them. Am I the stupid bitch that believed he'd get better?"

"You don't have to say that word," the counselor said.

"Sorry. Am I the stupid girl that thought he'd get better? I don't know. Maybe. I guess so."

"You're not stupid," the counselor said. "You were in love, and there's nothing stupid about that. Thank you for sharing."

We all clapped politely, and she looked at me once more and then nodded to everyone and gave a smile. Then the counselor started again. "Here at FSU, we have a lot of programs to help with your grief and your coping. There are many clubs and communities you can join. This is only one of them. Additionally, each of you are entitled to a free one-on-one therapy session here at the Wellness Center. Just ask me to schedule it, okay?"

>

Outside in the courtyard I unlocked my bike. The night had gone from light purple to indigo. The lamps along the brick walkways glowed a warm orange, orbs on black iron poles that attracted moths and flies. Students came out of small cafés and late-night lectures. Music was coming from the quad, the dying sound of some event winding down. The Filipina from the session came up behind me.

"Computer science with Robert Carmichael."

I turned to her voice, and it all fell into place. She sat behind me most of the time. I recalled her giving some presentation. Maybe another encounter at a party that same year, back when we were freshmen shotgunning PBRs over empty bathtubs. Maybe she and Ellery even spoke a few times.

"Shit. That's right. Good memory," I said.

"Alexa. You're Sam, right?"

"How'd you remember that?"

She tapped her head and winked. "This is a lockbox. Weird to see you in there," she started. "I mean, not *weird* but you know what I mean. I go all the time so this must be your first."

"I guess I never had a reason to go."

"Yeah. I figured as much. I'm sorry."

"Is it weird that I didn't share? Is that bad?"

"No way. You're doing what you gotta do. That's a big part of all of this. No right ways or wrong ways. Just troubling ways and healthier ways."

"That sounds like the same thing."

"It sounds less lecturey. Here. Gimme your phone. Take my number if you ever wanna talk or if you ever wanna go to a meeting but are too nervous to go alone. When I first started going I would only go if this one other girl was gonna be there. Felt clingy and weird, but hey, it helped."

I handed her my phone, and she put her number in. She gave it back with a smile and walked backward. "See you around, okay?"

"Sure. I'll see you around."

I gave a smile too and she turned on her heel and disappeared around the corner. I got on my bike and pushed off into the night. I wouldn't speak to her for two more years.

>

When I got back to my apartment, I poured myself a ton of whisky and lay in bed with my laptop. Something about that group therapy session felt off. Inauthentic. Something about Alexa felt disingenuous. I hated being vulnerable in public. I hated working through the same platitudes over and over again. I wanted to scream and lash out and break things, but nobody let you anymore. The only safe space to be weird was online.

You see, in the time since the incident happened, I had found myself on more and more websites that I had no business being on: 4chan forums, the YNC, disturbing Reddit threads, WorldStar, Best Gore, Creepypastas, cryptid myths, SCP wikis, stories about the dark web and red rooms, normal porn for normal people, 112Dirtbag, the guy that shot himself for Björk, and more. Just full-blown acid that consumed my hours between grieving and productivity, eventually gnawing at productivity and leaving me either in tears or consuming even more content in a vicious cycle.

You have to understand that it's very hard to be a guy on-line—you only get so many options. You're a lurker, you're a reply guy, you're a poster, or you succumb to insecurity farming and go full incel. In many ways, the only spaces that were for The Boys were the dank dens of freaks and monsters. Somewhere along my journey of grief, I shifted gears. I no longer had interest in learning how to cope from a therapist's Twitter thread. Instead, I wanted to see what the cartel did on a Sunday afternoon. And for some reason, it helped.

I clicked around and after a few videos and a few NSFL ("Not Safe for Life") links, I started to feel inspired. I had been toying with the idea of writing something spooky about Ellery, just like I did with Uncle Ted, but I could never stomach it. There was nothing I could make scary about her death that didn't already make my hands tremble, so, instead, I decided to log in to the old account I used back when my Uncle Ted died. It was for a lame ghost forum called CampfireFables.com and my username was Blue Bird for reasons I had forgotten. The memory was foggy, truth be told, but the big one I wrote, the one I got the most points on, centered on a kid in bed, glasses off, hiding from a creature who kept on crying. I called him the Wax Man and all my posts described the phantom as being tall and made of wax and wearing fine clothes like wingtip shoes, a long trench coat, and a silky fedora. He'd lay under your bed and weep really hard with the intention of scaring you and make you cry too, because he didn't want to cry alone. If you shed a tear, he got your ass. Looking back, I think my child psyche revealed itself pretty clearly. My favorite uncle died, and I was afraid to cry alone.

As I got into college some of the stories changed and I kept up with it, if only in secret. He'd trawl college campuses and look for the sad and lonely. Once he got you crying, you were doomed. Friends would find you caked in hard white wax, wax in your mouth, wax clogging your throat and nose, you fully drowned in it. There were some versions where even your organs were wax and the real ones were nowhere to be found. I won more and more internet points and people followed up asking for other posts all while staying in character. "Wax Man spotted at LIU!" a post would say, showing a blurry photo of a mannequin under a bed. "Wax Man got a girl at Yale!" said another. It was cute but tapered off after a few years when drinking and *being in college* became the priority.

Anyhow, the hits kept coming and when I logged into CampfireFables.com, I was met with more disappointment. All my posts were long deleted, and a mod note said: "Removed for violence against children." The ticker said I was last logged in two years ago, which would put me at nineteen and probably missing Uncle Ted more than usual. Now everything was deleted, and all the messages in my inbox were gone except for one. A recent one from a few months ago. Specifically, from the week Ellery died. I opened the message, and it was from someone named Haruspx. The message was a jumble of letters: chinsky.rekt.x. Total spam.

The night was a bust. I shut my laptop and stared at the security light across the alley.

I thought more about Uncle Ted and Ellery and felt tears run down my cheeks.

Shit, I thought. *Now I'm gonna die.*

>

In the morning, I decided I wasn't going back to therapy, but I tried to imagine what I'd say if I did. "Tell us about her," the counselor would say.

How do you pitch a person to a committee? Do you start with their accomplishments, their résumé? Or what they looked like? Maybe if I knew the words, I could describe how she sounded and tasted and what she liked and what she watched and the space she took up on my futon. I'd say she was tall and played volleyball. I'd say she had white skin and a lot of blemishes. A birthmark along her left arm. A skin tag behind her right thigh. She had dirty-blond hair and light brown eyes. When she'd get upset, she'd break out in splotches of rosacea. Sometimes she chewed at her nails or picked at her cuticles. If I were more poetic, I'd describe how when she looked in the mirror, it was always at an angle, keeping her face tilted to her shoulder, side-eyeing as if to catch her own profile, imagining how she'd look candid, or as a bust, or on some currency. Or maybe it was because when she stared at herself directly, she took too much of herself in, her gentle eyes sweeping and surveying every arbitrary flaw she had decided on that morning. Or maybe it was the opposite, not fully acknowledging her reflection lest someone call her vain.

Maybe I'd tell them about the first time we kissed, outside of the gym back at Hillsborough High School. I wished her luck on her game, and she trotted over and gave me a light peck on the lips. I blushed and she did too. She went to play, and they lost anyway but afterward we made out, her duffel bag at her feet, me in Chuck Taylors, marked up by Sharpies, not knowing how to stay still.

There are some nights in Florida that wash the state of its sins. When the breeze comes off from the gulf and spreads its long, cool fingers over the houses and through the trees. The cicadas chirr restlessly. Frogs sing in a mystifying Greek choir. The dew already forming on the blades of grass and thickening the Spanish moss that dangles down like the beards of old wise men, crouched in the trees, watching mortals move around and toil amongst themselves. Ellery kept texting her mom not to pick her up yet. The game was delayed. The game was interrupted. She was hanging out with friends. Getting food at Nico's Diner across the street. But really, we sat there on the steps behind the school and kissed as the rest of the city seemed to melt away. She ran her fingers through my hair. I rested my fingers on the black spandex of her uniform. She sighed into me. We were both a couple months shy of sixteen and already knew that whatever sat beyond the threshold we wanted to experience together.

Something relevant I'd share was that she knew who she was but didn't know how to express it. She didn't understand *online*. She didn't get it. She couldn't find her voice. When the socials were blowing up, she was adrift. It sounds trivial, I know, but she got bummed about it. Facebook was already washed, Twitter was too cynical, Instagram was too phony, Tumblr was too girly, so what did she have? Doing TikTok dances? Snapchatting locals from Tampa? Barf. I tried to explain that it was small potatoes in the big scheme of things, and that her not being online was actually *good*, and she agreed with me for the most part, but she still kept at it. Her biggest attraction, like a siren song, was YouTube. The girl wanted to be on YouTube. She tried her hand as a BookTuber but couldn't read fast enough, a SportsTuber but hated the fighting, and a FashionTuber, but then raged out when a mean comment remarked on her height.

I think it was a sense of FOMO. To her, everyone had their thing and their voice and their hot takes and their memes and their targeted ads, and she was getting frustrated with being left out and late to the party. And it's not like anyone was huge or popular, we just worked part-time at a job she didn't get. During lulls in conversation or parties, people would fish out their phone and retreat into it. They got their own little fill in their private little world. They'd crack a smile, get a dopamine rush, and then come back to reality. But she never could get the hang of it.

At the start of our freshman year in college, she was determined to have a real go at it, and as she was technologically inept, I helped set up her account. She settled on the username StinkySmellery and her password was the same for everything: TerrierSetter22 (a reference to our high school, volleyball, and her number). She posted short vlogs about campus and class and tips for incoming freshmen. I often made an appearance throwing up a peace sign. She'd spend all night editing them and it felt like she made a thousand, but in reality, she quit after four.

We hadn't been living together yet and I let myself into her dorm. She was sitting at the janky wooden desk and staring at her own face on her own vlog.

"This is just so cringey," she said. "It's cringey. Admit it."

"It's not cringey, it's earnest."

"Even worse. Ugh." She deleted the vlog.

"But you spent so much time on that," I said. I sat down on her bed and grabbed at her weed pen. "You even bought a light thingy."

"That's my whole point," she said. "It's like a monument to hours wasted. And for like three views. It's not that I don't want to be online, I want to *not want* to be online, does that make sense?"

"Mhm. Preach."

She closed her laptop and put her feet on my lap. "And it's

annoying because everyone is like, oh it rots your brain, save your attention span, blah blah, you're doing it right, but I feel like a Mennonite. Like *come on*, I want the juice! Let me *in*!"

"Honey, I promise you're not missing anything."

I convinced her to keep the other videos up, but in grim irony, I was the one to later delete them. After she died, comments of *RIP* came out of nowhere. Dove emojis. Prayers in the comments. Fs in the chat. She was blowing up for all the wrong reasons. One comment from a jumble of numbers asked: "Is this that girl? Lmaooooo." Disturbed, I deleted the videos and her channel entirely. And as quick as she came, StinkySmellery was gone.

What I kept trying to express to her, in my own confused way, was that I loved the space she took up and I loved how she only explicitly existed IRL. I had a friend in college named Conor who used to work at a furniture store. He'd make house calls and repair people's lamps, fix up their dressers, refurbish their table, whatever he needed to do. He was a strange duck that would describe people by how they treated their furniture. Does this person know how to sit in that chair? Does that person use coasters? If that person chipped the paint off a dresser, would they give a shit? One day, Conor, Ellery, and I drank Bud Lights in the sun and strolled through a tailgate party. This big guy ran to catch a Frisbee and thought he could step on one of those camping chairs. His foot ripped through the cloth and he twisted his groin and fell in agony. Conor just shook his head: "People forget they matter." He walked off, and Ellery and I looked at each other vastly unsure of what he was talking about. She cracked a smile and I laughed.

"People forget they matter, Sam," she said.

"You're right. They forget," I said, sipping my beer.

She crushed her empty can in her hands and said, "Look at how much I matter."

I stomped on mine and kicked it across the lawn. "I matter all over the damn place."

That night we had sex in her apartment, and I watched the bed frame bump against the wall, chipping at the mauve paint. I mattered there. When she was drunk at my place the next weekend and wiped out and pulled the shower curtain off its rings she mattered then. We both mattered when we went to the campus cinema and I inevitably spilled my soda onto the seats or she got nachos and wiped her hands on her shirt. And when a semitruck blew past a red light and sideswiped her Nissan, sending it into a drainage ditch, bursting out glass and metal, she mattered then. Even if it happened so fast that she couldn't let out a yelp of surprise, she mattered to pieces.

> Be me, 22
> See the folks
> Download Spyglass
> Enough Internet for today

What should've been a four-year program I stretched into five years with the hopes of stretching it even further until I died and became the ghost of Strozier Library.

Florida State University, for all intents and purposes, was largely a wasteland bereft of any culture more enlightening than a can of Natty Light. I fucking hated it. People told me that college is what you made of it. They told me that everyone needed to find themselves and that the various extra-curricular activities would allow for such self-reflection. The problem is that the campus as a whole, sun-soaked ninety per-cent of the year and bricked and steaming like a kiln, doesn't allow for much flourishing beyond being called a faggot by a truck with a Trump flag.

In my ever-growing list of self-destructive and masoch-istic habits, I resigned myself to stay forever. I drank more, I smoked more, and I wouldn't go to bed until I watched at least three or four people die online. My parents stopped foot-ing the bill after my fourth year and I took out loans, doing a course at a time, going from fifth year senior to "Goddamn, you're still here?"

My friend Jason, a real Italian type with skinny arms and big wrists, stayed in Tallahassee too. He and his girlfriend, Maria, a shrewish know-it-all, got a house in a cul-de-sac not far from campus. Maria got a job at the governor's office, and Jason worked remotely for some company based out of Atlanta, driving up whenever he needed to. Maria hated when Jason and I hung out. In the early days of my grieving, she was admittedly very sympathetic, but after a year, during a box party with some film kids, she called me an "emotional parasite." The type of presence that needed to cling to positive vibes and leech them off others because I wasn't capable of producing them myself. I said I preferred the term "emotional marsupial," but she didn't laugh. She hardly ever did.

The fact was that Maria gave something to Ellery that I couldn't really manage. Maria saw Ellery as her own person, removed from me entirely. It was not Ellery-and-Sammy Goals, but Ellery-by-herself Goals. Ellery-by-herself Dreams. Ellery Solo. Maria would often ask about her five-year plan and there was an unspoken energy that I wasn't a part of it. Not in a malicious way, just—whoops!—left out by accident. Obviously, I understood that Ellery was her own person and needed her own goals, but when you're in the sauce, it's hard to see people from a different slant. It's hard to make plans for someone that don't involve you when everything up to that point had. Maria was good for her, and honestly it was in those life-planning moments, she and Ellery at the corner of a party, laughing and strategizing, that both of them really took on a shine.

When Ellery died and I told Jason and Maria what had happened, Maria recoiled in such horror it seared into my brain. This person loved her. She clutched her face and her jaw dropped and she said, "No, no, no, no." Then she wrapped her arms around Jason and cried into his T-shirt. How could you dislike someone that cries for the same reason you do?

When I graduated from Hillsborough High, I had shit grades and couldn't get into the University of Florida. Ellery got into Chapel Hill. We balanced together on the edge of eternity, wondering what was going to become of us. I couldn't do long-distance, and, frankly, I was ready to lose her. All good things. A bildungsroman for this Florida Boy. But surprising everyone, she chose FSU. Maybe she did it for me. Maybe she did it to be closer to her family. Maybe it was just a matter of money. But suddenly, I couldn't drop the ball.

In her years at FSU she, like myself, rationalized that she had made a good choice. She saw her family more. It didn't get as cold here. The money really was a lot. So, I doubled down and had to make our relationship worth it. I loved her harder every day. When I saw her eyes wander to the window, her mind pumping out what-ifs and what-could've-beens, I mentioned ideas like marriage and having kids and moving into a house we saw a little outside campus. She smiled and it assuaged her for a bit, but I knew in reality that my time was limited. I didn't want her to marry me and then one day up and leave because she wasn't satisfied with her career or with her education or with her lot in life. I wanted to be with her forever, and I knew that by the end of our college career, I needed a plan. But I couldn't talk to her the way Maria did. I didn't have the vision. The best I could do was approach it from the negative.

"I know you hate it here," I said one night. We were drinking Sapporos at this cheap sushi place on Call Street.

"I don't hate it here," she said. She dipped a tuna roll into some soy sauce and just squished it around in there. She was wearing a long-sleeve T-shirt and shorts. Her long legs had bruises from falling on the court.

"We're graduating soon. It doesn't even matter."

"You should've gone to Carolina."

"I'm glad I didn't. I would've lost you."

And then she died. She died in Tallahassee. And while I wasn't so narcissistic to believe she was only there for me, there's got to be some superstition that if you die in the city you hate, you're legally allowed to haunt the asshole that brought you there. I deserved my nightmares. I deserved my pain. I deserved my guilt. So, when Maria called me an emotional parasite my first thought was, *I wonder if Ellery thought that too.*

>

All this to say, after that film-kid party, helping them move was an act of self-flagellation.

"Can you be nice to my girlfriend for like five seconds?" Jason asked. He was handing me a box of Maria's kitchenware. It was heavy as sin, and she was already in the house unpacking.

"I am being nice," I said.

"No, you're not," he said, climbing down from the truck. "You guys keep lobbing grenades at each other. It's driving me insane. I feel like I'm back between my parents."

"She called me an emotional parasite. In front of everyone."

"That was like three weeks ago, dude. You gotta get over it. And anyway, it got big laughs." To Jason, anything was justified if the bit landed. You could get away with murder if, in his eyes, it *crushed.*

"Well maybe I'm salty about this house then," I said. "You know this was the spot Ellery and I wanted." Not exactly true. Ellery and I had *one* conversation about staying in Tallahassee after graduation and we found this house. But here's the thing, in my mind, if I could reframe some of those past moments, it'd sound like I actually did ask her about moving in together. Which I always tried to do. In my own way.

Jason looked at me and leaned against the truck. "You're finding reasons to be upset," he said. He squatted down and lifted up a box of clothes. He was sweating through his T-shirt. It was around August, and it was boiling, and the laces of his sneakers were coming undone.

"This is just weird for me, man," I said. We stood in the sun and gnats buzzed around our necks and behind our ears. I brought my voice to a lower register. "I'm happy for you to be making this step, but I can't help but feel like, I don't know, that this should've been me and El. It's all I can think about, you know?"

"I don't know what I'm supposed to say to that. Are me and Maria never allowed to move forward?"

"That's not what I'm saying. This is just weird for me. That's it."

"Well, feel weird later and help me get this shit in before I have a heat stroke."

He passed me and I followed, stepping across the brown lawn. The sky overhead was cloudless, just the sun boring through the sky. Moving always made me think of Uncle Ted. The guy couldn't keep an apartment to save his life, so my parents always covered the cost to find him somewhere else. I always got to carry his books. For all the shit that guy got into, he was never without some paperback folded in his back pocket. I guess that's what called him to mind.

"Hey, do you remember my Wax Man stories?"

"Your what?" he asked.

"The Wax Man stories," I said. "I think I'm going to start them up again."

"Those creepy things you wrote online?"

"They all got deleted by mods. My whole account got nuked for some reason, except this one spam message. But I might bring him back. Help me cope, I don't know."

"That's a strange coping mechanism, dude."

"It's my only idea, to be honest."

"Did you ever tell Ellery about them?"

"No way. She never knew about those stories. They'd freak her out."

"Then maybe writing her into one isn't a great idea. For the karma and all."

"That's a good point," I said as I crossed the threshold into the shade of their home.

"Sammy, right over there," Maria said, pointing toward the small kitchenette.

"How many Le Creuset pots do you need?" I asked. The displeasure in my voice came out thicker than I had intended.

"You're supposed to cook in kitchens, Sam, not just smoke and eat Popeyes."

I heard a peal of laughter from Jason. I grumbled.

"And for what it's worth," she continued, "Ellery was the one who showed me Le Creuset sets, so, you know, take that."

That's the type of remark Maria often made. It was the type where you had to read between the lines. Hold the dollar bill to the light and see the watermark, because what she meant was, "You didn't even know the girl you killed." And that made me want to freak out and whip a plate, but Jason loved her, and he was my best friend, so what the hell could I

do? Like Jason suggested, I was forced to feel weird and depressive at a different time. So, at the housewarming party a
few nights later I did the old Irish goodbye and walked all the
way home with a stolen bottle of Kraken (and the lid of her
orange Le Creuset, jammed into my backpack).

>>>

A few weeks later I drove down to Tampa to, among other
reasons, pick up a shift at a gig I used to have back in the day.
My mother was a professor of medicine and, years ago, before
everything went to hell, she got me a job being a standardized
patient at a clinic. I reminisced on an experience I had there
that still, to this day, left an odd taste in my mouth . . .

I was nineteen at the time and met this guy named Ryan
Vasquez, who was about thirty years my senior. Along with
others, we came in each week with a new problem memorized
and these med students had to figure it out. It was a real-life
game of twenty questions. For each right question they asked,
we revealed something that'd nudge them to the correct diagnosis. That week I was Herman Shrew, 28, with pneumonia.
Last week I was Zach Ishka, 22, with AIDS. The week before
that I had a slipped disk. Next week I was going to have an
inflamed spleen though I didn't know my name yet. You get
the idea.

What Ryan Vasquez had started doing was crying after
each diagnosis. Like really *really* crying, hard and heavy
while clutching at the student's white sleeves. It happened
first when we each had to hear that our wife was going to die.
It was such a moving performance that the doctors watching
the footage and listening to the audio were getting misty-eyed
themselves. I heard it in the adjacent test room, and it threw

off my game. I ended up forgetting the line that I was supposed to say when they told me about my fake wife's fake
death. I just looked at the student and frowned.

The thing is, though, Ryan didn't have a wife either; he had
a girlfriend and that girl's daughter. But every week since then,
he made sure to bawl his eyes out over whatever the diagnosis
was. Once, the guy was crying like hell over eczema and soon
it was clear to everyone that he wasn't performing at all.

"It's therapeutic, you know?" Ryan said during one of our
breaks, putting his cigarette out on the curb. "You've never
been there so you don't know. You have nothing to cry about,
kid. You can't see yourself actually having these problems.
You got nothing at stake."

"What are you talking about? I have a girlfriend and I
have a family. I don't need to be forty-five years old to fear
death," I said back. I was angry at the claim of not having
stakes and the implication that I didn't fear death. I feared
death just as much as the next guy, even then at nineteen,
but Ryan rolled his eyes and rubbed his goatee. His earrings
caught the sun. He looked like a pirate.

"Yeah, but have you cried?"

"Not here, no."

"Why not?"

"Because I don't feel the need to cry out all my problems to med students. Go see a therapist for that," I said. I
remembered thinking that Ryan was an asshole who pushed
his grief onto other people. At the time, I thought it was self-
ish. Obviously now, looking back, maybe he had it all figured
out, never crying alone and all that, but dammit, those med
students had other things to worry about.

And where did he get off thinking that I had nothing to cry
about, thinking that he was the only one with *stakes*? What

would he say to me now if I told him my girlfriend of nearly a decade died? What would know-it-all Maria say to *him*? He had to be some sort of emotional parasite too, right?

We didn't say anything else for the remainder of the break, but when I got back into my hospital gown, I decided that I was really going to let it rip on the next student. I was really going to cry out my eyes and cause a big ol' scene and throw off Ryan's game before he could do it to me. That way he could see how obnoxious it was. A taste of his own medicine, so to speak.

The student came in and he was a young Indian boy with a soft brown face and fine black beard. He was nervous in his approach, and he was making rookie mistakes like not making eye contact and such. He started off by the books, though, which was how most nervous students did it. They got so caught up in doing it right that they came off as robotic and uninviting. My favorite ones were the laid-back cool kids that came out almost always failing but making me feel nice.

The student started off asking all the right things. I answered with rehearsed phrases like "Sharp Pain" and "The Cough Syrup Doesn't Help Much" and "I Can't Even Sleep." I watched the Indian kid take notes diligently, but on his paper, I saw the word *bronchitis*, which was wrong. If he asked me more questions, he would've realized that, and had he listened to what I was saying he would've realized I said my appetite was terrible, which is a signal for pneumonia because with pneumonia, it's hard to keep food in your body.

The student then failed to percuss my back, so I couldn't give him an index card with a clue on it. In fact, the guy didn't listen at all, and I saw flop sweat form on his forehead, but before the student could tell me the wrong diagnosis, a shrill cry erupted from the wall. It was Ryan and he was really letting it all come out and the crying was heavy and intense, and it was easily one of his best.

But because Ryan's crying was so goddamn loud and because this kid's diagnosis was totally wrong, I got really heated. It was *my* turn to cry but the kid wasn't listening to me so I couldn't. This Indian kid was about to tell me I had bronchitis and send me home with pneumonia and I clenched my fist and tried to count to ten. Ryan's deep, grown-man blubbering was loud and dramatic and the Indian kid looked at me, and referring to Ryan, said, "Wow, that's really authentic, huh?"

And I said, "Calm down, he does it every time."

And then I sat there in the hospital gown and looked up at the camera and wondered if it was watching me. If the microphones were listening to me. I looked at the student and said, "By the way, it's pneumonia," but he was listening to Ryan cry and didn't hear me.

Even then I missed Ellery, and when she picked me up after my shift, I told her all about the incident. All about Ryan. She asked me why I got so upset over some dude crying a lot. I said I didn't know.

To be fair, it had been years since I saw Ryan, and I wasn't doing any good getting myself worked up about it, driving through the rain to Tampa, but this is what you did when you drove for four hours. You just started to think and replay moments, and I had conjured up this excitement about grabbing a shift at the clinic and seeing if he was around and giving him a real reason to cry. The thought of fighting him titillated me. I couldn't explain why. There was a violence inside me that simmered on a hot plate, and as the memory of the event faded from my mind, I found myself pulling up to my driveway. I wondered now, what patient files I'd have IRL.

What would they say about me, Samuel Dominguez, across the spread of time?

Samuel Dominguez, 19, home from college, working a summer job.

Samuel Dominguez, 20, feeling like he trapped his girlfriend.

Samuel Dominguez, 21, grieving, loss, bereft.

Samuel Dominguez, 22, suicidal, arriving in Tampa to say hello to his parents before drowning himself in the lake in the backyard.

But the moment I cut the engine, I had a new one.

Samuel Dominguez, 22, finding Ryan Vasquez and crying harder than him.

>

The bedroom of my childhood home was nothing anymore. After Ellery died, and before I even had a chance to go through everything, my parents threw it all out and converted it into a guest room. They had kept the obvious items like stuffed animals and photos but had no sensitivity regarding the rest. A hoodie, a receipt, her diorama from our high-school science fair, the volleyball I made her sign after her winning game against Plant High. When I first came home and bore witness to my parents' cruelty, I think I screamed. I remember throwing a glass. Now I had gotten used to it and realized the truth: I was the biggest thing they couldn't get rid of. I was a dour reminder of the mercilessness of life. Even my father, having buried four members of his family before I could even walk, couldn't stand the sight of me. I was a walking memento mori, and I wanted my old room back.

Inside, the place smelled of arroz con gandules and my

father scraped the remains out of a pot and into Tupperware for his lunch tomorrow. My mom chirped on the phone about a lesson plan for the coming quarter. She came out of her office in her big glasses and slippers and shouted some Spanish at our cat and then looked at me. She gave me a gentle hug but was distant about it. She eyed me up and down and then shuffled away. My dad strung up some trash and handed it to me. "The recycling too," he grunted.

I wheeled the trash can and recycling bin to the base of the driveway and wedged them next to the mailbox. The rain had decreased to a light drizzle, and I stood there under a streetlight and tried to feel each drop. Across the cul-de-sac a neighbor watched his dog pee on the grass. He waved to me, and I waved back.

"You're back again!" he shouted, friendly enough.

Back inside, I told my parents how my courses were going. My mom sat in a deep couch with a heat pad on her shoulders. She listened to me lie and nodded along. My dad channel-surfed through four hundred ESPNs. I went straight to my room and laid in bed but couldn't get my eyes closed. I kept thinking about Ryan Vasquez and the memory of his crying. I reached into my bag and took out a small bottle of Wild Turkey 101. I sat up and drank it while I scrolled around on my laptop. I watched couples dance on TikTok, I watched game reviews, I watched gym bros pump iron, I watched girls explain the 666 Rule, I watched guys explain male disposability, I watched a high school bully pummel a kid, I read a story about a shooter, I read pasta about a goat man, I watched a LiveLeak of a Chinese factory worker, I watched a GIF of some redneck mishandling a grenade, I looked at a girl's OF, I read statistics about Nazis, I re-watched the LiveLeak.

Eventually, I looked up Alexa Ritter, that Filipina girl from that therapy session back on campus. It had been months since we spoke. I still had her number, and I thought about texting her but decided against it. I scrolled through her Instagram instead and something about her photos hooked into me. Even in a candid, it felt like she was looking through the screen, watching. Regardless, she was a pretty girl, and I got myself horny and jacked off to her. I fell asleep and had nightmares about the Wax Man, his crying so familiar, not Ryan's but someone else's, and in the morning, I woke up and picked at the cum on my bed sheets.

>

The initial reason I went back to Tampa was because Ellery's dad, Bill, had called me and wanted me to come over for dinner. It was approaching a year since the funeral. Phone calls turned to emails which turned to texts and then a few unnerving messages wherein he just took pictures of his laptop displaying Facebook images of his daughter and me. "You two were so cute!" some of the messages said. It was she and I at homecoming junior year of high school. It was she and I at a Renaissance fair. It was she and I at her cousin's wedding.

Claire set the table as Bill told me how he'd been. The Waterses' house was nice. It was in the richer South Tampa district and was old, shuttered, and symmetrical, but sloping with age. These houses were graceful in their size, not like the McMansions you saw pop up all around Carrollwood and Lutz. Granted, in South Tampa you couldn't go very far without seeing the Dixie flag flutter on someone's lawn. Bill and Claire Waters didn't have that though. Their lawn was crisp and clean and clutter free, much like the rest of their house. It was almost cavernous, really. The place was void of feeling, hermetic in its cleanliness. Back at my place there was the obvious energy of, "Please go back to Tallahassee, you're bumming us out." But here there was the opposite energy: "Stay and give this house a pulse." And that energy was directly coming from Bill who jabbered on about real estate, local politics, who is doing what, who I should I reach out to, who he can e-troduce me to. Beyond him, Claire moved like one of those egrets you saw tiptoeing through a pond. Every time Bill said "we" or "us" or referred to himself and Claire as a group, she winced. Even the vaguest allusion to cooperation had her back in the kitchen slamming cabinets and knocking dishes around.

I excused myself to the bathroom, and Bill sent me to the one upstairs because the bottom one was on the fritz. Up there, I moved down the hallway to Ellery's room. It was a guest room like mine and my heart broke all over again. I don't know what I expected. You see those movies of the devastated parents keeping their abducted children's room exactly as it was in case they came back, but this was just another reminder that she wasn't coming back from anything. The bed that used to be purple and pink was now a steely gray on a black bed frame. The walls that were light blue and had string lights and Polaroids were now just white walls with random landscapes hung up. Her vanity table was painted over to match the bed frame. The closet held winter coats and empty suitcases.

I looked at the carpet and tried to find the stain from when I fingered her for the first time and broke her hymen. When she shuddered and I panicked, and we both tried to shimmy her out of her shorts without making a mess. After I helped clean up, she cried and told me, "I think I love you," and I said, "I think you love you too."

But the stain was gone.

>

"There's more in his study," Claire said behind me. I nearly leapt. I turned and saw her standing in the doorway, the hallway light behind her making her a strange, narrow silhouette in an apron.

"I wasn't trying to snoop."

"It's okay. You can snoop. But the cute stuff is in Bill's study."

We looked at each other for a minute. I couldn't see her eyes, but I could feel them.

"You're a smoker now, right?" she asked me.

"I'm trying to quit."

"Everyone says they're trying to quit when they're just embarrassed."

I shrugged. I took the pack out of my back pocket and offered it to her.

"Later," she said. "After dinner." She walked down the hall and called back, "His study is on the right. Dinner will be ready soon."

I watched her go down the steps. The top of her head disappeared behind a banister and then sunk out of eyeline. I took a few steps down the hallway. The runner was long and blue with white angels and trumpets, faded from foot traffic. The door to Bill's study was ajar and I pushed it open, and the place felt warmer than the rest of the house. It was like Bill kept all of his beautiful emotions here, scattered and messy like a kid's playroom. His anger, frustration, and sorrow covered the drapes and shelves like streamers and confetti left behind. Even the pretty moments, memories of better times and blissful afternoons, bounced around like rubber balls or lay in colorful piles, toys covering the ground like Legos and pick-up sticks.

On a shelf were pictures of Ellery, but only a few. One of her as a little girl, younger than I ever knew her. One was high school graduation. There I was, laughing, my arm around her, both of us in shiny red gowns. Next to that was a thick booklet. It was her Chapel Hill acceptance letter and orientation guide. I remembered how excited she was when she got in. We were at Yogurt Mountain on Dale Mabry, and she kept refreshing her email. I spooned at my cup and prattled on about AP Euro this, and algebra that, and homeroom who gives a shit when—

"Let's fucking go, yes, yes!"

"What happened?"

She spun the phone around and showed me the acceptance mail. The word CONGRATULATIONS was big in the subject line.

"Yoooooooo!!!" I shouted.

"I gotta call my mom!" she said and grabbed the phone. She dialed Claire and hurried outside. Through the glass windows, I watched her pace back and forth in front of the yogurt shop. She pumped her fist, she ran her fingers through her hair, she laughed out loud. My heart was so full. I was so proud. Jesus. Why didn't she just fucking go?

>

"I'm coasting," I said as I passed mashed potatoes to Bill. "I'm definitely coasting. Graduation is in a few months though." I was lying through my teeth. It was college. There was a graduating class every semester, but I sure as hell wasn't doing it anytime soon.

"Are you going to stay in Tallahassee?" he asked me. Claire picked silently at her plate. No matter how friendly and gregarious Bill was, my gaze kept flicking back to Claire. Her high cheekbones. Her pursed lips. How her long fingers and big knuckles made her hands look like a collection of moving lollipops.

"I think I am going to stay, yeah. I have some friends in the area. I may do some work for the school and save some money that way. Rent is so cheap there, you know?"

"Absolutely. Oh, did I tell you the news?"

"He doesn't care, Bill," Claire said. It was ice shot from a cannon. I sat up straight and smiled at Bill and bounced my eyebrows as a signal that maybe she was wrong.

"They're gonna put more traffic lights at the intersection."

He was referring to where Ellery died. Monroe Ave running north and south next to a slight hill, and Marks Street meeting it like a T. The truck was coming down Marks. He had a red light, but Ellery coming up Monroe didn't have one. I hardly thought more lights would make a difference. Claire was right. I didn't care.

"I thought that they should put a fountain there, but—"

"They're not going to put a fountain at an intersection, Bill."

"I just think—"

"Think all you want. They're not going to put a fountain at an intersection."

Bill looked at her. His face dropped. He didn't even pretend to smile it off. He slopped more mashed potatoes onto his plate and put his head low.

Claire looked at me. "Let's go outside."

"Now?" I asked. I wiped my mouth with a napkin.

"He's in the middle of eating, honey," Bill said.

"I want to go outside and have a cigarette."

"But you don't smoke."

"Sam has cigarettes. I want to smoke one with him on the veranda. You stay in here and clean the dishes."

"What are you doing?"

"I just told you," she said. Then she stood up and tossed her napkin on her seat. "Come on, Sam." She moved out of the dining room with quick and precise steps. Bill looked at me, and I pushed my chair out to follow her.

On the veranda you could see the other rich houses along the street. I saw through big windows, family units watching CNN, pacing around, setting dinner, barking errands at each other. It was a humid, late-August night. I heard crickets and a mosquito buzzed in my ear and I flinched.

"Did you smoke with Ellery?" she asked me. She was leaning against the banister, and I was reminded of her height. Her long skinny legs reaching down into soft brown shoes. Her jangling bracelets on her bony wrists. Her reddish chest and face, like Ellery's, flush with more and more emotions every moment until she slept and restarted the next day.

"No. Well sometimes. She was better about it, though, and wanted me to quit." I took the pack out and offered her a cigarette. Ellery was a classic party smoker. She bummed one every single time. I kept telling her to just buy a pack and get it over with, but nah. One party, she solicited six people for a loosie before giving up. The next day I just bought the damn things. The week after that she had a preference.

Ellery Waters, 21, lung cancer.

Sammy Dominguez, 21, enabler.

>

"I used to smoke Parliaments when Bill and I first dated. Marlboro Reds, huh?"

"Ellery called them Obama Smokes. Because, uh, I think that's what he smoked. I think she heard that somewhere. Anyway, it's what she liked and now I guess me too."

I lit her cigarette, and she took a drag and blew the smoke toward the lamp overhead where moths and flies held convention. The ceiling of the veranda was painted a haint blue, and I felt my stomach churn. A car passed by in the street before us. The lawn was really so clean and crisp. Under the moon it looked like a plate of steel. Another mosquito buzzed, and I waved it away. She took a pause and closed her eyes.

"Stop coming over here," she said, opening her eyes at me, slowly, like a cat. "You know Bill and I care for you deeply, Sam. But the fact is that when I look at you, I see my daughter. Email us, call us, if you need help with anything obviously let us know, but you can't keep coming over like this. I know Bill likes having you over, but just tell him no. He doesn't seem like it, but he's a lot softer than me. I don't need him bawling in his study every night and you seem to really fill his tank with gas."

"Okay. I understand."

"Just looking at you," she scowled. She ashed the cigarette onto the veranda. "I'm never going to get over her death. Bill and I won't ever get over it."

"Me neither. I—"

"But looking at you makes me feel like I'm mourning on your behalf too. I can't give you Ellery. Okay?"

"I'm confused. What?"

"Just go. I love you dearly. You're like a son to me, but just give us some space. She was our daughter, Sam. Okay? *Our daughter.*"

I stared at her, nonplussed. She didn't blink. Her gray eyes were a bit red on the sides and her lips trembled. She held her ground. This was not like the Waterses. The Waterses I knew would let me come over until the world ended, feeding me, wrapping me in blankets of parental love that my own folks kept hidden away in gunnysacks like two Latin misers. But she looked hurt. With Bill falling apart every night, she had enough on her mind and on her hands. She didn't need me around. I was the straw that broke the camel's back.

"Okay," I said. I put the cigarette to my lips and walked down the concrete path that cut through the lawn.

"Thank you for the cigarette, though," she said to me. I nodded weakly and kept walking, my own shadow stretched long before me like some sleep paralysis ghoul, taunting me and luring me back to my car at the curb.

I stomped the cigarette in the gutter and climbed into the car. I started it up and heard, "Sammy! Wait!" and it was Bill, hustling down the lawn. He got to the car and tapped on the window. I lowered it, and he smelled like booze.

"I'm gonna stay in touch, okay?" he said. "Don't worry about Claire. I'm gonna still ring you now and then, okay? Is that okay?"

"Ignore him, Sammy! He's drunk and sad!" Claire called from the veranda. She was leaning on the banister. She had the tone of a schoolmarm.

"Don't listen to her. Please. Let me call when I wanna call. We can hang out without her knowing, you know? She doesn't control me."

"Listen, Mr. Waters, I—"

"I know what's best for him, Sammy. Just drive! Go!"

"What the fuck is wrong with you?" he turned and shouted to her. With his back to me, I had my escape. I put the car in drive, but he turned back quickly and placed his hands on the window. I didn't know what to say. I panicked.

"Yeah, man, just email me if you want."

Bill smiled with relief. He exhaled and his breath smelled like bourbon. He patted the roof of my car. "Good man."

I raised the window and took off. They screamed at each other before fading into silence behind me.

>

Driving home, I listened to the album *Juju* by Siouxsie and the Banshees. When we were twenty, Ellery told me about them and said it was her new favorite album ever. Of all time. Period.

"Don't you wanna wait before you make that claim?" I asked, needling her, just seeing what she'd say back.

"Nope. I don't have to wait. It jumped to my number-one favorite."

"Damn, that fast, huh?" I was grinning. We were drinking beers in a courtyard pool. It was late and we had snuck in. We didn't even live in that complex.

"Maybe it's just an absolute objective fact. It is the best album. Of all time. Kinda crazy that I'm just now listening to it at the tender age of twenty flat."

"You're ridiculous," I laughed. She swam over and dried her hands on a towel and synced her Bluetooth with a small speaker. She raised the volume loud as the first track, "Spellbound," came in.

"Not so loud," I said. "You're going to get us kicked out."

"Who cares? Let them all hear. They should pay me for this enlightenment." She cranked it louder. I swam over to lower the volume, but she climbed onto me, pushing my shoulders underwater. The heavy guitars and drums echoed loud through the courtyard, bouncing off apartment buildings that weren't ours. I heard it even underwater, the vibrations coming through like deep muffled yawns. I came up for air.

"Spellbound! Spellbound! Woo-oh!" she hollered. I was part laughing and part drowning, thrashing around in the pool. She wrapped her legs around my shoulders and tried to get me to stand up with her on top, but she was too tall, and we teetered back and forth. *"Following the footsteps of a rag doll dance!"* she sang, laughing. Lights in the buildings turned on. Some dick head in a polo shirt was about to kick us out. I learned the chorus and yelled "Spellbound" with her. Now it was the only album I listened to.

>

Back home in my bedroom-turned-guestroom I opened my laptop and logged back on to CampfireFables.com. I felt a bizarre sense of nostalgia as I scrolled through the trending submissions and the anonymous in-character posts of cryptid sightings. It was only after a moment before I felt someone in the room with me. This was how my stories always started. Some buffoon came home late at night and felt bad for himself (like me, right then) and shortly after, the buffoon heard the soft crying of a grown man under his bed. Then the Wax Man shimmied out, first the top of his hat, then his face, noseless, a thick layer of old wax covering his skull, the crying coming from *within*, muffled and desperate for air.

To me, before I quit writing them, the essence of the crying was always most important. It was never a crying of pain, but rather, a crying of despair. It was the crying of a man having fucked up so bad that he couldn't blame anyone but himself. The crying was always key. Some users submitted Wax Man posts that piggybacked off mine, but they never got the soul of it right. They had Wax Man crying with rage or crying from heartbreak, but that always missed the mark. If you put a gun to my head and asked me *why* the crying had to be just right, I'd just stare at you blankly. Somewhere deep in my lizard brain the gears would've turned, but I wouldn't be able to verbalize it. I've tried to dissect it myself a few times, but it always felt like one of those kitchen cabinets that never opened and seemed to just be there for design, but if you looked closely through the gap in the wood you could see *something* made its way in there. Something you forgot about. Something maybe you locked away on purpose.

I sat there in the dark and wrote a cutesy post titled: WAX MAN LIVES!! I made up a quick little paragraph about a young girl at a boarding school who found the Wax Man in her closet and he came in and had his way with her before she was found dead and clumped in white folds. Within moments of posting it, the piece was deleted. A banner fell across my page saying: *Detected harmful violence/sexual violence against minors/students.*

"Yeah, that's the point," I said, refreshing the page. "This is bogus." I tried to change some verbiage and post it again, but my post limit was maxed. "What the fuck happened to this site?" I heard myself mutter. I was about to close my laptop when a message popped on my screen. It was from Haruspx. They were online right now.

I noticed you were posting again.

Missed your stuff.

The letters were green against the black-and-gray background of the site. Skull sprites twirled in the margins of the screen. The site was hokey, no two ways about it.

I replied back with my initial thought.

Wtf happened to this site?

Woke mob got to it

I wasn't sure how to respond. I registered as a Democrat in Leon County my freshman year, but I figured Haruspx didn't need to know that.

Use this site instead.

chinsky.rekt.x.

Yeah you sent this already. I

thought it was spam

It's a good community. We're all big

fans of Blue Bird.

I was flattered at first by the comment, but then quickly put off by the idea that I had a following, and if that were true, how long had I had one? I clicked on Haruspx's page and found zero submissions and zero comments, but that they'd been active since around my freshman year. Maybe even earlier. I clicked back on the message thread and studied the combination of letters. I copy-and-pasted it in a fresh tab.

"Please don't give me a virus, please don't give me a virus," I chanted as I pressed ENTER.

The link took me nowhere.

I messaged Haruspx again.

It didn't go anywhere

Are you using a Mac?

Yes. Is that bad?

Download Spyglass. It's a browser.

thegoodbooty.org.

I clicked the link, and it took me to a picture of cartoon skeletons in pirate gear. It was animated, and a file, nestled in a treasure chest, blinked at me, asking to be installed.

Is this Tor or something?

Lol. Tor is for pussies. Spyglass

is legit.

> what is this site anyway?
>   Is it stories?

Lmao.

I started downloading Spyglass.

You see, links for the dark web don't look like Google or Facebook or often have intelligible words. They're random letters and numbers like 4uwjabfmr5i29qh.onion, onion being the domain a browser like Tor can access. But Tor was for pussies evidently and Spyglass, well, to be frank, I had no idea where to even start. In truth, the idea of crossing the threshold into the dark web had been kicking around my head for some time. I was getting bored of the casual gore I'd been watching and wanted the next thing. I still wasn't sure what that meant though, or if I could handle it. I looked at the link from Haruspx one more time. chinsky.rekt.x.

"Let's see what happens," I said. I ran Spyglass, pasted the link, clicked it, and the screen flickered and went gray and I got a pinwheel. My laptop fan started whirring and getting warm. Afraid it was going to keel over, I force quit Spyglass and let the little guy catch its breath. I messaged Haruspx again.

> the link still isn't working.

It took a while, but eventually they hit me back:

Uncover your webcam.

> Yeah fucking right.

don't be a fag

I studied the painter's tape on my webcam. Could it really be dependent on a visual? It made me uneasy. Fuck it, I thought. I restarted Spyglass and went to the site. I reached forward and ripped off the tape. First, the webcam glowed green and blinked at me. Then my computer whirred to life, not as mad as before, and settled into a hum as the page loaded.

The website was garish. Just hideous. Everything was neon yellow and the borders were red and dripped with blood. Even the ratio of the screen felt outdated, like it was meant for a computer with a cathode tube in the back. The contrast of the screen killed my eyes, and I waited a second for the page to populate. After a while there was only one link, and it was scrawled in some phony, scary font: CAR ACCIDENT ON MONROE AVENUE.

I went numb. It took a second for me to move. If the link was what I thought it was, there was simply no going back. I heard wheezing in my room. It was underneath me, somewhere close.

I clicked the video and watched it. It was CCTV footage from the nearby streetlight. It was unmistakably of Ellery's Nissan. The license plate. The bumper sticker of our high-school volleyball team. The Johnny Bravo bobble on the antennae. And just like that, I watched her get sideswiped by a truck going eighty. The car flipped over like garbage. The truck spun out and fell into a bar ditch. Scrap metal and glass blew out like fireworks.

I sat back and tried to catch my breath. I closed my eyes and the footage played in the murky dark. I saw it in my brain. The way her Nissan tumbled on its pitch and yaw, the doors flinging open like cut wings. Her neck probably snapped. The roof crushed down on her head. I shut my laptop and threw it into my hamper. I paced back and forth in my tiny room. I wanted to scream but imagined waking up my parents on the other side of the house. I stifled it and bit into a pillow. My lips quivered and I took a breath, and I sat on the hard wood and pressed my knuckles into the cold floor. After about an hour, I gathered my senses. I dug my laptop out of my clothes and opened it to see if what I saw had actually been real. And it was. The sole link was still there looking at me. And so, I watched it again.

>

In the morning, I had my SP gig at the University of South Florida. My name was Ronald Clayburn and I was thirty-one and I had a urinary tract infection. I was a little bummed, convinced there was no reason to cry over hot pee, but I took the role anyway. I didn't sleep last night for obvious reasons, but I didn't cry either which started to upset me. Haruspx, whoever they were, came out of the woodwork to rattle my cage. To show me Ellery's car wreck. My brain felt poisoned, and my clothes felt suffocating. Something in me was coiling up, tight and violent, but why the hell didn't I cry?

In the waiting room I saw Ryan. He had aged gracefully; the way fishermen do. Wrinkles got deeper. Salt-and-pepper hair turned to salt-and-sugar. All of his features looked more weathered and sun-soaked. Even when he looked at his lines, it looked like he was on a boat tacking left and right. I spotted that he had a wedding ring now. He must've married that woman he was dating, the one with the daughter. Now he was somebody's stepfather. I bet he cried about that for sure.

In the doctor's waiting room, I sat on the examination bench and looked at the cameras looking down at me. All I could think about was Haruspx. Spyglass. Ellery. Her Nissan. I tried to pull myself together. I had a series of index cards in my hand. Did it hurt when I peed? Yeah. Did it burn? Sure. Did I have a dull kidney pain? Yes, but not bad. Was my brain melting out of my ears? Probably. Did I witness something that altered my very DNA? Felt like it. Shortly, the student came in and she was a Chinese girl with jet black hair. She was tall and thin and kept her hair in a Looney Tunes bow that she probably bought in response to notes calling her cold.

When she asked my name, I didn't answer right away. I was distracted. I tried to get a sense of where in the building Ryan was. I had to listen intently. It was extra important now.

"I said, 'Hi, how are you doing today?'" she repeated.

"It burns when I pee," I said. I was looking at the wall. I thought I heard his voice. "That guy with the sunburn and goatee, do you know what he's sick with?"

"We don't know the other SPs' illnesses."

"Sorry. Go on."

"Do you have frequent urination?"

"Yeah, a lot. I can't sleep through the night." I stood up and crossed the room and put my ear to the wall. I had to be sure not to miss it.

"Guy, you're like totally messing this up for me."

An intercom buzzed in the corner of the room. It was a professor watching from a monitor: "Everything okay in there?"

The student gave me a look like, *You're fucking this up.*

"Sorry. Yeah, it burns when I pee and sometimes when I lay on my side, I feel a pain right here." I moved back to the bench and gestured to my kidney.

"On a scale from 1 to 10 would you say—"

"It's a dull 1.5 kidney pain. It burns when I pee, and I pee a lot. Come on. I'm practically feeding you this."

"This isn't a race—"

"For me, it kinda is."

"Okay, well I'm going over what you've told me, and I think—"

"Come on, come on, just say it, quick, he's gonna go—"

"Mr. Clayburn, I think you may have—"

"Spit it out already—"

"A urinary tract—"

I screamed as loud as I possibly could. The girl, startled, backed away to the cabinets. Her eyes went wide, and she held her hands up like I was about to pounce.

"Mr. Clayburn, it's just a UTI, I think—"

Before I knew it, the cry became real. Thank God. My bottom lip quivered, and I took in large gulping breaths. I pounded my fist on the wall.

"Fuck you!" I yelled. "Fuck you!!" I wasn't sure who that was for. Ryan. Haruspx. Myself.

From my peripheral vision the student had fully pulled herself into the corner. She looked up at the cameras and hollered, "This one does *not* count." She went for the door and left, and I heard her and some professors talk in a heated exchange. I returned to the examination bench and controlled my breathing, calming myself down, only feeling the real and pure embarrassment of it all when the door opened, and two white coats looked at me like I had four heads.

I caught up to Ryan in the parking lot. He was holding a Styrofoam cup of coffee and hurrying to a car that was waiting for him. He looked pissed.

"Hey!" I shouted after him.

He spun around, angry. "Was that you in there? Blowing up my spot?"

"How did you like being on the other side of it, huh?"

"*What?*"

"Three years ago, you told me that I couldn't fear death because I didn't have any stakes."

"What the fuck are you talking about, kid?"

A pair of students came out in lab coats. One of them was the Chinese girl, fuming, mid-rant that I ruined her exam.

Ryan took a pause and stepped back. He looked me up and down. In the car behind Ryan, a woman was waiting.

"Do I know you?" Ryan asked. Maybe he remembered my voice. To his credit, I sure as hell didn't look like I did when I was nineteen. My facial hair had come in, scraggly and long. My glasses were bigger and more scratched up. My teeth were already stained from tobacco and booze. I was skinnier too, like a man wasting away. But still, he cocked his head and said, "I do know you, don't I?"

"You told me I didn't have any stakes in my life and so I didn't have anything to cry about. Ellery got hit by a truck one year ago and last night I watched it happen. I want you to apologize."

"Huh?"

What Ryan was doing was fucked. Crying like that was performative. If you did it in front of people like Ryan, or in a group, then you were manipulative, throwing your burden onto other people, weighing them down. But conversely, if you cried alone, then you were weak, self-pitying, vulnerable to the darkness in your room and under your bed. And being raised Catholic, you were only allowed to cry for other people, and they had to go first, or you'd just make it awkward. So, what the hell could you do?

"Apologize for what you said about Ellery," I said again. My fists clenched, and he saw it. He turned his body at an angle.

"Man, fuck you, I don't know what you're talking about."

"Did you say Ellery?" a voice said. "Ellery Waters?" It came from inside Ryan's car. The person waiting in the driver's seat leaned her head out. It was a woman with sunglasses. She climbed out of the truck. She was athletic and tan and masculine.

"Honey, get back in the car, this kid lost his mind," Ryan said, but the woman came forward anyway. She was wearing a Chamberlain High Volleyball jersey. Then I noticed their pick-up truck and the net of volleyballs in the back.

"Who are you?" I asked.

"I'm Lisa Fischer. I'm the coach at Chamberlain. My daughter played against Ellery. She was at Hillsborough, right?"

"Yeah," I said. I was shaking, the inside of me bright and hollow like a gymnasium.

"I'm so sorry about what happened. We all talked about it. She was so good. Didn't she go to Chapel Hill?"

I drove back to Tallahassee with a black eye and a busted lip. I never went back to therapy, but I kept looking at forums. I kept watching that video, and I kept watching things like it. I had to desensitize myself. I had to put it all in my mouth at once so it all tasted the same. But most importantly, I had to find out who the hell Haruspx was.

> Meet new girl
> Jason & Maria get mad at me
> HaruspxHaruspxHaruspx

"What do you know about the dark web?" I asked Jason. It was Halloween proper, and we were at a bar. I was dressed in black nose paint, dog ears, a bandanna, and a gunshot through my head. I told people I was David Foster Wallace & Gromit. It was a grim joke that made Jason laugh a lot. Like I said before, anything worked if it landed, although the bartender didn't think it was too funny. I couldn't tell if he was put off by the suicide make-up or that he actually quite liked *Infinite Jest*, a book a friend once described as *Atlas Shrugged* for liberals. Either way, we got slammed on Yuengling and shots of Bulleit and I tried to beat around the topic of what I had seen online.

"You don't wanna get involved in that shit, man," he said. He was dressed as JonBenét Ramesses II, complete with a blonde wig and Pharaoh headdress.

"Do you know anything about Spyglass?"

"What's that?"

"It's a private browser. Like Tor."

"Dude, stop, you're gonna take one step into the dark web and get hacked and get viruses and then someone is gonna kidnap you for your organs."

"That's a myth."

"It's really not. Plus, the FBI monitor the shit out of new-bies. You need some real-deal security and privacy. You can't just go moseying on in. You'll be on a list in no time."

"A list for what?"

"I don't know," he said, then he started to grin. "They're gonna spy on you through your webcam, take one look at you, and be like, 'That's a pedophile.'"

I let out a sharp laugh. He doubled down: "They're gonna see your beard and glasses and be like, 'He's going for child porn stat.'"

"I'm not going for child porn," I said. I raised my voice and looked around the bar. "You hear me, guys? I'm not going for child porn!"

Jason laughed and countered me, "Sammy, put that cheese pizza away! I ain't into that shit, man!"

The bartender shot us a look, and it wasn't friendly. We quieted down, but only a little.

"Why are you so curious anyway?" he asked. "What do you want to see?"

"That's the thing, man," I started. I glanced around the packed bar. "I think I already saw it."

His face got serious. The implication hung between us. He whispered. "What did you watch? No. Don't tell me. What the fuck are you talking about? Did you watch—?"

"No! I didn't. I watched a different thing." I wanted to tell him about the Ellery video, but it didn't feel real yet. I mean it *was real*. It was CCTV footage, of course it was real.

"Brother, we have to get you out of this slump."

"I'm not in a slump."

He scoffed.

"I'm not," I said. "I'm fun Sammy. I've been fun Sammy for months now."

"Fun for who?" he asked. "You watch that shit and it eats at your brain and then you try to show all of us. Last month you made us all watch fucking *Cannibal Holocaust.* Then you get all mad and mopey when Maria yells at you like, hello, it's because you just walk around showing us creepy videos of amputees and shit."

He wasn't lying. Since seeing the Ellery video, I had begun to unravel in a real way. It shifted the plates in my skull and opened the floodgates for things I needed to see. Day and night I spent scouring the internet for the worst things possible. A video shows a woman getting killed with a Black and Decker hammer. A blog post tells of a coding teacher raping and killing his own son. A video shows a horse stable on fire, the horses inside whinnying in complete agony as they try to kick through the blazing wood. I couldn't explain why, but I kept two windows open: Ellery death cam & other stuff. Back and forth all day. A part of me believed that if I could find The Worst Thing, then Ellery's car crash wouldn't affect me as much. Remember how I mentioned emotional spikes? Buddy, I was spiking all over. And all the while, my webcam watched me.

"Okay." I nodded. "Point taken. I'll lay off the freaky shit."

"You promise? Because I have more news for you."

I raised an eyebrow and put the beer to my lips.

"Maria's got a friend you might like," he said. The clatter and hum of ski balls happened in the background. I rubbed the back of my sleeve on my nose, streaking it with black make-up. Jason kept going: "Her name is Becca Steiner. She's cute."

"I don't know, man. I still—"

"Feel weird. Sure. And you're allowed to feel weird for-ever. But she's cool. I'll leave it at that."

"She like some Jewish-American-Princess type? I don't know if that's my bag."

"Dude, Ellery was WASPy as hell. High-maintenance white girls are very much your bag. And anyway, no, what-ever the opposite of a JAP is, she's that type. An industrious Jew with lots of responsibilities who does everything on her own. That's what she is. She's cool. Trust me. Feel weird all you want. But trust that you'd like her."

"Okay," I said. He went on and talked about Becca and about me meeting her in a way that seemed rehearsed. I pic-tured Maria giving him flash cards and talking points, using him *to get through to me.* I knew he didn't like bringing it up, because in the time I've known him, he liked taking the path of least resistance. At that moment, he was out of his comfort zone, doing it for Maria. I guess I appreciated it and, surpris-ing myself, deemed it wholesome.

Maybe there was a part of Jason that felt he owed me something. After all, I was the one that coached him through his courtship of Maria. He was a shy, but sweet, loner when I first met him in a Rocks-for-Jocks class our freshman year. He was a transplant from New Mexico, and I invited him to come play role-playing games with Ellery and me and a few other friends I had made in the DeGraff dormitory. After that, we were routinely watching the *Die Hard* movies and pound-ing Miller Fortunes, making up drinking rules whenever we wanted. Drink when McClane did this, did that, killed a moth-erfucker, said a really good line. Shortly, we spoke a language that was near impenetrable; fortified with inside jokes, ref-erences, bits, and gags that began to eat its own tail in that bizarre ouroboros long-term banter becomes.

After our fourth round, I went out the back door and yakked along the brick wall, supporting myself with my right hand. Jason came to the doorway and, drunkenly swaying, said, "The bartender is cutting us off. I'll close us out."

"Thanks," I said and threw up again between my feet. Jason went back into the bar and let the metal door shut loud behind him.

>

"Feel weird all you want," Jason had said back in the bar. Over the next few weeks, I replayed it in my head. *Feel weird all you want,* I thought when I looked over my shoulder on the bus. When I looked under my bed late at night. When I scrolled CampfireFables.com to see if Haruspx ever replied. `fucking answer me`. *Feel weird all you want,* when I caught myself shopping online for wingtip shoes and expensive hats. When I had twenty different tabs open, all of them NSFW and NSFL. When I looked at Ryan Vasquez and his wife's Facebooks. When I looked at his stepdaughter and thought, for one fleeting moment, that she belonged to me. *Feel weird all you want.*

>

I ended up meeting Rebecca Steiner at a house party where she creamed me at beer pong. She was twenty-three and had come south from Tennessee to get her master's in sociology. At this point in my troubling lifestyle, I had graduated from my long and drawn-out undergrad program and gotten a job inputting data and numbers on a small terminal beneath the science building. I opted for the night shifts and the boss man,

Mr. Cathy, a pudgy and religious guy, told me, "We don't really have night shifts." I looked at him and made up some reason why I couldn't work days, but that I'd be happier to take on extra work if I got to work at night. The truth was that I consistently had trouble sleeping and, in a derisory effort of self-improvement, thought that occupying my nights with a steady paycheck would be better than the alternative—cheap whisky, internet slime, and watching Ellery die. It was a small change, but I was on an upswing and going to a house party with Jason and Maria felt like a well-deserved reward. Meeting Becca was even better.

She was short and narrow-framed and had waves of thick, chestnut curls. She was pale and wore little silver rings and had strong facial features. When she laughed her mouth went wider than expected and rows of big white teeth shined from ear to ear. She wore dark-blue jeans with a brown belt that was too long, so she tucked it back into the belt loops around her small hips. She was the sweetest girl I could've met, and I fell fast and hard.

She tossed the ping-pong ball and it landed in my cup and she shrugged like it was an accident. I chugged the cup and, doing my one party trick, spat the ball out of my mouth back into the cup. She laughed and in moments, we were on the couch talking.

"I swear to God the drop was like five feet," she said, explaining turbulence she experienced on a flight a year ago. I watched her talk and watched her move her hand around like a plane, simulating luggage hitting the ceiling, and re-enacting her and her mother freaking out.

There was a part of me that needed this to work, not just for me, but for everyone I had been dragging down these last few years. Jason was too friendly to say anything, but I knew how he felt. He'd come on walks with me and we'd talk movies and TV shows, rarely broaching serious subjects. I'd text him at night to come over and get drunk with me and sometimes he'd show up with a bottle of Jack and sometimes he'd show up with just one or two cans of beer, telling me, "I'll never let you drink alone." The minute the booze hit and I started feeling sad for myself, I'd see his demeanor change. Like a factory worker punching the clock. It wasn't fair to him. It became clear that if I could be happy with Becca, then it was proof I could change, and all of Jason's time put in would be worth something.

Becca kept telling me the story, and I watched her and nodded along. She had a knack for it. Her intonations rose and fell, her face was expressive. She had little asides and comments, even doing silly voices for the flight attendants and the screaming church group at the back of the plane. I was enamored with her. Her voice was high and a bit raspy. After each section of her story, she'd nod forward and ask, "You know what I mean?" And I nodded and said, "Yeah, definitely."

"No, you don't," she said. "You're not even listening to me. You're just staring at my lips."

I was caught. I nodded again and said, "Yeah, definitely," and she laughed.

Later, we walked outside, and I offered her a cigarette. She declined and said, "I don't like to kiss smokers." I paused and looked at her. It was December now. The house party was still going strong inside. She had a face that seemed like a permanent smile. She had freckles across her cheeks. She had messy eyebrows. She had the air of a girl that couldn't say no and whose selflessness had often led to her burning out and taking on more than she could handle. A girl that was a people-pleaser, that would spend her nights up and about, flitting around and running errands and doing last minute chores because she told some other people, *"It's fine, I can do it, I can handle it, no worries, I can do it."* But the fact of the matter is that she *could* do it. She had learned every lesson she could've learned from every misstep she'd ever made. In short, she never made the same mistake twice.

"You don't have to quit tonight," she said, smirking, "but maybe not right now before we go home together."

"I think I can make that work," I said, and I stepped forward and kissed her and brought her in close, my hands on the small of her back. "You know, for most women I'm a gentle lover. But for Jewish women I'm a Gentile one."

"Never say that again."

The kiss came easy, but the sex came hard. She was the second girl I had ever slept with. I only ever knew Ellery's body, and Ellery's routine, and Ellery's positioning. I only ever knew her smell and taste and the geography of her bed, or rather, the amount of space she occupied, the volume of water she displaced in a tube. I had to pull it off like a Band-Aid. I was a car going through mud and if I lost momentum I'd be stuck, stranded, and I'd potentially lose Becca who shined in the room like a beacon of adjusted health.

When we got into Becca's apartment, I went to the bathroom to hype myself up. I listened to her move clothes from the bed to the desk chair and send last-minute texts. I paced back and forth and silently scolded myself. I told myself I wasn't cheating, and I told myself I was allowed to do this. I told myself Ellery would be happy I moved on, but even then, I knew I was lying. The video of her accident flashed in my head. My psyche wouldn't let Ellery be happy for me. Not in a million years. But in some gross, masochistic twist, the thing that got me into bed with Becca was knowing that I didn't deserve it. Knowing that Ellery would hate me. Wanting to be hated. Wanting to be filled with shame and guilt. To be potentially harangued from beyond the grave seemed like a fitting punishment.

But the real fear and concern came afterward, in the morning, in the fresh light of the new day when Becca and I realized we liked each other. Surely, I didn't deserve that.

>>>

Quickly thereafter, the casual sex turned into coffees and lunches which turned into dinners and breakfasts and then, in the iconic youthful way, made a full one-eighty where the most intimate thing you could do was lay in bed together, fully clothed, and talk about your various scars, emotional and tangible. *How are your folks? How are your siblings? What was your bad breakup? What do you wanna do with your life? What are you afraid of?*

Becca told me she had an autistic brother back home in Tennessee. He was older than her and her parents took care of him. She showed me pictures of him, and I said, "I'm sorry," and she said, "You're not supposed to say that." Then I said, "Okay, he looks like you." And she chuckled and said, "Sure, I'll let that one fly."

It was my turn to share, and I told her about Ellery, and she nodded along and said she knew. That Maria had told her. Fucking Maria. My initial anger that I didn't get to share my own memory was diffused and supplanted pretty fast when I felt Becca nuzzling into me. Her hair smelled like honey. She put a hand on my chest and said, "You don't have to tell me anything." I felt tears come to my eyes and I shuddered and listened intently for any crying, whether from me, her, or the man under the bed. But there was nothing.

I almost offered to show the video to Becca just to get her reaction, but I balked. It wasn't right. Haruspx meant it only for me. Instead, I closed my eyes and ran through the Rolodex of horrific things I had read or seen online. I didn't know why, but I needed to feel something icy cut through this haze of pink clouds and warmth I felt. I conjured up a video I saw months ago of a cinder block flying through a car windshield and killing a man's wife in the passenger seat. The way she went limp, the bottom of her jaw cracking inward, the top row of teeth falling out like Chiclets. The way the husband screamed and grabbed at her. And also the son in the back. How he yelled out, *"Mommy! Mommy, what happened?"* And then the dad had to swerve the car to the shoulder and call for help. Everyone was crying and screaming. The mom's eyes fluttered, the last images of her entire family falling like plastic blinds. Her tongue peeks out of the back of her exposed throat like a creature waiting to unfurl itself.

Becca looked up at me from my chest and shimmied forward and kissed me and snapped me out of it. We cuddled and fell asleep in our jeans and sweaters. In the morning, it was cold for Florida, maybe in the high thirties. We had sex and, possibly for the first time, I didn't think of anybody else. I just thought of her and looked at her and she made eye contact with me all the while. We came together and she shuddered, and my back went weak, and I fell into her chest and breathed the scent of her skin and the sheets and the morning warmth of a restful night.

Sammy Dominguez, 22, in love again.

Our relationship progressed and, in more ways than one, I was operating like a high functioning alcoholic. I transformed my dour and depressive drinking into life-of-the-party drinking, shouting and getting everyone to do shots, gunning forward with this idea that I will be fun with Becca and, thus, I will be fun with everyone. Beyond the Cutty Sark, Hornitos, Golden Monkeys, weed, and occasional key bumps with Jason and Maria (yes, even the shrew cut loose now and then) I had a new substance to abuse, one that was wholly a secret from everyone else.

I was addicted to the chthonic reaches of the internet and would read or watch multiple horrendous things a day and wouldn't stop until I wanted to vomit or sometimes even did. There were a few times, in my teens, when I was concerned that I was addicted to porn and I googled how that manifested itself. The common red flag was simple: you had an addiction if you canceled plans just to jerk off. I didn't have that problem with porn *anymore*. My sex life now with Becca was more wholesome and fulfilling. But there were times, for no reason at all, I'd get the urge to steal away from dinner, hustle to the bathroom stalls, and watch something macabre like an ISIS beheading or one of the BME Pain Olympics where a poor bastard stuck thumbtacks into the white meat of his testicles. I'd come back jittery and sit across Becca, beautiful as ever, and I'd act like I didn't just digitally dip my face into hydrochloric acid.

One time, post-sex, she was in the shower, and I laid naked in her bed and, like muscle memory, dug around on my phone for something to consume. I read a story about a young girl who spent her entire childhood folding herself into a luggage trunk every time her parents went on vacation. They'd padlock her in there and give her a potato if she got hungry. She explained how the first time she ate the potato she had diarrhea and nearly suffocated, shitting herself in an airtight trunk, slopping around in her own mess like a pig. Then she learned she had to suck on the potato and not eat it raw. I read the story but couldn't name the bizarre emotion it evoked in me. It took several moments before I realized Becca was trying to get my attention and I had to rub my eyes to see her as she was. The trunk, the girl, the potato, and the shit, quickly faded from my brain, but not without leaving a trace of keloidal pinstripes that I could go back to and follow like a trail of breadcrumbs.

Throughout all of this, I was still spamming Haruspx, but message after message, they were ghost. I was still in the dark about Spyglass, chinsky, the video, where it came from, who uploaded it, everything. I was on the breaking point. Until finally I got a response.

Becca had gone to bed, and I left her apartment and travelled back across campus to clock into my job. The campus was mid-transition. Students, dressed for the night, were in and out of the dining hall, moving across Landis Green, and pre-gaming at each other's dorms. Dark bronze statues looked black and menacing beneath large trees, bolted into concrete benches with ornamental plaques.

I keyed into the back of the science building and moved through the hallway and down the stairs into the basement. The station I worked on, a blocky thing from 2009, sat in its own room next to a more modern Seminole-branded laptop. Essentially, the blocky bastard had outdated software and contained loads of backlogged and archived files and paperwork and anytime someone needed it, they'd spend an hour and a half hot-keying through pages of frozen graphs and blurry scans. My job was to modernize it, file it, input it into something not from the Mesozoic era and, at the same time, get rid of redundancies or things deemed "inconsequential."

Ignoring Mr. Cathy's request, I didn't take my smoke breaks outside and instead sat on top of a steel cabinet and opened a sliding window that fed onto the grass of a back alley. I heard the custodian shuffle along the floor above me. My phone lit up with a sleepy text from Becca: Be good at work then come back to meeeeeee

I smiled and leaned against the wall and blew the smoke out of the small window. The smoke lifted up, moved, and disappeared in the cold wind of February. Then I started working.

After a few hours, I moved on to personal affairs and opened up my own laptop. I logged onto CampfireFables.com and was tense to find a new message from Haruspx.

new links up, was all it said.

go fuck yourself, I typed back. I had been rehearsing this rant in my head for weeks but was suddenly choking.

Take that video down. Please.

But they logged off.

stop ghosting me you little shit.

Nothing.

I sat there for a moment. The custodian moved down the hall, opening and closing doors.

You see, in a strange way the original video helped. It gave me context. The void that was in me was now filled. The footage was so sterile, so unbiased, so unflinching, it gave me the answers I needed, or, rather, confirmed that there were no answers. It was just a horrible accident. There was no solace to be had and, in a way, that was the solace. As shattering as it was to watch, it removed some of the mystery. I was able to breathe. Big screaming, raking breaths, but breathing all the same. I wondered to myself: what other links could there even be?

I opened chinsky and uncovered my webcam. The page loaded more links this time. The titles were: HOT SLUT MUR-DERED, BITCH GETS DRAGGED, EMPTY CLIP INTO GIRLS HEAD. Typical stuff really, but I felt a chill run down my arms. I hustled over and locked the door. I couldn't risk getting interrupted. This time, the page kept loading. It was fuller. More fleshed out. There were tons of links, all of them dripping red, but something was new about Ellery's. It was circled with a gold and blinking ring. It shimmered around the video like a pennant, like this video won something and the other red links didn't. I clicked on it again and saw the video that I had committed to memory. The high angle CCTV, the collision, the horrific silence. I backed out and examined the other links. BITCH GETS MAULED BY WOLF, YOUNG GIRL FALLS DOWN ESCALATOR, CRANE CRUSHES HOUSE. None of them had the gold banner. I clicked on some of them.

But they were all of Ellery.

A man unloads a .38 snubnose into a girl's head. It's Ellery, begging for her life. The first round blowing through her right eye. The next five blowing her skull apart. She's on a dirt road somewhere. It's hard to make out. I clicked another.

Two men take machetes to a young girl. It's Ellery. She's in her favorite sleep shirt getting dragged down the hall of her house, her feet kicking at tables, bringing them down, everything clattering on the wood floor. She's begging for help. The first blade lops off her hand. She holds her wrist, blood pumping in arcs. She looks at the camera seconds before the other blade lodges into her head at a slant. I hear nothing but the sound of meaty thwocks.

A car wreck sends Ellery out of the windshield. Freak scaffolding falls on Ellery and crushes her. She jumps out of a burning building. She gets beheaded. Torched. Lynched.

Drawn and quartered. I stood up and I rubbed my eyes. I was still at work. The custodian was lumbering around. He was gonna knock on my door any second. It was night out. The campus was dying. I needed something to drink. I needed drugs. For a second, I remembered the first time I did coke. I was with Jason in the garage of a Christmas party. Ellery walked in on us and asked for some. God, Ellery. She was cute and sexy, giggling with nerves and excitement that we were doing our first line as college students. "We're like the show *Skins*," she said, laughing, leaning her head down to a black leather trunk. Was a young girl on all fours in that trunk? Sucking on a potato and shitting herself? No, wait. My mind was shuffling the deck. Memories were falling beside things I had read and seen. I wanted Ellery high with me right now but that was impossible. Right now, she was in a buffering video where a Russian girl pushes her off a rooftop and the camera whips down just as she smashes against the concrete and her skull grapes open and shiny blood splatters everywhere like a Pollock mess.

I collapsed back into my chair. I kept my eyes open, and no matter what, I kept watching. Pages and pages of the stuff. But here's the kicker, not all of them were violent. Some were peaceful. Serene by comparison. There was one of her dying of cancer and one of her having a heart attack.

There was one where she was eighty years old, frail and small in her bed, surrounded by loved ones. NATURAL CAUSES was the title of the video. The camera was angled in the corner of the room. Her adult children held her hand. They stifled sobs. Ellery, white-haired, a fading gossamer, closed her eyes and passed away.

The knocking on the door made me jump.

"Hey, big man, I gotta get in there to clean," a voice said.

I closed my laptop and pushed myself away from the desk. I caught myself in the reflection of my little smoking window. I looked undead. Like someone between planes. Like I dunked my head into the pool of Hades and was back to speak to the droves.

The man knocked on the door again, and, paranoid, I was quick to open it. He was tall and Dominican and stood with his supply cart.

"I know you're working, but I gotta clean this spot and go home."

The clock said 2:00 a.m. The Seminole work computer blinked with spreadsheets.

"You good?"

"I'm good."

"I found a pair of shoes in the other room. They look expensive. They yours?"

"No. Not mine."

"Okay, well if anybody asks about them, they'll be in Lost and Found."

I nodded, gathered my shit, and hurried out, desperate to get to Becca's before the sky turned pink. Once at her place, I let myself in, tiptoed past her roommates, and got into bed with her. It was a few moments before she rolled over and held me. I closed my eyes tight and dreamt I saw the Wax Man in the corner of the room. Only now he looked a little more like Uncle Ted. Now he looked less hostile. He kept repeating one phrase: "Now that's something to cry about."

In the morning, I didn't tell Becca about what I had seen. I didn't know how. I had promised Jason that I'd lay off the freaky shit and, fine, while I technically *didn't*, I stopped *showing* people and, socially, things were getting better. Even Maria and I stopped fighting. But I needed to investigate.

CUTE GIRL CHOKES ON VOMIT, BITCH TRAMPLED, PINATA PARTY. All of them just scrolled through my mind like movie credits. Ellery was dying over and over again right on my screen, but there was something to it that I couldn't figure out. I couldn't approach people with this until I was sure. Sure of *something.* Sure of *anything.*

>>>

In the spring, my parents had a barbecue and Becca and I went down to Tampa. Despite my deteriorating mental state, our relationship was progressing, and she wanted to meet the folks. My family sat outside on the lanai my dad prided himself on. My Uncle Sal (on my mother's side, her last living brother) passed around margaritas and people sat and talked. My Aunt Dev on my dad's side (his last living sister) started talking about the past. Not just the immediate past, but also the past she wasn't there for. She started on about family drama from before WWII and passed around these faded old photographs she always brought to these types of things.

My mother decided to get drunk with Sal. He was a big burly guy with a sleeve of tattoos and when the two would tie one on together, it was impossible to keep up. Remember the impenetrable wall of banter I had formed with Jason? Siblings did it even worse. And adult siblings? Good fucking luck.

To my mother, death was just science. The old photographs of dead relatives that passed between their drunken hands meant little to her or, at least, that's how she played it off. Any talk about Uncle Ted and she just shook her head and fell into herself. She'd chalk it up to "bad choices" and say his body "couldn't handle it anymore." Death had a clinical sterility for her. Not for my dad, though. My dad's parents and most of his sisters had been dead and gone for years now and the old photos meant a lot to him. Death waited around every corner and through every doorway and should be respected but not engaged. Heard but not seen. Spoken to only when addressed.

After a while, the sun headed for the horizon and my father passed around cigars that he and the other men in my family smoked. I took one and briefly recalled my role as Jerry Smith, 34, who smoked two packs a day and experienced poor circulation. With my father's cigar in one hand and yet another of my uncle's margaritas in the other I felt like an asshole, but the tobacco kicked the alcohol into high gear and my body felt warm and full. Becca scooted her chair over and sipped on her own drink and we took turns taking puffs of the maduro.

"You hanging in there?" she asked.

"I'm alright." I looked at her. Her face was serious with worry. The string lights of the lanai reflected in her eyes. Her paper plate of barbecue food was in front of her, the crumpled-up napkin stained red and brown. She put both hands on my wrist and squeezed it. I could only pay half-attention. The other half was rewatching Ellery get lowered into an industrial shredder.

"Thanks for coming down with me," I said.

"Or what? Miss a Dominguez barbecue? I could never."

I smiled at her.

"Are they gonna ask me about Ellery or like bring her up?" She nodded her head to the photographs of dead people being passed around. The thought hadn't crossed my mind, but it was a valid concern. Did my Aunt Dev have a photograph of Ellery? I couldn't be sure. Did my Aunt Dev have . . . videos of Ellery?

"I doubt it," I told her. "All of those pictures are of relatives."

"All of them are rancheros," she joked.

"Tons of rancheros," I confirmed.

Not long after, my mother click-clacked her way over, high-cupping her drink. High-cupping, among the women of my family, was a tell-tale sign of intoxication. The higher they held their drink, the more they had to drink. I had explained this tell to Becca on the drive down, and we snickered when my mom approached, cup at shoulder height. I took a large draw from the cigar and kept the smoke in my mouth. I let it sit and sting.

"You look beautiful tonight, Becca," my mother said. "I'm so glad Sammy brought you down and we got to meet you."

"Thank you so much," she replied, giving a smile. "I'm happy I came."

"Look how nice she looks," my mom said, "and you're going out like that. Mira este."

"I think he looks cute," Becca said and patted my head.

"I don't envy your position," my mom started. "Being the one who has to follow Ellery? Yikes, chica. Yikes."

"I—" Becca stammered. "I'm not sure how to respond to that." She looked at me for rescue. I shot my mom a glare.

"You ever think about what you say?" I remarked. I finished my margarita and started on Becca's. I filled my mouth with the smoke from the maduro. I figured if I kept my mouth full she'd take the hint and leave us alone for the night. I looked across the table and my dad gave a look and then engaged Dev about the old photos again.

"Big shoes is all I'm saying," my mom said. Becca got quiet.

I thought of Roger Hall, age 40, stress ulcer from sup-
pressed rage. I suddenly got that familiar itch to go to the
bathroom and look at the worst thing I could find. Anything
on my phone would do. A thread of dog fights. Anything. But
I was too cross-faded and would've wiped out if I stood up
too quickly. I decided to source the misery from elsewhere.

"Tell Becca about Uncle Ted," I said.

My mother's face went sober. "Why?"

"Everyone's talking about Dad and Dev's relatives, but
she doesn't know anything about Uncle Ted."

"I don't really need to know," Becca said. She gave me a
look with wide eyes.

"I'll tell you about Teddy, I don't care," my mom said. She
pulled out a chair on Becca's right side and sat down. She put
her hand out for my cigar, and I refused, and she flipped me
off and then grabbed her margarita. "My brother Teddy was a
very troubled man, Becca. He had been in and out of jail. He
had AIDS. He was a drug addict. And he fell on really hard
times. He couldn't keep a job. Sammy's father and I tried our
best to keep a roof over his head. We paid for his apartment,
we gave him an allowance for groceries, even though all he
bought was beer and cigarettes. We did everything we could."

"That sounds really hard," Becca said.

"It was," my mom slurred. "And Teddy loved Sammy so
much. Loved Sammy more than anything. Sammy was his
favorite nephew. And one day his body couldn't handle it anymore and he had a heart attack. And that was that. It's very
sad. Sal and I miss him very much. We all do." My mom finished her margarita and went over to the stack of photos Aunt
Dev had. She took out two photos and tossed them our way,
then went into the house. Becca took one photo and I looked
at the other. He was tall and had darker skin than the rest of

us. He had stubble and a wide head like a boxer's. He had kind eyes and a big smile and large ears that kind of drooped lower the older he got. He wore paint-splattered jeans and mud-crusted boots and had a red bicycle with him that he rode everywhere after he wasn't allowed to drive anymore. My Uncle Sal looked like if Ted did steroids and went to the Army. My mother looked like if both of them were mashed together, given breasts, and sent to college.

Becca examined the photo she picked. It had the three of them in it, but I didn't take a good look. Instead, I got up and went to the glass table by the pool and grabbed two more margaritas that Sal had been setting up on autopilot. The sun had completely set at this point, but the sky was still a modest purple. It was a hot and sticky night and the tiki torches, these cheap guys my dad got from Walmart, burned and flickered and my family got rowdier as the night went on. Everyone was getting more drunk. Even Becca. And especially me.

Shortly, Becca and I walked out to the dock. My parents lived in a small neighborhood where they all shared a retention pond. Becca sipped on her margarita, and I nearly finished mine. The dock creaked under our weight, and we sat without speaking, the noise from the party still going on in the background. I was drunk and lightheaded and had trouble concentrating.

"You ever want to just hit her?" I asked Becca.

"No," she replied. "I think she means well."

"Yeah, you would," I replied and puffed at the cigar, the orange end casting a light on my face. "She wasn't being honest," I said. "About Uncle Ted."

"What do you mean?"

"He used to drive me to soccer sometimes when I was younger. He didn't have a car, but he'd borrow my grandpa's back when he still had this white rust bucket on their driveway. Anyhow, this particular soccer field was far away, like an hour out, and he'd drive me to practice and would keep a small cooler in the back seat with beers in them. I didn't know he was plastered the whole time. I really couldn't tell. Or maybe I did, but never wanted to admit it. I think I was like eleven at this time.

"So anyway, one day I'm at Publix with my mom and I'm just, you know, following her around the store. She gets to the beer section and starts getting Coronas for her and my dad and I see a four-pack of this fancy craft beer. I don't know why, but my stupid brain makes this dumb remark and I say, 'We should get those for Uncle Ted for our drives.' And, obviously, my mom figures out that Ted had been drunk driving me this whole time."

"Oh no," Becca said.

"It gets worse," I said. "It turns out that he had a history of doing this and years ago when I was like three or four and my parents thought he got his shit together, they paid him to take me to the zoo. I don't really remember this but apparently, he got high there and driving back, he jumped a curb on the road and rear-ended this lady. It became a whole thing.

"So now my mom has all of this flooding back to her and her and my dad are obviously fucking pissed so they scream at him and cut him off for good and my Uncle is looking at me like I ratted him out. Like it was my fault and like I should've kept his secret. I started crying and trying to backpedal and fight for him, but it wasn't really working.

"Anyway, about a week later my parents left town and I was home alone. That night, when I was asleep, he used the garage-door code to get into the garage. Our back door was still locked though, and he couldn't get into the house, so he kept knocking on it and calling for my name, I think. I don't know. I was sleeping. But he must've raided the fridge in the garage and got drunk. He had a heart attack and died there, and I found his body in the morning, surrounded by cigarette butts and empty beer cans."

There was a long pause. The moon was behind Becca, and I could just see the silver outline of her big hair and white arms. "Sammy," she started. "I'm so so sorry."

"I'm drunk," I said.

"That's okay," she said.

I looked at her over the rim of my glass. She was looking at me. Waiting for me to speak again. The shape of the glass distorted her body, and I moved it out of the way so I could admire her. I was lucky to be with her. I loved her, and I knew this was true and I got all depressed. How could I love this girl and give her my all when Ellery was dying online a million times over? How could I be here and be healed if this monster wasn't dragged into the light and beheaded?

"Here," she said and handed me her full glass. "You can finish mine too."

I took a large draw from the cigar, now at its endnote, a spicy-hot-cutting mouthful, and threw it into the lake.

"Did you really expect her to tell that story?" Becca asked.

"I don't know. I guess I wanted her to blame me."

"But it's not your fault. She wouldn't blame you for that. Nobody would."

"I think my parents do though. I know it sounds wild, but they look at me like I did it."

"You carry a lot of resentment around and sometimes you don't know where to put it or who to direct it at. It's just aimless resentment."

"I know."

"Come on. Let's go inside."

>

In my bedroom, I was absolutely hammered and nearly spinning. The rest of my family had gone home, and my parents were asleep on the other side of the house. I tried to sleep with Becca, but she laughed at my efforts. It wasn't in a malicious way, I could tell. I was just too fucked up. I took off her top and I admired her small chest and her white bra and a small golden necklace that rested in her cleavage.

"You can't even get it up. Look at you."

"Give me a second."

"No way. It's late. I'm going to sleep."

"Come on," I said, and I tugged at the waistband of her jeans.

"Go shower," she said. "You're all smoky."

I nodded and decided she was right and climbed off the bed.

In the bathroom, I started the shower and kneeled in front of the toilet. I could feel my head high washing around my skull, moving my brain up and down like a boat. My cheeks were heavy, and I kept spitting. I tried to puke but nothing came out and I stood back up and eased myself into the shower. The hot water fell over me. I was dizzy and watched my feet rotate back and forth like a carnival ride. I rubbed a bar of soap over me and felt my chest and my soft dick and the sensation beneath my knees was all rubber, the warm tapping of water like those reflex hammers doctors used.

"Come on, Sam," I said to myself. My eyes were sandbags. After a second of resistance, I nodded off, standing upright. When I opened my eyes, the bathroom was filled with steam. I turned off the water and stepped out. It was later than it was before. I could tell Becca was asleep. The whole house was. The sounds of it settling had gone mute, leaving behind a still and quiet yawn barely heard working through the wood and drywall. I felt a touch more sober, and I sat on the toilet, naked and wet.

I took out my phone and fiddled around looking for something juicy. I couldn't get chinsky on my phone, which was a bit of a blessing. Instead, I watched a Japanese guy's house burn down, him crying and all, filming it in the snow. I forgot it snowed in Japan. It's not something I thought about a lot. I remembered this Reddit thread of rapists justifying their actions and I dug it up. I read it, letting the slime pour over me, and then I heard it. A soft crying, no, a wheezing. I froze. I put my phone on the sink counter and sat there. Dripping wet. The room still tilted left and right, the white tiles of the bathroom floor pixelating and spinning like pinwheels. The crying was soft and there was a tapping. I stood up and pulled on my jeans.

Outside of my bathroom the hallway of my home stretched downward to the wing where my parents resided. Their office. Their living room. Their Diego Riveras all over. The chimney with the bric-a-brac and hardcover books: medical journals, clinical guides, and textbooks that my mom was featured in. Moonlight came in through the windows of my home, throwing up gnarled tree branches like black hands reaching in. On the gray wall I could see the pencil markings of my height over the years. From the kitchen I saw the lanai and beyond the lanai one tiki torch still flickered softly, an orange tongue licking at the cloudless sky. I almost went to snuff it out when I heard *tap, tap, tap . . . tap, tap, tap . . .* And then the wheezing. God. The wheezing. A sharp painful inhale. A labored phlegmy exhale.

I was too fucked up to think. I was shirtless, in jeans, and barefoot. My lips stung from the cigar. My hair dripped down my back. There was a chill in the house. The A/C working overtime. *Tap, tap, tap . . . Tap, tap, tap . . .*

The taps continued and I followed them to the utility room. I stopped short with my hand on the doorknob. I made a mental catalogue of everything in that room that could be the source. The laundry machine? No, that's turned off. The dryer? Nah. Sink? Buckets? Cleaning supplies? Would any of those make a sound?

On the other side of the utility room was the back door that led to the garage. In that garage was a fridge with beer. A few bikes. My mother's Jeep. A pull-down ladder that climbed into the attic. *Tap, tap, tap.* Maybe Becca went out to the garage to get a water bottle and the door shut behind her. *Tap.* Maybe my dad was in the garage, doing his end of the day putz-around. *Tap.* Maybe my mother left something in the back seat of her Jeep. *Tap.*

I kept my hand on the doorknob. If I opened it and stepped in and turned on the light, I would see whoever was there in the garage tapping on the glass window of the back door. I'd see who it was that needed to get in. I opened it and flipped the light switch and when I saw his face, pressed against the glass, tapping his index finger on the window, I leapt back. He had a Coors in his hand, and it was upside-down, dripping out, and he was wheezing, tapping his long yellow fingernail on the window. *Tap, tap, tap, tap, tap. Taptaptaptaptaptaptaptaptap—*

"Come have a beer with me," he said, a cigarette hanging from his rotten lips. He was in a stained, white T-shirt. He had a pack of Pall Malls rolled up in his sleeve. His eyes pinned on me like a parrot's, wide and skinny and wide and skinny and adjusting back and forth to the light. *Taptaptaptaptap.* He took a breath and started coughing, flecks of blood and

phlegm sprinkling the glass window. He took his brown thumb and smeared the mucus along the windowpane. *"Come have a beer with me, buster."*

Then I heard the crying. It was Becca. It was everyone. The house swelled with crying, and I fumbled backward, out of the utility room, landing hard on the tiled hallway, smacking my head against the wall. His tapping turned into aggressive knocking. Then open palm slamming, shaking the frame, shaking the door. *"Come on, Sammy!"* he yelled. *"Have a beer with your uncle! Come on! I know you can hear me! I know you know I'm out here! I'm out here waiting for ya!! Come on!! Una cerveza por favor, eh? Hola!!! Hola, mi sobrinoooooooo!!"*

I got up and hauled ass down the hallway. Becca's crying turned to choking. She was dying in my room. I barged in and saw it. A trench coat whipped left and right like a rat's tail, slipping under the bed. A fedora fluttered in the corner, tossed aside. Becca was turned to wax. I woke up in the shower screaming.

>

"You scared the shit out of me," she said. "I thought you slipped and broke your neck."

"I'm sorry."

We were driving back up to Tallahassee. She was at the wheel, and I was nursing a hangover from hell, trying not to get queasy as the bland landscape of Florida passed by the window. We were driving toward clouds, ashy and gray like a smudge of graphite.

"I think maybe you should try therapy again."

"I don't like crying in front of other people," I said.

"You can do it one-on-one," she said. She changed lanes and overtook a car. She made decisions fast and efficiently. She planned ahead where we'd get gas and where we'd eat. If there was an accident up ahead, she already knew the alternate route, gliding to the exit without a hitch. This is how she was.

"I don't like to put myself onto people like that."

"Well, you do it kind of a lot, though, babe."

"What do you mean?"

"Just because you don't actively talk about what you're going through doesn't mean you're not putting a certain energy onto people."

"Are you calling me an emotional marsupial?"

"What?"

"Never mind."

"Can you at least tell me what the nightmare was?"

"It was Uncle Ted trapped in the garage."

"Fuck. Because we talked about it?"

"I guess. And you started choking and when I ran into the room the Wax Man killed you."

"Who is the Wax Man?"

"It's stupid."

"Tell me." She put a hand on my hand and squeezed it. She quickly looked from the road to my eyes and raised her eyebrows. She nodded and her hair shuffled forward. "Please?"

"It's this fake character I made up and wrote spooky stories about. He wears a fancy hat and a coat and has nice shoes. Kinda looks like a detective."

"Like Ted?"

"Huh?"

"The picture that your mom showed me last night. It's your mom and Sal and Ted and they're at some Halloween party. And he's dressed like a detective. Is the Wax Man just Uncle Ted?"

I felt something tighten in my chest.

"Are they related or something?"

"I don't feel so good." My hands started shaking and I wiped a tear away.

"Sammy, look at me, you need help."

"I'm fine," I said.

"You're clearly *not*. Just tell me. Talk to me. Flow into me. I'm your ocean. Flow into me. I can handle it."

"Flow into you?"

"*Yes*."

Something in me started to fall apart. That locked cabinet in the kitchen was starting to open. I was stained glass, breaking, scattering into shards on the pavement outside.

"It's in my head, Becca," I started. "I just hear crying. I hear crying and I get fucking scared. And I wrote little things about it because it freaked me out. And I think he's dressed like that because that's when he was the happiest. That's how I want to remember him, but I can't, my brain won't let me, because he should be *alive*, Becca. He was having a heart attack in the garage and begging for help, and I hid under the bed. That's the part I didn't tell you. I saw him outside trying to get in and I ran to my room. I hid under the bed, and I listened to him *die*. And he should be alive and now my fucking brain won't let me move on," I broke down.

My heart started racing and I started to feel dizzy. My hands shook. I started breathing hard.

"Sammy, you're having a panic attack," Becca said. Her eyes flicked to the rearview mirror. She started moving to the emergency lane.

"I can't breathe," I said, sucking gulps of air.

"Just calm down," she said. "I'm pulling over."

"It's me," I said between sobs and gasps. "It's *me*. I killed him just like I killed Ellery."

Becca brought the car to a stop and turned on the hazards. "You didn't kill *anybody*," she said. "Just breathe. Focus on breathing. Relax. Close your eyes and focus on breathing."

I closed my eyes and did as she directed. I leaned my seat all the way back. My palms were clammy, and I clutched her hand and tried to count my breaths.

"You didn't kill anyone," she said. She held my hand to her lips and talked in a soft tone. Cars whizzed by. Overhead the sky turned gray and burnt.

"I look at awful things. I consume awful things. I need it in me like poison."

"I don't understand," she said.

"I can't let myself feel good. Uncle Ted is dead because of me. Ellery is dead because of me. I can't let myself feel good. My brain won't let me feel good. If I feel good and I feel happy, then I'll fucking kill myself. I just can't do it to them."

"You don't need to feel like shit for them. They wouldn't want that."

"Becca, I can't negotiate this."

"But you can't go on like this."

"Listen, I'm so close. I really am."

"To *what*?"

A big raindrop landed on the windshield. Then another. The sky broke and started pounding the car.

"I used to post Wax Man stories on this stupid website and now it's for pussies. Someone sent me software and a link for something really fucked up and I've been watching it."

"What are you talking about? I know what you look at. Maria warned me. Watching more isn't gonna help!"

"I'm gonna fucking kill that girl."

"*Sammy!*"

"This site is different. Trust me. I can't talk about it because I can't explain it. I just need to get in there and figure out who Haruspx is. Figure out who is uploading this shit. It's like a big dial in my head and if I can crank it up to eleven then maybe I can break it and bring it to zero and be free of it, you know?"

"So what the fuck is your plan? Push yourself deeper down a hole until you hit rock bottom? Then what? Then you'll find help?"

"I don't know. I have to get to the bottom first."

She looked at me for what felt like minutes. She put my hand back on my lap. She checked the mirrors and then we pulled back onto the road and drove through the rain. I loved her and felt loved by her, and I knew that the sentiment was mutual. It was a real bummer that we had to break up.

>

It happened at a Beef O'Brady's, this tacky chain of sports bars all through the area. The Tampa Bay Rays were playing and, urged on by Becca to get healthier hobbies, I had forced myself to become a fan. It felt like homework, and it was impossible to give a shit. I was detaching from society, holding on by a thread. The siren song of chinsky and Haruspx (ghosting me, still, that fucker) was glowing from my laptop every moment I was alone. Just earlier that day I watched a video of a Brazilian gang banger pitch a brick at Ellery's head. Becca was out for a jog, and I watched, through dreadful video quality, more guys come up in jeans and motorcycle boots and drop brick after brick right onto her cracking, collapsing

skull. Baseball was clearly the better option. There are troubling ways and healthier ways.

I had an idea of what Becca was going to bring up about a
month or so beforehand. She had been taking various phone
calls and was being jittery and excited, padding around her
apartment and staying up late answering emails and doing
Zoom calls. It was her idea to come here for lunch and when
the plate of hot wings was set before us right next to a large
pitcher of beer, she extended her hands softly and held mine.

She started to tell me about a career opportunity. She had
more time left in her program but this small company out of
Portland wanted to poach her and fast-track her. The pay was
fine. Sociology majors weren't exactly raking in money, but
she wanted to get out of Tallahassee and start her life and this
job seemed to provide an opportunity. It was a starter pistol
loud and undeniable. She had been looking at apartments for
the two of us, and she had some friends with a house east of
the Willamette that offered their guest room for us to crash
until we got settled. She even started looking at jobs for me,
which I first thought was kind but then convinced myself was
condescending and offensive. But I couldn't be mad at her.
She wanted to start her life and, when you got right down to
it, I wasn't ready. Not with this mystery still out there.

"I just think it'd be a very good move," she said. "A very
important move."

"For me to come with you?" I asked. I moved my hands
away from hers and poured myself more beer. She hadn't had
any yet and I already felt myself slowly falling into my old
ways. Being the drunkest one at lunch. At dinner. Getting
shots. Doing whatever I had to do.

"Yes. Come to Portland. With me."

"I don't know," I said.

"I'd be making solid money," she said. "I could support you until you found a job. I'm not saying you have to marry me or get me pregnant or anything like that. *But.* I just think it'd be a nice change."

"But I like it here."

"In Tallahassee? No, you don't. Everyone knows you don't."

"I'm starting to like it."

"What's to like? You've been out of school for a year. Why are you sticking around?"

I didn't say anything. The Rays were up 2–1 against the Braves, bottom of the fifth. This meant nothing to me. I just had to look at something that wasn't revolting and wasn't Becca, her big eyes pleading, her big mouth forced into a thin line. She still hadn't touched her food, and I knew she wasn't going to.

When someone is on their deathbed you can gauge the quality of their life by looking at the list of people they wished they had said yes to. If there are only a handful of opportunities they wished they'd said yes to, then that's a fairly solid life. If it's pages and pages of potential lovers, first dates, jobs, road trips, new drinks, different clothes, different apartments, different favors, then that's a life that wasn't lived. That's a life that was softly hugged in the shadows. A life that was barely caressed, jaded even from shirked experiences. But I couldn't say yes to Becca. I simply couldn't. I took too long to answer.

"I thought we had a serious thing," she said. She wasn't crying. She just sat upright. Years of dealing with her brother who was vulnerable to any overstimulation had trained her to be the master of composure. I thought about Ryan Vasquez. If I started bawling my eyes out right here, I could turn the tables and she'd let me off the hook. But no. That'd be fucked up and manipulative of me. I had to be better.

"We do have a serious thing," I said. I was stalling, trying to think of anything to put off the inevitable.

"It doesn't seem very serious when you can't even look at me." The Braves tied it up. Top of the sixth. Another brick fell on Ellery's face. Her teeth shot out along the dirt. The Brazilians laughed and jabbered in Portuguese. The video buffered. I looked at Becca and cleared my brain. I poured myself more beer. The pitcher was nearly done.

"I'm going to stay in Tallahassee because I'm going to do that grad program here."

"For what?"

"I was gonna get my master's in data and integration."

"Bullshit. Since when?"

"I've brought it up a couple of times."

"No, you haven't. You're making it up right now. You're talking out of your ass."

"That's not true. I've always wanted to do it. And I applied already and decided to enroll."

"Dude, you're full of shit."

"I'm not."

"Don't do this. Why are you doing this?"

"I'm not doing anything."

"You're lying to me." Her voice cracked. She blinked away the mist from her eyes. She swallowed hard and pressed her knuckles into her thighs. She started kneading her legs. Measuring her breaths. "Forget it. Just forget it."

I filled my glass again. The pitcher was empty. The game was tied and went into the 7th and—

"You can't just stay here and mourn her forever," she said. I looked at her. "I've never lectured you about how to mourn

Ellery. Never once. I've let you do what you had to do because I knew how special she was to you. Still is to you. I was happy enough that you were with me even if sometimes on darker days your mind was somewhere else. I loved you. And I still do. You cannot stay here and just mourn her."

"She didn't die in Portland," I said.

"What?"

"She died here. In Tallahassee. About two miles west of where we're eating." I shrugged. I didn't know what else to say. "She stayed in this city because of me, and this is where she died so this is where I have to stay."

"Until *when*?"

"I don't know. Until something changes. Until . . . I don't know. But I can't just go to Portland and act like it didn't happen."

"Nobody is asking you to do that."

"I need to stay here," I said. "I told you, I'm getting my master's."

"Right. I must've forgotten." She sat up again and held her elbows. I sat up too and tried to flag down a server, but she caught me. "Maybe one pitcher is enough for lunch, huh?" I lowered my hand into my lap. "Just know," she started, "that some people go through breakups and they feel like they've wasted their time. I don't feel that way. I don't think this was a waste of time at all. I love you and what we had was special. I just regret that I have to leave you behind. But I am going to leave you behind. And maybe at some point when you're ready and you're done haunting this city, you can catch up and find me. But listen. I love you now. I love the Sammy here. Back in the car, when you had that panic attack, you said you needed to go deeper because, in your head, you deserved it. I can't and won't stay here and coach you through it if you refuse to get help. And if you become a monster and come looking for me, I will not greet you with love."

She pushed her chair out and grabbed her bag and left.

The Rays lost the game.

That digital Ellery died in Brazil.

I ordered another pitcher.

That night she came by my place and grabbed some of her things. A sweater. Some books. Shampoos and conditioners she kept in my shower. A razor. Some underwear and T-shirts. She kissed me on the lips and gently tapped her forehead into my chest.

"I'm sorry," I said as she edged for the front door. She balanced her box of things on her knee and reached for the door. I offered to help.

"I got it," she said. "I'm a big girl." She opened the door and held the box and headed down the open stairs of my complex. She stopped short and turned around to me. She was orange from the security lights. It was summer and bugs chirped, and the horizon was hard to make out. "Do me a favor," she said. "Wait like a year or two before you decide to drunk-text or call me. I don't want to think about you while I'm getting my life together."

"Deal," I said. I kept my hands in my pockets. I leaned against the doorway like some farmer or maybe like one of my ranchero ancestors, faded in photographs, long-dead and buried in the badlands. Somewhere in the past he probably watched his lover leave the ranch. Maybe he found her later. Maybe he died in a saddle.

"Bye, Sam," she said, and she moved down the stairs, the top of her curly hair disappearing around the corner. I thought of Claire Waters going down the stairs back in her house in South Tampa. I thought of Bill banging on my car window. Of when I drove from their house that night. I thought of Ryan and me fist-fighting in the parking lot, him putting me in a choke hold. Then I thought of Ellery. In the sky, her ghost drifted. On the streets of the sprawl, her spirit lay. There was something that was keeping me here, and I knew it was evil.

>

"You're such a shit head," Maria said. She was sitting cross-legged, doing a puzzle. Jason and I were having beers in the kitchen, and she undoubtedly heard me telling Jason what happened.

"Thanks, Maria," I said.

"She had her life together. She offered you a golden ticket to get the fuck out of Tallahassee and you turned it down. For what?"

"I know, I know," I said.

"But do you?"

I looked at Jason with eyes like *get her off my back*, but he shrugged and drank his beer. Traitor. "You two are still here, aren't you?" I said. "How come I'm the only one that has to leave?"

"It's not about leaving," she went on, "it's about having a plan."

"Oh, fuck off."

"Hey, man," Jason said.

"Sorry."

"We're in our mid-twenties, Sam," she said.

"I'm twenty-two!" I interjected.

"Even still. There's no more hand-holding. We need to have a plan. Jason and I have a plan. We're saving money.

We're making small steps to be real fucking adults. What's your plan? You have nothing."

"I'm doing the best that I can."

"No, you're not. You're just falling into a spiral and taking everyone down with you."

"Who am I taking down? You? Jason? He's doing great!"

"Yeah, that's because I try to limit how often he sees you."

"I'm right here, guys," Jason said. He was being meek again. Years ago, when Ellery and I set him up with Maria, we knew they'd be a good fit because he needed someone strong to take him down the proper roads. "Someone to put starch into his clothes," is what Ellery said. But now my grip on him was slipping. Maria was pulling him too far away.

"Am I the only that still gives a shit about Ellery?"

There was a silence.

"Sam, that's not fair. We—"

"Don't say, 'We all miss Ellery' because I don't think that's true. Not the way I miss her. I loved Becca. She was amazing. But she wasn't Ellery. How am I expected to start my life and go forward with a *plan* when Ellery is dead? *She* was my plan! Don't you get that? She was my fucking plan. She was everything. She was the future. She was the blueprint to how I was going to be an adult. It's all gone. The plan is gone. I'm totally without a fucking plan."

"I know that, Sam, but—"

"You don't know that." I cut her off. "Neither of you really know that."

"Can everyone just calm down?" Jason asked. "Let's just breathe and take a few steps back from this."

"We're moving to Atlanta," Maria said. "Jason wanted to wait to tell you but we're moving before the fall."

I looked at Jason. "What?"

"There's nothing here for us in Tallahassee," Maria said.

"I can't work remotely anymore," Jason told me. He looked at his beer and avoided eye contact. "I won't be that far. We'll still be friends."

"Good. Just fucking go. I don't want to bring anyone into my *spiral*." I set my beer down and went to the door.

"Don't be like that, man," I heard Jason say, but I shut the door behind me.

I rode my bike to the liquor store and the Pakistani guy was there, and when I asked for a 750 of Cutty he said, "Things will improve, my friend."

"Things are going great," I said. "I'm living the dream."

"There you have it. Good for you."

> Be me, 23

> logging into hell

I turned twenty-three a few days after my breakup with Becca, and when my mother called to wish me a happy birthday, I broke the news to her. There was a pause for a few moments before she just sighed.

"You should've gone with her," she said.

"Things are picking up for me down here," I replied.

"Si tú lo dices."

Mr. Waters reached out as well. Told me happy birthday and then informed me that there had been another car accident on Monroe Avenue. The stupid traffic light didn't do shit. No deaths, though, Bill wrote. Thank Christ for that I suppose! He asked if I wanted to come over for dinner in the coming months. Claire has been leaving on the weekends so it can be just us guys, it said, and the sadness of the email poured out like a flood. I marked it as UNREAD and made the mental note to get back to it later.

Shortly, on top of all that, I was tasked with helping Jason and Maria move out of the same house I had moved them into only a year ago. I was sad to see Jason go, but happy to see the house empty once again. In fact, a part of me was happy everyone was leaving.

After I loaded up the U-Haul, I came around to the

driver's side and gave Jason an awkward hug through the open window. Maria was already up in the new place. I felt a pang of loneliness echo through my chest and the real and first wonder of whether I'd ever see him again fell across my mind like a cut tree.

"You gonna be alright down here, boss?" he asked. He started the truck and it started humming, his skinny arms even smaller against the weight of it. He fixed his rearview mirror like he wanted to make sure of the things he was leaving behind.

"Yeah, I'll be okay," I said. A warm, sticky wind came down the road and rustled the dark-green leaves in the trees above us.

"Come up sometime. I want to see you a lot. It's not far."

"You got it, man."

"You're gonna lock up the doors for me?"

"Yes, sir."

We gave another awkward hug, and I smelled the sweat and dust on his garnet Seminole shirt. He put the truck in drive and disappeared down the road.

I walked back to the empty house and let myself in. The place held its breath. Every step I took, its true form hid from me, ducking around corners and pulling itself into shadows. The last time I was there, I was running away from a fight with Maria, but now, alone, I felt Ellery in the stasis of the home. I felt Becca too. I felt her against the wall and in the kitchen and in the bathroom, now gray and empty, two curtain rings left abandoned on the shower rod. The energy of the place felt diametric. Maria and Jason had moved on with life. Becca extended me her hand and I brushed it away. And now the place sat like an empty terrarium. Ellery was in the stuffy corners and the cobwebs and she was holding me back, but I wasn't mad at her. Being held back was still an embrace.

I went to a beer garden a bit off campus and sat with a drink and a smoke and a yellow legal pad. I just needed a place to think. I was racked with guilt about how things ended with Becca, but I knew how to make it right. If I could unravel this cursed website, then I could somehow rectify the broken things in my mind. I imagined calling her after a few years and telling her the news. I wondered if she'd be happy to hear my voice. If the invite to Portland would still be open.

The place was half full but buzzing. It was sunny out and the beer I sipped cooled my gears. I felt sweat form on the back of my neck, on my forehead, under my arms. Students shuffled around and drank and played cornhole. Some were on their laptops studying. Some were alone, reading in the shade of bright-green and blue umbrellas.

I wrote down all that I knew about this chinsky.rekt.x. It had videos of Ellery, but how? Were they deepfakes? Her face pasted over actual recorded deaths? I had seen my share of deepfake pornography and while they all looked pretty compelling, a close eye and common sense could show the truth. Emma Watson wasn't actually getting her back blown out. It was just some crafty creep with time to spare.

Another thought that dawned on me, as silly as it sounded, was the idea of parallel dimensions. What if Spyglass wasn't just a browser for the dark web? What if it opened 'windows' to other worlds? There really were millions of Ellerys and they really were all dying at different stages. Maybe it was because, lately, every movie was about other universes, and my mush brain was jumping at shadows, but I couldn't shake it. I scribbled it in the far corner of the pad and kept my head low, embarrassed should anyone see.

Of course, the most obvious answer was the scariest to write: I was losing my mind. I hadn't shown anybody the website because I was afraid of scaring people off. But what that really meant was that I had no witnesses. Nobody saw what I saw.

"Sam from group therapy at the Wellness Center!"

"Jesus!" I leapt out of my skin and knocked over my beer. My legal pad got soaked and I quickly crumbled it up. I turned to the source.

"And before that, computer science with Robert Carmichael," she said. It was Alexa Ritter, that girl from way back, when I was relatively sane.

"Holy shit," I said. I snuffed out my smoke. "You gave me a heart attack."

"Sorry about your beer. You weren't doing homework, were you?"

I looked at the soggy ball of paper. My secrets and hallucinations totally smeared.

"No, it's fine. It was just scribbles."

"You never came back," she said. She sat on the bench next to me. "I was waiting for the text. I didn't scare you off, right?"

"No. I just . . . Never came back," I started. "God, that was over a year ago. How do you even remember that?"

She tapped her head. "A lock box. How've you been?"

She looked at me like she was watching for strange behavioral patterns, like her eyes were set behind thick observation glass. She sat, half in the sun, half in the shade of the umbrella, with her tan skin and black hair and slim figure. She asked me again because I took too long to answer, "Well?"

"I'm good," I said. "I've been okay. I'm still here. I'm going for my master's now which seems smart. I don't know. Can't tell yet. What about you? Why are you still here?"

"I live here, buddy. I love Tallahassee."

I choked on my beer. *She* was the crazy one. "No way," I said.

"Yeah way. I just moved back."

"*Why?*"

"Okay, relax with the attitude."

"I'm sorry. That was mean."

"When I graduated, I went to grad school in New England and now I'm back to start an early residence training type thing here at the psych department. I love Tallahassee. I'm a southern girl."

"Okay. I take it back. Cheers to you."

She clinked her glass on mine. She took a long pull. "I gotta run," she said. "But seriously, text me. Let's hang out. I can show you some local places so you're not, like, wasting your time at bars with freshmen. Unless you're into that. Picking up young girls with fake IDs. Is that your whole thing?"

"I don't think I'm at that point yet. But I'll get there."

"Text me. You still have my number, right?"

"I definitely do."

She smiled. Her hair was fine and fell in straight rows past her shoulders. She was cute, but I didn't trust her. I couldn't explain why. Maybe it was her aggressive kindness that put me on edge. Maybe it was because she saw in me someone who could relate to her. Having met at the group session way back when, it was logical to lump us together, but I didn't know her experience much beyond the facts. Her boyfriend died and my girlfriend died. As far as I was concerned, the similarities stopped there, especially when considering recent discoveries. But if she thought that she could help me or that I could help her in any way, shape, or form related to coping, we'd both be wasting our time.

She waved as she left the beer garden. I turned back and looked at the spilled beer and soaked pages. All my ideas, smeared.

>

That night, at work, time crawled by and even then it wasn't slow enough for me. I thought of work as a haven where I could turn my brain off. I sat at my terminal in the basement of the science building. I did my tasks. I looked at data and charts and cells that meant nothing to anybody. I rubbed my eyes and looked at the clock. I climbed onto my smoking cabinet and opened the skinny window. The night grew long, and I listened to the building purge itself of faculty and students. Eventually the custodian came by again and nodded at me and moved on down the hall. I checked my email and looked at Bill's invitation. I replied that I'd happily come down and have dinner. Dollars to donuts he was getting divorced. He needed someone around, and I felt like I was running pretty low on good karma so a quick dinner might do the trick. The idea of showing him chinsky crossed my mind, but that'd be cruel. He'd crack. I couldn't do that to him. But I had to show *somebody.*

I followed up on the email, on impulse, asking if I could stay the night. The thought of seeing my folks made me nervous for some reason. My mother and I hadn't been on the level since I cornered her into talking about Uncle Ted. That was back with Becca. Shit. The image of him at the window tapping his finger was tattooed on my brain, and I forced myself to think of something else. Bill replied faster than I anticipated.

SOUNDS GREAT!!!!! the email said.

It was settled. I'd drive down to Tampa in a week.

When I got off work it was around midnight, but the campus was still buzzing. The movie theater was opening its doors for a midnight screening. Students stargazed and gossiped on the grass of Landis Green. Suwannee Hall was still open, serving bad food to stoners and pledges in suits and khakis. I felt more and more like a ghost, and I unlocked my bike and rode out of there fast.

I wasn't ready to go back home. I needed some sort of plan before I jumped back into the digital hell that waited for me. I texted Alexa and asked where she was. We ended up meeting at a craft bar called Proof far out past my apartment. I was happy to bike away from my place, the further the better, I thought.

The bar was hip and cozy and there were students my age and other Tallahassee locals that didn't go to FSU. It felt right and when I got inside, I sat with her at a booth in the back.

"This town ain't so bad when you actually leave the radius, right?" She sat back with her beer. She had changed since I saw her. She wore a thin sweater and business pants. She caught me sizing her up and said, "I look more professional, don't I?"

"I feel underdressed," I said.

"Don't. I had a mixer I had to go to. There's a lot of ass-kissing in my field. And you know, everyone is sipping little chardonnays and asking terrible icebreakers. I ended up wanting a real drink, so good timing."

"I'll be honest," I started, "I only came out because I didn't wanna go back home."

"Someone waiting for you at home?" Her eyebrows raised. The question seemed innocent though.

"No. Nobody there. I've just, uh, been forming some bad habits."

"Just like gooning all the time or something?"

"Yeah, something like that." I drank some beer and felt myself relax a bit, and then immediately resented myself. I wasn't allowed to relax. I had to stay *on*.

"You okay? You just went ghost on me." She was leaning forward, reading my face. Saw my internal dialogue. "It's okay to have fun," she said. "I've been where you're at."

"I don't know how true that is," I said.

"It took forever before I started letting loose."

"I think I've been letting *too* loose is the problem. I could probably stand to tighten up, honestly."

"Tighten up tomorrow. We're already here."

I looked at her and decided to go for it. "Have you ever seen or watched something that really fucked you up?"

"In what way?"

"Like something you never had to see. Like a morbid indulgence."

"When I was a kid my sister and I used to Google car accidents."

"Yes!" I said. I leaned forward. I brought my voice down and looked around. For some reason I thought they were all listening. "Exactly. Car accidents. And you keep pushing your boundaries a little bit further and further until you see a car accident that tops all other car accidents and then you're like, 'Holy shit, that's enough internet for today.'"

"Yeah, it's happened," she said. "A few years ago, I was on a forum somewhere and I stumbled on a video of, like, an ISIS beheading. I don't know why the fuck I watched it. I didn't eat the rest of the day. *But*. What I did realize after that was that the morbid indulgence is rarely worth the damage to my psyche. You know? I try really hard to watch and consume good things. I'm not like a pansy though. I can watch horror and see some shit. But putting myself in that headspace . . . I don't know, it's not for me. I'm already dealing with so much, the last thing I need to do is tack on some digital trauma as well."

I nodded. I liked listening to her talk. She spoke with intent like a teacher might.

"Is that what happened to you? Did you see the mother of all car accidents?"

"Yeah," I said. "Something like that."

"I remember you mentioned in group that your girlfriend died in a car accident."

"Did I really? I don't remember talking. I was too nervous."

"Oh. Maybe it was in the paper. Or maybe I just heard through the grapevine. Either way, you shouldn't watch that stuff, man. It can be really triggering."

"It was that car accident."

"What do you mean?"

"I saw the CCTV footage of that accident. The one that killed her."

Her face dropped. She leaned in. She leaned back. She blinked a few times.

"Holy shit. Oh my god. Dude."

There it was. Her reaction. It suddenly grounded me in a way I hadn't felt since I started watching all that shit. Her reaction was a normal, well-adjusted human's reaction. I hadn't reacted like that in years. I chased it.

"It was surreal," I said. "Just absolutely surreal. But in a weird way it brought solace because there were no more questions. It was right there in front me, literally in black and white."

"So, then what?"

"I, uh, I don't know. I freaked out and stayed up all night."

"Fair. Okay. And then after that?"

"I watched a bunch of other videos."

There was a pause. She sipped her beer. She was formulating some sort of thesis on me. I had fallen into a therapy session without even realizing it, only this one was sneaky and came from an angle I hadn't expected. Her face was the lesson plan. Her narrow eyes and stern lips. I could see the gears turning in her head. She was flipping through pages she'd read about maladjusted loners, or, maybe just hairy guys who drank too much.

"I'm gonna get another beer," I said.

"Actually, let me get it. You got the first round." She stood up. "I thought we were gonna get drunk and fool around but now it's turned into a whole thing." She walked off to the bar.

"You thought what?" I called after her.

>

In the morning, at her apartment, I sat on the edge of her bed and put my sneakers on, and she watched me, naked, half under the covers. Her body was lithe. The sex was good. She bit a strand of her own hair. "You're not gonna be weird, right?" she asked.

"Nope," I said.

"You're not gonna text me and get all clingy?"

"No, ma'am."

"What's the last relationship you had?" she asked. I was

suddenly watching Becca go down the stairs again. I was the ranchero. She gave me a chance. I blinked away the memory.

"Broke up this summer actually. She left for Portland, and I stayed here."

"Oof. Gotta hurt," she said. "I haven't dated anyone. Doesn't feel right. Most people I say that to are like, 'Come on Alexa it's been years,' but like they can fuck off. Right? You know?"

"Believe me. I know." I got up and grabbed my bag. She didn't even make an effort to get out of bed. There was no walking me to the door. There was no feigning an interest in coffee.

"I don't want a boyfriend or anything. Not yet. I just want to fuck someone that's as broken as me."

"That's a crazy thing to say to someone."

"I'm just saying. If you want a girl falling all over you, get one of the freshmen from Pots."

"What's with you and freshmen? Do I have that energy?"

"Yeah. A little. You could sweep up there. You're not ugly but you're not too intimidating. Girls will think you're smart."

"But you know better."

She laughed. Didn't even deny it. She smiled with her hair between her lips, and she nodded.

"I had a good time," I said. "Maybe we can do it again."

"That'd be fun."

I paused for another moment.

"Make sure you close the door hard when you leave."

And so, I did.

>

When I returned to my apartment, I felt a wave of caution come over me. I walked slowly, unsure of who or what was around every corner. My laptop sat there on my desk right where I had left it. There was an empty bottle of Cutty where it had fallen. I still smelled like beer and Alexa's sheets. I dropped my bag and stood there for a spell, staring at my laptop. I crossed the room and opened it up and went to chinsky. For a moment nothing happened. The screen wouldn't load. Then I remembered the webcam and I peeled the tape back and let the green eye blink at me a few times and then the page came up bright yellow and caustic.

I grabbed some cold cuts from my fridge and ate them with my fingers and I scrolled the red links casually. I took out my legal pad, ripped off the first few damaged pages, and was determined to take notes. Determined to approach this with some sort of investigative science. I froze for a second. Wasn't sure where to start. Some of the links were different, but the car accident one remained. The gold ring shimmering around it. In the top right was a search bar. Hadn't seen it before. I typed in ALEXA RITTER and it worked. The red links loaded slowly. The words made me balk: KILLED BY DAD, SUICIDE, CAR ACCIDENT ON US-18, MUGGING GONE WRONG, SHOT IN ATLANTA, BITCH DROWNS ON SPRING BREAK.

I clicked the first one and the video loaded. It was Alexa on her knees in her kitchen, and I guess maybe her father stood in front of her. He was big. Huge. Had his sleeves rolled up and showed his hairy arms and thick knuckles. "Daddy, please!" she screamed and begged with her fingers laced together. But the guy palmed the side of her head and smashed it against the kitchen granite. *Wham! Wham! Wham!* The side of her face swelled up like a purple valley and her teeth were coming loose. "Daddy . . . please . . . stop . . ." *Wham! Wham!*

Wham! And the video ended. I tucked some ham into my mouth and kept looking.

I clicked the link that said, SUICIDE. It was her naked in her bathtub. She had a large kitchen knife and cut her wrists downward. She gasped when the wounds opened up and then she shuddered and sank underwater. Blood came up in small faint clouds until they darkened at the surface and spread. For a moment I wondered how the video knew how she looked naked. Then her hair rose to the surface like La Llorona. I x'd out. None of the links had the gold ring that Ellery's had. I wrote down on my pad, *Alexa is still alive.* I looked at the sentence. I underlined it a few times. Then I called an old friend from middle school. A kid named Lucas.

"Hello?" His voice was deep. I hadn't spoken to him since high school when he went to the all-boys Catholic joint and I didn't.

"Hey, is this Lucas Melendez?"

"Yes?"

"This is Sammy. We went to Villa Madonna together."

"Holy shit, man, what's up? How've you been?"

"Yeah, yeah, I'm fine, but hey, listen, I got a weird question."

"What's up?"

"Do you remember Dominic Cooler?"

"From Villa?" he asked.

"Yeah. Do you remember his brother?"

"Terry. Why?"

"How did Terry die again?"

"Jesus, man, you call me out of the blue to ask me that?"

"I know, it's fucked up, but I didn't know who else to ask. I wasn't gonna ask Dominic. Just tell me. How did he die? I can't remember."

"It was a motocross accident. I think he was a sopho-more at Chamberlain. Broke his neck. Remember? We had that vigil in the courtyard and Sister Theresa was all mad that some of us weren't crying enough. What a bitch. My mom made me swear to never ride a motorcycle."

"Right. Dirt bike accident. Okay."

"Why?"

"Nothing. It was good talking to you. Hey, I'm gonna be in Tampa in a week. Let's hang." I hung up and scribbled down on the note pad: *TERRY. DEAD. MOTOCROSS*. Then I looked up Terry Cooler in the search bar. A few of the links that popped up were: SCHOOL SHOOTING, WHITE BOY GETS STABBED, BOATING ACCIDENT and then, there it was: DIRT BIKE WIPEOUT shimmering with a golden ring.

"Winner, winner," I muttered to myself.

I clicked the video and watched. Terry, on his bright green bike, took a ramp and wobbled and then took another ramp and wobbled some more. Shortly, he approached a steep in-cline and took it and soared, but then came down hard and his wheel got stuck. He flipped over himself, and the momentum of the bike flipped him hard and fast and his ragdoll body flew catty-corner off another ramp and he landed hard in the mud on his neck. People screamed and ran to help. The video ended.

I was twelve again and standing next to Lucas in the court-yard of our middle school. It was a winter morning and we all held hands in silent prayer as Dominic cried his eyes out. There was a picture frame of Terry on a lectern. Sister Theresa watched to see who wasn't grieving enough. I watched a bat fly toward the chapel.

I snapped out of it and looked at the yellow screen and the blood-red links. Someone was keeping score. The way the page was laid out it seemed like the least plausible deaths were further down the list. HOT AIR BALLOON CRASH. GUYS FALLS OFF EMPIRE STATE BUILDING. What the hell was going on? I moved over to CampfireFables.com to see if Haruspx had messaged me back. No dice.

Their account was still empty. Our message thread was still there but there was no other activity.

"Okay, motherfucker," I said. "You showed me this on purpose."

I looked at the search bar and thought of the people I knew that died. A teacher at my high school had a heart attack when I was a freshman. I typed in Bert Steeling and got it. OLD FART CROAKS ON FOOTBALL FIELD. It shimmered gold. When I was a junior a girl's mother died of breast cancer. I searched for Josie Baker. There it was. Shimmering gold.

"Who is playing this game?" I asked the screen. "And what are you winning?"

I dug a little deeper. Went a little more personal. The first of my father's sisters to pass died of a stroke back in the '80s. I never met her. I searched Angelina Dominguez. Nothing came up. Too old? Too long ago? His other sister died right after I was born. I must've been one or two. Eliana Dominguez. Only one video appeared, and it had the gold. LADY TAKES PILLS. I clicked it and it was just a mounted angle of a woman sleeping in bed, face down. In the video a phone is ringing somewhere. My stomach went sideways and I x'd out.

"Rest in peace," I said to nobody. I didn't know Aunt Eliana went out like that. My dad always told me she had a heart attack in her sleep. Granted, maybe the website was full of shit and didn't actually know how she died, but all of the other Gold Videos were true. I typed out Uncle Ted's full

name in the search bar, but then I quickly deleted it. I didn't
need to see him. See that. I typed Sam Dominguez in there
and the page loaded fast. There were thousands of links. More
came in as I scrolled, being added in real time: *KID KILLS
HIMSELF, SUICIDE BY POLICE, ASSHOLE IS KILLED ON
BLOOD MOUNTAIN*. I clicked it.

I looked older, tired, and I had a gun in my hand. I'm
climbing up the side of a mountain. I kick open the door of a
shed and someone inside sends a buckshot through my chest.
I fly back and land in leaves and mud. I'm gasping for life.
I'm trying to piece my chest back together, but a man comes
out of the cabin, and he pumps the shotgun again. The video
goes a bit grainy, and I can't see who the gunman is, but he
kicks my gun out of my hand and then shoots me square in
the face and my head bursts sideways like a melon.

"Fuck me," I said to the screen.

More links came in: *DIES OF ALCOHOL POISONING, DIES
IN PRISON, GETS TWO IN THE CHEST, FAGGOT HANGS
HIMSELF, WETBACK GETS MOWED DOWN OUTSIDE OF
GAS STATION, GIRLFRIEND FINDS HIM*. I clicked that one.

The video starts and I'm dead in my own bathtub right here
in my apartment. There's a pile of pills on the toilet and I'm
half-sunk underwater, puke coming down my chin. The door
comes in and a girl says, "Goddammit, Sammy." She comes
into frame and it's a girl I've never seen before. She's skinny
and Black and bald. She's wearing a ratty hoodie and she's got
a ton of earrings. She tries to pull me out of the tub but can't
and water gets everywhere. She doesn't even look that upset.
More disappointed. She makes a phone call just offscreen and I
hear her say, "He did it. He didn't even wait." The video ends.

"Who the hell are you?" I asked the screen. I kept looking at links: *BOY DROWNS, BOY DIES IN TALLAHASSEE*

FIRE, CAR ACCIDENT IN ATLANTA, HOUSE FIRE IN PORT-
LAND, and finally, the one that got me in the gut, DIES
LIKE UNCLE. I clicked it and tears came to my eyes almost
immediately.

The camera is hidden somewhere in the corner of the garage. I'm in jeans and a T-shirt and I'm trying hard to get into
the back door. I'm banging on the glass. I'm calling someone's name, but there's no sound. I'm forty years older and
am stumbling side to side, wasted, a twelve-pack of Coors
Lite at my feet. I put a cigarette to my lips and my hands
are gnarled and twisted with arthritis. I have a five-o'clock
shadow. The cigarette bobs in my lips and then I start coughing really hard. I drink another beer. I bang on the window. I
keep calling someone's name. I'm trapped in the garage. I'm
hammered, wobbling around in blown-out sneakers, a used
rag hanging out of my back pocket. Then I clutch my chest
and fall against the fridge. Then I scream for someone and
start coughing some more. Then I fall to the side. The video
keeps running in silence. My body just lays there. The video
kept playing and I watched and I wiped away tears because I
knew what was coming.

"Please. No," I said to the screen.

My sixty-something-year-old body stays there, slumped
on the side, and a small kid comes to the back door.

"Don't open the door," I said.

The kid is young. Looks like me. He's peering through
the glass window into the garage, my dead body just out of
eyesight, behind the fridge.

"Don't look at me," I said. "Please. Just go back to bed."

The kid opens the door and steps into the garage.

"It's not your fault, it's not your fault, it's not your fault,"
I started saying to the screen. My old body is there, dead,

crumbled, and the boy steps forward and sees me. I started crying hard. "It's not your fault. It's not your fucking fault." And the kid, startled, starts touching my dead body. Poking my neck. Trying to wake me up. Then the kid starts crying and hyperventilating. Then the kid backs up and hurries out of the garage and shuts the door behind him.

"No, no, no, no, no," was all I could say.

I x'd out and saw another link load for me. Brand new. Hot off the presses.

JUMPS FROM BALCONY RIGHT THIS SECOND

"Fuck you," I said and shut the laptop.

>

That night, at work, Alexa sent me a nude. I sat on my smoking cabinet and opened the picture. It was her in a desk chair with her knees up on the wood and her shirt pulled above her chest. Her face wasn't in it. Then she sent me a text: Woops wrong person.

Then more: Jk.

netflix and chill?

Hulu and oral

disney+ and u finger me idk

At her place, I was rough with her in a way I had never been before. I couldn't explain why. The videos I'd seen had violated me and coiled me up and filled me with dark and evil emotions that I needed to put somewhere. I went at her from behind and grabbed a fistful of her hair. I pulled.

"Not so hard. Ow."

But I didn't listen. I gathered more of her hair and wound it around my fingers. I wasn't even thinking about the sensation of me inside her. I wanted to yank her head back. I wanted to make her back arch more than it could. She moaned softly at first, playing along, but then—

"Dude, stop, that shit hurts."

I ignored her more. I was in a fugue state. I wondered if I was a link now. I imagined a video of me killing her. Would it have the gold ring? I pulled again.

"What the fuck? Stop!" She broke from me, spun around, and slapped me across the face. I fell back onto my butt. She was rubbing her head. "What the fuck, man? Are you trying to scalp me?"

"I—I'm sorry. I wasn't thinking."

"You were ripping my hair out," she said. I saw the fear in her eyes. The anger too. It felt right. It felt human.

"I'm sorry. I was getting carried away."

"I'm not gonna let you get off on hurting me. You can forget about that."

"I wasn't tryi— I'm sorry. Can I take a shower?"

She looked at me. Studied me. "If you're gonna jerk off on my shower curtains, we can just finish this up." She studied me again and saw that I had already gone soft. "Okay, go shower, you weirdo."

I got out of bed and shuffled to her bathroom. While showering, I studied the tub. I studied the white-and-pink tiles. It was identical to the video I had seen. How could they know this? Down to the detail of the bath mats. She came in with a ceramic pipe and sat on the toilet.

"Are you done being psycho?" She took a pull and waved the smoke away.

"I'm really sorry. I don't actually do that. That's not who I am."

"Whatever you say, Patrick Bateman."

"Jesus."

"I'm kidding. It happens. One time I dug my nails into a guy so bad he bled."

"I don't know where my mind was." I felt the hot water run down me. I was trying to find some difference between this real place and the one in the video.

"You're really distracted by something," she said. I looked at her. She was naked with her legs crossed. She offered me the pipe and I leaned out of the shower and accepted it.

"Can I ask you something?"

"Shoot."

"Would you ever kill yourself?" I asked.

"I mean. I've thought about it a few times."

"How would you do it?"

"Are you just asking to ask?"

"Yeah, entertain me. Would you ever cut your wrists? Right here in this tub?"

"Are you getting hard right now?"

"*No*, I'm just asking."

She raised her eyebrow at me. I gave the pipe back. She took another pull and blew out the smoke. The bathroom was getting steamy. I had stopped washing myself and just stood there, hands on the wall, head down, waiting for her response.

"Nah. Probably not. I'm squeamish and if I tried to cut myself, I'd probably fuck it up."

"So how would you do it?"

"My dad has a gun at home," she said. "He doesn't think my sister and I know, but we know. So, I'd go home and visit the parents. Spend some time with them and then when they leave to run an errand or something I'd go and get it. Then I'd drive out to a Publix or something and do it in the parking lot."

"Does your dad ever hit you?"

"That's a pretty personal question, Psycho Boy."

"You don't have to answer it."

"He used to hit me and my sister and my mom," she started. There was a measured sadness in her voice. I thought about her face smashing against the granite. She had talked about this plenty of times, I could tell. "Then one day when I got older, I knew my shit and I pointed a knife at him and told him if he ever laid a hand on any of us ever again, I'd cut his dick off and I'd take everyone and leave. He never did it again and now he just sits on his fat ass and drinks."

"That's intense."

"You know what's the craziest part? Sometimes I wish he would. I'd jab that blade into him so deep he'd feel it scrape his spine. And I'll do it to you too if you ever get rough with me again."

"I promise I won't."

She took a pull. "Unless I want you to, of course." Then she laughed, got up, and left. I looked down, and I was hard.

We attempted sex again, and this time it worked. She mounted me and ground into me. She was focused. Her eyes turned fierce, and her eyebrows went straight in concentration. She had a flat stomach that extended up to her small breasts and dark nipples. She dug her fingers into my chest and rode me and made me cum hard inside her. On the way down I decided Ellery would've hated this girl. Becca too, probably. I don't know if I much liked her either to be frank, and I bet she didn't care for me, but she was there and so was I.

In the morning, when I got home, I looked to see if the videos had changed. There Alexa was, sitting in a car in a parking lot, dabbing tears from her eyes. The camera seems to be a type of dashcam. In the background there is a Publix. She reaches into the back seat and takes out a small leather satchel. She opens it up and takes out a GLOCK 43. She makes sure it's loaded. She tucks the gun under her chin and pulls the trigger. The bang is loud. A flume of blood shoots out of the top of her skull. Her head lolls forward and blood pours out of her mouth and nose. The video ends.

I sat back and watched it again. I looked at the other links. The video of her cutting her wrist in the bathtub was pushed down to the bottom of the page. Guess someone was wrong.

"I'm on to you," I said and then the webcam turned on and blinked at me once more before I shut my laptop.

I had some time to kill before my dinner at
Bill's. I pulled my car into the driveway of my house and when
my dad came out with the trash, he looked surprised to see me.
Then his shoulders sank, and I saw him shout something back
into the house. I got out of the car, but I didn't shut the door. I
had to keep it open to remind myself that I wasn't staying long.
My dad threw the trash by the mailbox and climbed back up
the driveway. Behind him some white clouds drifted along over
the tall trees that stood over the cul-de-sac. Tampa was always
called hot New Jersey and, for what it's worth, that was right
on the money. The general pockets of green and lake and storm
clouds reminded me of something more ominous, though. Like
if Florida wanted, it could just sink under and allow the limestone of the state to crumble into the gulf and swamp of the
eras before it. The lush jungles that Ponce de Leon cut through
would climb back with a vengeance and reclaim what was
taken. Florida always felt like borrowed time.

"What are you doing back?" he asked. He kept his hands
in pockets. He stayed a few feet from me, eyeing me like I
had a knife or something. "Are you staying long?"

I studied the man. His cropped beard. His eyes. His dark
mane of hair that brushed his shirt collar. Cicadas chirred in

the trees. There were vague memories of him plopping me in a laundry basket and racing me around the perimeter of the house, my mom counting off laps like an announcer. Even still, even then, there was a distance. He was the type of man that had a hard time showing love. He was a Latino for Christ's sake. There were no two armed hugs. I-love-yous were scarce. He showed his love by providing food and shelter and I was too naïve and innocent to predict that it wasn't going to be enough. I was twenty-three now and self-sufficient for the most part and I wondered how he loved me when he didn't have to provide for me. Perhaps he never loved me at all.

"Why didn't you tell me Aunt Eliana killed herself?" It came out faster than I had expected. I didn't know my mind was going there. My dad backed up. He didn't look away but stared me down like a chess player.

"Why would I tell you that?"

"Because we're family."

"You were two years old," he said. "You were hardly family." He started back for the house. The garage door was open and for a moment I saw my own dead body by the fridge and the young boy at the window.

"Why'd she take the pills?"

He stopped short and turned around. Hands still in pockets.

"You tell me."

"What?"

"She babysat you for a week while your mother and I went away. When we returned she killed herself the next day."

"What are you implying?"

"I didn't think of a connection at first. I thought she took pills to cope with Angie. But then Ted died, and you were the only one in the house. And then Ellery died and well, you know."

I was floored. I stammered. I felt adrenaline come out of nowhere, my heart rate going like a hummingbird. "No, actually, I don't fucking know. What are you talking about?"

"Your mother thinks you're cursed. I think it adds up okay. When you were here with Becca for the barbecue she woke up and heard you screaming and crying in the shower."

"Yeah, because—" I stopped. I didn't have a real reason. Because I saw Uncle Ted tapping at the back door? Because I saw Becca dying in wax?

"Dad, I don't think I'm okay."

"Us neither."

"Can I come inside?"

"No," he said, "I'm sorry, but your mother likes to know in advance before you come. She's not ready to see you right now." There was a pause before he spoke again. "How did you know Eliana took pills? Who told you?"

"I saw it," I said. I couldn't explain chinsky or anything, but if he saw some superstitious cloud over me, I had to lean into it. I wanted to scare the old bastard. "She died face down in her bed while you tried to call her." His face went white, and he made a fist. I got back in the car and slammed the door shut. I pulled out and watched him disappear in the rearview mirror.

>

Bill showed me around the house. He pointed out new renovations and fun "man cave" things he'd done in Claire's absence.

"She's been taking a lot of trips," he said in a monotone voice half at me and half at the wall. The subtext in the statement was heavy. I didn't need to pry.

"I like the energy here," I said and gave him a polite smile. I wasn't lying either. Bill let himself be sad in a way I could relate to. He bought little tchotchkes. He kept the TV on as mindless noise in the background. He started a decent bar cart with a modest wine rack. The absence of Claire was palpable though. Bill's grief turned into a sentimental virtue. Claire's turned malicious and sour, and she left behind that energy. It clung to the corners of the rooms and along the rafters, floating along like a specter. If you turned around too fast you saw it pull its head around a corner. At the wrong angle in a mirror, you saw her resentment glare back with red eyes.

"Let's eat," Bill said.

He was an alright cook and the two of us enjoyed a peaceful dinner. He played a Rolling Stones compilation that wasn't right for the mood but felt right for him, so I didn't protest. We ate pork chops and asparagus and drank wine, a Sangiovese he had clearly done a lot of research on. "Aged in an amphora," he said. "I didn't even know they did that. How cool is that?" I nodded and drank hard.

"It's been so long since we had dinner," he said. The gin blossom on his nose was getting worse. His eyes looked wet and shiny, the rims slightly pink. He wore a light-blue button-down that was pulled taut at his belly. He had shaved recently, and his jowls looked like raw meat. I thought about it for a second—the last time I had dinner with him was the time I went over to beat Ryan Vasquez's ass. The notion of attacking him again crossed my mind. Maybe showing him chinsky . . .

"You there?"

"Sorry," I said. "My mind wandered."

"What have you been doing up there?" he asked. "Have you been seeing someone? It's okay if you say yes, you're a young man. You should be dating around and trying to be happy."

"I met someone, but it didn't work out."

"Sure, sure." He dragged his knife against the pork. He slopped it around in the pan sauce he made. He chewed it like a cow. "Claire is seeing someone else."

I put my wine down. I let him know I was listening.

"I'm happy for her. She had to get out of here. She comes back sometimes, you know, but I just need her to find out what she needs. Do you know what I mean? Like a help me, help you, sort of thing."

"That's pretty noble of you, Bill."

"I still love her. Plus, I don't know what the alternative would be. Fight her on it? Neither of us have that energy. I'm too old for a divorce. Too sad as well. Remember when she told you that you reminded her of Ellery? I think it's the same here," he said and pointed to his face. "I mean how can she not be reminded? That girl had my nose and eyes." He laughed a small and quiet laugh. He drank his wine and sloshed more into his glass. He took a sharp breath in and kept cutting his meat.

"You can sleep down here if you'd like. Or Ellery's room. Or there's a guest room across the hall. It's up to you."

"Thanks. I appreciate it."

"I don't want to be intrusive, but why don't you want to stay at home?"

"My dad thinks I'm cursed."

He laughed.

"Is that an, uh, a Latino thing?"

"I think it's just an asshole thing."

We both laughed.

"I think we're all a little cursed," he said.

"Agreed."

>

I laid on the bed in Ellery's room and opened up chinsky. In the search bar I looked up Claire Waters. I scrolled through red links. I wanted to see how these people? computers? dimensions? thought she'd die. Various links were flat-out horrific with only a few of them seeming, to me, plausible. WOMAN SLIPS DOWN STAIRS made sense. Car accidents always made sense to me now. There was even a video of her with a man, not Bill. Bummer. But what about the ones orchestrated in hell? Where did they come from? OLD HAG GETS FIRECRACKERED, and it's a video of someone lighting the tail of a rocket that's duct-taped into her mouth. She whimpers and the bottom of her jaw blows downward, swinging off its hinges. Her tongue flailing and the skin on her cheek bones flaring up in smoke and soot. How the fuck would that ever happen? In what parallel universe did that happen? If it was a deepfake, fine, it happened to some poor bastard IRL, and they put Claire's face on it, but then a thought occurred to me. If in some heinous ordeal Claire actually went out that way, then this video would get a gold ring. Okay. So what? What did the gold ring really mean? And to that end, who or what was receiving it?

I was in the weeds, and I felt dirty. Grimy. I felt cursed like my old man said. This site wasn't meant to be dissected like this. But it was a Chinese finger trap. I realized that I couldn't just pull all the way out and act like nothing's happened. I'd have to go all the way through and free myself on the other side.

I snuck downstairs to Bill's bar cart. I poured myself some bourbon into a crystal tumbler. When I tiptoed back up to Ellery's room he was standing there and looking at the laptop.

"What is this?" he asked.

"Shit."

"What are all of these videos of Claire?"

"They're not real, they're—"

"Did she act in these or something? Jesus Christ."

"No." I took a step off the landing. I felt like Nosferatu, my silhouette bent and contorted from the weak lights. The glow of the screen was like a bright blinking eye staring at me from behind Bill's frame. It looked like the eye of a giant squid. Bill turned back to the laptop on Ellery's bed and then back to me. I had yet to cross into the room. I was a vampire now. I had to be invited.

"What the fuck is this, Sam?"

"It's fake, man. I don't know." I felt myself getting more flushed. "It's like a dark web deepfake thing. I don't know!"

"What the fuck are you talking about? What?"

"I can't explain it but—"

"Get out."

"You weren't supposed to see that."

"Then who was?" He was shaking. He was stained glass collapsing onto the chapel floor. He was me in Becca's car. When I was a boy in middle school I knelt in a chapel and looked at the trees through the red of Jesus's feet. Bill was in shards.

In truth, I had imagined myself showing him the website. Wondering what he'd say or do. But I always put it off because it felt cruel, and his reaction wouldn't be right. You see, there was the reaction I got from Alexa that scratched the itch. Hers was tinged with "The world is so scary, and I'm sorry you're a part of it." It kind of let me off the hook. But Bill's was colored: "You did this on purpose. I know you did." Which hooked me even deeper.

"Is Ellery in this too?"

I couldn't see the features of his face. He looked bluish-black in Ellery's room and the squid eye stared at me from behind him.

"Yes, but—"

"Get out. You're fucking evil. Get out."

"Bill, it's—"

"Get the fuck out!"

I held firm, but he approached me faster than I had anticipated. He shoved me and I stepped backward off the landing, missing the step. I fell down the stairs sideways, clocking my head along the way. The momentum took me, and I twisted my wrist, and my ankle came down clapping against the hard lip of the wooden step. The back of my head slapped against the tile of the floor and my mind went shutterbug. For a split second I tried to remember the links I saw for my own death. Was any of this familiar?

Bill had disappeared from my eyeline and came back out of Ellery's room with my stuff. He hurled my duffel bag from the top landing and my clothes scattered along the steps. I climbed to my feet and tried desperately to pack the bag. He came out of the room again with my phone and laptop. He hurled the phone, and I went for it but was too slow. It cracked along the tile and pinwheeled into the front door.

"Fuck man! Come on! Not my lapto—"

He Frisbee'd it over the staircase and I leapt, arms out, legs straight, soaring, boy would my dad be proud, an athlete *finally*. I caught the laptop and landed on my chest. Thought I felt a rib crack on the tile.

"Get out before I call the cops. Get out!" Bill yelled. I gathered my shit, and he started crying up there. "What did you do?" he kept asking between his sobs. "What did you do?"

I swung open the front door and took a half step out. My rib was definitely cracked. I touched my chest. I tried to breath. I turned back to him. "Mr. Waters, Bill, please, you have to believe me. I didn't do this. But I'm trying to get to the bottom of it. I'm trying! I swear!" Before he could yell again, I shut the door behind me and hurried across the lawn stooping low like a goblin.

I drove back to my place and parked a few houses down. I keyed in quietly through the front door and went to my designated guest room. I set an early alarm to wake up and leave before my parents knew I was in. Death had come home.

In the morning, the left part of my chest was a greenish purple. I snuck to the kitchen and grabbed a bottle of Advil. My mother was at the table watching me.

"I know, I know, I'm out of here," I said.

"Did someone do that to you?" she asked.

"What do you care?" I tossed three of the coated Advils into my mouth and forced a dry swallow.

"Do you want breakfast?"

"Not from you."

I limped to the hallway but stopped. Without turning to her I said, "I saw how Uncle Ted died. I can see how everyone dies. Even me. Even you."

"Please, go," she said. I heard fear in her voice.

I limped to my room, grabbed my stuff, but returned with venom. "Show me the pictures Aunt Dev passed around. The one of you and Uncle Ted at that party."

"Por qué?"

"Because I need to see it," I said. I was leaning against the entrance to the kitchen. It was a bit overcast and the morning was gray. In our lanai, where we gathered in the summer, dew was collecting on the bug screens.

My mom stared me down. Her face looked sick. I noticed how old she was. How tired. Her glasses were perched on her brown nose like Scrooge McDuck's. She slowly stood up and shuffled to a drawer in our hallway. Behind her, her coffee slowly steamed and got cold. She pulled out a photo album and opened it to the page.

"You've seen it a million times," she said. It was just like Becca had described. My mom, Ted, and Sal are arm in arm, drunk, smiling. They're standing in front of some garish 1980s wallpaper. Sal is some safari explorer. My mom is the Cat in the Hat. Uncle Ted is a Humphrey Bogart detective, his face bleached white from the camera flash.

"It was right before I got pregnant with you," she said.

I studied the picture. It was the exact outfit I had always described. The one in all my posts.

"When he died, you looked at this picture every day. I didn't know why. I still don't. You'd steal away to your room with it and talk about how weird he looked. You wouldn't let it go."

"Do you blame me for his death?"

There was a long pause. She held her arms and took a long breath.

"What are you asking me?"

"I think it's pretty clear."

"He was a hurt man that needed a lot of help at that moment, and nobody gave it to him."

"So that's a yes."

"It's hard for me to know that you watched him die. Right there. Just like that. I . . . I don't know what I'm supposed to say to you. There's nothing I can tell you."

"Do you think I'm going to end up like him?"

"I'm certain of it. When I see how you drink and smoke and how you're hard on yourself . . . I think Ted is living out his final years through you, and that scares me. I think you two are locked in some sort of dance together. You two always had a connection. He loved you so much. He put you on his job applications as his greatest inspiration. You, Sammy. He'd try to get a job at a fucking deli and talk about how his eleven-year-old nephew was his hero. And then he died, begging for your help. I think a part of you broke off when it happened, and his spirit packed itself into that hole and grew bigger and bigger. All I see is him when I look at you."

"What do I do?" I felt tears run down my cheek and I wiped them away. My lips grew tight and started to tremble. I hadn't cried in front of my mom in over a decade. She smelled like breakfast. Her eyes were misty behind her glasses. She grew clinical, sterile, she blinked away the wetness and looked at the floor and then the walls and then back to the picture.

"Mom, look at me."

"There's nothing to do," she said. "I saw the stories you used to write as a kid. The scribbles you'd make after he died. Your little sketches. He's a part of you now. He's always going to be. But when you went to college, that energy left here, and your father and I had a chance to breathe again. It was like the air got cleaner."

"That's why you never want me home."

"How could I? You have so much attached to you. Wherever you go, you never go alone." There was another pause before, "You should leave before your father wakes up. Here." She took the photo out of the plastic sleeve and placed it in my palm.

Then I left the house, and the next time I saw them it was on a laptop screen.

Sammy Dominguez, 23, cursed.

>

I had planned to go to see Lucas, my friend from the Villa days, but he wasn't around quite yet. He said his roommate would be home in a few hours to let me in, so I had some time to kill. Before I knew it, I found myself driving to the USF clinic with the hopes of finding Ryan Vasquez. I decided that I'd be doing him a favor if I showed him chinsky and how his new wife and stepdaughter will probably die. This whole time he had been crying about the *possibility* of it happening, and maybe showing him what it'd look like would really fry his circuits. I didn't have a real noble reasoning behind It. It just made sense to me. I wanted to break him.

Once there I prowled around the parking lot and scoped the place out, looking for the pick-up truck his wife drove earlier. Deciding the sadsack probably got dropped off again, I pulled into a spot and headed inside where a Haitian woman behind the desk eyed me up and down. I didn't recognize her, but she seemed open to talk.

"I'm looking for an SP named Ryan Vasquez," I said.

"And who are you?"

"I'm Sammy Dominguez. My mother is Chandra Dominguez."

"Oh, how is she doing?" the woman asked. She leaned forward and smiled.

"She's fine. Does Ryan Vasquez still work here? Does he still do this?"

"Let me see if he's scheduled today," she said. She typed at the computer and her golden bangles clattered against the bottom of the keyboard. She read something on the screen and then pouted. "It looks like his last session was a little over a year ago. Hasn't been back since."

"Hm. Okay. Do you have his email?"

>

Lucas's roommate, a tall Black guy named Horace, let me into their apartment. He said I could crash in Lucas's bed and that he wouldn't mind. Lucas said that when he got off work, we'd hit some bars around USF. I told him that I was pretty banged up and not feeling it, but he insisted. Horace told me their Wi-Fi, and I got comfortable.

I lay in Lucas's bed and examined my chest. It was hard to take a deep breath in. My phone was cracked to shit, but it still worked. Triangles of light and shards of screen blinked and twitched like an organism. I opened the laptop, and it was in good shape. I thought about searching my name. I imagined a video of Bill strangling me at the base of the stairs, or better yet, me breaking my neck in the fall, a stream of blood coming from my ear.

Instead, I looked up Ryan Vasquez. I thought long and hard about my undying grudge against this man. It had been a year since our brief showdown in the parking lot where he trounced me. But this was a war, and I was ready to go full PSYOP on him. I typed his name into the search bar and the red links populated the screen. When my mother told me that I had so much attached to me, I wondered if it included a guy like Ryan and all of his output. Crying doesn't just disappear. The energy to weep and scream and thrash, that shit doesn't dissipate, it lingers. Bill Waters managed to turn his into toys. Colorful marbles and Legos and chattering teeth that sat glossy and plastic in his study. Among other reasons, it's likely why he scolded me and shoved me down the stairs. I had broken his toys.

But Ryan didn't have any space in his life or in his backpack for it. So, he tossed it out and, evidently, I was a magnet for it, so I piled it on my back like a sweater of iron shavings. Admittedly, there was a part of me that liked it. Somewhere deep inside me I knew I had a quarry to fill. Whether it was mine or Uncle Ted's or even Ellery's for that matter. But even still, Ryan Vasquez was not my friend.

FLORIDA MAN METHS OUT, GUY DROWNS, FAMILY KILLED IN BOATING ACCIDENT, GAS EXPLOSION KILLS THREE. As I watched them, a deep sense of nostalgia came over me. The death videos, the smell of Lucas's room, me huddled up in his bed. I was ten years old again. I had a new and fresh secret. I kept clicking around when a new link popped up and caught my eye. It was trending: KILLED BY WAX MAN.

I paused. I listened to see if Horace was nearby. After a moment, I clicked the video. It took place in some sort of dungeon and Ryan, dehydrated, weak and gaunt, was on all fours, crying, crawling for his life. Behind him the Wax Man, with his white face and detective coat, stalked him with a metal rod. The Wax Man slammed the rod into the back of Ryan's skull. It cracked and hissed as air and blood shot out. Ryan gasped, coughed, his eyes twitched backward. Then the Wax Man got on his knees and put his mouth to the back of Ryan's head. And he started sucking. I dug out the picture that my mom gave me and studied Uncle Ted. It was a perfect recreation.

I downloaded the video as an .mp4 and sent it to Ryan's email. I sent them from a burner and the subject came to me naturally: HERE'S SOMETHING TO CRY ABOUT.

Feeling satisfied, I closed my laptop and nestled into bed. I closed my eyes and let myself sink into the gray comforter. It smelled like deodorant and body spray. It smelled like lotion. It smelled like sneakers.

I could dial it all back to Lucas, I thought, laying there, drifting off to sleep, my breath rattled and strained. He was the first person to show me something. It was in fifth grade and Austin and I went to Lucas's house for a sleepover. He opened up eBaum's World or some other early 2000s website. I couldn't remember. He showed me Split Face. Some brown kid that looked like me in cargo shorts jumped off a bridge into the river below, but he didn't clear the landing and he cracked his head open along the concrete pylon. Everyone gasped and shrieked, and his body slumped into the water— an immense blossom of red quickly darkening around him. People leapt in and swam after him. Then the video cut to some overhead angle where doctors were trying to save him. But he was Split Face now. His head was like an open book. The doctor kept trying to push and hold the two halves of the skull together, but they'd fall back apart like bat wings, his brain and skull shifting and sliding out with each attempt. His right eye loosened in the socket and squirmed out of his skull like a dog backing out of its collar.

He had a name before he was Split Face. Uncle Ted had a name before he was Wax Man.

Sammy Dominguez, 23, with many names yet to come.

>>>

"You really look like shit, man," Lucas said. He was a boxy, barrel-chested guy that pushed paper for a construction company. He had fat wrists and wore a tight, leather watch on his left hand. He had a tight necklace with a crucifix. He had a big round head with low-cropped brown hair. He had stubble on his round cheeks. But he had nice eyes, they were small and deeply set in the flesh of his face, but they were kind. I never realized before. He drank his beers fast and kept refilling his glass.

We were at some on-campus gastropub that broke off to what USF students called the Avenue. Just shoulder to shoulder bars of decreasing quality. My body was still sore, but I tried to keep pace and drank beer and did a shot of Bulleit when he ordered it.

"Hey, do you remember Split Face?" I asked him. I forked some food around and slid a piece of steak into sauce. I wasn't very hungry. I was content with getting drunk, Ubering to his place, and then getting back to Tallahassee in the morning.

"No, what's that?" he asked.

"It was that video you showed us back in fifth grade. At your sleepover with me and Austin?"

"Oh, where that fucker got his head wrecked?" He started laughing wide-mouthed. He banged his big fist on the table. "Yoooooo," he said, "that shit was gnarly. Man, you got all pale and were weird the rest of the night."

"I did?"

"You don't remember? You kept going in and out of the bathroom like you were gonna throw up. I had to get you ginger ale and like saltines or whatever." He kept laughing. I nodded and laughed a little. Panicking and getting queasy sounded like me for sure, but I had come a long way since. If only he could see me now, I thought. I can beat his Split Face a million times over.

"How is Austin? Do you talk to him?" I asked.

"No, not after Jesuit. He joined the army. You know how he was. Liked those war videos a little too much," he said, grinning. He pantomimed shooting a rifle and yelled in gibberish, trying to sound Arabic. People at other tables looked over, offended. "There was an old Villa kickback a year ago. I think he might've been there. I was pretty fucked up to be honest.

"This feels kind of surreal," he continued. "We've never really hung out like this. I was always bummed about how we grew apart."

"I'm glad you're doing well down here," I said.

"Man, this place rocks. Everyone busts my balls about never leaving Tampa, but dude, the girls here are the best. Did you know we're the strip-club capital of the world?"

"Is that true?"

"I don't know. I heard that somewhere."

"By the way, I can show you something worse than Split Face," I said.

"Maybe not here while I'm eating," he laughed.

"You should really see it though," I said. I needed to show him something terrible. Close the loop.

"Listen, we're gonna go out tonight and we're gonna get laid. These bars are like all eighteen-year-olds with fake IDs and nobody checks anything. I clean up here."

Shit. Alexa called it a mile away. Picking up freshmen.

"I don't know, man," I said. "I had a rough night last night. I think my ribs are fucked up."

"I know you didn't come all the way down here to show me a snuff film, right?"

"No, I guess not." But as soon as I said it, I had to wonder. I wanted to show more people. I needed to show someone to remind myself what a normal reaction looked like. I needed to show someone and absolutely break them. Bill screamed, but it wasn't right. Ryan might not even open that email I sent, and even if he did, I wouldn't see his reaction. Wouldn't feel his energy. I needed immediate gratification. Someone quick and dirty. Someone like an eighteen-year-old girl with a fake ID.

"I want to catch up," Lucas started, "but I'm not exactly the kaffeeklatsch type of guy."

"I don't even have any condoms on me or anything."

"Bro, you're too old school," he said. He took a baggie out of his jacket. It had a bunch of white pills in it.

"Molly?"

"Plan B."

"That's insane," I said.

"No, it's not. You cum in them and give them one of these. It's easy and it's a win-win for everyone. I'm actually kind of a gentleman if you think about it."

"What about STDs?"

He sunk his head down. He massaged his temples.

"These girls are right out of high school. They're good to go. You don't get STDs until you're like in your twenties, ya know? Their pussies are too resilient."

"I'm starting to remember why we grew apart," I said.

"Fuck you. I got sent to Jesuit and was deprived of pussy for four years. Every day I got bullied by douchebags in ugly suits. You got lucky and fell in love with the first girl you fucking met. I'm making up for lost time. My ripe years were stolen from me."

"You're twenty-three," I said.

"And I'm loving it."

"Alright," I conceded. The plan was slowly forming in my head. "But if I pick up a girl, can I take her back to your place?"

Lucas looked at me and raised an eyebrow. "Why? You don't wanna fuck in a dorm?"

"My laptop is back at your place."

"You need it to have sex? Alright," he said. "That's weird, but alright."

>

Alexa had predicted it near perfectly. I was twenty-three years old and looked relatively mature and smart for my age and the girls at Darby's had no clue I was more or less carrying a digital hunting knife. It was easy enough to buy them drinks and talk to them, but I had to find the right girl. I had to find the one that would go reeling into the night, pulling at her hair. The girl that would scream in the life-affirming way I needed.

Weaving through the throng of people I felt a sense of melancholy. I missed everyone. Jason, Ellery, Alexa, Becca, and oddly enough, Mr. Waters. I looked over at Lucas buying some girl a vodka Red Bull and remembered us as kids in uniforms walking into a chapel in single file. We had reconciliation every other month and we'd all have to sit in front of an old priest and confess our sins. We always joked about what we were going to tell the priest. We would conspire to lie about an insane transgression just to see the reaction on the old man's face, but we never went through with it. At least I never did. I always chickened out and sat there before the man, picking at my cuticles. So many times in my life I was prompted to lay bare my emotions in a way I was never ready for. Confession in the chapel, being a standardized patient, going to group therapy, being at funerals, my mother not looking at me, my dad handling the mourners like they were all too hot to touch. If I found the right girl tonight, I could dig my hands into the soft of her stomach and rip out her raw emotions and possibly relearn how to be human, or, maybe, I thought, just drag her down with me for the company. Maybe

I can stuff her into my crevices and push out all the other people that were taking up space. There's a confession I could tell that dawdling old priest.

Or maybe all of that was rationalizing and the real confession was that I was just angry and resentful. I was upset at Becca for leaving me. I was upset at Ellery for haunting me. I was upset at Alexa for calling me broken. I was upset at my mom, at Maria, at Claire, at everyone who kept acting like everything was normal. I just wanted to find someone and scare them. And luckily, I did.

There was a skinny girl with blue hair bopping around the outside of a larger group. She had a cheap beer in her hand, and I approached her. She was wearing black jeans and a striped T-shirt. She had black boots on. Her legs were spindly, and her knuckles were pink and spider like, clutching the neck of the bottle. She looked like she thought she was edgy and artistic, and when we walked outside to the patio area, I got her another drink. Her name was Cece and she was nineteen and probably 100 pounds with stones in her pockets.

When she was ready to go, she started kissing my neck and I called an Uber and texted Lucas that she probably won't stay the night. He replied back that if I fucked in his bed, then I'd have to Venmo him for laundry.

Cece told me I didn't need to wear a condom because she was on the pill. She asked if I was "clean" and I said sure. With every thrust my fractured rib screamed at me. I had to get on my back and have her go on top. She felt tight on my dick. She was frail and waifish and her bony body was light and my beer belly felt heavy and my hair felt greasy but she didn't seem to mind. Maybe she thought I was artistic and forward-thinking. That my body odor was because of some statement. She didn't know that I was actually a troll. Or maybe she did know and craved it. Regardless, she felt unsure and awkward on top and so I grabbed her waist hard and fucked her.

"Cum inside me," she said and so I did, and she trembled, and her knobby knees shook on the bed. She fell beside me and purred to herself. My dick was wet and sticky.

After a moment, I went for it. "Do you want to see something cool?"

"I'm tired," she said. She didn't open her eyes. I ignored her response and got out of bed. I opened up the laptop and went to chinsky. I was crouched over, naked, the glow of the screen outlining me. I looked like one of those demons in that copy of Dante's Inferno. Her eyes were closed but I could tell the bright glare of the screen was disturbing her. She folded the pillow over her face and groaned. "Sleeeeeepy," she said.

"Just watch this really quick," I said. I took the tape off of the webcam and took her ID out of her wallet. I typed in her name: CECELIA DUNN. I turned to her and she was still not having it. The webcam blinked on and flickered and the yellow of the screen came pulsing. She lay in Lucas's bed, tangled in the sheets. Her legs looked even longer, and her blue hair sprawled in all directions. I brought the laptop to the bed and showed her the screen.

"Come on, man," she said. "You're being weird."

"Just really fast," I said. "I promise."

She groaned and, without sitting up, pulled the pillow away and opened her eyes. She flinched and blinked at the bright, yellow screen and forced her eyes to adjust.

I was sitting on the bed next to her and patted her shoulder as a gesture of comfort. She furrowed her brows and looked at me.

"Is this gonna be porn?" she asked.

"No, just give it a second."

She looked at me and propped herself up on her elbows. "Are you secretly a weirdo?"

I couldn't help but laugh. "No, I promise."

She moved some hair out of her face. Slowly the page loaded up. Blood-red links started appearing. BLUE HAIRED SLUT GETS DRAGGED BEHIND CAR, SKINNY TEEN GANG RAPED, TIGHT BODIED GIRL FALLS DOWN ELEVATOR SHAFT, SLIMEBALL KILLS GIRLS IN TAMPA.

"What is this?" she asked. I could hear the weight in her voice. It wasn't soft and sexy anymore. It wasn't drunk and horny either. It was heavier. No flirtation anywhere.

"Just click one," I said.

"I don't watch these things," she said, "They freak me out."

I reached over and clicked a link. A video loaded up of Cece getting dragged behind a purple lowrider. Her wrists were tied with chains and the lowrider peeled out down a freeway, dragging and skinning her along the way. People cheered and shouted. The car did a drift at the end and her body whipped around and caught itself under the tires. Her throat snagged under the bottom of the car. She died screaming.

I turned to her in bed. Her lips quivered.

"Was that me?"

Before she could react, I clicked another video: SLIME-BALL KILLS GIRLS IN TAMPA. It was me suffocating her on the floor of Lucas's room. Pressing my thumbs against her neck. Her eyes bulging out and her face going purple. She reaches up and scratches at my face and my cheek opens up and drops warm red blood on her eyelashes and hairline. I turned to her again.

"They're all you."

She erupted in a scream and kicked the laptop off the bed. I caught it before it hit the ground and she pulled up the covers and scrambled to the corner like a chipmunk. She screamed again. "Get the fuck away from me! Don't you fucking touch me!"

I clicked another link and showed her the screen. It shined on her and trapped her against the corner of the room. She was naked and terrified, and I could see the pink of her pussy and the red marks of my grip on her waist. "Get the fuck away from me!"

The video showed some guy with a monkey wrench caving her face in. Her teeth blew out. A deep fissure opened up from her forehead to her cheekbone, purpling the surrounding area in deep shades of bruise. You can see the brain damage sink in as her mouth goes slack and bloody drool starts flinging out in thick waving strands. The real her started crying in the corner. "Somebody help me!!"

Just then, Lucas barged in. Behind him was another girl. She was on the phone, dialing 911 presumably. They must've just come home to the shouting. Lucas saw Cece there, and she bolted for the doorway and fell to her knees in front of the other girl, crying. Before I could say anything, Lucas punched me hard in the mouth and I went sideways, knocking my head against his desk, and then falling onto my laptop cracking the screen off its hinges. Before I went under, I heard Lucas tell one of the girls about how we grew apart.

>

Back in Tallahassee I dipped into my savings and bought a beater laptop from another kid who was selling his. I downloaded Spyglass right away, didn't pass Go, didn't collect $200. The image of Cece screaming and recoiling from me, naked and flailing, was branded on my mind. For all intents and purposes, my goal of solving the mystery that was chinsky took a far back seat to my new interest: showing it to people.

The weeks started to peel away, and I let myself become the monster I had always wanted to be. I would sleep all day, go to work 'til late, swing by Pots or some other shitty bar afterward and prey on whatever young girl was there. I'd take them home and I'd show them how they died. Any semblance of "doing the right thing" and "catching" the "people" behind chinsky fell away. I simply couldn't do it. By the nature of the website itself there was nothing to click, nowhere to go, nothing to see that wasn't the hellish yellow screen and the grotesque red links. Haruspx was gone, the webcam flickered, and the machine hummed. I felt like I had failed Ellery and like I had pushed Becca away, all for a puzzle I couldn't solve. But here's the thing—I couldn't stop logging on. I couldn't beat the website, so I just had to indulge it. I thought, vaguely, of what Maria said about me spiraling and she was right. Everyone was right. I was lost in a storm. I didn't want help solving it, I just wanted to make people afraid of it the way I was.

I had a whole system down. I only did it twice a week and alternated through a series of bars. If I saw a girl or the friend of a girl at a bar that could somehow recognize me, I left quickly. I never gave my real name. I never gave a phone number. Sometimes I'd bring my laptop in a messenger bag and would be adamant to go to her place, unless they lived in some sterile dorm in which case the closed network would likely buck me off.

I stopped hanging out with Alexa mostly because I couldn't bear to look at her. She didn't seem too upset about it, but as her texts slowly stopped altogether, I wondered what her lasting impression of me was. Sometimes I toyed with the idea of calling her and taking her up on that offer all those years ago—to be my escort to a group therapy session. I knew I was close to the breaking point. My actions with these girls were like painkillers in a weird way. I could keep feeding off their screams like a vampire, but I knew, somewhere in my subconscious, that a deep internal wound was only expanding wider and deeper like a trench.

I'd have them over and do whatever they said. I used a condom if they wanted. Was gentle if they seemed anxious. Whatever. It was all about lulling them into thinking I was considerate and kind, which, up to the reveal, I mostly was. I never drugged them or got them too drunk because they needed to be conscious enough to see it. I was never rough and I never scared them away prematurely and if they wanted to quit, I did. On some occasions there wasn't even sex, and we would just get high and talk and I'd fall asleep, stoned, on my couch before even getting to the damn website.

The Pakistani guy at the liquor store saw me more and more, only buying things a little more appealing than a flask of Cutty: flavored vodka, mixers, Jack, Blue Moon, etc.

"Things will improve, my friend," he said.

"Buddy, they're the best they'll ever be," I remarked, hoisting up the large brown bag.

I showed a girl her lynching. I showed a girl her drowning. I showed a girl her dying of a rare blood disease. I showed a girl me stomping on her face, her head gushering open onto my own carpet. I showed a girl her fall down a well.

Months passed like this. From my first login to my awakening in Tampa, through the winter months and following spring, I haunted the campus. Christmas came and went, and

I spent it alone in my apartment, jacking off, getting high and watching people die. My father faked a phone call to me and wished me a Merry Christmas. I didn't say it back. I went through the motions at work, becoming more of an automaton, transferring and scanning documents from one screen to another. Ryan Vasquez never emailed me back, and I grinned at the thought of him going blind with fear like some Lovecraft protagonist.

On New Year's Eve I hopped the fence of Jason and Maria's old home. Nobody had moved in yet and I laid down in the backyard on the cold grass and watched the city's fireworks display. Bright circles of yellow and red colored the sky like a ringworm infection. I sat with a hip flask and drank pulls until the horizon wobbled on its axis. In the darkness, the fence at the end of the yard stood like a black wall of sentinels. A panel of shoulder to shoulder jurors soon to deliberate over my fate. Pointy heads. Straight backs. Chevrons to the night sky and the negative space between them pointing down to hell.

I took off my sweater and opened my shirt and felt for the people inside of me. I felt around for the deaths I'd eaten. The sorrows I'd gobbled up whole. In the creases of my palm I saw girls crying and running for the door. I couldn't remember my own rationalization anymore. Were they teaching me how to be human? Were they teaching me how to cry? How to feel? Or was I fooling myself this whole time? In my gums I felt their mouths and the salt of their tears. I thought of Uncle Ted and wanted a pack of Coors. I thought of Ellery and wanted to see her one more time, to hear her tell me she did, in fact, love me and that, yes, she actually wanted to be here at FSU. I was okay with the lie. Pink exploded in the sky and fell down in loud curtains. I wanted to see Becca one more time. I had a few more months before I could hear her voice. Sometimes I dreamt of her looking at me from the base of the stairs. I pulled my cowboy hat down and spat on the dirt and she got on a horse and rode into the mist. Green popped over blue and into yellow and for a brief moment the sky was light enough for me to see my own hands on my cold bare chest and the way my shirt fell to the sides like an open coat.

"Pobrecito," I said aloud to nobody, my voice sounding more like a spic than I remembered.

It was January 1st, and my flesh was as cold as the dead.

Soon, the nights got warmer. In the mornings, when the sky was still pink, I'd stand on my rusted balcony and look out over the humble skyline. The downtown stretch of politicians. The campus to the west. Somewhere out there, rivers and lakes and just even further, the gulf. Ellery was in the breeze. Energy lives forever. One night I found myself riding my bike to the intersection where she died. The metal rod and flowers that her friends planted years ago were gone without a trace. I was turning twenty-four that year, but I had gone backward. I still listened to *Juju* but in a way that was too familiar, like simulacrum. It had played so many times it started to lose its meaning. Semantic satiation. Saying the word "wonderful" nonstop and then asking yourself what the hell it even meant. Saying her name too many times and questioning if that was actually right. It scared me. I couldn't lose *Juju*.

Soon it was the summer, and I was about to go out. I didn't have work that night and had plans for this seedier bar called Poor Paul's. Smoking was still allowed. They had communal bars of soap in the rest rooms. People threw darts and shot pool. I had been a few times during the day to tie one on and started seeing a younger crowd pour in over time. There was this Black girl I kept seeing. Small chested.

Dark-skinned. Hair in Marley twists. She kept seeing me too, but I always hesitated. There was something in her eyes that seemed wrong. But she looked familiar. I had decided that if she were there tonight, I'd get her.

Before leaving I stood on my balcony and called Becca. It had been a year since she walked down the concrete steps and left me like a ranchero in the doorway. It rang a few times, and when she answered I felt my stomach drop. I had forgotten her voice. Her intonations.

"You really waited a year," she said.

"I really did."

"How have you been?"

What a question, I thought. I white-knuckled the rail of the balcony to keep upright. My mouth went dry. I grabbed a bottle of Blue Moon and took a swig. Called it pre-gaming.

"I'm doing my best," I said. It's all that came out. I could hear her soft breaths. "My birthday is next week."

"Got any plans?"

"No. What are you doing?"

"For your birthday? Nothing."

"I meant right now."

"I'm driving home. Just had a nice dinner."

"With a guy?"

"With a friend."

"That's a guy?"

"Why are you calling, Sam?"

"Because I miss you," I said. Saying it aloud made it worse. A pang of guilt that Ellery might hear. A pang of guilt that Becca would know I felt guilty about Ellery. A pang of guilt for what I'd been up to. I started crying on the phone in a way I didn't expect. I heard her voice shake. She took a breath.

"Sammy," she said softly. A whisper. I heard it in her voice too. She was driving, talking through the Bluetooth of her center console. "Why are you crying?"

"I think I'm fucking up down here, Becca," was what came out. I was crying harder. I couldn't keep it together. My jaw hurt. The night sky over Tallahassee shined back only a handful of stars and streaks of black clouds. It was probably seven o'clock over there, the orange sun heading toward the green and blue mist of that wonderful west coast. Wonderful. Wonderful. Wonderful? "I think I'm being really bad," I said.

"Sammy, you're gonna make me . . ." She tapered off. "You can't just call me like this, okay? It's not fair."

I tried to keep quiet. My breaths were fast and shallow.

"It's not fair for you to call me like this," she repeated. She was cracking too. Then she went for it. "I gave you a chance to come here. And you rejected me."

"It's not like that. I'm trying down here. I'm just working some stuff out. But I'll come to you. I promise."

"What? What are you saying?"

"I don't know," I said. "But I can't stay here much longer. I want to be in Portland. I want to be with you."

"No," she said.

"What do you mean 'no'?"

"I mean no to this. No to you calling me and dropping this on me."

"I'm not trying to drop any—"

"Then why are you calling, Sammy? Really? Are you drunk?"

I examined the Blue Moon in my hand. Definitely not drunk. Not yet at least. Not in the way she knew me to be.

"Don't call me," she said. "I'll text you. Okay? I'll text you. I just need to think first."

"Okay, but—"

"Goodbye, Sammy. Goodbye. I'll text you. Goodbye."

And then she hung up.

>

At Poor Paul's, the girl was there just as I had anticipated. She was sitting at the bar, and I sat next to her. She had piercings in her nose and on her lip. She wore a hoodie with her thumbs through the sleeves. She had checkered Vans. Her hair was thick and beautiful. She had a glass of beer and a pack of cigarettes with her.

"I was waiting for you to talk to me," she said when I took my seat. I was a little put off by that remark. Suspicious. I looked around as though someone was going to spring up with a billy club.

"I'm Sammy."

Shit. I forgot to give a fake name. Had to play it cool.

"I'm Jay."

She half turned to me. She offered me a cigarette, but I brought out my own. I lit it and tried to get comfortable. She was older, I could tell. Still younger than me but not a freshman. Maybe not even a student. There was something uncomfortable about her gaze. It was lazily seductive. She knew she didn't have to try so hard. She just had to not scare me away. I ordered a beer and we chatted briefly, perfunctorily.

"Are you going to take me home or do we have to ring up a tab first?"

"Do I know you?" I asked. I took another drag. I couldn't place her. I had never met this girl before, but she examined me differently. She kept her back straight and pushed her chest forward. She had a turquoise necklace and several rings and stones on her hands. Her skin was dark, and her teeth were stained. I felt watched. Alarms were ringing.

"Come on, let's get out of here," she said. She downed her beer and stood up. She laid her hand on my shoulder, and I felt the small pressure from her fingers. Her nails were painted dark blue. They were chipped.

"I can't help but feel like this is too easy," I said.

"You don't always have to work so hard," she said. "Not if we're after the same thing."

I got up and followed her out.

On the sidewalk, I called an Uber. She lit another cigarette and blew the smoke to the sky. "I have a boyfriend, you know."

"Oh."

"He knows I'm out though."

"Okay," I said. I felt myself getting hard. This girl was different. Something was happening.

As soon as we got into my apartment she went straight for the bathroom.

"Give me a second to get clean, okay?"

"No problem," I said. I went into my room and got ready. I took off my pants and my underwear and my shirt, and I got my dick hard. I took out my laptop and peeled off the webcam and the light blinked at me. Slowly the itchy déjà vu grew stronger. It was her voice. I didn't recognize her at first because of her hair, but it was the voice that I knew. I didn't type in her name, but instead found the video of me dying in the bathtub. The Black girl that finds me and pulls me out. This was her. I heard her come out of the bathroom and approach.

"Hey, do I—"

Before I could finish, I was met with pepper spray. Searing pain. Tiny hooks in my sclerae. I dropped the laptop. "Motherfucker!"

"Found you, bitch!"

"Fuck me!" I clenched my eyes and felt around. I was swiping. I was scared. I moved past her and tumbled down the hallway to the fridge. My eyes were on fire. Tears and snot ran down my face. My throat burned sickly and bitter. I could taste the chemicals on my tongue. I fumbled for the fridge and quickly grabbed some half-and-half. I opened it up and dumped it on my face. It was cold but only helped a bit. I wiped away my eyes just to get a glimpse of her again, still dressed in her jeans and shirt, raising her foot fast to my groin. I doubled over in pain and threw up on the ground.

"How do you know about chinsky!?" she yelled.

"*What?*" I shouted.

She grabbed me by the hair and threw me. I landed hard on the tile of my kitchen floor. I was still naked. My bare feet slipped around in my own vomit. She took out a pocketknife—blue and silver like her jewelry—and measured it at my cock. Her other forearm was on my neck. "Move and I fucking castrate you, you sick fuck."

"What the fuck are you talking about?"

"You're the one showing girls how they die!"

"No, no, please, I wasn't—"

"How do you know about chinsky? Are you behind it?"

"*What?* No! I'm sorry. Please. I'm sorry."

"Answer my fucking question!"

"It was sent to me!" I yelled. "It was sent to me by a stranger!" The feeling in my balls was returning. My eyesight was still blurry, but my eyes stung less. The point of her blade was inches from the soft flesh of my scrotum. "Please," I said. "I'm sorry. You'll never see me again."

"Show me who sent it."

"Okay. Go get my laptop. Bring it here. I won't move."

She got up and kept the knife leveled at me. She back-pedaled and disappeared down the hallway. I quickly scanned the kitchen for a weapon. The first thing my eyes fell on was Maria's Le Creuset lid. I groaned and rolled my eyes. Even still, she was fucking with me.

"Show me," Jay said again. She was standing over me with the laptop and she tossed it on my stomach. I logged on to CampfireFables.com to show the thread from Haruspx. "Look," I said, presenting the screen.

"Who the fuck is that?"

"I have no idea. They deleted their account. I know nothing."

"And you're Blue Bird?"

"Yeah. That's my username on this site. I don't post any-more though, I swear to God."

"And you don't have any idea who Haruspx is?" she asked. Anger was leaving her voice. There was still disgust though, make no mistake.

"No," I said between strained breaths. "It's not my web-site. They sent me the link, and I just go on it."

"To show girls how they die."

"Yes," I said. "I admit it. But it's not my website."

"Do you post?"

"What? No. I don't even know how."

"How long have you known about it?"

"Since September."

The kitchen started to smell. The half-and-half, my vomit, cigarettes, booze, pepper spray, and the general sleaze of how I've been keeping the place. She looked deadly. There was not a doubt in mind that she wouldn't drive that knife to the hilt right in the soft meat of my perineum.

"You've been torturing girls since September?" she asked.

"No," I said. I was begging at this point. Maybe not through my words exactly, but she could tell through my tone. "I wanted to solve it but had no clue where to start. Then I got scared. Scared of what it was doing to me. So, I showed it to other people."

"But why?"

"Because I'm fucked up, okay? I'm fucked up." It was a shitty answer, but it landed. And like Jason always said, it just needs to *land*. She stood up and kept her knife at her side, blade still out. Her T-shirt was stained, not sure from what. Above her the dome light of my kitchen backlit her. She was a silhouette. An angel of judgment. I went into the fetal position and cupped my balls. Counted them. Felt my dick, soft and sore.

"You're pathetic," she said.

"You hunted me down?"

"You deserved it."

"How do *you* know about chinsky?"

"That's not important. But I'm gonna end it," she said. She slung her hoodie over her shoulder and headed for the door.

"Wait!" I said. I got up and nearly fell over from dizziness. I had to walk in a crouch. My balls were turning purple, my rib was re-fractured, and my eyes burned. I grabbed some gym shorts from my room and limped down the concrete steps after her.

"Back the fuck up," she said. She pointed the knife at me. It was almost midnight. People were in the parking lot. Parties were being had in other apartments. The two of us looked insane.

"I'm sorry," I said. "I mean it. Let me help."

"Yeah right," she said. She leaned against a car and pulled her shoes on. I kept my distance.

"You can't leave me in the dark about this," I insisted. "Let me help. At least tell me what the fuck it is."

People were starting to see. Three friends with a case of beer were watching us from a balcony. A couple near a car was staring. She put her knife away.

"I have to know," I said. "It's eating me alive."

She paused for a moment. It was hard to imagine that I had seen her at Poor Paul's. That we were flirting. But in a way, really, that wasn't her at all. It was a ploy. A bait and switch. It wasn't even her on top of me in the kitchen with a knife to my taint. This was the closest thing to the real her. Scared. Confused. Angry. Nervous. But in need of help just like me.

"Give me anything," I pleaded.

"It's a betting site," she said.

"So not other dimensions?"

"What?"

"I thought—forget it. What do you mean a betting site? Who is betting?"

She paused and studied me. "Fine," she said. "Saturday. The Crater. Come around the back. But if I hear one more thing about a creep that's been scaring girls, I won't even double-check. I'll come right here and cut your fucking balls off. Got it?"

"Got it," I said.

"Yo, is he bothering you?" We both turned to the source. It was one of the guys from the balcony.

"Mind your business!" she shouted back. She turned to me and scowled. Then she walked off down the sidewalk and climbed into a Kia that was waiting for her.

"Stop being a creep, my man!" one of the guys shouted. "You're scaring the hoes!" The others laughed. They had no idea.

> Be me, 24

> meet Jay & Izzy

> learn about the videos on page 40

A week after my encounter with Jay I turned twenty-four. It was a somber affair. I fielded more obligatory phone calls from my family. My father called and we spoke for all of twenty seconds. I asked if Mom wanted to talk to me and he said no and that she was busy. Then, covering it up, he said that she was feeling sick, then, not wishing to manifest anything, he doubled back and said, "She's just tired."

Jason called me and we talked about my toiling in Tallahassee.

"I'm out of here pretty soon," I said.

"What about that grad program?" he asked.

"What do you want me to say?" I asked in return. "Nobody wanted me to do that anyway."

"Relax, man," he said. "We just wanted you to do *something*. Anything, really."

"You sound like Maria," I said. I heard him sigh. I heard Maria shuffle around in the background.

"You gotta fuck off with that," he said.

"I'm just saying."

"Right."

"So, when are you going to come down and visit? We can get a *Die Hard* session going."

"I don't know. I'm pretty swamped."

"Yeah. I get it."

"Happy Birthday, man." Then he hung up and I looked around my apartment for a place where the old me might be hiding. How long could I go on like this? Surely, the troll under the bridge gets tired of it all too. I thought of Jay's anger. Her violence toward me. How justified it was. This was someone who had seen the same things I had seen but was doing something about it. I went full tilt into the dark side. I let it consume me whole, but she fought, and not just for herself but on the behalf of my young victims who I sent screaming and twirling into the night like pinwheel sirens. She should've killed me right there in my kitchen.

I ran a bath and thought of the video I had seen of me, dead, with Jay pulling me out of the tub. The website knew about her before I even did. I lit a cigarette and let myself sink into the water.

>

The Crater was a sprawling nightclub toward the north of Tallahassee. You had students, townies, and even politicians pull up and party down in allotted sections of the building. The pit was for the students, shoulder to shoulder, sweating, and screaming. The back bar was for the townies, bending their elbows, wearing their nice jeans and nice work boots, shouting over each other about what real Leon County folks do. And the top floors were for polished, crooked, suit-and-tie-wearing politicians that just got off their shift sinking Florida deeper into the hell pit it was destined for.

I locked up my bike on the far end of the lot and kept my distance from the throngs of people lined up and pre-gaming around the club. Behind the Crater was a steep hill with a chain-link fence and beyond that, through a forty-minute walk in the woods, was the border of Georgia. I walked through shadows and gave a wide berth around the right side of the building toward the back. Loud music sounded dense and muffled and vibrated the dumpsters on the side. Glass windows, now blacked out, shook high along the walls. I had heard the building used to be a notch below a megachurch. The old crucifix that stood atop was taken down and had somehow found its way to a skate park near Thomasville. Jesus's face was sideways, all spray-painted and chipped away from failed kick flips and successful grinds. Ended up in some edgy zines.

I had been to this club exactly one time before with Ellery, Jason, and Maria. This was when I was losing her to herself, and our arguments of what could've been became more frequent. I was pulling out all of the stops to show her Tallahassee could be fun. She knew I hated clubs because I got insecure and self-conscious, but I put on some cheap cologne and took her there. We got drunk on kamikazes in plastic cups. In the morning she said she hated it.

Around the corner people of all types smoked and drank. Little groups formed at the chain link fence, against the walls, sitting on the dumpsters, and pissing along in the darker corners. The door of the back flung open and a bright square shone like a spotlight. It gave birth to a small guy throwing out trash and recycling, everyone cheering him and laughing and him hustling back inside to shut the door behind him.

I moved down the alley and weaved between people. I tried to recognize Jay in the small pockets of activity.

"Sammy!" I looked. A tall, skinny guy waved me over. He had a tight jacket over his button-down and wore blown-out Nikes. I approached him.

"I'm Isaiah." He put out his hand. I shook it and it was dry and rough. "You can call me Izzy. I heard Jay caught you red-handed."

I didn't know what to say. I looked down and my cheeks went flush. It was an embarrassment I couldn't fight. People jostled around, drinking and roughhousing near the chain-link fence. I was afraid to be overheard. I looked back up at Izzy and his glasses caught the moon and they appeared like white disks, all-knowing and all-judging.

"Yeah," I started, "about that—"

"Heard your dick was out and everything," he said. "She fucking got your ass, bro, she's on it."

"On what?"

"You know"—he moved his hands around in a gesture to mean everything, the alley and the fence and the new state past it—"everything."

I furrowed my brows. I didn't know what he meant. I didn't know what was happening.

"I'm not really like that," I said. "I, uh, I think the website just kind of got its hooks into me."

"It's okay, hoss, there's plenty of time to make up for it," he grinned.

Before I could reply, the back door opened again, and people cheered. Out of it came Jay in a black uniform. She wiped her hands on her work pants and waved at someone who knew her name. She approached Izzy and me.

"You work here?" I asked.

"You got a problem with that?"

"No," I stammered, "I just—"

"Then let's go," she said. Then to Izzy, "You ready?"

"Always."

We went back out of the alleyway toward the parking lot. Someone clapped Jay on the shoulder and whispered something in her ear. She laughed it off and then flipped the guy the bird. Someone else offered Izzy a sip from his beer and Izzy declined and said, "Got a long drive."

As we crossed the parking lot a group of girls climbed out of a Toyota. One of them recognized me. I had shown her a video of her being mauled by a bear. A GoPro helmet watched the thing rip her stomach open with ease and she yelped and cried for mommy. The girl went pale when she saw me, and I averted my eyes and kept pace with Jay and Izzy. I looked back, and she was still watching me go. One of her friends, unknowingly, tugged at her shoulder to bring her toward the Crater. I wanted to throw up.

Izzy was tall, maybe around 6'6", and he had to fold himself into his small Kia. It was the one that picked up Jay from my place. They were clearly some sort of team. Jay took the passenger seat, and I climbed into the back still unsure of what was ahead. He started the car, and we slowly left the Crater behind. We were headed south. Out of Tallahassee.

"I didn't think you'd show up," Jay said. She turned toward me and leaned down the center of the car. I plucked at my seat belt. Her Marley twists hung low and coiled around the leather of the car seat. In the darkness she was hard to make out. Each passing street light burned her skin a dark orange like the dying embers of a hearth. Only her piercings flashed in the light. She was like a fish at the bottom of the sea luring me in with shiny doodads and bobs and then opening her mouth wide to swallow me whole. She fiddled with rings and put each one back on her hand. She put her turquoise necklace back around her neck.

"I feel really bad about what I've been doing," I said.

"Actions speak louder than words, pal," Izzy said from the driver's seat. He didn't take his eyes from the road. "We can all sit around feeling bad for our shittiness, but one day we gotta make steps to *not* being shitty."

Jay nodded. "Well said."

"Well, I'm taking those steps," I said.

"Yeah, we'll see," Jay said. She turned back to the road and put her feet on the dashboard. Izzy slapped them down. Jay put them back. Izzy shook his head. "If I stop short, your knees are gonna go through your eye sockets."

"Then don't stop short," Jay said.

"Where are we going?" I asked.

Jay turned back to me again and looked me up and down. She wasn't smiling. "Let's talk about the website first," she said.

"I told you, that account sent it to me. I don't know anything about it," I said.

"I know you don't. But let's talk about what you *do* know."

"Okay," I said. We were on the highway. FSU was disappearing in the distance. The same alarm that rang when I first met Jay started up again. I had to embrace it though. I wasn't going anywhere in a hurry. "You said it's a betting site right? So, it's a bunch of people predicting how people are going to die and the winner gets that gold ring and probably some sort of money. Some sort of crypto I guess."

"You're almost there," Izzy said. "They're AI-backed algorithms, but you gotta remember that humans make algorithms, right? Humans make AI too, it doesn't just come out of the sky."

"Sure."

"So, people are designing these little bots that surf online for two things: violent videos and personal data. Then it tries to match your data with some snuff vid they're synthesizing. It's all numbers. Zeros and ones."

"Are they deepfakes or are they totally made up?"

"How do you mean?" Izzy asked.

"When I see a video of a guy getting beheaded and he has my face, is that a real video that's been edited or is the whole thing fake?"

"Well, that's where it gets tricky. The best of the best is completely fake but entirely convincing. The sloppy guys are using pre-made material. Depending on how original your work is, you'd get a higher payout. These are freaks we're dealing with, but they fancy themselves real artists too."

"Okay, sure, but what are *we* doing?" I asked. "Where are we going?"

"*So*," Jay started, "on the front page you see these videos of you, me, our friends, and parents, dying, right? And some of the videos are so outlandish and preposterous, it's like how are *these* on the front page?"

"Because it's curated," Izzy said. "But not in the way you might think."

"If you keep clicking through the pages and get to, say, page forty, you'll find other solid videos."

"Then why are they pushed to the bottom?"

"Because they're sloppy," Jay said. "They're fucking sloppy."

Izzy started again, "The videos on the front page are polished and re-polished so that they're nearly impossible to trace, at least not without the creators finding out about it. But the videos on page forty? They're full of EXIF data.

Some of them down to the coordinates where the damn thing was uploaded from. Sometimes they're rookies in way over their head. Sometimes they like leaving their flair. It's like breaking into a house and tagging the walls. The real concern is if it's a bug or a feature. Because chinsky must know that some of their users are vulnerable. And if they know that, then maybe they encourage this sort of infighting. This sort of hunting."

"Hunting?" I asked. "You mean—"

"We can find them," Jay said.

A car flashed its high beams behind us, and Izzy winced. The bright light shone from behind my head and covered Jay in a white sheet. She recoiled, like the undead. "Fucking assholes." The car moved to the right lane and sped past us. Jay lowered the window and screamed, "Turn your fucking high beams off, dipshit!" She was distracted. I thought about opening the back door and tumbling out, but she turned back around, and her face was back in the shadow of the interstate. "We know where one is," she said. "And he's gonna pay."

"What exactly are we going to do?" I asked. I could see Izzy look at Jay. He had been wondering the same thing. I looked at the clock on the radio. It was almost one a.m. I spoke again. "I can't imagine we're rolling up at this hour just to talk."

Izzy looked at me in the rear view. "That's the thing," he said. I just registered how high and squeaky his voice was. He sounded all pinched and stretched out like Gumby. "There's a good chance he'll know we're coming."

"I don't think I can do this," I said. "Whatever this is."

"You don't have a choice," Jay said. "I saw that girl look at you back there. You know what you did to her. You're coming with us now."

There it was, laid out plain and simple. We were going to get revenge on one of the bad guys. What that entailed, I wasn't sure, but this was my redemption staring me in the face. Izzy's car hit eighty as we glided into the night, cutting onto US-19. Giant trees stood tall, reaching for the stars in thick coats of blackish-green and dripping moss. I felt caged and lowered the window. It was cool out and I took in big gulps of air, only realizing I was sweating when I felt a coldness on my face. I wasn't sure what was expected of me, but I prepared for the worst. I thought of revenge. I had decided that if I brought this bastard to his knees, mine was coming down the pike right behind him. I imagined coming back home to my apartment and seeing that girl from the parking lot. The one who recognized me. I tried to think of her name. Dani? Savannah? Erin? I'd walk in and find her in my desk chair with a handgun pointed at my head.

That was only a video of a bear mauling too. Not all that outlandish given the other links on the website. But then I thought of the other videos I'd seen. Someone getting their head tucked under a table saw. Someone getting whipped from the top of a carnival ride. Or the video of Claire Waters with the firecrackers in her mouth. Jason did a lot of prop bets in college. When a big game would come on, he'd hit the sites and there'd be bets for all sorts of things. One he always bet on was the over/under on how long the national anthem would go. These gruesome videos were the equivalent of betting that the national anthem would go on for an hour and a half. It's not *impossible* but it's incredibly unlikely. And then I grew cold. Unless someone *made* it likely.

If, theoretically, some computer pitched that Claire Waters was going to be kidnapped, tied down in a backyard, and then have half her face blown off with illegal fireworks, *and then* someone set out to make good on their promise . . . Well, that'd be a pretty hefty payday. That'd be like making the national anthem go an hour and a half. Was the driver that killed Ellery in on it? Did he get a cut of the pay? Or was it really just a freak accident, predicted by bots?

Suddenly, Alexa texted me: long time no talk, r u up?

I didn't answer.

>

We drove to this small town called Horseshoe Beach about two hours south. It sat on the gulf directly west of Gainesville. Izzy pulled off of US-19 and onto a narrower dirt road that moved through high trees parallel to marshland. I started to sweat more. I looked at Jay, sitting calm and calculated in the passenger seat. Her jaw moved softly like she was reciting something to herself. Counting through the steps maybe. Hyping herself up.

"You don't even go to FSU, do you?" I asked.

"Nope," she said.

"And what about you?" I asked Izzy.

"I go wherever she says," he said back, almost smiling, his eyes flicking up to me in the rearview. He cut the headlights and we rolled to a soft stop. In front of us, gray in the moonlight, was a chipped wooden sign that read: HORSESHOE BEACH. GET AWAY FROM IT ALL.

"This is all happening pretty fast," I said. Jay turned back and looked at me incredulously.

"Is it? Because you've known about this website for almost a year. I'd say it's happening a little too slow, don't you think?"

"It's just that—"

"You've been in Tallahassee since your girlfriend died, what, three years ago? You've been farting around, terrorizing people, losing friends, and main-veining evil shit on the internet. If you ask me, it's about time you started doing something."

"How do you know all of this?"

"Just go with it," Izzy said.

"I'm not talking to you," I snapped back.

"You're done talking entirely," Jay said.

"Just tell me what we're gonna do!" I implored.

There was a pause. Jay and Izzy exchanged another glance. Jay turned back to me and spoke like a mom explaining a punishment.

"We're gonna find him. Talk to him. Then we're going to put him down."

My hands started shaking. My mouth went dry. "We can't kill an innocent man," I said.

"You'd just as quickly watch someone else do it," Jay said. I balked. She was right. The observer was getting pushed out of the plane. Free falling. Build your parachute on the way down, motherfuckers. "And besides," she continued, "this guy isn't innocent. He's literally gambling on how we die. We're taking back our fate."

"That's a little dramatic," Izzy said, and Jay hit him on the shoulder.

"Shut up," she said. She turned back to me. I couldn't see her face, just the light gray of her teeth and glimmer of her piercings. "Someone made money off of Ellery's death. Think about that."

The words felt like hot iron on my chest. I needed to do this for her. I needed to do this for myself.

Before I knew it, Izzy was sliding into the back seat and

pushing me to the side, then Jay came in after him. Izzy opened up his laptop and plugged in a USB with a thick antenna. "Let me show you the real shit," he said, typing away. "The guy that lives here is named Lou Harding. He works a white-collar job as some insurance broker in the day, who cares, but at night he's betting on chinsky just like the rest of 'em. Now why is he on page forty? Maybe he likes to leave bread crumbs. Or maybe he's a dunce that's in over his head."

"I can relate," I whispered.

"Anyway, his biggest winner was this." Izzy showed me the screen. A video showed a small Indian kid getting backed over by a truck. The mother came out and started screaming and banging her fist on the side, but it was over by then.

"Fuck me," I said.

"Right. Cleared some serious coin on this one. And I stayed close on him, seeing him pop up again and again. Most of his videos are small time. Lots of factory accidents."

"Jesus. Why?"

"Probably a numbers game. But he did upload one video that took place in Tallahassee."

"Ellery's?"

"Maybe."

"Okay," I said. It was like trying to make sense of a new card game when I was already five hands in.

"The point is he's bad," Jay chimed in. "But show him how this night goes."

"Right," Izzy said. He started typing. "Everyone is playing whether they know it or not. So when I search Lou Harding on chinsky, we'll see how people think this is gonna go down."

The page flickered and loaded its bright yellow glare. The top link was *HEADSHOT, MY BOYO!* and Izzy clicked it. In the video a guy with a ski mask points a shotgun at a man bound and gagged and on his knees. The person pulls the trigger and the man's head bursts backward like a tipped-over galaxy.

"Is that us? With the gun?" I asked.

"Ideally," Jay said.

"But there might be videos of us dying too, right?" I asked.

"We don't like to watch those," Izzy said. "It psychs us out." Then he closed the laptop.

We went around the car, and Izzy popped the trunk and unzipped a duffel bag. He pulled out a small .38 Special. It was grimy in the moonlight and had tape on the handle. He put it in his jacket pocket. Jay pulled out three ski masks and handed one to me.

"What about my glasses?" I asked.

"Put it over 'em," she said, like I was an idiot.

Izzy and I looked at each other. He put his on first and his mask slanted his glasses. He rearranged them like some slapstick gag. I followed suit. "This is fucking insane," I said under my breath.

"Don't forget this," Izzy said. He produced from the bag a sawed-off shotgun. Double-barrel. Heavy as shit. Looked like something they'd use in the old times.

"What the fuck is this?" I asked. "Am I robbing a stagecoach?"

"Make jokes," Izzy said. "But anyone who has never shot a gun is a pro with this. Just point it at whatever wall you want to destroy. You gotta get up close and personal with this guy." He was smiling through his mask. I turned to Jay; her twists were coming out from under her mask like the tentacles of something else. I started to panic. I looked at the gun in my hands. I looked back at the narrow road out of here.

"Don't even think about it," Jay said.

>

Calling Horseshoe Beach a town was a bit generous. The place was hardly a neighborhood. It looked more like those retirement communities you saw in pamphlets when your grandparents were on their way out. Small and narrow roads crisscrossed each other, and golf carts sat parked outside of little bungalows. Every resident here put their money into their boats. The marina cut right through the center with sailboats and pontoons and kayaks and sheds and trucks and maintenance winches and then opened up to the sea proper. Even in the daylight this place would be a sleepy fishing town. Now, at this hour, it was dead. From the gulf, the smell of the tide was rich. I hadn't smelled the beach proper in years, I thought. I wondered if it'd be too cold to swim.

"He's on Tuna Lane," Izzy said. "Keep to the shadows."

"Tuna Lane. That's so cute," Jay said, barely audible. So she thought things were cute. Who was this person?

"We're looking for a very unique home. Shouldn't be hard to find," Izzy said. We stayed low, moved in a crouch. In the distance, to our north, the town's sole diner glowed a dull yellow, empty, with one or two lights on inside. We moved along, crossing over lawns and through barren yards, cutting from sidewalk to street to alley.

I felt my knees strain. I was out of shape. The gun was heavy. The mask was itchy. The beach smelled bad. I was scared and had to pee. Then the realization occurred to me. I wasn't even all that afraid to potentially kill a man. I was more afraid of what would come next. Would chinsky know what we did? Would this be the inciting salvo that started the war? This was the beginning of something truly terrible, and I wasn't ready for it. Wasn't even close.

"And there it is," Izzy said.

We stopped and stayed low behind a shed. Up ahead was a geodesic dome with pink lights on the top. Think about the big golf ball from Epcot. It was a sphere with panel facets, about the size of a three-story home. Izzy spoke again: "Those homes are weatherproof and energy-efficient. A guy with a lot of hardware needs to keep it dry and keep it cool."

In the driveway was a small pick-up truck. I couldn't tell if any lights were on in the house. I couldn't even imagine how the house would look inside. I remembered a story I read on Reddit about a farmhand who found an intermodal shipping container in the desert. It was heavily air conditioned with whirring generators and when he and his boss went in, they found nothing but beeping monitors and humming computers. That and child porn. Terabytes of the shit. "Real deal pizza meal," it was labeled. He ran away, called the cops, and when he returned the place was already on fire. He mentioned he was positive he had been seen. By who? I don't know. The owner of the container probably. That farmhand inadvertently ruined some creep's million-dollar industry. Everyone wanted updates on that guy's life, but he never posted again. Completely dropped off the site. That's what happens when you walk into homes you weren't invited to. Hell, maybe we were all vampires.

"I can't kill a man," I said. It was to Jay's back. Izzy looked at me and then looked away. Jay slowly turned.

"Then I'll kill you right here," she said. She put her gun under my chin.

"This is crazy," I pleaded. She pushed the gun up, and it hurt my jaw. I was looking at the stars. "It's not too late for us to go back to Tally."

"It is though," she said.

"Please."

"Are you a good guy like us or a bad guy like him?"

"I—" I stopped. I had no argument. I was petrified.

Jay pulled back and pushed forward and after a moment Izzy nudged me to follow. Quick steps took us to the back of the guy's truck. The home was humming softly. It was evil. We could tell. The hair on my arm stood up with static. I was grinding my teeth.

"Shit," Izzy said. He pointed to a camera looking right at us. A soft red light blinked.

"He ain't calling the cops," Jay said. "He doesn't want them in his house."

"What do we do?" I asked. I felt the gun in my grip. Over a decade ago my father gave me a BB gun and told me to never shoot a living thing. If he saw me now he wouldn't be surprised. He thought I was cursed after all. I looked around at my current situation and considered it myself.

"Fuck it," she said. "Let's try his door." Jay moved to the back door, a skinny rectangle cut into the lowest panel of the dome. She tugged on the knob and nothing happened. I stayed put behind the truck and looked at the camera looking at me. I was certain that if I checked chinsky right there, the top video would be *THREE WANNABE HEROES GET DOMED*. A gold ring would flicker.

"Let's fucking bail," I said to Izzy. "She's a psycho."

"Shut up," Izzy said, but I could tell he was nervous. He could be swayed.

"Come on, she's gonna get us killed," I urged.

"Don't be a pussy, I'm not leaving her."

"Guys," Jay called in a stage whisper. "I think I hear—"

Gunshots exploded out of the door. Jay dove to the right and landed face down in the dirt, just dodging them.

Pinholes of light came out of the doorway. Then more bullets. "Help!" she yelled. I spun to Izzy, but he clammed up. I moved fast.

I got out from behind the truck and hugged the side of the golf-ball house. Jay was crawling away on all fours and the door swung open. A guy came out with a polished looking pistol. He was in a button-down with his sleeves rolled up. He had slacks on and was barefoot. Izzy said he was an insurance broker, but I didn't expect him to still look the part. He approached Jay, who scrambled to get on her feet, but she kept losing her balance and falling on her knees. I saw blood in the patch of light from the dome. She was hit.

"This is gonna be big for me," the man said. He wasn't facing me, but I heard his voice. It was articulate. It sounded educated. Sounded like he had polished it for meetings and interviews and pitches and conferences. He was not the scummy rat-king I had expected. I expected a burnout, some guy that slept in a hoodie and jeans, someone that looked like me. Someone it seemed okay to kill. Trying to hurt this man, this person who seemed like he had, at least at some point, contributed to society felt wrong. The butt of the pistol winked at me. Jay was running out of time.

I closed the gap fast and, with the sawed-off in my right hand, swung it down like a flyswatter. I heard the guy's teeth click together, and he fell forward in a slump. I looked up and Jay was climbing to her feet. Her shoulder was clipped, dark blood coming down along her sleeve, dripping off her fingernails.

"Holy shit, holy shit," Izzy said behind us. "I totally froze."

"Let's get him inside," Jay said. "Quick." She reached down to grab the guy, but the pain in her shoulder fought back. She winced and backed away. Izzy grabbed the guy's shoulders, and I grabbed his feet. We brought him inside up the steep and awkward steps and laid him out in the main area of his odd little dome. Jay grabbed the man's pistol and put it in her jeans. She shut the door behind us.

His home was filled with computers and terminals and giant, blinking towers. Wires and cables ran in zip-tied bundles left to right along the floor like the chevrons of a hospital. Empty cartons of AriZona Iced Tea were piled in a corner. The place was freezing.

Tied up, the guy became feral. Gone was his articulate tone and upright posture. He gnashed and spat and swore at us. He laughed at certain questions. He had been so deep in chinsky and the inner workings of it all, he was certain, just as Izzy and Jay were, evidently, that all of us were being watched at that very moment. He called it being *generated*. Called the videos generations.

"You mean *simulation*," Izzy said.

"No, *generation*. A simulation is for an outcome. A generation *is* an outcome."

"I don't understand."

"You wouldn't. At certain points generators learn from generations. They propagate their own. The real Bettors don't even go on their computers anymore. They just set the little balls in motion and collect at the end."

"You don't do that?" I asked.

"I don't have the rig," he said, disappointed. "Yet."

"So, we're being generated right now?" Izzy asked.

"You know that answer," he said with a grin. His face was forgettable. A small nose in the middle of a flat head. Brown eyes. Lightly buzzed haircut. Clean face. Slightly yellow teeth. "I know the one you saw of me. But I also know the one I saw of you."

I thought of the video Izzy showed us. I felt like one of those on-rail shooters you played at an arcade. Every step moved you along a designed path, you either shot first or got eaten.

"What happens next?" I asked.

"You're gonna get spooked and drop that shotgun. It's gonna go off in this faggot's leg. I'm gonna bust out of this tape, kill you, then skull-fuck your girlfriend back there. It's the hottest link. I'm not worried at all. Let's log on and see."

I turned to Jay to get her opinion. She was sitting on the floor with an ACE wrap tied around her shoulder. Even through her mask she looked gray, but the blood was stopping. "How are you doing?" I asked.

"I think it went through me. Don't open the site." Jay slowly got to her feet and supported herself on a tower nearby. "You said this was gonna be big for you. Who is paying you out?"

He struggled at the tape around his wrists. He took a breath. Exhaled. "It's like a casino and this is a betting room. I don't know the name of the guy paying."

"Is it bitcoin?" Izzy asked and the guy laughed.

"Man, y'all are years behind."

"Then what is it?"

"Fuck you."

Jay came in fast and kicked the guy across the mouth. The exertion tired her, and I caught her from falling over. She brushed me off, and the guy was seeing stars. Blood came from his nose. His eyes were purpling. "Did you see *that* generation?" she asked.

He spat some blood on the hardwood floor of his home. It shined bright under the lights. "That gun is looking heavy in your hands," he said to me. "Looking like it might slip soon."

I wiped my palms on my jeans. Held the gun waist level. I shot a glance at Izzy's skinny leg. This gun could blow it to pieces.

"If we kill you now," Izzy asked, "is someone else going to get paid out?"

The guy started to chuckle to himself. "Now you're getting it."

"What do you mean?"

"Someone else *always* gets paid," he said.

"Did you bet on Ellery Waters?" I asked. I stepped forward with the shotgun. I didn't know where the question came from. To that point my head had been so flighty and adrenalized. Moments ago, I was about to run out on Jay and let her die. I was only just done processing that we had a hostage, but my brain had already moved forward to the interrogation part.

"Who?"

"Ellery Waters."

"Man." He looked up. His eyes were a dark indigo now from Jay breaking his nose. "I bet on a lot of shit. But I don't remember that name."

"She died in a car accident three years ago."

The guy shrugged and shook his head. I almost believed him.

"It was in Tallahassee."

And there it was. He stopped moving. His ears perked up. Slowly, he looked up and grinned. "Monroe and Marks Street." I tightened my grip on the gun. I had to make sure the video he saw wasn't the winner. My heart raced. Adrenaline coursed through me again, only it wasn't numbing and fun like the first round. This round was salty and made of vinegar.

I could taste spice on my tongue. "Yeah," he said. "I remember that girl. She was cute."

"Did you bet on her?"

"Relax," he said. "I lost."

"Fuck you. Don't tell me to relax. Who won?"

"I don't know their names."

"Did they pay someone to hit her car? So they could win?"

"It's possible. Why you got such a hard-on for her?"

Jay tried to shout for me to stop, but I ripped off my ski mask. I fixed my glasses. I took in deep breaths. The guy looked at me like he recognized me.

"Holy shit," he smirked, "you're Blue Bird. It's Blue Bird!" he shouted to nobody. "The Blue Bird! It's the kid from the garage! Ya hear me?? It's Blue Bi—"

Jay hurried over, grabbed my gun, and blew the guy's head off. The sound was deafening. So loud it made my teeth rattle. Bisected at the jaw, the guy's skull snapped back and exploded in shards like an overturned jigsaw. A vomit of gore erupted, and the buckshot shattered monitors and circuitry popped and blood flumed out in a spiral. He flopped to the ground with a wet slap. I stood there caked in it. The gun was smoking. Izzy was pale. Jay was weak but she stood, legs locked, with the gun still trained on the body. Around us, the man's house seemed to wheeze and cough. Processing units whirred with anger. Lights surged and settled. The air conditioning felt oily.

Coming out of the man's dome, we saw a woman outside in her pajamas walking her dog. She looked at us three.

"Is that computer man gone?" she asked.

It was a moment before Jay said, "Yeah."

"Thanks," she said. And then she turned and kept walking.

>

It was an hour before the ringing in my ear faded and, on the way back, I told Izzy to bring us to Jason's old place. I grabbed the spare key from under a loose rock and we carried Jay in. She was weak and lightheaded, and it was just after dawn when we attempted dressing her wound. We laid her down on the center of the carpet. The bleeding had stopped, but the odds of it getting infected were high. Jay insisted on going to the hospital, but Izzy was paranoid. He said the hospitals had a mandatory reporting of gunshot wounds, but Jay didn't care.

"I'm not going to lose my arm because of that shithead," she said. "Take me."

So we did. Izzy came to a rolling stop and Jay walked inside, clutching her arm. Before she left us, she swung around to the passenger door. "Nobody goes on chinsky until I say so." We nodded. "*Nobody*," she said, glaring at me. "And thanks for getting my back." I nodded numbly and she walked inside.

Izzy and I grabbed some beers, and we went back to the cottage and sat in silence. The smell of Jay's dried blood settled low at our feet like a dark, iron substrate. I felt drained and dehydrated and threw the beer up into the toilet, then kept dry heaving until mucus and saliva spun out. All I could think about was the constellation of that man's head. The wet spongy sound it made when it hit the ground. And him shouting *Blue Bird*. Who was he shouting to? Who was listening? Izzy picked at the label on the beer.

"What nightmares do you have?" he asked behind me. A furtive, quiet voice like a boy in trouble.

"What?" I said, pulling back from the toilet.

He had followed me to the bathroom. All the lights were off but the early sun was coming through the windows, showing how empty and barren the home was. He sat in the doorway.

"Before I met Jay I couldn't sleep a wink without seeing this creature in my dreams," he said. "It's like this white thing with long arms and legs and an upside-down face. I read about him in a post when I was a kid. It's haunted me ever since. I know it's stupid. It's not real. But the more I fell into this shit, learning about chinsky, learning about the dark web, seeing everything that *was* real, I started to grow certain that the monster was too."

"What's the monster called?"

"He's called Spindly," he said. "Now I'm fairly certain that anything good online is fake, but everything bad online is real. How'd it get like this?" He looked up at me. He was sad. Scared. His glasses were too tight for his nose. He had small beady eyes. His Gumby voice was cracking. "I froze back there really bad," he said.

"Yeah, and I wanted to run away."

"I won't tell Jay if you don't."

"Have you been brainwashed? We're not supposed to be quick to kill someone."

"Jay was."

While saving me, I thought. I kept it to myself though.

"So, who do you see? In your sleep?"

I studied Izzy for a second and wondered if he was fucking with me. They had seemingly done so much research on me, but now he was prodding for secrets. The morning light behind him reached along the floor. The window in the bathroom started to light up.

"I see my uncle. Not so much anymore, but he died when

I was eleven, and I could've saved him. I loved him more than anything, but I think he was a bad man. Did bad things. I don't know. Now a part of him lives inside me. Makes me do bad things too. Well, that's what my mom says at least. I wrote pasta about it when I was younger."

"What's it called?"

"The Wax Man," I said.

"I know that one. If he finds you crying alone, he kills you and turns you into wax."

"Yeah. It probably doesn't need explaining, but when Ellery died I started crying alone *a lot*. Then he started showing up in my dreams. I don't know why. It was like my subconscious was mocking me. Crying is supposed to be healthy, right? But for some reason my own brain turned it against me."

"Why did that guy call you Blue Bird?"

"It was my username when I wrote about him."

"Guess he was a fan."

"Something like that."

"That makes me nervous," he said. "Didn't someone message you the link to chinsky? Sent it to your site?"

"Yeah."

"That means somebody has had their eye on you for a long time."

"What am I supposed to tell you? That I'm fucked? Have been fucked? Will be fucked? We killed someone hours ago and I'm still processing that part."

"I'm just trying to get all the data," he said.

"I have no more data for you," I said back. I was starting to get annoyed. "If these people know my face and know me as Blue Bird then my cover is blown, and I didn't even know I *had* a cover. That's how far ahead they are. And to be honest I'm a little pissed off that you guys dragged me into this fucking mess. I'm not some cyberpunk vigilante. I was fine before. I was doing my own thing. I was doing alright."

"You were terrorizing the campus."

"I was trying to get answers."

"Bullshit, come on." He fixed his glasses. I could tell he was getting nervous. Jay seemed to be the heavy hitter and he was the yes-man. Now he was on his own. The house was getting hot. The A/C hadn't been on since Jason and Maria moved out. I took a breath. Changed subjects.

"What about Jay?" I asked. "What's her story?"

"When she was in high school, her brother was tripping on drugs and he jumped off a building. This was before she knew about chinsky. The video of it was trending on the YNC. She was able to piece together who filmed it and she hunted them down."

"Did she kill them?"

"She never told me. But that guy wasn't found again. Then I met her at a public library in Alabama. She was watching snuff films in the corner. Been friends ever since."

"When I picked her up at Poor Paul's she said she had a boyfriend."

He blushed. "She's funny like that."

"Is she talking about you?"

He blushed some more. "Kinda. Not really. Sorta. I don't know. She's got a real soft side to her. I don't think she gets a lot of chances to show it, you know? She's gotta be *on* all the time. But yeah. I'm kind of obsessed with her."

"I think she'll pull through."

"I hope so," he said. "I really need her. *We really* need her. Anyway, I'm going to head out." He stood up tall, towering over me still by the toilet. He finished his beer. "We'll hit you up later. Remember, don't go on chinsky until she says so." I nodded my head in acknowledgement and then he left out the front door and when it shut behind him the house felt the quietest it had ever been. Alone, I cleaned the blood off my face in the bathroom sink. When I finished, I paced through the house and looked at the carpet. The bloodstains were already browning. It was clear how much Jay mattered.

>

Back at my apartment, I collapsed on my bed and then woke up to a FaceTime call from Alexa. I was half asleep, my face sideways in my pillow, but I answered. The screen opened up on her standing outside on a staircase.

"Hey, I'm here, are you going to let me in or what?"

"What are you doing here?" I said. I had to find my voice. I was half unconscious.

"I was in the area and wanted to see you. I saw your car outside. Let me in, I gotta pee."

I sat up and hurried to the main room. I saw my sneakers on the ground speckled with blood, and I tossed them into my closet. I opened the door, and she was there in work clothes. Slacks and a cute cardigan. Her hair was in a bun, and she had office makeup on. She moved past me into the apartment straight to the bathroom.

I came to the door and she was on the toilet, pants at her ankles. She was never embarrassed. I remembered liking this quality about her. "I haven't seen you in months," she started. "Are you trying to ghost me?"

"Guess I'm not doing a good job if you're here right now using my bathroom."

"I refuse to let you ghost me. I don't get ghosted," she smirked.

"I figured you wouldn't miss me that much," I said.

"Were you fucking freshmen like I predicted?"

"It wasn't my proudest year."

"I forgive you," she said. "Where were you last night? You didn't answer my very obvious booty call."

"I think I was already in bed."

"It was like one a.m., you stay up until four."

I shrugged.

"Damn, are you really over me? Is this it?" Still smirking. Good humored.

"No, I'm here."

"Do you wanna come to a Sisda with me?"

"A what?"

"A Sisda. SSDA. Sober Session, Drinks After. It's a bit of an older crowd but it's nice. My friend is hosting it at her place, and you still owe me a group therapy date."

"I don't know," I said. "I kinda had a long night. I'm pretty beat."

"Thought you said you went to sleep early."

I leaned against the door. Already caught. Her smirk turned into an open-mouthed smile.

"Alright, I'll come," I said.

"Excellent. Let me go home and change and then I'll pick you up."

>

Her friend had a cozy house hidden behind a thicket of trees in the back of a twisty neighborhood. Alexa offered to drive and I let her. I was still thinking about the Computer Guy back at

Horseshoe Beach. Lou Harding. There was something about his death that had yet to feel real. Yet to sink in. It was like I had viewed it, once again, from behind a monitor. I blinked several times and watched the shadows pass by on the manicured lawns. I tried to take note of everything that passed. I had to convince myself they were real. That I wasn't looking at my laptop anymore. Hear the sounds. Smell the scents. Some houses were partying. Some were barbecuing. A group of friends crossed the street with handles of vodka and bourbon.

I remembered a story I heard in high school about a group of Holocaust survivors that went out hunting old Nazis that were hiding in plain sight. Some thought they were heroes. I tried to imagine the long-term feasibility of Jay, Izzy and I driving around in Izzy's Kia, blasting through homes and shooting at weird techie loners. Even then I knew it wasn't exactly a long-term career. Realistically, we could only get in one more, maybe two, before the whole damn site, mods and all, had a bounty on us. Suddenly it gained gravity.

"I don't feel very good," I said. I turned to Alexa. She had changed into a black skirt and white top. She had too much perfume on and I lowered the window and turned my head back out. The air came past the window fast and crisp. It was dry on my lips. I convinced myself I could still smell the beach and the gun smoke. I was making myself queasy.

"We're almost there," she said. "You can have some water inside."

"What am I supposed to say to these people?" I asked.

"Say what you say in group."

"I don't go to group."

"Just act like you're talking to a room full of me. And don't tell them we fuck. I don't think there's a rule against it, but I'd rather not get into it at all."

"Well, there goes my opener."

The place was warm and well lit and Alexa was right about the crowd being a bit older. They were in their early thirties, and they dressed hip and casual. There was a counter full of wine, all unopened, and a case of good beer in the fridge. A pretty woman with dyed white hair had me place my half-empty bottle of whiskey on the table for afterward. There was a pumpkin candle in the living room and we all took our seats. Alexa sat in the center of the couch and nudged me to the edge. She knew these people well enough, and introductions were had. I tried to place faces from the one session I had way back when but couldn't. The woman with the dyed hair smiled at me. It was her home and her gaze was comforting. Her boyfriend sat next to her and placed a large palm on her back and rubbed it. He shook my hand and it was warm too and he placed it back on her shoulder and nodded toward the booze counter.

"You bring the whiskey?"

"Yeah," I said, "I didn't have a lot of time to get something nice."

"Whiskey is nice as far as I'm concerned," he said. He had nice teeth and wore a blue plaid sweater with the sleeves rolled up. There was the edge of a tattoo just peeking out.

The session started, and I sat quietly for most of it. It was a far cry from that first session when I sobbed and pulled off my glasses and my lips quivered at the thought of speaking. I picked at the fabric of the couch and reflected on who I was back then versus who I was now. My heart sank at this budding idea, but I knew it was certain that I hadn't evolved at all. Except for becoming a deviant-turned-murderer I hadn't changed. Not even a little bit. I relapsed beyond zero. Ahead of me, among the circle of faces I sat in, were people on this healthy climb to re-adjustment. To healing. Everyone around me had their ropes and carabiners and belays and ascended the mountain of grief the proper way. I hadn't even left my truck. My boots were back at home. I was leaving the trail. What made me want to cry was the notion of hopelessness. The grief I felt for Ellery had calcified. It wasn't going any-where. Now I was stuck with myself and just hours earlier I watched a man's head get blown clean off. I saw my reflec-tion in the glass top of the coffee table and wanted to scream. I was glossy and transparent and had the hue of warped wood. Everyone else was alive and teary-eyed and faintly orange from the pumpkin candle. I couldn't even hide from myself. I took off my glasses.

Alexa spoke in a rehearsed manner, but it didn't surprise me. I don't think it surprised anyone. She told the story of her boyfriend who died in his hospital bed. She had foolishly, like all of us, put all of her eggs into that one basket. When she told the story, she articulated and intonated every sentence and phrase as if to make it more real than it was. She had this quality when speaking that felt as if she was reminding her-self what reality was lest she allow herself to daydream for too long. It was like asking a patient, "What year is it? Who is the president? Why are you sad?"

In a lot of ways this idea of constant reminder carried out in most of the facets of her life. When we had sex, she was deliberate and focused and felt with her hands all of the mise-en-scène. She breathed in the moments. Her eyes doc-umented the room, my face, my flaws, and everything in between. She had decided that she'd never take a moment for granted again. If everyone around her died tonight, right here in the living room, she'd be able to recount and remember all of us for eternity. She'd maybe verbalize it late at night, describing us all to a sketch artist. She let herself cry and be vulnerable and she turned to me with her thin eyes and she was blushing. She made a fist and gently tapped her knuckles against my thigh and then she kept on with the story.

When it was my turn I stared like a deer in headlights. I put my glasses back on. The friendly guy in the blue sweater nodded at me, encouraging without being pushy. His girlfriend with the white hair kept her fingers laced over her knee.

"This is his first time," Alexa said. She had a tissue and wiped her eyes. She sniffed and smiled and turned to me.

"I watched someone die today," I said. It was the only thing going through my head. It wheeled around in there like a slot car. The room was silent. I had to pivot before the questions came in. "It was online," I continued, "but it felt real."

I settled in my seat and kept talking. There was a half-truth I was digging up, I just had to be careful not to mention names or sites. The paranoia was real. I was Blue Bird to somebody who was listening. "I can't stop watching these videos online. Of people dying. I'm addicted to something I never saw coming. And if it doesn't make me feel like throwing up, or like cutting my wrists, I keep searching for the video that does. I don't know what type of self-harm that is, but it's what I've been doing. And I think about what Ellery would've wanted for me. Sometimes I think she's happy I'm doing this to myself. I think she kind of resented me in the end of it all. When I go outside and the air is right, I can feel her sneering at me, wanting me to be worse and to *do* worse. But then I think I'm just projecting. And then I think I'm going crazy."

"Do you think you watch these videos to feel closer to death?" the white-haired woman asked. She had patterned glasses and looked like Blossom Dearie. Her boyfriend took his hand off of her and she leaned forward.

"I think it may have started like that," I said. "But I don't know where it's going. Sometimes I have this feeling that I just need to watch the right one to be done forever."

"Have you sought professional help?"

"Does this count?"

"No," she smiled, "we're just a support circle that likes to have dinner and be real every now and then."

"So, do you have any advice?" I asked.

"My advice is always the same. Keep trying your best and keep your support group close. I know Alexa brought you here and I'm glad she did." Alexa smiled at me and then back to Blossom. "I think we all have stories of odd habits or un-orthodox addictions. We find these small things we can plug into the blank spots of our mind that would otherwise be used for grieving and remembering. But then we realize that those blank spaces are infinite and that this plugging isn't really pragmatic."

"Right."

"So just stay strong. And maybe do your best to self-limit and self-moderate. Replace it with a more constructive and self-affirming habit."

And perhaps those were the words I needed to hear. Shooting Lou Harding in his home was the most self-affirming thing I'd done in ages. When I stared into his eyes, gun inches from his face, and asked about Ellery, it didn't matter if she hated me in her final days. It didn't matter, the things I'd seen on chinsky. It didn't matter that my folks thought I was cursed. I was the one who arrived after a two-hour drive to bring justice. I chose myself. Even if I was a coward up to the final moments, I chose *me*. Even if Jay technically pulled the trigger, I was right there front and center. Suddenly I was aware of an urge to call Izzy and Jay right away. We had to go again. We had to push forth with our mission before the walls closed in and darkness fell like a shout.

After the session we drank wine and ate food. The blue-sweatered boyfriend, a guy named Jed, drank whiskey with me. We stood in the corner of the kitchen and chatted and he raved about his girl, Blossom, really named Mackenzie, and how kind and generous she is for hosting these events. Then he pointed to Alexa and asked, "So are you guys . . . ?"

"No, we're just friends," I said.

"How do you know her?"

"We had a class together freshman year."

"She's an intense one," he said.

"What do you mean?"

"You know she's full of shit, right?"

"What?"

He moved to the freezer and grabbed a fistful of ice. He plopped it into the glass and poured more Jack Daniels over it. I had bought that bottle for my marathon of freshmen. It had been used once prior when I took shots with a buzz-cut girl in a tube top and then, after it was said and done, I showed her a video of her getting shot in the back of the head by the Taliban which, looking back, was a risky bet because the Taliban weren't even that prevalent anymore and, honestly, it would've made more sense if the generation was of ISIS or even an unhinged white guy, but I digress.

"Okay, maybe I'm being unfair," Jed started and then brought his voice to a whisper. We were the only ones in the kitchen. The rest of the group went out to the backyard and was playing Kubb, the perimeter of the yard lit up by string lights. I caught a glimpse of Alexa with a glass of wine tossing the wooden rod and laughing. "Nobody knows exactly if she's full of shit or not, but there's this rumor that she made it all up."

"Made what up?"

"Everything," he said. "She had a boyfriend and he got sick, but he never died. That's one story. Then another version is that she's never had a sick boyfriend and she's one of the crazy people that need to feel the sadness of others. Like that movie *Fight Club*, you know the one?"

"Sure, yeah."

"And there's another rumor that she *killed* her boyfriend, but that one is definitely bullshit. Anyway, she's really sweet and outside of that seems perfectly chill so Mack lets her come around now and then."

"She thinks this rumor is true and lets her still come around?"

"Well, Mack's logic is that if she's making something up just to cry and feel supported then there's probably something *real* bothering her, and if Mack can help, then Mack will help. That's her motto at least."

"Haz bien sin mirar a quién."

"What's that mean?"

"Do good and don't look around for approval or rewards. Something like that."

"I'm gonna steal that," he said. He came to the counter where I was, and we watched the group play. Mackenzie tossed a wooden rod to Alexa and said something, smiling, and Alexa laughed. "So maybe be extra kind to her," Jed said. "When I was a kid, my dog died, and I was crying a lot at school. I was so embarrassed that kids were gonna make fun of me for crying over a dog that I lied and said it was my brother. I don't even have a brother. I have a sister who's like ten years older. Anyway, people lie for all sorts of sad reasons. I wouldn't go interrogating her about it."

"No, I won't."

"Come on," he said, "let's play some Kubb, baby." He left through the back door, and I regarded Alexa. She moved her hair out of her face and looked at me and waved me over. It felt like her Instagram photos from way back. Like she was watching me even when she wasn't.

In the car ride back to her place I studied her profile. The passing of cars and traffic lights flashed her from yellow to green to red to orange. The sheen of her black hair and eyes and the dark paint of her nails glimmered like gentle stars in the darkness of the car. Jed's words bounced around in my head, and I had to catch myself several times before bringing anything up.

When we got back to her place, she unlocked her front door but didn't come inside with me. "I have to make a call," she said. "Get comfortable, I'll be in shortly."

"I don't know if I can stay the night," I said. She was barely listening, already punching in numbers on her phone.

"Then don't," she said, "I won't force you. Let's just hang."

"Alright," I said.

"You were really strong today. I'm proud of you."

"Thanks."

"Be right back."

I moved through her apartment with a different sense of familiarity. Jed's story convinced me that I barely knew her. The things on her fridge, on her bookshelf, the toiletries in her medicine cabinet, now all felt like props. But at the same time, I didn't want to let some rumor I heard from a guy I met four hours ago change my view. When she cried in group or talked to me about her boyfriend, all of those emotions felt real. Whether they were linchpinned on a real person or not didn't make a huge difference in the big scheme of things. And plus, who the hell was I to judge?

I moved to her room and sat on her bed. The comforter was lilac, and sitting on it, I let myself recall the times we fooled around. There was a sincerity in the way she moved and fucked that couldn't just be for show. But then I thought of the coincidences around her. Having met her at the first session so long ago. Then the Haruspx message waiting in my inbox from the week Ellery died. Then I saw her again at the beer garden and she remembered me exactly. She knew about Ellery's car wreck even though I never brought it up. And what about her text last night on my way to Horseshoe Beach? And then her at my door this afternoon? And how did she know about the freshmen? It was like she was keeping tabs on me. Or collecting data.

I stood up and stepped away from the bed. I looked at the pool of shadow under the frame and wondered if someone could fit under there. Maybe with a mask and a knife. Everything began to show its seams. I backed out of the bedroom into the main space. Furniture and picture frames began to look fake. Plastic bargain-bin purchases from Sears. Nothing felt lived in. Nothing felt right.

I hurried out to the hallway to find her, but she was gone. The long corridor stretched forward. No sounds of conversation. No signs of life.

"Alexa?" I called out. My voice fell thin and muted. "Fuck this."

I hurried down the stairwell and out of the complex.

I scurried back across Tallahassee, hurrying from sidewalk to bus to campus to bus again looking over my shoulder. Paranoia gripped me by the scalp and kept my neck strained. Nearing my apartment, I got texts from her.

Where did u go? the first said.

I ignored it.

I was getting beer and food.

I ignored that too.

its 50 leb if you die in the kitchen.

I suddenly got sweaty. I had no idea what that meant, but I deleted our message thread and blocked her. Suddenly everyone looked dangerous. A hipster on a bike approached opposite and I half expected him to drive by, blowing holes in my chest with a 9mm. But he zoomed past as silent as he came.

At the base of my apartment, in the parking lot where I confronted Jay, the building looked like a death trap. People walked around and drank and music came from some open windows, but evil shimmered from the roof like the mirage of a highway. I couldn't stay there.

I cut back across the main road through various subdivisions half running half scrambling to Maria and Jason's old house. I tried not to draw attention to myself but flinched anytime passersby came too close.

50 leb if you die in the kitchen. That's what the text said. She was in on it. Maybe always had been. A phone call came from a number I didn't know, and I ignored it. I stepped onto a curb and picked up my pace. The summer night was hot, and my shirt started to stick to my chest. Twenty hours ago, I saw a man's head get blown off. Karma chased me like a dog.

I let myself back into the old house and breathed in Jay's stale blood. The place was quiet. Dead. It was late and a faint sodium streetlight hugged the front window. A ghostly orange eased into the house, giving shadows a sharper edge and corners abrupt blackness. The number called me again, but this time I answered.

"Who is this?"

"Who do you think?" she said. "Don't you block me again."

"What the hell is going on?" I asked.

"I've seen how this ends," she said. "You're back in the house. Someone is in there waiting for you. Now I just wait to see if he cuts your throat or rips your guts out."

I heard her laugh and the line went dead. I kept my back against the front door and examined the home. In its dark emptiness it looked like a cave. Cars passed by in the distance behind me. Some turned down the subdivision and their headlights, only for a moment, washed over the house. I convinced myself I heard breathing. Someone was further inside.

"You don't have to do this," I shouted.

A dark laugh came from around the hall.

"Hey, Blue Bird," the voice said. It was deep and vicious. There was a snarl to it. He was speaking through a mouth covering, something made of thick fabric.

I tried to stay still but couldn't. My hands trembled and my breath came in fast and out of control. I thought about turning back and exiting but pictured him on the ground, scrambling toward my ankles. I'd once seen a video of a guy's heels getting cut. The sickening snap of the tendon. The way he went down with not so much as a gasp.

"I killed a guy just last night," I said.

Lou Harding, 30s, Up Close and Personal'd.

"I know," the voice said back, lost in the house, impossible to pinpoint. A minotaur in a maze.

I don't know why, but I decided to ask, "What do you look like?"

There was a long pause after that. Probably caught him off guard.

"I'm tall," the man said. "I'm a tall man. I have a big man-chest and broad man-shoulders. I have hairy man-knuckles and a big man-cock. And if we go to the bathroom, we can do this the way I predicted."

"Yeah, and how's that?"

"I dunk your head in the toilet tank and fuck your ass 'til it bleeds."

A moment snuck by. My knees started to tremble, and my heart pounded. I realized what I had been looking at this whole time: Izzy's beer bottle. Well within reach.

I slowly crouched down and grabbed the bottle. Then with my back still on the wall, I reached over and grabbed the doorknob to feign like I was leaving. I opened the door and backed into the shadows.

The guy hurried out of the bedroom to stop my escape. He was all business. He wasn't scrambling but charging. Straight legs and pumping arms. He ran fast, and I swung the bottle in, smashing it over the back of his head. He grunted, recoiled, and then swiped with his knife and caught me on the bicep. A thick strip of blood formed quicker than I imagined it would. It was hot and stinging and cold as the wound kissed the air.

The man was exactly as described. A big, tall balaclava'd motherfucker with the type of hunting knife you saw in *Scream*.

He came in close with the knife underhand and, with both hands, I caught his wrist. He was more powerful than me. Easily. I had to be smart or the next time he got close he'd get me under the ribs no doubt. My teeth clenched at the thought of the serrated edge eating my bones. I did a move I saw in a movie once and headbutted him and we both toppled over, the attack hurting me more than him. My head went cloudy and he laughed and as I scrambled away, he swiped and caught me behind the thigh and I lurched forward in pain, blood racing down my jeans, pooling in the fresh sneakers I had worn for the SSDA.

I climbed to a fast limp and rounded the corner into the bathroom. He had mentioned the toilet tank which had to be the heaviest thing I could swing in here. But I had to play it smart or I'd be feeding right into his generation. I locked the bathroom door behind me and lifted the ceramic lid. I held it with both hands.

"You're right where I want you, kid," the man said from behind the door. He kicked at it and the wood rattled. The thing was cheap and thin, designed for some college asshole to throw a fist through.

I primed the tank lid like a baseball bat and tried to imagine that he was the driver of the truck that killed Ellery. I tried to talk my body into overcoming fear, but my hands were sweaty, and the rough underside of the lid was cutting into my palms.

He kicked at the door again, and my eyes darted to the fetid water in the tank itself. He said I was going to drown in that while he fucked me. Moments of physical weakness flashed in my head like the greatest hits of defeat. Jay pepper-spraying me and kicking in my nuts. Ryan Vasquez landing a few blows, knocking me sideways in the parking lot of USF. Lucas clocking me in his room late at night when Cece ran screaming. His large black boots hit the door again.

"I'm warning you!" I pleaded. Sweat got into my eyes, and I blinked it away.

Then it happened quickly. The bathroom door busted off its lock and swung open to me, and I responded not with a swing but with an overhead throw. He put his arms out to block. The lid made contact with a loud crack and he yelped and stepped backward, moving his feet out of the way so it missed on the way down. It hit the ground and burst into heavy shards. I lunged for his knife.

The wrestling was pathetic. He threw me around the bathroom, breaking the sink, the medicine cabinet, and smashing the toilet. I held on for dear life, waiting for a window of opportunity. My vision was going from exhaustion. My forearms were cramping. The man's breath smelled like liquor, and he seemed to be having fun with it.

The trick was that he was expecting me to fight him, so I had to follow his lead like a dance. The second I put weight on the knife he'd simply angle it at my chest and overpower me. When he swung me back to the door I let go and fell among the shards of ceramic. One dug itself into my lower back and I gasped, reaching behind myself, feeling the blood spread on the tile. There was my chance.

"It's not too late for the jackpot," the man said and he grabbed at my ankles, trying to pull off my jeans. My waistband fell below my ass, and I grabbed the fattest shard I could and swung it wide into the side of his head.

He grunted and his eye filled with red and then blood came out fast from beneath his mask. He dropped the hunting knife, and I grabbed it and plunged it into his stomach. The knots in my back twisted around my open wound. I felt slick everywhere. The smell of iron and mold filled the room. Soap scum and blood.

I was on my knees before him like I was ready to take him in my mouth. His blood ran down the handle of the knife and down my arms and he looked at me with wide eyes. He took in large gulping breaths. He palmed my head and bashed it against the wall. Black stars of pain scattered through my vision.

"You little faggot," he coughed up. I heard blood and spit clogging the fabric that covered his mouth. He grabbed my head and smashed it against the wall again. My right cheek ripped open. My teeth were loosening. My grip on the knife was slipping, and the pain of my skull was orbiting. He grabbed my head once more, but before he could crack my skull open, I angled the knife downward and dropped my weight on it. It pitched deeper and lower into his abdomen, the handle stopping at his zipper.

His knees buckled and he fell backward, cracking his head along the bathtub. I stood up, leaving the knife in his stomach. The guy started to choke and he pulled his mask under his chin and coughed up globules of blood. He was just some white guy. Older. Maybe Polish. It was hard to tell because the wound in his face was deeper than I thought. He was letting out some sort of death rattle. He tried to sit up, but when his neck was at the rim of the tub I kicked my foot forward and cracked his head back. He started spazzing on the ground, his black boots hopping around and shaking, his arms flailing in small, jazz-like death throes. Then he died.

I was shaking. Adrenaline filled me like helium. I was aware of every sensation. I could feel the quivering of my insides. I could smell my own piss and blood and the clotted pus and brain matter of his skull wetting the knit of his mask. My cut arm throbbed, and my shirtsleeve stuck to my skin. The back of my thigh was cold and tight. My left shoe was filled with blood. The side of my face was swelling and broken, and I tongued a tooth loose in the back of my mouth. My lower back had a hole I could fit my thumb in. I hugged the wall and limped out of the bathroom, eventually giving up and falling to the floor of the hallway.

I was on the ground trying not to die when my phone rang.

It was the number she used earlier. I pressed a bloody finger on the screen to accept the call.

"How'd you kill him?" she asked. Her voice was soft, like she knew I was weak and didn't want to overwhelm me.

"What?"

"Was it with his own knife or did you have one? And where was it? Did he get you over the toilet or no? He was really banking on that. Had a prop bet and everything. You know, we generated the house because you can't seem to let the place go. Houses are hard though; the interiors always smudge."

"You're a fucking bitch," I said. It was a whisper more than anything. My lips were dry, and my tongue felt like cotton. "Did you bet on him too?"

"That's a silly question, Sammy."

"How long have you been doing this?" I asked. I wasn't physically ready to have it answered. I just had to get it out. Had to clear my head to focus on not dying.

"I've been a fan for a long time," she said. "Ever since the beginning. You tapped into a community. I clamored for you."

"You're crazy," was all I could say. I was starting to sway. The hallway elongated and shrunk and closed in and twirled. Behind me the man's corpse remained in the bathroom, sitting wrong.

"What part of you did he cut?" she asked. It sounded like she had a pen and paper.

"Fuck you," I said weakly.

"Did you break his neck on the tub?"

"I'm not playing this game."

"You're always pla—"

I hung up. The last thing I remembered was calling Izzy to come over quick.

"Don't let her find me first," I said. And it's strange, because as I said it, I knew I meant Alexa. But as I sat there, nodding off, feeling my blood, I wondered if I meant all of them.

>

Sammy Dominguez, 24, multiple lacerations, probable hematomas.

>

Days passed in the empty cottage and I woke on an air mattress feeling like dog shit. My arm was stiff, and my thigh was sore. I had welts and purpling bruises all over my torso and back. One of my teeth had come out. Eventually, when I opened my eyes, I saw Jay sitting on a folding chair opposite of me. Her arm was in a sling, and she had bandages where she was clipped in the shoulder.

"Hey, look, you're alive," she said. It was early and the sun came through the bedroom window. She sat half in light and half in shadow. Her head was shaved. She looked like some prophet from another world coming to visit and take note. She came to measure the scales of the human race and deal its final punishment. "You good?" she asked.

Ah, the million-dollar question.

"Not really," I said. It was hard to breathe. I touched my rib. Cracked again. The poor thing.

"Izzy got your call, and he came right over. He found you in the hallway. You do that guy in the bathroom?"

"In a manner of speaking."

"We're not staying long," she said.

"Where are we going?"

"Far away. Off the grid. Izzy went to your place and grabbed some clothes for you. He destroyed your laptop and your phone."

I laid back down and focused on the ceiling. I tried to will it to come crashing down on me.

"Alexa got away," I said.

"She'll show up again," Jay said. She stood up and the right side of her face was yellow in the sunlight. Her eyes were pretty.

"How's your arm?" I asked.

"Just get your rest," she said, and she left fully into the gray of the empty home. I heard a door open and shut behind her. She spoke to someone else, Izzy I presumed, and the two shared a muffled conversation. I kept my eyes on the ceiling and tried not to cry. I fell asleep and for the first time since Ellery was put underground, I didn't dream a thing.

>

In the morning we loaded up Izzy's early 2000s Kia Rio. He packed for me and I examined the contents of the duffel bag. Some jeans. A few pairs of underwear. Shirts and sweaters and a hoodie. No technology to speak of.

"I did the best I could," he said, hand on the trunk, waiting for me.

"I just feel a little naked," I said.

"That's the idea," he said back.

I threw the duffel bag into the trunk and climbed into the backseat. Jay was in the passenger seat with sunglasses on. After a moment, Izzy joined us and turned the car on. Within minutes we were on the highway south.

I wanted to call Jason. I wanted to call Becca. I thought of my parents and, even still, after knowing how they felt about me, I wanted to call them too. Just to hear my dad's stammered silence and my mom's brisk conversation. I was stuck with these two strangers in a car barreling down the interstate. A week ago I didn't know they existed and now two different people were killed by our doing.

We left a sign that marked the border of Tallahassee and my heart skipped a beat. I was finally out. I was never going back. I knew it for sure. It took three years for me to leave Tallahassee after fundamentally killing Ellery here, and I thought I heard the scream of her ghost whizz by. I thought of that night so long ago, of us eating at Asian Rox, pushing cold sushi around, staring at each other. Her eyes showed betrayal. They showed her realization that I had trapped her there, but she was out of Tallahassee now and I was too.

"We're going down to Webster to grab a trailer that we'll be living out of for a bit," Jay started. "Izzy has been collecting the locations of various Page 40s. There's a few small timers in the area we can wipe out. Lake Yale. Sanford. Sylvan Shores. Then we're gonna reorganize and collect some data before we go for the bigger fish."

"How long are we gonna be living in the trailer?" I asked.

"As long as it takes."

"What's that mean?"

"The Page 40s are easy, but they'll be dangerous," Izzy said. He looked at me in the rearview mirror and then back at the road. "Eventually they'll catch on but who knows. If we want a Front Pager we gotta go ghost for a lot longer than that. I mean we really gotta disappear off the earth."

"Like how long?" I asked.

There was a long pause in the car. I couldn't tell if they were thinking it over or were just hesitating to tell me. "To get a Front Pager," I reiterated, "how long do we have to disappear?"

"I'd say twenty years," Jay said.

"What? Why? That's insane."

"A Front Pager sees our every move," Jay said. "We'd have to disappear for real. They need to think we're dead. And since that's their whole business, it's a hard thing to trick them on."

"I can't disappear for twenty years," I said.

"Why not?" she asked. "What are you missing? Who needs you? Where do you have to be?" She got louder and turned to me from the front seat. "Or did you have some big five-year plan? Because the last I checked you were throwing your life away and drinking yourself to death. So, unless you started some career path in the week that I've known you, I'd say you're capable of disappearing for one-hundred years without so much as a fucking inconvenience to anyone."

"Jay," Izzy said. He moved his hand in a way that said, *ease off.*

Jay turned back to the road and crossed her arms.

I sat back in the seat. It had finally come full circle. In the same way I stole Ellery's years, Jay was stealing mine. My just deserts were given in a Kia Rio.

"You saw what happened back in Tallahassee," she continued. "You're Blue Bird and you're wanted. That guy that came with a knife was on easy mode. What happens when it's a convincing car accident? Or some long-gestating heart attack? What happens then?"

"Then I just die, and it can all be over," I said.

"You fucking wish," she said.

>

In Webster, a small hicktown in central Florida, we pulled up to a run-down home, nestled deep behind an overgrown lawn and various trees, old and crooked, like they were melting in the heat. Mosquitoes buzzed and bit and the humidity of the air felt like soup. I could hear the screaming of the sun, beating down on the broken asphalt of the driveway.

Peeking out from behind the home was the face of an old camper. A large rectangle on back wheels, tilted forward into the packed dirt. It had brown rust along the sides like racing stripes. I climbed out of the car and, limping, followed Jay around the home.

"Can Izzy's car even carry this?" I asked.

"Don't doubt the Kia," Jay said.

The back door of the home swung open, and a little dog came out yapping and sniffing at Jay and I. Out of the home came an older woman with tattoos and short red hair. She had a cigarette in her lips and she studied Jay and myself. "Guess you're here for the camper, huh?"

"That's right," Jay said.

"I'll get the keys," she said and disappeared back into the house.

"How can we afford this?"

"We did her a favor and she's giving it to us."

"What was the favor?"

"Remember that guy at Horseshoe Beach? He cleared a cool million on a video of her son being killed in the woods. In the video, these men shot him up and went through his wallet. Izzy zeroed in on some specifics. We found his mom, showed her, and we worked something out."

"How much did you tell her?"

"Not a lot. Wasn't worth it. I said, hey these guys got your son and I know where they are."

"Jesus Christ," I said. "Is she safe? Are they going to come after her now?"

"That's not really my concern," she said.

The woman came back out of the home with a small pair of keys. "It ain't good to gossip, ya know," she said. She took a drag of her smoke and spat into the dirt. She tossed the keys to Jay.

"I'm sorry about your son," I said.

"Don't be. He was a shithead. But he didn't deserve to die like that, I reckon. At least not by some nerd that lived in a ball."

"Are you going to be safe here?" I asked.

"I'll make do," she said. "Just get on out of here."

We took her orders to heart and Izzy backed the car toward the camper and we locked in the hitch. Inside, the place was stale and stuffy and only a few yards from one end to the other. A small cot sat bunched against the laminate walls. A tiny Formica table was wedged between the foot of the bed and the sink and a hot plate. Moths had eaten at the cloth curtains. A narrow toilet and shower were jammed in the far corner, the curtain just a thick and broken slide of plastic.

We moved all of the duffel bags to the trailer and Jay pulled out the .38 Izzy had failed to use in Horseshoe Beach and she taped it under the sink. She put another handgun behind the mattress of the cot. Then she turned to me with the sawed-off.

"Where do you want to put this?"

"I have no idea," I said.

"Then here." She handed it to me. "You can figure it out." She left the trailer and the delicate door shut behind her. I examined it in my hands. It felt more comfortable even though I technically hadn't fired it yet and only used it like a cudgel on someone with their back to me. I put it in my duffel bag with my underwear and pants and zipped it up. I sat on the cot and felt the Kia start. The small thing bucked and wheezed and eventually we pulled out of the lady's backyard. I stayed in the camper and felt it tilt. From the stained and dirty window, I saw the lady smoke her cigarette and watch us leave. She shielded her eyes from the sun and her little dog chased us down the driveway. I hoped that she would be okay and found myself wondering what chinsky would show me if I searched her name. I sat on the cot and felt the trailer's rocking turn into an easier, smoother glide as we climbed back onto the highway. I checked my bag once more and realized that Izzy didn't pack any booze or smokes.

"Motherfucker."

> They Go Tech
> You Go Crude

It was late afternoon when we reached Lake Yale. I laid on the cot and let the camper rock me in and out of sleep. I felt my arm and thigh, the fresh bandages already getting red. I touched my ribs and my back. Somewhere out there Alexa was scrambling to find me, looking at the pages of her chinsky user account. She was making a simulation or, rather, a *generation*, setting up the algorithm that tried to locate me, pinpoint me, spotlight me like some old-time bandit breaking out of jail. I thought of my family and wondered if they were safe. If there was a chance that some folks could go after that lady back in Webster, the odds were likely higher for my family. I was Blue Bird. That name meant something to people.

The plastic door opened, and Jay stood there in the frame. Behind her, palm trees lined the edge of a gentle lake, slowly touching the shore that wasn't much of a shore at all, but rather just grass and a stretch of marshland. Our car and camper were on a sturdy road, but any closer and we'd be sinking in muck.

"Izzy went to find some food for us," she said.

"Okay."

"How was the ride?"

"Bumpy."

"Wanna come out? It's pretty out here."

I stepped out of the trailer and onto the grassy road where we parked. She was barefoot and she sat on the ground and kept her back against the wheel of the camper. I stepped toward the lake and scanned the horizon. The lake was big, and the sun was behind us, lighting it up like a tray of bright orange. Small waves cast shadows like a series of black triangles moving outward from some growing epicenter.

"He's in the houseboat on the other side of the lake," Jay said behind me. "We're gonna take a canoe over there and take him out and canoe back quiet as a mouse."

"Last time wasn't all too quiet," I said. I turned back to her and watched her pluck at the grass.

"Well last time was our first time so let's call it a teaching moment."

"When you killed that guy, what did you feel?"

"You answer first," she said.

"I felt like part of me broke."

"Something did break. The old you."

"I'm not a killer," I said. "I mean. You've made me one."

"Go ahead and blame me if it makes you feel better. But don't get it twisted. You're not a good person. Maybe you were at some point. I think you probably were. But you were shown a dark corner of the earth and you immediately turned rotten. You were planning to fuck me and then show me how I die."

I felt my chest tighten. I looked at her and she was right, obviously, about everything. "I'm sorry," I said. "I don't know what happened to me. I think I just felt so helpless and frustrated and like I was being toyed with. And I wanted to feel powerful. Like I was in charge. I don't know. I'm sorry though. I really am. The day when that guy attacked me in the house, before that, I was at a group session with Alexa. Everyone was talking about life-affirming habits and proper steps to heal and this and that. I hadn't been making any of those choices, but I've gone down such a fucking rabbit hole that, now, the choices don't make any sense. The choices in front of me now look nothing like my choices three years ago."

"Here's the thing," she said. "When I blew that guy's head off you know what I felt? Ecstatic. I was thrilled. It felt like I was killing the guy that filmed my brother die. That feeling was owed. That feeling was *mine* to have. Nobody else's. You haven't gotten that yet. You haven't earned shit. You have a lot more work to do before you get that feeling." She was Ryan Vasquez telling me I didn't have stakes.

"You're gonna get us killed," I said.

"Don't even try that," she countered. "The moment you logged onto chinsky looking for a thrill you locked your fate. If you weren't with us now, you'd be a murder case in your little cottage. Or you'd join them, and it'd be *me* kicking down *your* door and shooting you in the face. This is the side you're on. And it's sure as hell better than the other sides. So, the way I see it is you're with me and Izzy for good. Because if you leave us, then you know too much, and I'll end you. Or you leave us and join chinsky and guess what? I'll end you. Or you escape my grasp and start stalking girls again. And guess fucking what?"

"You'll end me."

"Damn right."

"I just can't figure any of this out. How long did Alexa know? How long has she been gaming me? I'm trying to think back and remember if I fucked her over or something, and this is all for revenge, but I can't think of anything. I feel like I'm losing my mind."

"I doubt it's revenge," she said. "These people don't take anything personal. Everything is content and points and currency. Nothing means anything to them. She probably saw a really damaged person in you early on, and then decided to extrapolate. You were a long-term investment that's now paying off."

"That can't be it."

"Makes you feel kinda used, huh?" She took a pause and sized me up. "We all have our obsessions."

I looked at my hands and picked at my cuticles. The sun had leveled itself behind the camper. We were both in shadow. She was right. I had more obsessions than I knew what to do with. I had little grudges I kept in my backpack like protein bars. Little innocuous phrases people uttered sucked at my blood like leeches. My head was a steel trap for anything that came its way.

"Izzy told me about the Blue Bird thing," she said. She sighed. "That really sucks. You were a kid and you saw something that fucked you up. You went online to cope, and you made a persona where you can be angry and weird, and the internet liked it. And then it decided to eat you. There are a billion people out there and they saw a weak kid struggling and so they sunk their teeth into you. Then they showed other people. Then others. Maybe Alexa read your stories first and finally met you. Maybe she met you first and then read your stories later. What difference does it make? You're not the chosen one. You're just one of many poor bastards that they decided to fuck with. But there's a chance you can win. You can change and be better and come out on top, or you can give into them, do what they bet on, and lean into that persona. I've seen how this can end." She looked at me. Her voice shifted gears, became more vulnerable and curious. She had such a beauty to her. It was golden hour and she rested her shaved head against the side of the camper. With her other hand she massaged her hurt shoulder. She looked back at me. "Have you searched your own name?"

"Yes."

"But have you searched all of your names?"

I leaned back against the camper next to her. Wasn't sure what to say. The lake in front of me turned to a bruised scarlet. A warm breeze rustled the grass and trees. Down the walk came Izzy with plastic bags of groceries. He saw how Jay and I looked, and he came to a slow stop, sensing the tension. I moved away from Jay and grabbed my food from Izzy and climbed back into the camper. I ate in the dark and I ate in silence.

>

Jay and I pushed the canoe into the water, and Izzy stayed behind in the car in case anybody came snooping around the camper when we were gone. It was around eleven p.m. and we paddled along Lake Yale at a quiet speed, not trying to splash the oars or make a fuss. Jay was in all black and her handgun was on the bench between us. My old-Western-looking sawed-off sat at my feet wrapped in a towel. Our masks were on and mine smelled clean. Jay or Izzy must've put them in the laundry. The thought rang funny to me, and I felt myself grin.

The plan was to pull up to the houseboat, tie onto it, and then sneak around to an open window. After a moment, when the house revealed itself in the darkness, I felt braver than last time. A tiny percentage but noticeable. The place was shaped

like a shoebox with a few small windows. A small porch of
sorts sat on the end facing the lake and our slowly approaching canoe. On the roof were a series of antennas and satellite
dishes.

"If anything happens," Jay whispered, "run in different
directions."

"Is anybody else in the house?" I asked.

"Dunno."

"What if there is?"

"Dunno."

So many of the videos I'd seen were of home invasions.
Ski-masked degenerates breaking into a sleeping home and
killing people in their beds, stabbing them to death next to
mounted pictures of loved ones, or blowing them away next
to a stand of trophies. And now here were Jay and I doing the
same thing for, ostensibly, the right reason. I was getting nauseous from how cyclical it was becoming. Everything keeps
layering on top of each other. You don't know you're in the
loop until your second time around.

Jay leaned forward out of the canoe and held onto the side
of the porch. She used her hips to bring the canoe around the
side into the shadow of the house. She tied us to a cleat and
then we waited for what felt like eternity. She slowly stood
and eased herself onto the porch, being sure to keep her back
to the wall, away from the sliding glass door. She peered in.
She gave me a look and beckoned me over. I unwrapped the
sawed-off and followed her onto the porch and felt it dip beneath our weight.

I crouched down and tried the door and slid it open. Cold
air conditioning spilled out of the black house. I crept in low
and shuffled past a small kitchen table. I rested at the counter
and Jay came to me.

"Don't shoot that thing if I'm in front of you," she said.

"Then let me go first," I said. She nodded and let me pass.

I moved down the hallway with the gun at my waist. Anybody that turned the corner too fast would get cut in half. The house was quiet and the gentle rocking from side to side made me carsick. The halls were narrow, and everything smelled like fish and low tide and it was cold. The hall I was in continued to what looked like a den with a little branch to the right. I stopped at the branch and turned the corner. It was another smaller hallway that led to what I presumed was the only bedroom. The door was shut. I kept moving to the den proper and stopped when I saw the computer. It was still on. A big, curved desktop with flickering lights and strips of glowing neon blue and green.

Jay came over and the two of us went to the computer. I moved the mouse around and the screen came alive. There were various windows opened. One of them looked like some sort of bank account. 15 LN was transferred into an account recently, but the account was just a long string of numbers and letters and the bank showed something similar.

"Fifteen Lebanon," Jay said behind me.

"That some kind of a crypto?"

"You bet," she said. "When that guy denied it was bitcoin, Izz and I did more research. That's about two million last I checked."

"Just from chinsky?"

"Probably not," she said. "He's probably doing the most."

I sat at the computer and went to the window that had chinsky displayed. I was in his user account and it looked different from the side I'd seen prior. It was all numbers and columns and rows like some checkerboard of code. I started to work at it.

"What are you doing?" Jay asked.

"Getting some information before he gets back," I said.

I typed in ELLERY WATERS and the page loaded up more technobabble, but further down the page was the video of her death. There was a number showing how much he lost on the bet (-3 LN) and next to that was his own video submission. It was her being strangled and raped in a back alleyway outside of the Crater.

"Do your research," I said to the screen. "She didn't even like that place."

"Huh?" Jay asked behind me.

"Nothing. Just keep an eye out."

I clicked the winning video, and a different page loaded up. It was the profile of the user who won. Finally. I had found him. The name of the profile was just numbers: 7100000cvc9e. The video won 20 LN. His videos had won a lot. This was a Front Pager.

"Is that your girl's page?" Jay asked. She was talking about Alexa.

"I don't think so," I said. "I have no idea. I'm never gonna remember all this shit."

Jay grabbed a pen and a paper from the desk and it slid it to me. "Get writing," she said. I scribbled down the profile name 7100000cvc9e, this guy's profile name (098001000ti), and even his bank account with the 15 LN (zz13alhdvsghiqaxvbers).

"He'll probably be home soon," Jay said. "Let's hide."

I stood up, but before leaving I paused and looked back at the monitor. A tab on the screen caught my attention. "RED CRIB." I clicked it and regretted it. It was an overhead shot of a naked baby on a table. It was trying to scream, writhing in pain with tape over its mouth. A pair of hands reached from the top of the frame and toyed with him, pinching him and pricking him with long needles, little rivers of bright blood pooling around the outside of the baby. The bottom right of the screen was zooming with donations and comments and whirling sprites. There was a meter counting up. If they hit a certain number the poster was going to fuck it. If Jason could see me now.

"I'm gonna be sick," Jay said, looking over my shoulder.

"This doesn't make sense," I said. "He wouldn't have kept all this shit up and running if he wasn't—"

"Still here," Jay finished my thought.

I got out of the desk chair and raised the sawed-off again. "Did you check everywhere?"

"I thought I did," Jay said. "His bedroom and bathroom were clear."

I thought for a moment. I felt the houseboat rock side to side. "There's gotta be a utility room around here. Someplace with a bilge pump. Check the walls."

We moved to the tiny hallway again and we pressed our hands along the walls. I kept the shotgun pointed forward, but my arms were getting weak. Then headlights swerved toward the house and panned across the den. "Someone is coming," Jay said.

"Hide." I motioned her toward the bedroom where she disappeared around the door.

I kept tapping the wood paneling and finally one gave. It clicked and eased open and revealed the small interior shed. Water heater, purifier, bilge pump, fuse box, etc. All complete with the homeowner, slumped on the floor with a self-inflicted gunshot wound bookending both sides of his head. His limp hand and pistol lay on his lap. The gun had a black handle and looked expensive. I heard the front door open, and I hurried into the bedroom.

Jay kept her back against the wall with her gun pointed at the doorway. I kept low and hid behind a small dresser. Both of us sat in silence before we heard the visitor.

"Donnie, I'm here!" he said. "Where are— Oh Jesus fucking Christ. Why did you do this? Oh fuck, man."

I caught Jay's eyes in the darkness. She lowered her pistol. The sound of the visitor retreated back to the den. I heard him typing and clicking, all panicked. He was deleting the evidence of his scumbag friend. I moved without thinking.

With the shotgun raised I turned into the den and fired at his legs. The kickback was immense, and I stumbled back and caught myself on a countertop. The blast reverberated off the walls and floors and paneling of the small boathouse. My eyes stung from the powder and the smoke. The pellets ripped through his knees, and he let out an agonized scream. He tried to pull a gun from his waistband, but Jay was quicker, kicking it out of his grip and across the room.

"Stop! Stop! I won't kill you," I said. I felt my voice shaking. The recoil from the gun had sprained my wrists and I felt them starting to swell. The man couldn't focus. He was screaming too much from the pain. In reality, looking at the blood, I had already killed him.

"A little warning next time?" Jay asked.

"I'm sorry, I was just *ready*."

The man kept screaming.

"Shut the fuck up!" Jay said.

The guy took in large gulps of air. "What do you want, man?" he said, putting his hands up. His legs pumped out a dark red stream onto the messy carpet. I motioned for Jay to keep her gun trained on the guy and I took out my folded notepaper.

"Who is user 7100000cvc9e?"

"*Who?*"

"Seventy-one-hundred thousand—cvc9e! He wins a ton of the fucking chinsky rounds. Who is he!"

"I don't know the fucking numbers! They mean nothing to me!"

I got angry and shot at the ground next to him.

"That's fucking loud!" Jay screamed.

The guy flinched and tried to crawl away. I had to reload and opened the gun and tucked in two more buckshots. My wrists were swollen and tight and it was hard to pinch. The smoke from the barrels wafted up and made my eyes water.

"He probably doesn't even know," Jay said. "They're just numbers."

"No," I said. "They can't just be numbers."

"It's all anonymous, man," the guy said. He was going white. He was bald with earrings. He had tattoos on his neck. He had blood on his fingers either from gripping his legs or from earlier when he found his pervert friend.

"But I know someone who might know," he huffed out in a labored breath.

"Tell me."

"It's a website like any other. It has admins and moderators and servers."

"Just say his name."

"He's the Skunk. Upstate New York. He's a moderator to make sure the site doesn't just put random videos up. He knows the accounts. Sort of."

"How do I find him?"

"Fuck if I know, man. His whole deal is *not* being found."

"Tell me anything."

"Okay," he said. He was getting weaker. "He plays big time poker at a bar called the Wet Stone. They all bet Leb. It's high-stakes but low-key. These guys look like scumbags, ya know?"

"Few more questions."

"I'm gonna bleed out, man, I'm gone."

"Then talk fast," Jay said. She pressed her heel on his open thigh. The man spat out and screamed and punched at her ankle.

"Mother's *cunt*, okay! Just ask."

"Does the name Alexa Ritter mean anything to you?"

"No."

"Ellery Waters?"

"No."

"What about Blue Bird?"

He shook his head.

"What about—"

"Don't say your name," Jay said.

"They already know my name. What about Sammy Dominguez."

He looked up at me. His face was white. I could tell his eyes were having trouble keeping focus. His pupils wavered and sagged, and he looked up again and then back down, nodding, although I couldn't tell if he was nodding as in *Yes* or nodding as in, *I'm dying.*

"He's done," Jay said.

>

I pulled the trigger and opened his chest. I sent the next shell into the computer tower. Then Jay and I left in the canoe, and Jay did most of the paddling. Izzy pulled us out of town, and we cut east across the state to Sanford. In the camper, rocking along the road, Jay and I stood across from each other and changed out of our dirty clothes. The passing cars and moon-light came in through the dirty windows.

"You really popped off back there," she said. The camper took a turn and she held onto the counter to balance. She took off her shirt and the small curves of her figure were lost in the darkness. She stepped out of her jeans and kicked them to the side. She was in her underwear, and I tried not to stare, look-ing at the ground and her clothes in the pile. I started to feel bad again for that night after Poor Paul's, and my balls ached with the memory.

"We gotta get to the Skunk," I told her.

"New York is a long way."

"But we're mobile now, what's stopping us?"

"You're gonna turn this into a whole revenge mission," she said.

"Is that not what we're doing?"

"I just want to be careful," she said. Headlights came and went and for a moment she went from shadow to white to shadow and I saw her body shine bright and disappear.

"Our clock is ticking," I said.

"Your clock," she said. "The Skunk is not my problem. Or Izzy's for that matter."

"But isn't he? He's a mod. He could answer for all of this."

"He's also probably untouchable and we'd get smoked on sight."

I kneeled down and tucked the sawed-off back in the duf-fel bag with my underwear and socks. I became aware of my odor, and I dabbed at my armpits with my T-shirt.

"Are we worried about the cops?" I asked.

"With the Lebanon these guys are talking about, we're playing in a different league. We're not even playing the same sport anymore. Here's the deal," she continued. "Let's take care of Sanford and then Sylvan Shores and then we can head up north and take our time. Let the heat cool off before we get got being careless."

"Deal."

Izzy's Kia left the highway and headed down a county road. The ride went from smooth to bumpy.

"If you wanna sleep, you can," I said to Jay. She nodded and moved to the small cot. She laid down and pulled her knees in. I moved to the ground and sat with my back against the cabinets under the sink. The place smelled old and broken. Blood from the man in the boathouse had sprinkled my jeans and now they lay crusty and folded in the far corner.

I crossed my legs and tried to get comfortable. I tried to make myself small. I felt like I was back in Uncle Ted's car, headed to practice. The sway of the camper sent me back. It was the same way he would gently swerve, a Coors in his hand. I'd look out the window and watch the suburbs of Tampa pass by stunningly bright and shockingly hot. Before it all went to shit, he talked about taking me camping. There were grounds around Fort De Soto. My mother always made remarks about how that wasn't real camping.

"It's glamping," my uncle said. "Glamour camping. And we're some glamorous dudes."

I closed my eyes and tried to imagine Uncle Ted climbing out of a camper. He probably had a beer in his hand. He had paint-splattered jeans and dirty boots. He had a bicycle he rode around the city. He told me about jail and about women and about his first wife. He told me about putting a knife into someone's side. I was able to ask about anything. What would he say now? About all of this? About Lebanon and generations and chinsky and Bettors and Betting Rooms? About how I was twenty-four years old and had killed three people. About what I did to those girls before I met Jay.

I thought of what my mom said the last time I saw her. Maybe Uncle Ted still lived in me. Maybe he saw what I was seeing. Was getting his last rocks off. Maybe some of my urges were his urges.

"I know you're in there," I whispered. "I'm really sorry for letting you die."

The camper hit a bump, and I heard Jay growl her disapproval on the cot. A memory came loose from the rafters. It's of my father and Uncle Ted fighting in the backyard of my Tampa home. They're tumbling on top of each other. My dad had confronted him about drunk-driving me. He's beating him to a pulp in the hot summer grass, the lawn uncut and wild, the sprinklers going off with a loud *siksiksiksiksiksik*, Uncle Ted calling him a cocksucker and trying to push him off.

More memories started coming undone. Uncle Ted asking me to grab money from my mom's purse. Uncle Ted telling me about how he got HIV from a needle. Him telling me about how to fuck a girl younger than you, how to hold them tight. Telling me about drugs. A body high versus a head high. Teaching me how to lace a spliff. Watching him take a bat to my Uncle Sal's car on Christmas Eve and breaking the mirrors off.

I was eleven and we sat on the hood of his truck, and he let me drink from his beer. He had parked a long way back from the soccer fields and we watched my team run around and do drills. The coach was a squat Italian man and I was terrible at the game and he always let me know it. The sky had a few clouds moving around, but the sun sat away from them all, indignant, bearing down on us with the contemptuous heat that Floridians know about. This had been our pattern toward the end of things. I got a buzz on before practice, belching when the Italian man told me to hustle.

"Your father doesn't like me, you know that, right?" Uncle Ted said to me. He had a dirty bandage around the palm of his hand. He had black oil on his shirt and legs.

"Yeah, I know," I said. I was wearing shin pads and tight cleats.

"I had a lot of things. Used to be like him. Then chose different things instead."

"I know."

"And I bet he gets mad at your mother for still wanting to be my sister. Still helping me out now and then."

"He gets mad at a lot of things," I whispered.

He put his hand on my shoulder and squeezed it. He rubbed my back and brought me close and kissed the top of my head. He smelled like beer and cigarettes and grease. "Do you feel loved by me?" he asked.

"I do."

"I know what your folks say about me. And they're not lying, not usually. But I love you so much. Gun to my head, I love you more than they love you, that ain't a lie, not even a little bit."

"Okay."

"Do you believe me?"

"I guess. Yeah."

"Then why are you crying?"

"The sun's in my eye."

"Sometimes I think I love too much. Love too many things. That's why I get into trouble so much."

"That's kinda nice."

He handed me his beer and the can was heavy. I took a sip

and my mouth watered and my face got hot. I felt it hit my stomach and get me drunk quick.

"But just think about this," he started. "I'm the worst person you know, but I love you the most. Love you more than your friends or Uncle Sal or your asshole dad or your mom, God, man, she's a real tight-ass sometimes. I'm the worst person in your life, I know that much, but I love you the most. And do you love me the most?"

"Yeah. I do."

"I know you do."

"I ever show you this?" He opened his shirt and there was a scar down the center of his brown chest. Next to it was a poorly tattooed bird over his heart. "You read poetry?"

"No," I said.

"Let me ask you this, if we bail on soccer practice and go see a movie are you gonna tell on me? Are you gonna screw up the works?"

"No," I said, smiling. "Let's go."

"Alright, Blue Bird, let's go."

>

I felt myself get misty-eyed and I don't know what compelled me, but I crawled over to Jay and slid myself beneath her cot. I made myself as flat as possible and stayed there in the dust. I listened to her snore softly. I stifled my cries until I fell asleep.

>

Izzy had pulled us into Black Bear Forest just outside of Sanford. The camper was hot and I woke in sweat, and climbed out from under Jay's cot. She was already outside talking to Izzy about what we had discussed earlier. I pulled on my sneakers and came out, wincing at the sun. We were certainly in a forest and the Kia and its camper looked like something out of a post-apocalypse movie. Birds chirped and I watched a massive spider pick its way over the grass into the shade of a thorny bush.

"Thought we oughta stay off the main roads," Izzy said. He had sweat stains under his arms.

"Thanks for driving," I said.

"I'm the Gate Keeper and the Kia Master," he said, smiling. "I heard we're going north."

"After we're done here," Jay said. She was setting down a blanket on the grass. "Hey, weirdo, why were you under my cot?"

Izzy looked at me, bemused.

"I don't know," I said. "I just wanted to be there."

"I know you have some sick tendencies, but try to dial them down, okay?"

"Yeah. Sorry."

"*Okay*," Izzy said. "I'm going to get some shut-eye." He climbed into the camper and shut the door behind him.

"I'm going to go into town," I said. "Try to find some food or something to drink."

"The point of coming to the forest is for us to not be seen," Jay said. "You get that, right? You're not going anywhere."

"I'm going to get heatstroke out here," I said. "It's fucking Sanford. It's a bum town, I'll be fine."

"You're staying here. That's final. You're not leaving the woods."

"Fine. I'm going for a walk then. I'll stay in the woods."

"And you're not going into town."

"I won't."

"And you won't be seen by *anyone*."

"*I won't.*"

>

The town was a sparse little place with wide roads and one-story homes. Every other block had a tapioca-colored church. Skinny palm streets shot up like fireworks frozen mid-ascent. It was about thirty minutes of walking before I found shops and basic civilization. Namely, a small strip mall with exactly what I was looking for: a record shop. Inside, the A/C chilled my sweat in place. The shirt on my chest went cold and my red face cooled down. The place had a dingy carpet and bright lights overhead. An older man with a ponytail and glasses nodded at me and I moved through the aisles of the rock section.

I found *Juju* for a decent price and asked the guy if they sold CD players.

"I got a pretty old one, but it's used," he said. He had a crucifix hanging on a thin necklace and a long green shirt with the sleeves rolled up.

"Does it work alright?" I asked.

"Well enough," he said. "Just don't shake it around a bunch."

"I'll take it."

I paid with two twenties and he gave me some batteries for free. I put the CD in and walked out and listened to *Juju* for what felt like the first time in my life. Different context came flooding in with each line and with each track. I wasn't listening in Tallahassee anymore. I was listening in bumfuck Sanford, but I was listening with intent. I was listening *on a mission.* I looked out onto the hot parking lot and at the starbursts of sun off the roofs and windshields of cars. Heat shimmered in the distance. The sky was cloudless. I felt for Ellery in the air, but she wasn't there. Just sticky humid heat. I looked at the coins in my hand and spotted what must've been one of the last remaining pay phones.

A yellow phone hung on a receiver and the box around it was painted with pink flamingos and green palm fronds. A manatee was painted on the wall above the phone. I walked over to it but paused for a moment. I tried to remember Becca's phone number but couldn't. The only phone numbers I had memorized were my parents', and I looked at the keypad wondering if it was even worth it. What could I even say to them? *Hey, Mom and Dad, I'm not coming home ever again and also, I'll probably be dead within the year.* That wouldn't be so bad for them, I thought. I was their memento mori after all. But then I considered what was said at the Sisda. Healthier, reaffirming habits. I sighed and tucked a quarter into the slot and dialed my mom.

It rang for a while and went to voicemail. They probably didn't recognize the caller ID and ducked it as spam. When the beep came, I wasn't ready.

"Hey, Mom. It's Sam. I'm calling from—I'm calling from. Uh. Tallahassee. Anyhow, I wanted to say that I've found some new friends and that things are getting better. I'm getting out of FSU really soon and I'll be starting my life now. You were right all along and I should've left with Becca when I had the chance. In fact, I'm going to meet her and be with her. Yeah. I just need to tighten up some things before I go. But listen, I don't know how to say this, try to stay offline. I know it's impossible, but just, maybe, try. And, you know, I forgive you, by the way. I'm mad at you, but I forgive you and, uh, yeah,

I think this is my first step to being . . ." My thought was cut short. In the reflection of the pay phone, I saw an open-roofed Jeep slow to a stop. I kept the phone to my ear and rambled some more. " . . . my first step to being better. But I'm also realizing that being better is kind of subjective and . . ." I cheated out to get a better look at the riders. A big-bellied guy sat at the wheel and in the back was a skinny girl who looked too tall and cramped in the car. I met eyes with them and they drove on out of the parking lot. I should've stayed in the forest, I thought. "I don't know who I'm being better for, so don't get mad at me if it's not for you." I hung up the phone and ducked into a Publix. I made sure to be quick about it and got Gatorades and pre-made sandwiches. I paid with the rest of my cash and hurried out of the store and back into the forest.

Jay was sunbathing on her stomach, and I tossed a Gatorade onto the grass next to her.

"I think someone saw me," I said.

"Goddammit," she said. She sat up and put her top back on. "What the fuck did I tell you?"

"They were in a Jeep and they saw me and drove off," I said. "Maybe tonight is too hot for this."

"It's gotta happen tonight," she said. "We're already here."

"It's too dangerous. They'll see us coming."

"So, you blew it. Now what do you expect us to do? Wait here for a few more nights?"

"I don't know," I said. "I'm sorry. I should've stayed."

"What was so important that you had to get? We still had some food in the car." She stood up and approached me. She pulled the bag out of my hand. She took out the CD player. "You're fucking joking, right?"

"It's important to me," I said.

"You really are broken in the head, aren't you?"

"It was her favorite album," I said.

"Who gives a shit? She's fucking dead," Jay said. She opened the player and took out the CD and before I could stop her, she snapped it in half. I felt a sense of rage I hadn't felt in a long time. I slapped her across the face and within seconds she had me on the ground. She was trying to punch my teeth out and Izzy had to pull her off.

"What the fuck is going on!" he shouted. She was trying to squirm out of his grip.

"You're a fucking asshole, you know that!" I screamed. I spat blood into my lap. I was running out of clean jeans.

"She's fucking dead, you loser!" Jay screamed. "You listening to that isn't gonna bring her back. Okay? You get that? She's dead as shit and you killed her."

"Yeah! Okay! Fucking fine. I killed her," I said. I climbed to my feet. Izzy still had a tight grip on her. "But I'm allowed to remember her."

"Not if it means going into town and ruining *my* mission."

"You went into town?" Izzy asked.

"He went into town and someone spotted him. All for a fucking CD."

"Dude, not cool."

"Fuck this," I said. "I'm out of here." I stormed into the trees.

"Yeah, go and get us killed, you fucking psychopath," she shouted.

I stepped over bushes and into the overgrown forest. I walked a few minutes before I heard Izzy rustling behind me, catching up. I felt my cheeks go red from embarrassment. There was a small slope coming up and I picked my way down it carefully. I wasn't even sure where I was headed, I just had to be away from Jay.

"Yo, wait up!" Izzy said. He caught up and placed a hand on my shoulder. "You gotta come back, man." He looked more red than me. He was skinny and blended in with the trees behind him. His little glasses showed me the sun up ahead, a searing white hole in the sky and now on his face. I stood on the slope a few feet below him.

"I don't think this is going to work," I said. "We can't work together."

"Bullshit. You guys are great together. We've already taken down two of these guys."

"She's unhinged, dude."

"Don't call her that. She's just determined."

"She broke my CD," I said. It was all I could say. I knew how childish it sounded. I knew how childish it *was.*

"I'll find you a new one. When we get out of here, I'll get you a new one."

A few seconds passed. I exhaled and let the fire in me cool.

"I'm sorry," I said. I let out an exhausted sigh at Izzy babysitting me. But he was right, and I was wrong. "I freaked out on her," I started. "I shouldn't have gone to town. But . . . I just. Jesus. I don't know what the fuck we're doing, man. I called my parents from a payphone. I don't know what I'm supposed to *do.* I have so much going on inside that I don't know how to reconcile."

But Izzy wasn't looking at me anymore. His face had gone ashen. His attention was elsewhere. Behind me. I turned to follow his gaze and saw it too. Coming up the slope, through the trees and under the low-hanging branches, were three people with rifles. Within seconds they stopped climbing and the five of us stared at each other. Two of them were the drivers from the Jeep and they were in ski masks. The third one was short and muscular and didn't need a mask. He had red eyes and his faced looked like the Devil's. I heard Izzy take a step backward.

"What up with that guy's eyes?" Izzy whispered.

"Go to Jay," I said.

"His whole face is modded," he replied, taking another step backward. "Why is his whole face modded?"

Then I spun to him. "Run!"

The two of us sprinted through the forest. Fallen wood and vines and thick-leafed plants whipped past my arms and jeans like angry switches. *Crack!* A gunshot fired through the trees. I heard the impact on a trunk a few yards to my right. Birds took off. A fat squirrel fled for his life. *Crack!* Another shot whizzed past my head and broke through some tangle of vines toward the right. "Keep running!" I yelled.

In the clearing, where the Kia sat, Jay was already primed with the .38. Izzy and I came bursting out of the tree line full tilt. She tossed the other handgun to Izzy, and it landed on the dirt and he scrambled for it and kept running.

"You brought them right here!" Jay yelled. I didn't argue with her. She was right anyhow. My little trip to town alerted the guards. Jay produced the sawed-off next and tossed it at me. I caught it, surprising myself. Braver now by another percent.

"They're gonna try to surround us!" Izzy yelled. *Crack!* A bullet blew through the plastic door to my left. I leapt to the dirt and scrambled for cover behind the Kia. Jay fired off a shot into the trees, but I didn't hear an impact.

"I'm not dying in fucking Sanford!" I screamed. Jay ran around the camper and put her back against the edge. From what I could tell, two of them were still right across from us.

The other one might've gone around and, God willing, Izzy was confronting him head-on.

Another shot banged out and packed itself into the side of the Kia. I felt the whole car shake. I got low and tried to crawl around to the front. Jay drew their attention to the camper, and I saw my window. The bigger guy who was driving the Jeep stepped out of the tree line. He had a greasy white T-shirt that showed the bottom of his belly. He had combat boots with red laces and dirty jeans. His rifle was brown, long, and bolt-action. He cranked his fat hand back and around and I saw the casing pop out and glint gold as it fell in an arc to his feet. He fired again at the camper, and I fired at his legs.

He yelled and went down hard, his weight pitching forward in a rude angle. Blood and meat scattered outward along the clearing of dead grass. He spun the rifle around to me and I shot again, wetting his chest. The rifle fell to his side.

"Get his gun!" Jay called. She leaned out of the camper and shot a few rounds. I ran for the rifle, grabbed it, and tried to keep moving, but the guy reached out and grabbed my ankle. I tripped hard and bit my tongue on the ground. I tasted blood.

"Meg! Shoot him!" he yelled. His chest was a muddied red-and-crimson display. He didn't have long. The woman, his riding partner, *Meg*, came out of the woods with her rifle. She was shaking more. This was certainly a ride-along situation gone south, and she probably hadn't penciled in "gunning down twenty-somethings" in her itinerary.

"Put it down!" Jay screamed. She was on one knee with the gun trained on the woman. I tried to do the math. She probably had around three shots in the cylinder. "Don't make me shoot your redneck ass."

"You killed Mankey," she cried out. Her voice was higher than I expected. She was crying under her mask.

"I ain't dead yet, hun," the big guy said, but he was close. I tried to pull my leg away, but he kept his grip. He looked up at me from the ground and growled. Just then gunfire screamed out from behind us. It was an exchange. Izzy and the short guy were going at it. Time was running out. Jay fucked up forcing us into this standoff. She should have wiped this lady out before anybody had time to think.

I grabbed the rifle and, still on my back, spun toward the woman. She turned to me and fired, but her gun clicked.

"You short-stroked it!" Mankey yelled and the woman yelped and stammered and tried to work the bolt again, but I shot her in the neck. The rifle kicked back hard into my stomach and I grunted, feeling a dry heave come on. She fell onto her butt, gasping for air as her blood sprayed across her knees.

"I'll fucking kill you!" Mankey said and with his new strength he climbed on top of me and pushed his thumbs into my larynx. The blood of his chest smeared across my shirt. He banged my head against the dirt and choked me for too long before Jay shot him in the top of the head. His eyes twitched sideways, and he fell down, pinning me to the ground. Jay didn't help get him off. She was already running toward Izzy.

Once I joined them, Izzy was shaking pretty bad, and Jay had stabbed the short muscular guy a few too many times with her pocketknife. Izzy sat and leaned against a small log. His hands were going crazy, and he tucked them into the bottom of his shirt.

"I'm here! I'm here, I got you," Jay said. She tried to hold Izzy's shaking hands, but she couldn't still them.

"I keep lucking out," he said. "I keep chickening out and getting saved."

"You didn't chicken out, you did great. Look. I'm not gonna let anybody hurt you, Izz, you know that." She pulled his head into her chest and held him. She petted his hair. I watched from my place near some trees. Mankey's blood darkened my shirt. I was exhausted and held the sawed-off at my side. Seeing Jay coddle this guy broke my heart in a way I didn't expect. She was such a hardass to me. She hated me. And sure, I understood *why*, but it still didn't prepare me to witness how much love she *did* have. She cared so much about this dork. She loved him. It was actually kind of sweet.

After a second, Izzy calmed down and stopped shaking. Jay held his cheeks and looked into his eyes. With her thumbs she wiped his tears away. He pulled from Jay's embrace and fixed his glasses. "I'm okay. I'm okay."

"You sure?"

"Yeah. Sorry."

"No sorries."

Jay squeezed his hands and stood up. She examined the dead guy. "What's with his eyes? What's with his face?" Up close we saw it better. He had tattoos and prosthetics to look like a demon. High, sharp cheekbones. Nose shaved down to the vomer. Earless. Deep grooves carved into his chin to look like the dripping teeth of a naked skull.

"Body modifications," Izzy said. He glanced and then recoiled and then glanced back, but I couldn't look away. It captivated me. Held me in a sense of wonder. Wonder? Wonder. This person had chosen who they wanted to be. I imagined that at some point in his life he also called his parents and said he was going to be better. Whatever that meant.

A drippy, smelly form of respect slithered down from the ceiling inside of me.

"Who did that?" was all I could ask.

"He probably did it to himself," Jay said. "Or, you know, paid someone to do it to him." She kicked the dead guy over with her foot. She dug out his wallet and took the cash. There was no ID.

"Let's lay low for a bit," I started, "then we drive to New York to find this Skunk guy. Is that cool with everyone?"

"Fuck that plan," Jay said. "You almost got us killed just now. You don't call the shots."

"Okay," I said. "Then what?"

"We continue with Sanford and then do Sylvan Shores and then we get the Skunk."

"*Jay*, that's crazy," Izzy said. "Everyone already knows we're here."

"Then get mad at him," she said, pointing to me. "My plan doesn't change."

She folded the pocketknife back into her jeans and shoulder-checked me as she passed, stomping through the dry grass and twigs to the camper. I helped Izzy up.

"You gotta be a better shot," I said.

"Then give me the shotgun back," he said.

"No way."

Back around the camper the lanky woman still sat on her butt before the fat corpse of her husband. She stammered quietly and blood sputtered from the hole in her neck drizzling on her jeans and lap and making it look like she just gave birth or maybe did earlier.

"Let her suffer," Jay said. She stood alongside the camper and examined the bullet holes in the doors and side paneling.

I watched the woman try to take a breath in, the hole in her throat giving a beleaguered and clogged whistle. Her lips quivered behind the mask, chapped and dirty from the brief gunfight. Mankey had begun to smell.

"She came from the church," I said. I was certain, and because of that, I was guilty.

The Page 40 in Sanford was out of a church on the edge of town. It was a pastor named Victor Markelli who, Izzy determined, was using some bulky desktop in the church's basement. While it was true everyone was out to get us all of the time, my little jaunt into town likely tipped off the target.

"But how can you be sure?" Izzy asked.

"I don't know. Context clues? Critical thinking?"

"Just ask her," Jay interrupted. She had finished examining the bullet holes and turned to us.

"Did that creepy pastor send you?" Izzy asked.

The woman wheezed in response. Her head jangled up and down.

"Listen, we're going to the church tonight," Jay said, leaning against the camper. "Is he gonna expect us?" Her arms were crossed. It seemed like Jay had no expectation that our hostage would answer, but it surprised us all when she groaned a long and painful, "*Yesssss . . .*"

"We got our intel. Just finish her," I said.

"Hang on," Jay said. "You went into town and she came here and got shot. This is your doing."

Jay walked over to the woman and tapped her on the head. "Can you lift your head?" The woman swayed her shoulders left to right. "Lift your head for me, come on, don't be weak," Jay said.

Jay stood with her back to me and with her hands in her pockets. Her shaved head and thin neck opened like an estuary to her skinny shoulders. She was bonier than I had remembered. She looked back over her shoulder at me. Her eyes were dark and cutting. Her lips were thick but her face was narrow like it was squeezed in a vise. She was like wet granite; move too fast and you'll break something.

"How do I get close to your friend without being seen?" Jay asked. The woman said nothing. "I'm gonna take off your mask, I can't hear you." Jay moved behind the woman. She pressed a hand on her shoulder and stripped off her mask. The woman groaned in pain. She was just a white woman with a shaggy bob. Had a tattoo of stars on her cheek. She looked like a smoker. She looked like a redneck. "How do I get into the church without being seen?"

" . . . back door . . . key in truck . . ."

"Look at that, Psycho Boy," Jay said. "Guess your fuck-up got us somewhere."

"I don't like watching this," Izzy said. He kept his hands wrapped in his shirt like a boy that fidgeted too much. "Jay."

Jay stood behind the woman and held her chin up exposing the wound to the sky and air. She took out her blue pocketknife and put the blade to the neck hole. "I guess I can just open this up a little more, huh?" The woman coughed in return. She was choking and something bubbled out of her neck and dripped down her shirt. "But I'm not the one who did this," Jay said. She tossed the pocketknife on the ground between the woman's legs.

"You can do it," she said to me. "Izzy and I are gonna find the truck and get whatever keys she's talking about. When I come back, she better be dead."

She turned and headed into the woods, and Izzy left my side and followed her. I stood before the woman and raised the bolt-action.

"And don't shoot her," Jay said from the tree line. "We can't waste the ammo, and you're just gonna attract more people." I lowered the gun and she disappeared. When I turned back to Meg, dying, I saw that she was weeping. She had no energy left to do it properly and so the tears just came slowly and her mouth hung pathetically.

"Are you crying?" I asked quietly.

She didn't answer.

"Are you dead?"

She cried a little more.

I felt a charge of electricity. My jeans tightened around my cock. Disturbed with myself, I grabbed the knife and quickly plugged it into her throat. The force pushed the woman back and she died, choking, more blood flowing around the knife and then pouring down either side of her neck. She turned her head and closed her eyes and stopped crying, but in my head, it played a little longer.

>

The New Voice of the Holy Ghost was the name of the church. Jay's plan was about as simple and straightforward as the ones before it. Go in quietly, probably make more noise than intended, and then leave out the back. We were still role-playing as Luddites, so all of our intel was based on whatever Izzy managed to scribble down before we left Tally. He had the coordinates of the upload, the guy's name, and that was pretty much it. Fortunately, with the keys to the back door the mission proved just slightly more achievable.

"What are the odds of him still being there?" I asked Jay. She was massaging her feet in the camper.

"Pretty low," Jay said.

"Then why are we risking this?" I asked.

"Because I want him dead," she said without looking up.

"Okay, but why him specifically? Why these four locations specifically, I don't understand. The dome guy, the houseboat guy, this pastor, and who is at Sylvan Shores?"

"What difference does it make?"

"It makes a big fuckin di—" I stopped myself. I took a big breath in. It was dark in the camper and Izzy was out in the woods dragging the corpses to a ditch. I stood opposite of Jay, both of us in swathes of dark. "I know I'm pretty much working for you and the Boy Wonder, but I'd like a hint at the bigger picture."

She didn't say anything. My eyes slowly adjusted to her shadow. She was sitting, facing me, with her hands on her knees, but I couldn't see her face or tell where she was looking.

"Well?" I asked again.

"You know, I looked up your girl. Ellery Waters."

"What do you mean you looked her up?"

"I mean on chinsky. I looked her up. I saw the videos. The car crash and everything."

"What are you doing?"

"I'm trying to connect with you, man."

"Why?"

"Because when I'm around you, I get a strong feeling nobody has connected to you in a very long time."

She couldn't even see me. The camper was too dark. But somehow, I felt humiliated and embarrassed and why was she doing this?

"The video was really bad," she said again.

"Yeah. Well. They say she died on impact. Where is this going?"

There was another beat. She made a sound like she was sniffling. For a second, I thought it was me. Just like when I saw her hold Izzy to her chest, the sudden vulnerability caught me off guard. Her shadow put a hand to her face, and she sniffled again. It sounded like she was holding back tears, but I couldn't see it. I could barely hear it really. The whole place was still. Even Izzy out there, putzing around, fell silent.

"It's just not fair," she whispered.

"What's not fair?"

"Your girl dies so suddenly. It's painless and there's no malice behind it, but it still fucking hurts. And you, Sammy Dominguez, allow yourself to have so much hate and anger and fury for what happened to you, that you freak and start wildin' out on campus and attacking people and losing your mind. This thing happened to you, and you lost your mind. But here's the thing, jackass, it happened to me too. Worse in fact. But for some reason *I'm* supposed to have a grand strategy. I'm supposed to stay calm and collected and methodical. It's not enough for me to stop you from being bad, I also have to direct you into being good. What the fuck is that? Why can't I break shit? Why can't I scream? You think I want to be the team captain here? You think I was made for this? Izzy can't lead us because he can't even shoot a gun. I can't trust *you* to do it because I find you under my fucking cot crying to yourself. So, it's on me. All of this thing that we barely understand is on *me.*

"You know, when Izzy picked me up from your apartment, and I told him that I invited you to the Crater, he looked at me like I had three heads. He said to me, 'Why did you invite him, he's dangerous.' Those were his words to me. And you know what I said back? I said I needed help. That's what I

said. I just needed help. I know I broke your little CD. I know
Izzy is gonna get us killed. But Jesus, man, I had zero when I
met you and . . . and . . ."

"And what?"

"And I'm *still at zero*."

She took a breath and I saw her touch her face again.
If she'd still had hair, she would've been running her fingers through it. "Izzy," she shouted to the door, "are you
eavesdropping?"

"Yeah," he called back. "Sorry." He walked off, his foot-
falls crunching leaves away.

"You two really love each other, huh?" I said, trying to
change subjects.

"These people have taken everything from us, but we still
have to try."

Another beat. I felt her gaze push needles in me. I was
still unsure about her. Scared of her. It had been proven over
and over again how dangerous all of this was, and she had yet
to lie to me about the nature of the game, but even still there
was something troubling about her. It was in the severity of
her actions. The maximum strength in how she moved and
decided and spoke. Considering the circumstances, she had
no choice but to move with severity, there was no question
about it, but the way she looked at me, even in the darkness,
was like she wanted me to fuck up. She placed me on thin ice
and walked backward from me, stomping her feet, making it
crack more and more. All she needed was one more reason to
put me under. Because of this, I felt a mounting resentment
toward her, but examining it made me feel gross. More gross
than usual at least. She was right about *Juju*. She had been
right in all our fights. But I still felt a blade forming inside of
me, and it had on her name on it. I had to choose my words

carefully. I couldn't give her an inch. What can I say? I hate a know-it-all.

"We can get this pastor guy," I said. "But we don't have to connect."

I left my end of the camper, and I opened the plastic door and the moonlight came in like a wedge. For one second, over my shoulder, I saw her face. Her eyes were red, and her cheeks were wet, and her tears were freshly wiped away. She winced at the moonlight and turned to the floor.

Seeing me exit, Izzy quickly squeezed by me and stepped into the camper. When the cheap door clattered shut, I heard him ask, just barely, "Why are you crying? What's wrong?"

A big part of me got all depressed. Why couldn't I ask her that? What was stopping me?

Then he asked her, "What did he do now?" and I got mad all over again.

>

We left the Kia in the woods and took Meg and her friends' Jeep instead. We pulled up to the front of the New Voice of the Holy Ghost around midnight. The building was a bland one-story box with a nice lawn and small parking lot. I climbed out with the sawed-off and the keys to the back that Meg gave up. Jay and Izzy stayed behind.

I stepped through a passage around the back between the back wall of the church and a chain-link fence. The grass was uncut and the brick walkway was cluttered with groundskeeping toys. Through the stained-glass windows, I saw the small emptiness of the church inside.

I crouched low and kept moving down the garden path, hugging the exterior. Finally, I got to a small white door and used the key. It unlocked and I eased it open. Before me was a passage that seemed to lead to the church proper where everyone sat, but also in front of me was a small staircase leading down.

A basement in Florida always seemed out of place. Stairs should never go *down* in Florida. The limestone of the land refuses it. For fear of sinkholes, most basements, if necessary at all, are shallow with low ceilings and only used for storage. There are no fun man caves with pool tables and popcorn makers. There are only spongy walls and a ground beneath your feet that seems destined to crumble and eat you alive. But this staircase was different. The walls seemed sturdy, and the ceiling seemed higher than usual. I decided that if any deranged pastor was working out of his church he'd likely be down here. Right now. Waiting for my arrival like the boss in a video game. I opened the sawed-off and counted the shells, one, two, then closed the gun again and descended.

When I was a kid, back in my Villa days, Lucas and Austin and I snuck into the chapel after hours. There was some festival happening on the campus and our parents were drinking cheap beers and talking to each other and to the teachers about grades and other things. Inside, the place was ghostly and barren. Long sheets covered the pews. Stained glass of the Virgin hung pale in moonlight. Lucas did an impression of Father Larry and chased us around. It was Uncle Ted who taught me that priests were bad and now he was inside of me, holding the same gun I was and hunting for the same man of God too.

The place was empty. Pastor Markelli had fled the scene, and everything was in shambles. A pile of desktop computers and monitors sat in a corner, destroyed by some blunt force. A coffee station sat in the far end of the basement with some folding chairs, also toppled to the ground, the glass coffeepot shattered on the floor. Overhead, the lights were on a low, dim setting and I moved through the place quietly, my footsteps barely making any sound. Nobody was in the bathroom, nobody in the kitchen, nobody upstairs in the church proper.

You're born a Latino and you're raised Roman Catholic, and you can never shake the quiet, oppressive reverence that's expected in churches. Everything is about death and guilt. Sin and redemption. The highest calling is to be a martyr and then come back with a few new monikers. It's pretty liberating if you think about it. You're only you until somebody smokes you.

"Anybody in here?" I called out. My voice echoed. The place was small but still had the acoustics. The altar sat in a gray, dead light and a large wooden cross stood over it. I heard Jay pull the Jeep around to the front doors. Whatever action she was expecting, she was going to be disappointed. Maybe it was the dreariness of the church talking, but I was starting to feel fatalistic about all of this. The talk with Jay, the Page 40s, the Skunk. There was a video I recalled of me getting blown out the door of some shack. If that link came true and that's how I went out, would people watch that video when I was gone? And if they did, was that my resurrection? I thought of what Ellery said back in her dorm with her vlogs. "I want to *not want* to be online." You and me both, baby.

"What a bust," Jay said, later, as we climbed out of the Jeep. She closed the door quietly, looking around the forest. We had driven back to where we picked the Jeep up, at the base of a large hill still away from the camper. "I guess we're skipping Sylvan Shores after all."

"It's too hot," Izzy said from the other side. He started picking through the trees and I followed close. "This is a good idea."

"I'm not happy about it, though," Jay said. "In fact, I'm really fucking pissed. I had a whole plan."

"I think this was bound to happen," Izzy said. "I know Sammy fucked up with his CD, but we were hardly going unnoticed. I mean with the grocery runs, getting gas, plus we're literally dragging a camper around."

Jay shot him a look.

"What? I'm just saying. We got two. That's *good*."

"Whatever," Jay said. She marched up ahead and Izzy followed. I turned back and examined the path we had come from. It was around one a.m. and the forest had yet to settle for the night. The place buzzed with energy. Twigs cracked and branches fell and bushes rustled with night moves. Somewhere out there, Pastor Markelli was laughing and wheezing about his narrow escape. He was probably telling everyone about us. The walls were definitely, *definitely* closing in.

>

Izzy and Jay climbed into the camper, and I opted to drive. It was still hot, even at night, and the little A/C in the car wheezed cool air. I cut onto the interstate and rural Florida passed by. With the moon out, the long, flat planes of green and brown were all the same shade of dark night-blue. Behind me, in the rearview mirror, the camper jostled around quietly. "What's going to happen to me?" I asked the mirror, thinking that maybe Jay could read my mind and tell me the next time we spoke. Maybe I didn't want to hear that answer though.

You can only be so broken before people get tired of pointing out the cracks.

Hours passed before we broke out of the Florida border and it was a few more hours still before we pulled into a gas station in Atlanta. The sun was coming up and the air was a touch cooler and it was nice to see a city again. I kept my hands in my pockets as the pump filled the tank. From the camper I had grabbed my hoodie and zipped it over the blood-stain of Mankey. I stood there and smelled the gas and the blood and the smoke that still lingered in my hair. The city proper was sitting across the interstate, and Jason wasn't far away. I thought it'd be nice to go see him, but after the stunt I pulled walking into Sanford, I was on a pretty tight leash. Still though, I hoped he was okay.

Jay came out of the camper and stretched her legs. Cars pulled in and out of spots and a convenience store glowed bright with red and yellow signage. "I've been thinking about the Skunk," she said. "And how things went down earlier."

"What's the consensus?"

"There's a trailer park in Pennsylvania," she said. "Izzy told me about it. It's more of a commune, really. Public land. People live there long-term."

"I can't do twenty years."

"I know. I agree. But technically this Skunk isn't Front Page so it might not be that long. But we have to take *some* time off and lay low, like really lay low. If we went now, after everything that just happened, we'd get hit within a mile of the guy."

"We've been together a week and we're at each other's throats," I said. It came out meaner than I wanted, but I didn't take it back.

"There's not a real choice," she said. She kept her fists balled in the small pockets of her jacket. She was shorter than I realized. She wasn't in her boots this time. She was back in the checkered Vans I had met her in. Her necklace danced in the harsh overhead lights of the gas station.

"You really like that necklace," I remarked.

She pulled at it and fingered the blue shapes under the bright lights. "It was my birthday, and my dad gave my brother some money to get me something. He went to TJ Maxx and got this for like twenty dollars. It's my favorite thing I own."

"It's nice."

"Thanks. You ever buy Ellery jewelry?"

I thought it over for a second. Surprising myself, I didn't get emotional about it.

"She wasn't much of a jewelry girl, but she wore a ton of those woven camp bracelets. She'd even shower with them and they'd reek. It was hilarious. I didn't really buy her a lot of things now that I think about it. I never had the money. But I always did stuff for her or tried to. Like she never had to ask me for a favor. In high school, I had a car before she did and her parents were always traveling and doing business and I remember one morning I woke up at like four a.m. to get to her house to go pick her up and take her to a volleyball game in Daytona or something. I think somewhere along the line I forgot how to do things for her, but I also think she stopped needing it. And that kind of hurt too. Like I only knew one love language and when your partner stops speaking it communication kind of breaks down."

"I know I give you a hard time, but I actually like it when you talk about her. It makes me think we have a chance."

I shrugged. "My best friend is here in Atlanta," I said.

"That's not happening."

"Yeah. I know."

I turned my attention back to the gas pump, but she didn't take the hint.

"How did Izzy say we met?" she asked.

"Public library in Alabama."

"That's not true."

"No?"

"He was the first Bettor I found," she said. She kept her eyes locked on me. "Or maybe hunted down is the better word. We go after Page 40s now, but Izzy was like a Page 100. A reckless kid who was just sort of good at computers. He was sloppy on chinsky but he was smart on other sites. Made some decent Leb too. That's how we paid for this little adventure. The guns. The food. My hospital bill."

"Why type of stuff did he bet on?"

"I only saw the one. When I found him, he was scared shitless. Quit the game right then."

"Why didn't you kill him?"

"I gave you a chance too, didn't I?"

"Yeah, and we've been *crushing it*," I said. Surprising me, she let out a laugh. It sounded nice and soft and totally opposed her face and attitude. I smiled and started laughing too. When it faded, she looked down at her feet then back up at me and she was serious again.

"When we get to Pennsylvania, he's gonna score us some new IDs and passports. Nothing crazy. But if your family comes looking around for you, they're gonna have a hard time."

"I feel like I'm being kidnapped."

"You're not the only one who likes to control people." She winked.

"And what about your family? Are they gonna come looking?"

"My family thinks I'm dead."

"Jesus."

"It's better this way. Have you chinskied your mom and dad yet?"

"I searched some relatives but not them."

"It's more real than you can imagine." She took a step forward and gave a hitchhiker's thumb to the camper. "Why don't you take a nap? Me and Izzy will drive."

The pump gave a metallic cough and the numbers stopped counting. I took it out and closed the Kia's gas hatch. "With all his Leb, he couldn't have bought us a decent RV?"

She smirked and I moved past her to the skinny door of the camper. Izzy climbed out and smiled at me. I stopped short and turned back to her.

"Wait," I called. She had moved to the driver-side door.

"What?"

"What was your plan?"

"Huh?"

"Lake Yale. Sanford. Sylvan Shores. You said you had a whole plan, but you never told me. What was your plan?"

She looked off at the skyline and then back to me like she was thinking it over. "I drew a circle on a map and said I'd kill everyone in it that I could."

"And then what?"

"I don't know. Make a bigger circle?"

> Be someone else

When we pulled into the trailer park, Izzy made no bones about it. He said the place was a shithole but that he could swap the Kia and the camper for a proper trailer home that was stationary. "We're not going anywhere for a while," was how he put it. He tossed this old man the keys and the old man did the same. Inside, the place was more spacious with more obvious room to sleep and with better amenities, but it was still a fucking trailer.

It was the thick of summer and early on I found a bicycle in the woods that I was able to fix up. I started wearing paint-splattered jeans. I started smoking again. I wore short-sleeve T-shirts. I was off the Cutty and started drinking six packs of Coors. My new ID said my name was Teddy.

"Are you fucking with me?" I asked Izzy.

"What do you mean?" He dug into his bag and passed Jay her new ID too.

"This name you picked. It's . . . Forget it."

You don't know you're in a loop until . . . Yeah, you get it.

Jay, Izzy, and I had become full Luddites. No phones. No laptops. No Wi-Fi. Nothing. We started to get skeezed when we were even *around* techies. A few kids had come to visit a relative in the park and they were talking about hotspots and

Snapchat and FaceTiming their friends and I felt myself break into a cold sweat. I had to hurry to our trailer and lie down.

Right when we got settled, Izzy took my bike and duffel bag all the way to Pittsburgh to find a crypto exchange. Said he knew a guy. He had to move it from Leb to Elfen to Varion to Condor and then to cash. He loaded the bag with stacks of hundreds and biked back over several hours. Said it was the most stressful ride of his life.

"I can't exchange money like that again," he said. "Now they know I was in Pittsburgh, but it should fade."

"We'll make it last," Jay said.

Izzy took the duffel bag under the trailer and stuffed it into a hideaway beneath our feet. He peeled off a couple of hundreds and handed it to the "landlord" of the park—a broad-shouldered man in a wide-brimmed Stetson, stained with the sweat of his brow. The Kia and the camper were for the trailer itself. The monthly "rent" was so the Stetson didn't bust our balls or tell the locals what we were about. Not that he'd have any idea. I was Teddy Dameron from Connecticut. Jay was Eliza Jackson. Izzy was Norm Lennel. To anybody who asked we said we were college dropouts that got tired of the liberal elites of the coast. I don't think anybody bought it, but after seeing us around for longer than a month, people just let it slide. Even to commit to their lifestyle as a bit proved grit and determination, which was all we needed to get by and not have knockers on our door. In other words, the bit landed.

Did I miss my family? Of course. Did I miss Jason? Absolutely. Becca too. And always Ellery. But when the days started dropping by, it almost became a matter of meditation. Sometimes I couldn't even remember what the chinsky site looked like. Sometimes I'd fall asleep without images of death and murder scuttling across the back of my eyelids. But the peace was never long. I'd wake up sweating on my little cot. The trailer would be dark. The faint sounds of animal life were heard in the distance. Even further would be the hum of cars on a raised interstate. Being the gentleman I was, I took the personal cot and let Jay and Izzy have the bed. While they weren't exactly the cuddling, nuzzling couple, sometimes in the gray of the morning I'd see Jay as the little spoon, wrapped in the gangly and gawky arms of her man.

My days warped. They lost all shape and meaning. They began to take the form of, you guessed it, a simulation. Or a generation. Or whatever the fuck they called it. My days were not Sammy's. They were the days of Teddy Dameron of Pine Lake Park. Ted Dameron, or T if you knew me, did whatever he did. He biked around and scavenged garbage. He went fishing now and then in a small pond not far from his (their? my?) backyard. I wasn't Sammy again until I had showered and got into my sweats, but even then, Sammy was receding into fog.

Back in Tallahassee I would close my eyes and feel Ellery in the air. Feel her depression in my bed. But she wasn't here in Pine Lake Park. There was something worse. When our first autumn rolled around the air turned metallic and the sky grew taut. I'd walk outside and it'd feel like a plastic bag over my mouth.

Oftentimes I'd catch myself in the small circular mirror of the bathroom. Uncle Ted stared back. I drank his beer. He had my eyes. *Hola mi sobrino.* I started to grow out my fingernails and tap them along the windows of the trailer whenever Jay or Izzy stepped out. *Tap, tap, tap, tap, tap, tap* as I watched hicks and drug addicts shuffle around in blown-out hoodies and ugly rain boots. There were no garages in the immediate area for me to die in and that proved to be a spot of relief. But still. I was poisoning myself.

The thought driving me forward was a two-parter. I needed to know who made money on Ellery's death. And I needed to get back to Becca. If I got to Becca before solving the first part, I'd live in fear for her life. Someone would be keeping tabs on me and, thus, her. That was a given. It could happen at any moment. A Front Pager orchestrates some freak accident where she falls into a manhole, or a hunk of scaffolding beams through her skull outside of Powell's Books. They clear 100 Leb and I'm pushed into going postal at the nearest cybercafé. Conversely, if I solved Ellery's death, but then didn't get back to Becca, I'd be resigning myself to a life of vengeance on the road with Pocket Knife and Squints. After the shootout in Black Bear Forest, I was quite certain that I had pushed my luck as far as it could go. At least with these two.

There were also times where I felt I had pushed my soul as far as it could go. There was a lesson in that church back at Sanford, and it had latched onto me. I'd look at my hands and my feet and my scars. Sammy Dominguez was done. Some parts of me were happy to be Teddy. To feel the calluses of his palms and the beer in his belly. And if this new form got beaten down, well, I still had my life in cyberspace. Never overlook the appeal of a digital ghost.

Our first Thanksgiving as refugees came like a beggar to the door. The holiday stood in the dirty Pennsylvania fall and panhandled for gratitude, begging us to be thankful for anything, begging us to look at each other like people with emotions and hearts and lives. But we didn't budge. Izzy went to the store and got Vienna sausages and the world's smallest turkey, something he could chop into pieces and put on a hot plate. Jay bought one bottle of sparkling cider that she kept for herself. I contemplated doing whippets with some urchins a few trailers next door but opted against it. In jest, Izzy said he was thankful for the space heater. We nodded in silence. The gloom of the holiday fell on us like a weighted blanket.

That night though, after I cleared a six-pack and lay on my cot, something in my mind blinked. It was the notion to start being thankful for what I had. I felt my lips part in a wide-mouthed smile. I was deranged. I thought of only one thing: I was thankful that my shotgun had a wide spray.

>

More than expected, the isolation started getting to Jay. The routine of our hidden existence coupled with the start of a dreary winter seemed to push her into a quiet sadness. She'd sit in a folding chair before a bent and twisted fire pit. She'd unfurl clothes hangers and prod the long wires into the ash and burnt carbon. She'd spend hours in bed curled up under a blanket. There was a part of me that thought she was conserving her energy. She was hibernating. What would even be the point of shaking her out of it? She had the right idea. Still, though, something was leaving her eyes. At the gas station in Atlanta, she made a show of not missing her folks, but I was starting to doubt it. *Folks* meaning everything. *Folks* meaning the old life. *Folks* meaning the blue pill.

"She gets like this in the winter," Izzy told me. "But this is the worst I've seen it."

We were walking through the woods outside the trailer park. It was cold and the snow was half mud. I didn't have proper boots and was doubling up on wool socks, the outer layer baring fewer holes than the inner. "Is she going to be okay?" I asked. I was surprised by my own voice. The sincerity of it. I was hard-pressed to call Jay a friend and the word *partner* didn't really hit the mark either. I didn't know who she was to me, if anyone at all. At least Izzy had the warm virtue of being able to be beaten in a fight if it were to come to that. Jay still scared me. That was the truth. How quickly she could've made me a eunuch in the poorly lit kitchen of my old apartment. It's hard to call someone a friend after that. Even if I did deserve it.

"She's scared just like us," Izzy said. "She has to put on a hard attitude or else people wouldn't fear her, you know? She's gotta go extra just to get the same."

"What's her nightmare?" I asked.

"What do you mean?"

"You mentioned that you always see this creature called Spindly. I see the Wax Man. What does she see? We all have one."

"She's never said."

I nodded and breathed on my hands. They were dry and cracked. I wasn't entirely sure why that question popped in my head. The way Jay had been moving around reminded me of myself after a string of night terrors. I had the energy of a Jenga tower on its last block. If something wormed into Jay's mind, a memory, a fear, something she'd done, then it was slowly eating her. We could all tell.

"How long are we gonna be here?" I asked.

"Jay thinks two or three years."

"And how long have we been here?" I asked.

"Like six months."

"Jesus," I said. I turned and climbed back through the trees.

>

The days moved like sludge. We made small journeys to this ramshackle market that fed most of the trailer park. Canned meat. White bread. Marshmallows. Beer. Lots of beer. My bowel movements were rancid, and I lost weight fast. Soon my jeans were big on the waist and, not wanting to risk a trip to a store, I made a belt out of shredded rope. When new trucks pulled into the park, we'd cut the lights and stay up, alert, crouched in the trailer, each of us armed. When the car doors shut and we heard them talk we listened closely, trying to suss out their intentions. If they were a threat or not.

A lot of the nights we just talked and told stories. We'd sit cross-legged on the small floor of our little trailer, huddled in blankets and layers, the junky space heater doing what it could. Izzy's first job was at Cold Stone Creamery. Jay's first kiss was on a field trip to MOSI. Izzy's favorite movie was the original *Total Recall*. Jay had never seen *The Godfather*. Izzy's second uncle was a writer on *Late Night*. Jay missed her brother a lot. That was the worm.

"What was his name?" I asked one night.

"Marcus."

"What was he like?"

"He was the best."

"What did you do to the guy who filmed it?" The room went quiet. Some kids walked with a dog outside among the twigs and fallen trees. A little radio was heard from a trailer at our diagonal. It was snowing hard, heavy flakes pattering against the plastic windows. Izzy looked at me and then back at Jay, who sat closest to the space heater. It felt more and more that I never saw her in the light.

"He was just a shithead that went to a high school nearby," she started. "His name was Rob Richie. He played football and sold drugs. He was with my brother and some others, and he laced my brother's joint with some intense hyphy shit. Watched him tweak and freak out. Apparently, he did that a lot and had a running video log of people spazzing. He was a sicko."

"So, what did you do to him?"

The space heater moaned softly. She was a pile of rags in the corner. The moonlight tried to come in through the snow, but it was failing. A little red light on the heater glowed against the wall like some faded crimson spotlight. Even Izzy was in the dark.

"It's not a very exciting story," she said.

"I wanna know," I said. "You saw how Ellery went. Let's *connect.*"

There was a beat. Something cracked in the woods, and we all looked. Then, slowly, she moved her gaze onto me.

"He never went to college and stayed in town. I found a way into a house party he was having. Nobody knew what I looked like. At this point my brother was dead about two years, I think. Something like that. I knew he'd overpower me if I tried anything physical. And I'd probably go to jail or something which I was only half willing to do. So, I went into his room and laced him back."

"How? With what?"

"Maybe we should drop it," Izzy said.

"What else do we have to talk about?" I asked.

"I'll tell you," Jay said again. Her voice sounded cool but drowsy. I cracked another Coors. "I had to do my research before I went to his place. Those two years I was trying to find the right way. Think of the perfect way. Saving money and shit. I found drug dealers that sold pot and coke and acid, but I needed to find someone that sold the real hard shit. I was looking for fentanyl. But the minute I go snooping around for it, I'd probably get got. Eventually I found a Craigslist guy who knew a guy who knew a guy. There was this forum about Asian massage parlors where these horny randos would post addresses. They weren't just parlors though. You could pick up loads of intense stuff. I had a guy go fetch me some stuff and I picked it up in a parking lot outside of a Kinkos. Still sat on it for months after that.

"Finally, the day of the party comes. I sneak into his room and find his stash. Coke. Weed. Salvia. Ket. I find a purple bag of hyphy shit and flush it down his toilet. Then I lace everything with the fentanyl. And I mean everything. You only need a minuscule amount, but even still, I was generous. I put the stuff anywhere he'd potentially ingest. I even caked some into his bong. I figured that eventually he'd use one of these things and he'd be a goner. Just a matter of time, you know?

"Anyhow, nobody gets to his stash at that party. Guess he was being stingy. I make myself scarce and go back to my life, just waiting. Having faith. A couple weeks later I guess he has some friends over to get high. Seven people died. All overdosed. Him included. The town painted it as a horrible tragedy. The brightest of our youth dead from drugs. Everyone's crying and shit. Even though two years ago they didn't give a shit about Marcus. Didn't even care that it was online. Did you know his video had a share button? The video of my brother jumping from a roof had a motherfucking share button. I'm happy I did it. I slept the best sleep of my life."

"You killed innocent people?" I asked.

"Let's not cast aspersions now," Izzy interrupted.

"No, it's fine." Jay shrugged. "I killed one guy who definitely did it and six others who were probably involved."

"You did what you had to do," Izzy said. He reached over and touched her blanket. She nodded quietly.

>

After that, story time kind of slowed down. I never got a lot of information out of Izzy, but it was abundantly clear how much he cared for Jay, yet I couldn't figure out the lens through which he looked at her. I had only seen her in shadow and night and with a blade in her hand, but he seemed to notice the exact opposite. He regarded her with such tenderness and love, and whenever he did, she looked at him like she was about to burst into tears, like an orphan being offered a hot meal. Even if they had spats or fought there was this very clear chemistry between the two. It was in glances and laughs and in the way she'd always ask what he thought of things just to hear him nerd out and wax poetic. They moved through each other's personal space with a casual air like they'd seen each other naked more than once. Even in the silence of the nights when we were in our beds I'd hear them whisper, maybe a laugh, maybe a sigh and gentle caress.

I knew their relationship was firmly romantic, but it started to blossom in a bigger, odder way. It was hard for me to understand. I mean, it's true that she was beautiful, but it's also true that she wasn't for me. So many things were *for me*, or at least I was under the impression they were. I snatched at things and grabbed them and pouted and kicked if I didn't get my way. But she sat on the other side of the glass.

She was the girl that caught me for my crimes. She was the girl that threatened to castrate me. She was the girl that, in some other iteration, pulled my dead body out of a bathtub. She was the girl that needed my help. The girl that wanted to connect, wanted to team up, wanted to save me in more ways than one. She wanted to reach into my chest and study my heart.

She kept me at a distance and while I wasn't offended or even surprised by it, I was more shocked to see the full spectrum of engagement she had with Izzy, a Bettor she supposedly found on Page 100. While I wasn't entirely convinced of that story, considering Izzy had already lied to me about their meeting once before, I also knew I wasn't going to be hearing the truth any time soon. Our three-way partnership was a bubble. We coasted with each other on a shared goal, but the minute loyalty, truths, and intentions were questioned, the entire thing would burst. And I was smart enough to know that I'd be on the wrong end of two versus one.

I kept quiet. I stopped asking questions. I let Jay and Izzy grow closer and closer, flirting in their own specific way which was usually Jay telling Izzy to shut up or Izzy asking her if she'd seen this thing or that thing. There was a thought that I kept in my head though. A thought that I played with and massaged. If it was possible that a Bettor could put boots on the ground to fulfill a generation, like say, the firecracker scenario, or Alexa paying that brute to slice me up in her kitchen, then it would stand to reason to not trust or get into bed with Bettors. And if a Bettor wasn't making any money and was bad at chinsky and was only on, say, Page 100, then it'd behoove said Bettor to get in close with a rising stock. Like a girl with a vendetta and a low-life with a moniker like Blue Bird. And maybe, just maybe, this Page 100 Bettor was playing the longest con imaginable for the biggest Leb payout in history. But it was just a thought. Too early to tell. But a thought nonetheless . . .

Another thought, adjacent to this, concerned Ellery and her car wreck. There were seemingly two types of AI generations on chinsky: fully "organic" unmanipulated ones that require no human interference, and the rigged, improbable ones that require a human touch on the Rube Goldberg machine. Ellery's sat right there in the gray. A car accident. In the first version, it really was just a freak prediction of data and intersections and car collisions and the road pavement and tire pressure and the mass and velocity of the truck and the this and the that. Sterile numbers. Just input and output and 7100000cvc9e plugged it all into his mean, ugly calculator. Or it's the second option. 7100000cvc9e said she'd get hit by a car at this time and then paid a trucker to do it. Which one was better? Off top, the better one was the mean ugly calculator that predicted all the factors of Ellery's demise. I had already come to terms with it. It's cold and sterile, but it's a grim reality. $X+Y=Z$ and here's the video depicting it. In that capacity, the elements are being used as tools. No more dangerous than a screwdriver and an abacus, or at least that's what the Computer Boy would have you believe. But the fact is, the person wielding the screwdriver and abacus can't just shrug off their work, and they should subsequently get killed by a firing squad. But that's just me. Which one was scarier? Now this one troubled me. Somehow there was a scarier development than Computer Boy and his Calculator. It was when the AI started generating its own things, hallucinating data and outcomes, and the Computer Boys, so enamored with it, set out to make it come true. Now the cause of Ellery's death could go either way, so the real, easier question is, which one gave me a better chance at shooting him in the head?

>

Christmas came in a similar fashion to Thanksgiving. Jay and Izzy exchanged gifts. Izzy told her he celebrated Hanukkah and that it was already over, and she told him she didn't care. That night Jay shared her sparkling cider, even pouring me a small amount in a plastic cup.

"Christmas was Marcus' favorite," she told me unprompted.

"Ellery was more of a Fourth of July girl," I said.

"Why do you sleep like that?"

"Like what?" I asked.

"Sometimes I wake up and you're underneath your own cot."

"I am? I never wake up down there."

"Maybe you sleepwalk."

"Sleep haunt is more like it," Izzy said. He was pouring himself more cider. "The Wax Man lives."

"I'll work on it," I said.

>

Things got hairier in the spring when the weather turned. Patches of mud covered the land. Dead trees were born anew, climbing out of the snowfall like soldiers reanimated. Birds chirped loudly and sang us awake. I was skin and bones. The Spam and Gatorade we'd been surviving on had turned my shit into a green liquid. Jay cut my hair down to the skin, but I refused to shave. I don't know why but I was still holding onto some idea of a beard, scraggly pubes that twirled out of my chin and cheeks. A spic mustache that made me want to say *andale andale arriba.*

Teddy Dameron, 24, a mess.

The man in the Stetson hat, the "landlord" of the place, started coming around more and more. Not harassing us, but one of the other trailers catty-corner from us. A woman and her young daughter, a thirteen-year-old girl, lived there. The mother was a burnout, and the Stetson would take the daughter on long walks into the woods and return her crying.

It was Jay that wanted to do something about it. She went over to the mother and found out the truth. They didn't have any money but were still on the run from some bad dudes. A gang-banger father was on the prowl for them. The Stetson kept threatening to turn them out and kick 'em to the curb because they stopped paying the rent. Then they came to an arrangement involving the daughter.

Jay suggested that Izzy should pay the mother's rent, but he was adamant against it. "I do that and then people know we have money and we're fucked," he said. He put his hand on the floor paneling that concealed the duffel bag. His eyes darted around.

"If we do anything, we'll blow our cover," I said. "We're almost a year in. We have over a year to go. I'm not restarting the clock."

Jay looked at us and knew we were right. We were on a mission with very strict guidelines. A side quest like this—stopping a rapist and saving a little girl—sounded noble and true. A real redemption for all of us. But what was the cost? More ski-masked hunters come and light up the park, spraying pell-mell at anything that moved? We'd been cut off from society for almost half a year. That's not something I was willing to nullify.

"We can do it and save her and stay hiding," Jay said.

"Unlikely," Izzy said. It was weird seeing him stand up to her. Even she felt a shift in energy. Her eyes made a plea for his good nature. They said, *I'm the bad one, not you.* He pleaded back and shook his head side to side. It was the saddest lover's quarrel all told in gaze.

"We can find him in the woods and take him out quietly," Jay said. "Nobody has to know."

"But someone will find out," I said. "Maybe the local police. Maybe some other, worse, hat-wearing rapist. It's not worth it."

"How can you say that?"

"This is just like Sanford," I said. "I learned my lesson from that."

"That was different. You went into town for a fucking CD. I'm talking about saving a girl's life."

Izzy and I didn't budge. Jay lost the vote. She shook her head, spat in the small sink, and went to my cot. She didn't talk to us the rest of the night. All three of us lay awake and listened. In the middle of the night the girl came back to her trailer, her faint sniveling just audible through our thin walls. I was bunking with Izzy that night. I turned to look at Jay across the trailer. Her shadow stayed there, immobile, curled in her sleeping bag. The mission had strict guidelines.

Around the summer the mother and her daughter disappeared. My birthday came and went, but I didn't tell anybody. Besides, Teddy's was December 1st and that's who I was now. Sammy was almost entirely gone, only remembered in old habits and burnt passions.

Everything felt like jail. I went on small walks through the woods outside but always stopped at the same marker: a small sewage drain in a shallow ravine. A few yards beyond it, through the trees, was the interstate. Cars and trucks sped past behind a wall of leaves and bushes. I was a type of cryptid, only spotted by imaginative kids watching from their backseat windows. The worst part was that I had yet to reach imago. I had so many more transformations inside of me, itching at the center of my palms, bending at the back of my knees. I knew that when I died, I'd be someone only slightly familiar. A figure from a nightmare. A Creepypasta in my own right.

I found myself wondering about Alexa. If she was out there looking for me and playing chinsky, how deep would she press her hooks into my old life? How long had my friends been dead? Becca? Jason? My family? How long ago did she cash the check for orchestrating some machine that turned an outdated pilot light into a blazing inferno, trapping my parents, screaming for help? Was she trying to flush me out of hiding? Like moving the furniture away from the wall? Or maybe she wasn't after anybody. Maybe my parents were fine. Maybe everyone was. I had no way of knowing.

I walked back through the woods toward the park and found a shallow grave. It was the mother and her daughter, rotting, dead, barely hidden by loose soil and branches. The grass around was green. The trees had blossomed and made a lush canopy of sorts, but the two were dead. The mother had a dark black hole in her cheek. The daughter's shorts were ripped and bunched up at her ankles. I turned away from the smell and kept walking.

>

Teddy Dameron, 25, missing the point.

>

Izzy kept paying the rent on time to the Stetson. Nobody bothered the three of us. On the Fourth of July the residents of the park had a little firework ceremony. We joined them and grilled hot dogs and sausages. Junkies got high. Kids ran around in sandals, stepping over broken glass. Izzy went to the crappy market and splurged on cigarettes and the biggest, most plastic bottle of whiskey there. The three of us sat in our lawn chairs and got fucked up. We didn't talk much.

When the fireworks went off at night, I watched, quiet, drunk, and smoky. Brilliant blossoms of red and blue and green. Sparkles of colliding colors and heat. The rise, the arc, the jazz fingers on the way down. Far-distant claps of explosion just above our heads, shining on our dumb faces with magnificent hues, painting our eyes and clothes and the cups in our hands. I looked at Jay, her eyes big and hopeful at the fireworks. She was sporting a buzz cut now and fingered at Marcus' necklace like she was praying to someone. We all lost a lot of weight and her Vans looked like flippers on her thin ankles. Even Izzy was wasting away, somehow skinnier than when I first met him. I saw his ribs in the morning. His elbows bent like the corners of safety pins. His Adam's apple was protruding like that cartoon vulture's. We were being consumed. There was a vampire in this park and we couldn't fight back. I reached over and poured more whiskey into my Solo cup. Around two in the morning, I collapsed on my cot.

>

In our second winter Izzy and Jay finally started fucking, or at least stopped hiding it. I'd stand outside in the cold, my fists dug into my jacket, and wait for the trailer to stop rocking and for them to get dressed. I didn't ask any questions, but the thought of Izzy being a Page 100 and playing the long game remained in my head. He was getting awfully close to Jay. Entwined in her life in a big way. I once daydreamed about outing him, Jay coming to his rescue, and me, with my shotgun and its wide spray that I'm thankful for, shredding everything in the narrow trailer, halving the two of them and then living with their corpses like a crypt keeper.

The truth was that there was something poisonous growing between Jay and me. I could tell she regretted telling the fentanyl story. I could tell she loathed me for not letting her save that girl despite the fact that her boyfriend agreed with me. The idea of her being a hero and me being the depraved psycho was being twisted. She was bad too. She was a murderer. Even Izzy was bad. There were no definite roles in our group, and I could tell it was bothering her. But I wasn't going to let myself be judged by Jay, not after she poisoned innocent people. Well. Potentially innocent. Screw it. Let her and Izzy fuck. Let anybody do whatever they want. If Izzy decided to turn on us, I'd kill him. It didn't matter anymore. Our loyalties were stiff and brittle. We had officially been there for a year and a half and had roughly one more to go. I could smell the Skunk.

"Who was the hit at Sylvan Shores?" I asked Jay once, early in the morning after Izzy went for a jog around the park. It was a stupid question to ask. It had been a year since that mission was abandoned. Jay looked at me from across the trailer. She pulled on her jeans.

"It was a mom betting on her own kids," she said. She slipped her shoes on and started brushing her teeth over the cluttered sink. She spat next to an empty tin of sardines, an odd addiction I had picked up much to her and Izzy's dismay.

"I'm sorry we couldn't do it," I said. "I mean it."

"It's okay. Getting the Skunk will be huge. He's probably got access to tons of Bettors." She spat again. Then she got her hands wet under the faucet and wiped down her neck and arms.

"Do you remember that guy in the woods with the modded face? Looked like a demon?"

"Yeah. Freaky. He almost got Izzy. What about him?"

"Why do you think he did that? To his own face, I mean."

"Are you asking me if he's 'hiding his face' or 'revealing his face'?'

"I guess."

"Honestly, he probably just thought it was hardcore and wanted to see people's reaction. I don't like to over-intellectualize these freaks. It gives them too much credit."

Then she looked at me and her face got sad. She relaxed her shoulders. "What's up?"

"I'm getting the feeling, more and more, that I'm supposed to be a different person," I said.

"You are a different person," she confirmed. "We all are."

"I'm not Sammy Dominguez anymore." My voice started to crack. "I'm somebody else. Before I became Teddy I think . . . I don't know, I think I have Ellery in me. I have my uncle in me. Even cowboys and monsters."

"What are you talking about?"

"It's like everybody has seen this play before and knows how it's going to end, but I'm still going through costume changes to catch up. And every time I run backstage there's a new costume I have to wear and a new set of lines I have to learn, and even though I don't know the lines and don't know what to say, everyone is acting like I'm saying the right things. And I've really thought long and hard about being crazy," I continued, "I lay awake in bed, or under my bed, and I think I *must* be crazy, but nobody treats me like I'm crazy. They all act like I'm doing exactly as expected. And that makes me feel even crazier."

"We have one year to go," she said. "I don't have time for an identity crisis."

>

The spring came around again, and then our third summer, and I turned twenty-six. I was down to 110 pounds. I felt light-headed and dizzy most days. I was always famished. I slept in more and when the A/C in the trailer stopped working, I just laid in the heat and sweat. I was being reborn. This was the gestation period. Spend two years trapped in a shithole and come out the other side bloodthirsty and ready to strike.

Sometimes I stirred awake and saw Ellery sitting at the foot of my cot. In my dreams her age was a sliding scale. Sometimes she was twenty-one. Sometimes sixteen, with back acne and a retainer. Sometimes she was older than she had ever lived to be. I saw her at thirty, sitting in the filtered moonlight wearing some outfit my brain pulled from a grade-school teacher some years ago. Sometimes she was younger than I ever knew her. Sometimes she was ten years old and a skeleton.

The Wax Man became a steady presence, only he had since stopped crying. He'd lay under my cot and wheeze. Ryan Vasquez would appear in the corners of my vision. Even the masked minotaur from the old house would make a cameo, his neck broken from the tub. All that carnage twirled around my head like a baby's mobile. When you don't do anything new for over a year you're forced to marinate in your memories. Reexamine. Reflect. I dissected and pulled apart every image I still carried from my old life.

>

In our third fall, we finally talked about the plan, who was still in, who was backing out. It had been two and a half

years. Two and a half fucking years. I had lost all sense of reality and was only living for the Skunk. Jay too, and somehow
our goals fell in line. I was to get the Skunk and find out who
won the Ellery video. Jay wanted to get a larger list of people
to take down, furthering her crusade, and Izzy, well, Izzy was
still murky to me.

"When we find the Skunk, I want some Leb," I said.

"That shouldn't be a problem," Izzy said. "He's probably
swimming in it. We're gonna be back on tech then so I can
make you an account and wire it to you like nothing."

"Nobody is gonna follow it?"

"Unlikely. The guy is a gambler. He's probably wiring Leb
in all sorts of directions."

"How do we get into Wet Stone?" Jay asked. "This isn't
Casino Royale."

"Oh, but you've seen *that* movie?"

"Shut up."

"Maybe we can fake something," I said. "Izzy, you used to
be a Bettor, right? Even if you were small time, you still had
an account. Had data. Played the game."

"Okay, so?" Izzy asked. He was already nervous about
being integral. Or maybe he was nervous about me reminding
him that I knew. Hard to tell.

"If this Skunk guy is a moderator, he probably takes his
job seriously. You go up to him and talk about your account
and lie about being cheated or something. The guy in the
boathouse said the Skunk's job was to make sure generations
don't go off the rails. Make some shit up. It's just gotta get us
close enough to him."

"That makes me nervous," he said.

"Good," I said. "We should all be nervous." I looked at
Jay. "It's almost November. When do we get out of here?"

"Let's go on Christmas," Jay said. "The Wet Stone is just outside of Poughkeepsie. It's like a four-hour drive. We go in one day, make no stops, and get close."

"He's not gonna be there on Christmas," Izzy said.

"Exactly. We get there, case the joint, and get comfortable and he'll walk in on us. It'll look less suspicious that way. Then you say you're a Bettor and you got cheated and want a refund. Sammy and I will sweep the bar and come in hot."

"Remember, I need some Leb," I said. "We don't kill him until I get some."

"Okay. You got it."

>

The next Thanksgiving came and went just like the two before it. We ate Vienna sausages and heated up a Marie Callender frozen turkey dish. We drank Coors and talked very little. There was nothing to glean anymore from our anecdotes. We had sponged up as much as we could from each other. I took the hint and went for a long, cold walk through the woods to let Izzy and Jay have the trailer. I came back and they were fast asleep.

>

On Christmas morning Izzy made another trade, just as he did when we got there. He tossed the keys of the trailer to some guy who, in turn, gave us the keys to a 1994 Isuzu Amigo. We loaded up the car with snacks, food, the bag of cash, and our guns. It was a four-hour drive to the Wet Stone and we set off through the fresh snowfall. The highway was barren. A car now and then passed in the other direction, its high beams on, blasting through the snowy fog of the day. I wasn't hungry. I wasn't tired. I was ready. I sat in the back and kept lacing my fingers over the sawed-off. A part of me started to miss firing it at people. A part of me missed their screams.

Leaving the three-mile radius of the park and entering the country again felt surreal. A lot can change in a year, but not much changes in two. The same types of billboards were up. The same types of drivers cut lanes and honked. Global politics changed and wars started but none of it mattered to us. Our future was so uncertain, so *unlikely*, that not much outside of the car doors was a remote concern. The same voices on the radio laughed and gamboled about nothing. Sound effects and lasers came through in tinny metal shrieks only long enough to give a break between Christmas songs.

"Turn that shit off," I said, and Izzy cut the radio.

The Wet Stone was a two-story pub with a large parking lot. It was built in the '80s but was designed to look like some colonial headquarters during the American Revolution. On Christmas Day strings of green-and-red lights hung gray and dead in loose arcs and drooping tails. A small tree and a smaller Santa sat on the front, secured down with bolts lest they be scampered off by the wind or some teenage hooligan. The place was empty as far as we could tell. More than empty. Closed. Shuttered. Abandoned.

"Goddammit!" I shouted and beat the back of Jay's seat.

"Just wait, relax," Jay said unhurried.

"Look at it," I insisted. "It's done." I slumped in the back. From the windshield of the Amigo the bar looked like a big, gray, out-of-focus tombstone.

Izzy came back from trying the front doors. He walked briskly across the empty road and held his coat up around his neck. He climbed into the car.

"Yeah, it's dead," he said, pulling the door closed. "Looks deserted."

"Two years for nothing," I exhaled. "Two years and the world moved on, because of course it fucking did. And why did we come on Christmas day? What were we thinking?"

"Someone should go inside," Jay said.

"The place is empty, Jay," Izzy replied. He was warming his hands over the heat vents.

"The guy said the Skunk played poker at a bar called the Wet Stone," Jay clarified. "That doesn't mean the Wet Stone had to be open. What did we expect? That these creeps would be playing in public with others?"

Izzy looked over his shoulder at me. "What do you think?"

"I don't want to admit that this was a bust," I said. "And since coming here was my idea, I guess I'll go in first."

"My thoughts exactly," Jay said and folded her arms.

I ignored the underlying blame in her voice. Instead, I fished out a protein bar and gulped it down. Then I tightened my sneakers and loaded the Personal.

"Hey, Sammy?" Izzy asked.

"What's up?"

"I don't wanna fuck up today. I don't wanna freeze."

"Then don't."

"Can I have the shotgun and you take this little guy?" He reached into his pocket and took out the .38.

"Watch it," Jay said, recoiling.

"Sorry."

I studied the small special in his hand. I exhaled and faced the truth. The only reason I was getting so lucky was because this double-barreled monster was doing all the heavy lifting. I couldn't hit a moving target to save my life, but I had seen how shaken up Izzy got, so I conceded.

"Yeah, man, okay," I said. He sighed with relief and handed me the .38, a little black thing with worn tape on the handle. I checked the cylinder and counted the rounds. I set the sawed-off on the backseat. Izzy had backed us into an alley between some café and a stationery store. The sky was graphite and a light drizzle came down, pattering on the top of the car.

"One more thing," I said. "Izzy, what's your username?"

There was a long pause where nobody said anything. Izzy looked at me through the rearview. He tightened his knuckles around the steering wheel. "Why?"

"Because if I go in and find the guy, that's my in," I said. Plus, I wanted to see if he had been betting on anything recently. But I didn't have to tell him that.

"You don't look like me, though," he said. "It'll never work."

"Why are you being cagey?" Jay asked. "Just tell him."

Another beat. Maybe I saw sweat form on his forehead. Maybe it was the reflection of the rain outside.

"TheDeliverator3132."

"What is that?"

"It's nothing. It's stupid. I used to be an Uber Eats driver. Just forget it."

"Remember how I said his was Page 100?" Jay laughed. "Everyone has coded names and his is after a pizza boy."

Izzy looked down, embarrassed. I almost felt bad for not trusting him.

Almost.

I opened the door and climbed out.

>

The small-town air had a different violence than the trailer park. We had left a place of desperation and resignation and were now visiting stunted ambition and claustrophobia. Well. At least that's what I was bringing. Being holed up for two years left me with an itch for engagement. I had felt like a car revving its engine, and here was a place to floor it. I was going to be twenty-seven in the summer and everyone that

occupied my new life sat in the Amigo just a few paces behind me. I looked back and caught Jay looking at me from the
passenger seat. We had our differences and our relationship
was strained, but she knew she could trust me in the field. We
made a good team when it came to shooting at people. Get in
where you fit in, I suppose. I put the .38 in my jacket pocket
and hurried to the boarded doors.

On our car ride over here we had discussed the following
steps. I was getting my Leb, getting my answers, and going
solo. Where at first, I was expecting Jay to be upset about my
bailing after hijacking her mission, if one could really call a
scattered murder spree a "mission," she actually seemed relieved to know that I was leaving after this. She had realized
that getting to the Skunk was beneficial for the lot of us and
knew that she couldn't do it with just Izzy. We had our uses
for each other, and we knew when to call it quits.

With my hands cupped against a window, it was just as
Izzy had said. The place looked abandoned. Furniture was on
its side. Strings of cobwebs dangled like ghostly tendrils from
the light fixtures. I saw my face in the reflection and jumped.
I had forgotten my mask.

"Fuck it," I said.

I tried the door in vain and then headed around the back.
At my feet was a small window that led to the bar's cellar.
It was about the size of the one I used to smoke out of, back
during my campus job. I looked around both stretches of the
alley and decided the coast was clear. I crouched down and hit
the butt of the .38 against the glass and it shattered, tinkling
along the cement floor.

I slid myself through the window and landed in a cool,
dank basement. It took a moment for my eyes to adjust before
I realized what I was looking at. It was a poker table, freshly

used with chips and cards splayed out and a pile of cigarette butts crowding an ash tray. The place still had the lingering scent of it. It had been used recently.

The basement was surprisingly festooned with Christmas garlands and holiday streamers. Perhaps they played a Christmas Eve round of poker the night before. It was a weird image that felt incongruent in my mind. These guys weren't the tech-bro billionaires you saw on TV and in the news. These guys were billionaires of a different sort. There were no flashy helicopters and newspaper scandals. These guys could afford that world, but they didn't want it. They moved and dealt and coded and traded with a sense of total resentment and misanthropic disdain for the world. If they could clear a couple hundred Leb from sourcing and providing torture porn, drugs, or even guns to African child armies, they would. Not because they wanted the Leb, but because the opportunity was there. They were slaves to the machinery of it all. They ate off plastic plates and drank red drinks with high sugar (as seen surrounding this room). They did cheap drugs and rented bad movies. And while their off-shore bank accounts expanded with fiat money that meant nothing to anybody, they still gathered around for what? Christmas? A gift exchange?

Perhaps so, because on top of a pallet of beer cans a large gift-wrapped box drew my attention. It was green and blue with little Santas on it. A tag was scribbled: *a skunks gotta spray*. I opened the box and my eyes widened. A submachine gun sat nestled in its holdings, black as night and polished like a shoe.

"Now I have a machine gun," I whispered. "Ho, ho, ho."

I took the gun out and put the strap around my chest. If I couldn't have the sawed-off that cleared any wall in front of me, I'd take the machine gun that could do the same. Let's work smarter, not harder, you know?

I held the submachine gun in my hands (the .38 still in my jacket) and eased up the basement steps into the main floor of the bar proper. The place was dusty and had the sweet sickly smell of mold. I reached over the counter and pulled at a beer tap. The spout sputtered and nothing came out. The fridges were dead. The lights didn't have bulbs. If their plan was to go unnoticed, they were doing an impeccable job.

I decided to scan the second floor before beckoning Jay and Izzy over. I climbed up the wooden stairs to an area I presumed was for administration work. A small office sat on the right with a couch and a laptop and a desk piled with papers. Through a window I could see down to the street below, to the Amigo waiting in the alley, like a turtle in its shell. I pilfered through the desk wondering what type of work would be done if this bar was ostensibly defunct.

I was too cautious to turn the lights on so I worked in the gray. Rain played against the window and the sky darkened, the underbelly of the clouds sinking lower, ready to pour. The papers meant nothing to me. Chicken scratch and code and printed-out matrices. Long thin sheets of binary folded atop each other. Candy bar wrappers and empties of Monster stuffed into the waste bin. This wasn't just where the Skunk played poker. This was his office.

I looked at the open laptop on the desk. I looked at myself in the reflection. My head was shaved to an uneven buzz cut. My chin and cheeks were overgrown with thin weeds of Taíno facial hair. I grabbed the mouse and shook it alive.

I brought up chinsky and the moderator page opened. A different perspective than the ones I'd seen. Surprising myself, the first name I searched wasn't 7100000cvc9e but, rather, Izzy's name, TheDeliverator3132. The first thing that popped up was his Leb account. He was loaded. He had been betting the whole time. He made Leb off the guy we shot in Horseshoe Beach. The houseboat on Lake Yale. When he was doing a currency exchange in Pennsylvania, he had uploaded a generation of the little girl and mom from the trailer park. This whole time he'd been in on it. His bets went back for years.

"You little fucker," I whispered.

"This is the most exciting moment of my life," a voice said.

I jerked, looked up, and aimed the submachine gun. In the doorway was a tall, slender guy with a long black ponytail. He had gauges in his ears and a spike through his bottom lip. He wore thin, wiry glasses that were bent over his small rodent nose.

"Don't move," I commanded. The guy raised his hands to show he was unarmed.

"I don't want any trouble," he said. His voice was high pitched, but he spoke low. Almost like in a baby voice. Like how an adult talks to little kids they're not sure around. "I'm just surprised is all. You really managed to go ghost for two years."

"It was easier said than done," I said.

"I expected you then, right from Donnie's house. Right when you heard about me. I was armed to the teeth," he said. "You shoulda seen this place. It was Fort Knox."

"Doesn't seem like it now," I said.

"Everyone got bored with waiting. But I knew you'd come."

"How'd you know I was here?" I said.

"You broke my window and I got an alert. Brinks." He shrugged and chuckled with a high-pitched wheeze. "I walked past your friends in the car, they didn't honk or nothing."

"I wouldn't call us friends," I said.

"I don't have any friends either," he smiled. His teeth were rotten. Eaten away from sugar.

"Looks like you had a party in the basement though. Someone gave you this," I said and gestured to the gun I was holding, to the gun I was pointing at his chest.

The Skunk snickered. "I don't really like any of them. Not in the real way I like other things. In the real way I like you."

"Why are you being nice to me?" I asked.

"Why would I be mean to you? You didn't do anything to me," he said. "Can I sit?"

"Okay."

He moved with an awkward gait to the couch and sat among the papers and printouts and bent and stained computer books and gadget manuals. His feet were small and he wore these childish rubber flip-flops. His toes were blue from his walk in the cold and his toenails were bright yellow from something else. He sat with his knees touching and he rubbed his thighs with his palms. "You have the gun, I guess you do the talking," he said, or rather, suggested. He was bashful. He kept shifting in his seat like he was nervous and had a crush on me.

From my pocket I took out the crumpled notebook paper from the houseboat: user 7100000cvc9e.

"Who is this?" I said and I showed him the numbers.

"You have the computer right there, silly, type it in yourself."

Something about this guy was making me nauseous. I think he turned the heater on because the building was getting warm and the room was getting stuffy. His body odor was sour and chemical-y and the room smelled like candy and looking at the moderator page made my head swim.

"You do it," I said. I backed up away from the laptop and pushed the chair to him. He got up with a grin and took his seat. I shot a look down to the street below to see the Amigo. Jay wasn't in the car anymore. Izzy was screaming and banging his fist on the steering wheel. I looked back at the computer when the Skunk started typing.

"Going after a Bettor is a bad idea," the Skunk said. "Highly inadvisable."

"I've done pretty okay this far," I said.

"That is totally true," he said and offered me a fist bump. I ignored it, and he kept typing.

"I should warn you," he started, "they'll ruin your life. They'll change you. They know everything about you, and they'll make your life hell."

"I'm already in hell. Just tell me who it is."

"I don't know his name, but we all call him '71 Civic and he wins a lot."

"Where is he?"

He typed some more and moved through the back channels of chinsky. He had tattoos along his hands, small skulls and sprites. Little video game things like Halo and the Triforce. Watching him navigate his mod account, I was shocked at the bland interface. No bright neon. No blood-red links. Just boring admin bullshit. "He's doing it out of somewhere in Georgia. A place called Blood Mountain. That's kind of spooky, huh?" He looked at me, smiling. "Right? Blood Mountain? Look." He turned the laptop to me and showed the coordinates. I scribbled them down on the crumpled piece of paper.

"Who is he?" I asked.

"I don't know. He just plays the game and is good at it," the Skunk said. "Your friend down there is good too," he said. He was referring to Izzy. "Pretty ballsy to be betting on the outcomes of your own adventure. That's some real 4-D chess, man." He laughed a light, squeaky laugh. There was no mocking in it, which I found more disconcerting. He seemed like a child.

"I want his Leb," I said. "All of it."

"Okay, I'll make you an account really quick." He started typing, and I studied his office a bit more. Pencil shavings littered the corner. Cigarette ash covered an arm of the couch. He had books. Many books. Piled high in shaky towers. All of them tech jargon and coding and software this and malware that. The room was getting warmer, and I pulled at the collar of my shirt.

"You don't play, do you?" I asked. I didn't need the gun on him anymore. He was harmless.

"No, not really. People don't like to play with me. I don't get invited to play much."

"You have a poker table in your basement."

"You know that friend that people keep around just because he's got the fun things?"

"Sure."

He gestured to the books and codes and bar around him. "These are my fun things."

"This is too easy. Why are you helping me?"

"You probably expected to come in and put a gun to my head, right? Torture me and beat me into submission, huh?" He was smiling ear to ear.

"Something like that."

"Do you know how many moderators this website goes through? Hundreds. You're not allowed to bet if you're a mod. You just watch and make sure nothing is screwy under the hood. Now imagine watching the same people over and over and over. All you're shown is how they're supposed to die. You never see how they're supposed to *live*. Then a mod falls for a subject or even a Bettor and they risk it all. They intervene. And it never works out for them. So if you had tried to come after me two years ago I probably woulda shot at you. Yeah. Totally true. *Totally true*. But then you went away for two years, and I missed you. Can you believe that? *Totally true*. I missed the three of you. Then I did a little looking inside, you know? A little soul-searching and I said, 'This ain't good, Skunkie, this ain't good. You can't fall in love with online people again. You're not allowed to intervene.' You know? But then I said, 'No way, Jose. This is the realest thing I've ever seen.' I'm tired of watching you die. I wanna watch you live."

"I'll try not to let you down."

"That's the best part," he said. "Because what I want from you is as sure as the rain."

"And what is that?"

"You are so scared and confused and you're just like us. You keep pulling and fighting and the future is dragging you on a conveyor belt and you're headed for a mouth that is big and scary, but you don't have to be scared. Not all the time. Sometimes it's good for guys like me and you. For guys like us."

"Sammy? Are you okay!?" Jay's voice called from downstairs.

The Skunk looked at me, deadpan. "There's a video where she kills me."

"I'd bet you're not alone in that," I said. "Jay, come upstairs! It's fine!"

I watched for the stairwell to make sure Jay didn't come in guns blazing. When she climbed up the steps she had her handgun poised. She was wearing her mask and because of how skinny she'd gotten, how skinny we'd all gotten, she looked like a needle. Like a pin ready to draw blood. But then she saw us and stopped. "What's going on?"

"This is the Skunk," I said. "He's helping me."

"Well, let's make it quick. Izzy is freaking out down there."

I studied Jay for a second. I had to break the news to her. "Yeah, well, it's for a different reason than you'd think," I said, and I grabbed the Skunk's laptop and spun it around. She looked at the page of Izzy's work and everything he'd bet on.

It was a second before it sunk in.

And another second before she found the video of her brother.

>

The rain clouds broke open just as we were leaving the bar. I had the Skunk's laptop and phone, tucked in a leather bag, and he followed us, stopping at the doorway, afraid of the rain. Before I left, he grabbed my elbow. "The new world is right in there," he said, pointing at the laptop at my waist, "so don't be afraid to hurt the people out here. IRL is in the past. Let them burn."

Something about that cut at my heart. The cruelty of it. The matter-of-fact way he said it, like he was letting me in on a secret. Jay was out of the bar and marching toward Izzy before I could speak. I pulled away from the Skunk, and I followed her out into the rain and the Skunk shut the door behind me and I knew he was good as dead. There was nothing else he could say that would make sense to me. The way he talked about Jay, me, and even Izzy was like his favorite show was on hiatus for two years only to come back for some grand finale. And as Jay marched through the rain toward Izzy in the Amigo I realized that he was right. The finale was starting now.

"Get out of the fucking car," she yelled. She banged on the door and banged on the roof.

"Listen, I can explain, please!" Izzy pleaded. The window was almost rolled up. He was terrified of her. Thunder clapped and the world shook.

"Get out!" she screamed and she raised her gun and shot at the window. Izzy shrieked as glass showered down on him. She reached in and opened the door. He tried to aim the shotgun, but she pried it from his hands and tossed it on the road. When it hit the ground it went off and for a second I thought lightning had struck.

"I was betting *for our side*," he screamed. She pulled him by the hair and threw him onto the street. Rain came down harder and he splashed in the cold, wet slush of the previous day's snow. "I was only getting money if *we won*!" he exclaimed.

"What about the girl and her mom—?" Jay asked. Her voice had cracked. She ripped off her mask and tossed it aside. She was crying in the rain. She was heartbroken.

"We needed money, didn't we?" Izzy yelled back.

"We looked at all your bets," I said. "You were covering all the angles."

"Because that's how you fucking *gamble*!" he screamed back. He scrambled for the shotgun again, and I pressed my shoe on it. He stared daggers at me. He tried to stand up and—

"Stay on your knees!" Jay commanded.

I looked up toward the bar where the Skunk's office was. He was standing in the window, watching. I stood in the rain with my little .38. I had already given his heat back to him, figuring he was going to need it sooner than I was. I decided this right here could be his Christmas present: a brand-new episode of the Three Musketeers. Live! 4:00 p.m. EST.

I bent down and picked up the sawed-off and tried to shake the water out.

I let Jay handle the rest.

"You bet on Marcus!" she yelled. She was full-on crying now. It was making me tear up. I couldn't listen to the pitch and waver of her voice. The whistle of her deep breaths.

"I didn't know at the time! He was just a kid. He was a burnout, I—"

"You take that back right now." She leveled the handgun at his head. He put his hands up and started weeping, begging for mercy.

"It was before I knew you."

"But then you did know me, and you faked it, and you lied to me. I feel so fucking stupid. You played me this whole time."

"No, it's not like that, I'm trying to tell you!"

"I really liked you. I really, really liked you. I thought I had you, but I have nobody. I'm back at zero. I'm back at zero *again*, I'll never leave zero!"

"You do have me, Jay, please. I'm sorry. Please. You have me. *You have me.*"

"No, I don't," she said. She motioned to the bar and to the Skunk upstairs watching us. "They have you. They've always had you." And then she shot him.

He fell backward into the muddy snow. Blood poured out of his narrow chest and he grabbed at it like he could stop the flow and put it back in. He stammered a bit and coughed and tried to crawl backward.

"Who wins now? Huh?" Jay called. She turned toward the Wet Stone. The Skunk was still watching from the window, enthralled. "Who's getting paid now? When I do this?" She put the gun to her head and then pointed it at me and I flinched and backed up. "What about when I do this?" she screamed and fired a few rounds at the bar and at the window. The Skunk ducked out of the way but then peeked back out, too hooked to look away.

"P-p-please," Izzy said. He was fading fast.

"I don't know who wins next, but it's not gonna be you," she said and then she shot him in the head. He fell back dead, and she stepped closer and emptied the clip. I waited by the car for when she was done.

>

Jay didn't speak much during the drive back, and I didn't want to push it. We were close to parting ways, the fork between us approaching, and I think we both wished it would hurry up.

"Leave me with the money at Pine Lake," she said. She was referring to the duffel bag of cash Izzy had procured.

"You sure?"

"I'm gonna get that cowboy rapist and take it from there."

There was a beat.

"I'm sorry about Izzy," I said.

"Fuck him," she said. She wiped her eyes and looked out the window. "Why didn't I look at his other videos? Why didn't I just scroll a little bit more?"

"I think you wanted to believe someone was on your side."

There was another beat. Minutes passed. The rain let up,

but only for a moment. It came down again trying to become snow.

"Are you gonna chinsky your family?" she asked.

"It's all I can think about," I said.

"Then they got you right where they want you."

"I'm pretty sure I'm not going to get out of this."

"None of us will."

>

At Pine Lake Park, I pulled the Amigo to the side of the road. Large trees flanked us. I took Izzy's duffel bag and counted out the cash. I gave Jay most of it and kept a few grand for myself. She took the money and her handgun and stuffed them into a small backpack.

"So, this is it, huh?" I asked.

"I don't have a lot of nice things to say about you," she said. "But I hope you get that Civic motherfucker."

"Thanks."

"What are you gonna do about that Alexa girl? She's still out there."

"I don't know."

"Do you think it's her?"

"I have no idea."

She grunted and shut the door behind her, but then turned and braced herself against the open window. "I'm not out of the game," she said. "If you do some fuck shit, I'll find you and kill you. Okay?"

"You've said that a million times now."

"Just don't be surprised when you see me again. I've searched all of your names. All of them."

"Bye, Jay."

"Yeah."

"And hey," I called. "If you can save that guy's hat, I'd love to have it."

"I don't know if you can pull it off, but I'll think about it," she said. Then she turned and moved down the path through the trees. After a moment she disappeared between the brown and gray of the forest. It was about thirty-five degrees and dropping. Patches of snow from the previous day had yet to melt away, collecting on twigs and moss and dead leaves. A few yards along she'd break the perimeter of the park. With the money in the bag, she'd find a trailer no problem. Find work easy enough too, now that she needed it. But if she threw it all away just to put two in the chest of that Stetson, then I'm sure she'd be happy enough still, even if she couldn't undo Izzy winning that round in the first place.

>

It was about a thirteen-hour drive to Atlanta, and I couldn't make it in one go. About halfway there, I pulled over to a gun shop and bought a box of shotgun shells and then I went over to a Red Roof Inn. I brought in my bags, the cash, the sawed-off, and everything I took from the Skunk.

The room was claustrophobic and ugly. One tiny bed sat like a rotten tooth a few degrees crooked from the wall. The curtains were heavy and plastic. In the bathroom, the shower head was too low, and I had to duck under just to get clean. I locked the front door and pushed a desk in front of it. I locked the windows and closed the blinds tight, even taking extra towels and hanging them from the rod to prevent anybody from peeking in. I flipped around furniture and plants looking for cameras. I caught myself laughing. It didn't make a difference.

On the Wi-Fi I loaded up chinsky for the first time in over two years. I started to sweat, naked on the bed, wondering who would have that golden ring. I looked up my parents first. I typed their names in the search bar and watched the page load. There was a golden ring, and my heart broke into pieces. It was shocking, that feeling. I thought I was too desensitized or broken or resentful. But it was just like Jay had warned: *more real than you can imagine.* My throat tightened and I couldn't find my voice. I burst into tears, crying for the first time in ages, my hands shaking. SPIC COUPLE GETS REKT was the link. I watched iPhone footage of my parents, bound and gagged, duct taped together in their king-sized bed. A man in a mask was stabbing each of them, alternating, back and forth. The blood poured down the silver of the duct tape and darkened the mattress. They tried to scream but couldn't. They died pale and gray, the bed they once bought together from Sears now a crimson platform like some sort of altar.

I screamed. I grabbed the lamp from the nightstand and hurled it against the wall. It shattered into pieces and the light bulb exploded in a tiny nebula of bright-blue glass. The room dropped into darkness. The shut-out curtains I crafted worked almost too well. I sat before the laptop. The gold around the link shimmered back and forth. The username that won, the one who uploaded the generation, was xx8243xug. I was still logged in as the Skunk. I clicked the username and saw what else they'd done.

I scrolled back two years ago and found it. The video they'd bet highest on and lost. It showed none other than myself being stabbed to death by the intruder in the empty house. This was Alexa's account. She was xx8243xug. Just as I feared, while exiled in Pine Lake Park, she had gone about trying to flush me out. She had set up my parents' murder and made an orphan out of me. The walls of the motel closed in. I shut the laptop and let the darkness swallow me.

In the morning, around dawn, cold rain attacked the front window and a clap of thunder woke me. I gasped, forgetting about the darkness I brought upon the room. I stayed there on top of the bed, naked, right where I cried myself to sleep a few hours earlier.

"I'm sorry, Mom," I said to nobody. "I'm sorry, Dad." The words floated above me and dissolved against the blackness of the room. The holes in my spirit were clogged with mold and detritus. I wanted to fit them inside of me but couldn't find room. The faintest light made a line on the floor beneath the blackout curtains and from it the image of my parents came back in hot detail. When I shut my eyes, the snuff film found its way there too, prying open my eyelids like someone looking under a bed. "I don't know how to get her," I said aloud. "I don't know where to start," I blubbered.

I had been gone for two years and my parents died thinking I was missing. They died thinking that I'd never return. For two years I was a sepia photo being passed around only for the roles to reverse in a Red Roof Inn. I thought of the voicemail I left my mom. Was she already dead then? Did she even listen to it? Then, a realization made itself clear. When the duct tape was out and the knife was drawn, my parents died *certain* it was the curse. And maybe it was.

I looked up others to see if they were killed because of me.

I searched Becca's name and jumped off the bed with relief. There were no golden rings. I clicked a video only to pause it and admire what she looked like now. Her mop of thick brown curls had been tapered and sheared into a more manageable and trendy cut. She was coming out of some hip coffee joint in Portland. She was pretty and wore tons of bracelets. She had a car and a cute little backpack and likely the dream job she left me for. I was proud of her. Proud of this digital generation of her. The video title suggested that she was going to shortly be murdered in a carjacking, but I didn't need to watch it. Her video was ringless. Which meant she was alive.

I clicked around and found a video of her being murdered in her house. I got the address and wrote it down. I had to get back to her. Me surprising her at her doorstep was reckless, but I didn't have a choice. It was a last-ditch effort to save myself and reclaim love and maybe even restart my life. If she didn't want to see me that was fine. But I had to try.

Jason was still alive too, but something was wrong. A video by xx8243xug was being bet on. It was Alexa and her fan base, and she had a streak going. Jason is going to enter his place, see Maria dead on their AptDeco sofa, and then he's going to get stabbed in the stomach by the same brutes who did my parents in. And it was going to happen soon.

But I was still logged in as the Skunk, so I had the power. I clicked Alexa's username and saw that the video was uploaded near Jason, not a mile away from his apartment, probably so she could help facilitate if things got bad. The little cheater. I had to beat her at her own game and bring her out to Jason's place. I banned her account and then deleted all of her submissions. She was now flying blind. That was sure to piss her off.

Now the agenda had changed. Save Jason from Alexa. Kill Alexa. Try to find and then kill '71 Civic. Go to Portland and live happily ever after with Becca, who hadn't seen me in four years. Maybe I explain everything, grapple with depression and PTSD, and then hang myself at forty, leaving her and some kids behind. A happy ending, all things considered. I

remembered a vague tip about coping with grief. Give yourself one mission every day. It could be getting out of bed,
or brushing your teeth, or making some coffee. Then you'll
do two missions. Then three. My favorite uncle was long in
the ground, then my soulmate was, and now my parents were
freshly dead, and here I was laying naked on a bed in a dark
motel. I had a few missions on the docket and I had to go
now. Just like what Alexa said about coping, there were troubling ways and there were healthier ones.

>

I pulled up to Jason's complex six hours later. It was almost
noon and it was cold and gray in the strange twilight between
Christmas and the New Year. I kept my head on a swivel and
held the sawed-off, concealed by the duffel bag. At this moment, Alexa was probably gnashing her teeth and making a
throwaway just to log in and see what posts were winning. It
was a mad dash for the gold. The gears were in motion, but
the website of chinsky was working against her. She'd be a
no-name account with zero wins under her belt and was likely
to get filtered to the bottom of the algorithm. The question
was a different one. Offline, will Alexa come after Jason just
to spite me? I knew I hadn't hobbled her fully. It was only a
matter of time before her bettors and fan base realized her
new account was legit, but by then I was expecting to have
her bleeding on cement somewhere.

   In the elevator, heading up to Jason's place, I felt another
particular sense of pride. It was the type that dipped into
jealousy. The nice carpet and heated floors and friendly neighborhood with the big parking lot and easy commute could've
been mine. Gone were the days where we got piss-drunk on

Rolling Rock and leapt from furniture to furniture playing True American with our other friends. Ellery laughing hysterically, high with someone in the kitchen. Me, talking out of my ass, trying to explain the grand plan of things post-graduation. *Do this, Jason. Do that. You'll get this. You'll understand later. Etc. etc.* Sure enough, the opposite occurred. I lived in a trailer park for two years as an unhinged gunman. He had made something of himself, and I couldn't let Alexa and whatever depraved henchman she'd hired take that away from him. I'd even save Maria if I absolutely had to. Kidding. Of course I would.

The doors parted and I peeked down the hallway. The white walls and brown-and-cherry carpet. Each white door with a little brass knocker and fun metallic number. Some had shoes outside. Some had kids' drawings taped under the peephole. "Leave delivery here." "The Robertsons." Cuteness all around. I hurried with the duffel bag to Unit 8J. I knocked on the door and Maria opened it, shocked, her face wide-eyed and confused.

"Holy shit," she said.

I remembered what I looked like. Rail thin. Jeans held up by rope. Shredded sneakers. Shaved head with pubic facial hair.

"Can I come in?"

"Yes, definitely." She backed up and let me come in. It was the apartment of a well-to-do couple. Everything on the walls and along the counters and side tables gave the unmistakable suggestion of what could've been. Even positing Ellery's death, this could've been mine if I made only a handful of different decisions. But here we were.

"We thought you were gone," Maria said. She was pale. She was in small shorts and a T-shirt and her home office was up and running behind her. A desk with a laptop, reams of articles, highlighters and pens. There was a cute coffee mug. A Keurig. One of those lamps that dim when you touch the base of it. Large glass windows with beige, well-woven blinds. The scent of a candle, probably Etsy'd over. And of course, her Le Creuset ware. Then there was me, looking like an urban castaway. She looked at me all over.

"Holy fuck, man."

"I was off the grid for a bit, yeah," I said. I passed her and looked around the place, unsure for what. I even caught myself checking under their master bed.

"What the hell is going on? What are you looking for?"

"Where's Jason?"

"He's at work. He comes home in a few." Then her face changed. It went to fear. "I heard about your parents. Sammy, I am so fucking sorry. That's just . . . What happened was . . ."

"Look," I started, "I don't know how to explain this, but the people that got my parents are coming here. For you and Jason."

"What?"

"Welcome to the spiral," I said. I dropped the duffel bag on their kitchen island. I unzipped the bag and took out the gun and she freaked.

"What the fuck is that?"

"Do you know how my parents died? They were murdered. Taped together in bed and stabbed to death by a big motherfucker in a ski mask. You get that?"

"I—"

"That same guy is coming here to cut your throat open right on that couch. Then Jason is going to come in and he's going to spill his guts all over the floor right here."

"What are you saying? How do you know?"

"Because I *saw it*, Maria!"

It was like when I told my dad about Aunt Eliana. How I saw Death. How we were buddies now.

It took a second before I saw Maria's wedding ring and her pregnant stomach. She saw me noticing and touched her belly. "Jason wanted you to be his best man, but we couldn't find you."

Tears stung my eyes, and I wiped them away. Then someone moved behind the front door. I raised the gun and, on instinct, surprising myself, moved Maria behind me. A moment eked by. We both felt the presence on the other side of the door. The subtle shift of weight only a few yards away. Something dark and sinister, breathing right in front of the peephole.

"She's pretty pissed, you know," the guy said. His voice was darker and heavier than expected. It wasn't raspy or guttural. It was a voice for radio. Eloquent and articulate. I could almost imagine the polished teeth and gentle smile behind the cotton.

"Who is that?" Maria whispered. I put a finger to my lips. "But who the fuck is that?"

"Your friend is in there too, right?" the guy said, and I winced.

"Don't worry about her. I'm gonna shoot through this door and cut you in half," I said. Maria backed away more and crouched behind a side table. She grabbed her phone and I turned and knocked it away from her.

"No cops," I whispered. She looked at me like I was crazy. I looked back at the door. "Tell her to come here herself."

The voice was quiet. The presence was still there though, like an unseen black hole. It swallowed our attention and our energy. If I kicked the door open, Maria and I would de-atomize in seconds, obliterated by its gravity.

"She doesn't have an account anymore," I said. "There's no payout. I deleted all her shit. She's back down to Page 1000."

There was a beat.

"I'm gonna wait outside for your buddy," the voice said. His heavy boots disappeared down the hall.

The seconds passed like slime. I backed away to Maria who was shaking, lips trembling with fear. I told her to call Jason and to direct him far away. "Don't say specific addresses. Just keep him away for a bit, on an errand or something," I said. It took her a moment to realize that, yes, I was still very serious, and she moved to their bedroom.

I opened the Skunk's laptop and went back onto chinsky. In seconds, I was probably going to be reported and kicked off the account fully, so I had to be quick. I found the yellow pages for Jason's deaths and I locked it. Now nobody was allowed to bet, view, or do anything. I pulled up Maria's and did the same. Becca's too. And right as I pulled up my own, the site kicked me out. "Fuck!"

Everyone was probably getting real mad right about now.

To be frank, I didn't have much of a plan, nor did I have the time to come up with one. I needed to bring Alexa to me, but I knew that, first, I had to get Maria and Jason far away from this place.

"Find out where Jason is going and meet him there," I started, "then don't come back."

"Ever?" Maria asked. She came out of the bedroom hopping into jeans and pulling on a jacket. Her eyes showed fear and sadness and a genuine concern for Jason and the life she had built for him. How can you hate someone who cries for the same reason you do?

"I'm sorry, by the way," I said. I didn't know where I was going with it, but I had to say something.

"What do you mean? For what? This?"

"No, well, kinda, yeah. I'm sorry I've been so shitty to you. The whole time we've been friends I was a shithead. But I was just afraid you were taking Jason away from me. I didn't want to lose another friend, but that wasn't fair to you. You were never taking him away, you were just making him better and I should've let you. So, I'm saying sorry."

"While holding a gun."

"Also, years ago I stole the lid to your orange pot. In case you ever wondered."

"You're such an idiot."

"I'm sorry."

"Just fix this."

"I plan on it. Go out and stay away and don't ever say aloud where you're going. Don't even Google it on your phone or anything. In fact, once you decide, lose the phone entirely."

"What are you gonna do?"

"Alexa wants her money, so I gotta bring her out."

"Alexa Ritter? Is she doing this?"

"Do you know her?"

"When you vanished, she kept asking us about you. We didn't know what to tell her. I don't even know how she got my number."

"Tell me her number, I need it."

She took out her phone and slid it across the dining table. I put the digits into the Skunk's phone. I slid hers back. "Come on, you gotta go."

I hurried to the door and slowly opened it. The hallway was empty. I almost tricked myself into seeing the footprints of the large boots that were just there a moment ago. I closed the door again and dug into the duffel bag and pulled out Izzy's .38 from Wet Stone. I handed it to her.

"I'm not taking a gun," she said.

"Maria, please. Take this. Point it at anybody that gets too close. Anybody."

She took the gun in her hand and examined it. She held it like it burned her. I put my hand on the doorknob again.

"Isn't someone out here?" she asked. She was scared. She had her bag on and running shoes.

"It's clear right now. Use the stairs, run to the car, I'll watch you from the window."

"Are you staying in my apartment?" she asked.

"Not for long. Go."

She hurried out and I spun the gun to either end of the hall. Whoever had been outside the door was no longer there. I ran with her down the hall to the door to the stairwell. I watched Maria disappear. Her panicked breathing and footsteps echoed loudly, bouncing off the concrete steps and metal railing. Then I shut the door and ran back through her living room to the far window by her TV. It looked out onto the parking lot, and I recognized her car from college. Jason and I used to make her designated driver so we could get ripped on Golden Monkeys and hot wings. It was a cute little Jetta. I stood there with bated breath and waited for her to appear in frame. It was a little after noon now and the sun was still trapped behind a fine layer of winter gray. Further in the distance the clouds broke and the pure blue of what was promised advertised itself. But that was far.

She appeared in the parking lot and hurried to her car. My eyes darted to the other cars nearby and to the strangers on the sidewalk. Within seconds she was in the Jetta and pulling out of the lot.

I moved to the Skunk's phone and texted Alexa: They're gone. I banned you from chin. Let's meet if u want back on.

She texted back: Ur bluffing.

I got the skunks phone and comp. who's bluffing?

monkey with a football

u sure? I've learned a lot since you last saw me.

It took a bit before she replied. I turned off the lights and drew the blinds. I stayed in the soft gray of Maria and Jason's place. I felt like a squatter. It was a strange sensation to see the adorned walls and bric-a-brac of them as a couple. Near the TV was a small framed picture of me and Becca with them at a bowling alley, the week before I decided I had to break up with her. I still remembered how upset Maria was with me. She had been right all along.

Finally, Alexa texted. Fine, where?

come up here to their room, you know where it is. and come alone.

I moved to the front door, unlocked it, and kept it ajar. I made sure the sawed-off was loaded and I hopped behind the couch and nestled the barrel along the spine nice and leveled, pointed at the small hallway where she'd be entering. There was a part of me that still needed answers, but what was the point? What answers could she give me? Why did she kill my parents? That was clear enough. Why was she doing this at all? I doubt she had some master scheme. That's one of the lessons I'd gleaned since hitting the road with Jay and Izzy. Nobody really had a master plan. They followed their guts. Followed the Leb.

I thought of what the Skunk had said before I left the Wet Stone. Leave IRL in the past and don't be afraid of who you hurt in the real world. I had to resist it. But every move I made set me further down the path. And the worst part was that I was still attracted to it. Deep down, I still had to see. Had to know. Ellery's voice rang again in my head. "I want to *not want* to be online."

A moment passed and I felt my hands start to cramp. I shook them out and placed them back along the gun. I hadn't eaten in too long and was getting queasy with anxiety. I heard the elevator doors ding open and I heard footsteps approach. I crouched lower. I was barely peeking over the couch, but I could spray down the few yards ahead. Softly, the door opened. Her silhouette was narrow-framed, thin, her hips defined in denim.

"I'm alone," she said.

"For real?"

"For real," she said. "Come out from hiding." She took a few steps into the apartment. Her face wasn't all that clear yet. From the shape along her side, I could see she was wearing a messenger bag. The light from the hallway backlit her and her shadow stretched toward me. I'd had a lot of nightmares about a lot of things and she was checking all the boxes.

"If I kill you nobody is gonna come avenge you," I said. "You're a nobody on chinsky. I made sure of that."

"I have to admit, playing the mod was a great move. Too bad they found the real Skunk and chopped his head off." She shifted and her head turned to me. "Oh, there you are." She waved at me from the hallway. I still couldn't see her face, but her voice was the same. The almost bratty lilt to it. The sound of: *Yeah, I'm a wiseass and you love it.*

"Why did you do all of this?" I asked.

"Ask something else."

"Did you plan this from the beginning? Since group?"

"Yes."

"Why?"

"I told you, ask something else."

"Why did you kill my fucking parents?"

"The Leb was great. The legend around you too. Really awesome stuff. Calling you Blue Bird, Civic and your girl, all of it. It's like you came to the underworld to bring her back, only you got lost too."

"You know I have to kill you," I said.

"I'm here, aren't I?"

I got nervous. Rearranged myself on my knees. Pulled back the hammer.

"Why are you making this easy? Why is everyone making this FUCKING EASY?"

"Because I've seen the end result of this all. And it's beautiful. The way things go. The way things end for you. I've seen it. The highest-rated one. The Skunk saw it too. It's something out of a movie. And if that's the part I gotta play, then that's the part."

"I die, don't I?" I asked.

"Oh yeah. And it's incredible. When you torched my account, I was pretty pissed about the Leb, I won't lie. But then I took a step back. Saw the bigger picture of it all, the path of things. And holy shit, you're not even ready."

"What happens to me?"

"Can't tell ya. After this you're going for '71, right?"

"That's right."

"That'll be fun for you."

"Turn on the light right there, I wanna see you."

She did. The lights came on and she blinked once or twice to adjust her eyes. Two and a half years had passed since I saw her, and she looked the same. She was in a heavy blue sweater and black jeans. Her brown leather bag, probably holding her laptop, rested against her hip. She was pretty. She had always been pretty. Her thin eyes and dark straight hair. Her high cheekbones and small mouth. Her olive complexion and thin, small hands.

But something seemed wrong. Something gnawed at the base of my skull. I hadn't seen her in so long, what if this wasn't even her? What if this person was just modded? Wearing the latest in Alexa Ritter plastic surgery? Alexa herself wouldn't just give up and walk over like this, like she was tired of the game, no chance. But she'd trick me though, one last time, have all her lunatic friends play with reality for one big finale.

This person, wearing a mask, showing up, wasn't so different from what I had been doing. I squinted at Alexa's face, her cheeks, her neck. Wasn't it her? Could it really be? I heard Jay's admonishment next: *don't over-intellectualize these freaks, it gives them too much credit.*

Maybe the truth of it really being her was just too much to bear. It was hard to admit to myself that I had been played. She was committed to some cause bigger than the both of us, but *cause* wasn't the right word. It was like she saw the glimpse of a painting and knew what she had to do. She knew what stroke she needed to be. Paint her the color of silver crud and watch her fall into place between black curves and chrome skulls. The painting looked like garbage until you took a few steps back and saw the entirety of it, at least to her, at least I imagined. It was actually a macabre masterpiece. Some ruthless Giger spectacle that made you queasy. She was in love with whatever she had witnessed and there was no going back from it. I was her painting just like I was the Skunk's TV show. The scariest option of all, people bowing to the generation.

"What was the post?" I asked.

"What?"

"The post you read that made you do all of this," I said.

"Freshman year you wrote about Wax Man stalking a boy and his volleyball-player girlfriend. I thought it was sad and beautiful and I read it on Campfire on a whim. I didn't know it was you, but I kept reading Blue Bird's stuff. All of your trauma you unloaded on that stupid forum. Then when I found chinsky myself I had searched name after name after name. One day I typed in Wax Man, and I saw that it was you. Saw that you were on my campus, going to class with me, eating at the same cafeteria as me. And you had no idea. The number-one-trending video for how Wax Man dies hasn't changed in the five years since I first saw it. Sometimes it dropped down a few spots when things got hairy, but it always moved back up. It became an obsession to everyone I knew. To everyone that played. How long could we keep this post trending. How long could we keep this generation accurate. We had all decided to make this prophecy fulfill itself. To set some sort of record. We knew that if Ellery graduated, you'd leave and move on and we'd all lose our favorite game. It was '71's idea to kill her off, and some of us pooled our money to make it happen. Sure, it was cheating, but we didn't care. We had our own game going. The internet knew who you were going to become way before you ever did. If that's not something to marvel at, dude, then you're just blind."

"It wasn't a real car accident then. Someone crashed into her on purpose."

"Correct."

"So some algorithm decided who I was going to be and that's it? The rest of you decided to make it so?"

"I know what you're thinking," she said. "If we didn't do anything would all of this have still happened?" She shrugged. "It's pretty fun to think about, isn't it?"

She stepped forward and the Alexa face smiled.

>

When I left, I had her blood on my sneakers. The bruiser from the hallway probably scrammed, realizing he wasn't getting paid out anytime soon, and I got down to the parking lot and to the Amigo in good time. I didn't feel safe reaching out to Maria or Jason quite yet, not with '71 Civic still out there doing their thing. I had to make sure he/they/she/it was gone first. Gone and never coming back.

> Be me, 26
> About to end it all
> Feels good, man

Which brings us back here. I climbed up the hillside on all fours like the animal I had been reduced to. I had a box of shells left and not a lot of hope. Five years had passed since I lowered Ellery into the ground and shrugged off any and every means of acceptable medication. I chose booze and violence and smut and sex and cruel, evil, manipulative behavior. The truth was, probably, that I didn't have anybody to blame. But I wasn't ready to hear that. The things I had consumed had exacerbated the problem. They were lighter fluid on the bonfire. And you can't really blame the lighter fluid without blaming the guy who squeezed it. If I could kick open the shed of this door and blow away whoever it was that made money on my Ellery's death, this cheater that *funded* it, then I could set something right. I'd be avenging her. With equal parts redeeming myself. Maybe add a healthy splash of revenge. Shaken and poured over misplaced rage.

When I approached the small cabin door, I didn't think to slow my momentum. I figured any hesitation would be my death. If the person inside, this '71 Civic, sensed the atmospheric change of my presence then they'd have more than enough time to prepare, but that assumption was operating on the belief that they didn't already suspect me, which they most definitely did. I think mostly, I was just ready to die.

I kicked open the door and fired the gun and someone fired back. I took it in the chest and stumbled out of the doorway and fired one more time, shearing the top of their head. Their skull jerked backward like a Muppet's and their computer burst into sparks and flames. I fell onto the mud, covered in my own blood and I went cold. It all happened too fast. I tried to crawl backward, but I kept slipping and losing my grip on the wet leaves and cold dirt of the mountain. Up ahead the sky was ashy and gray and cold rain started to fall, touching my cheek and wetting my shoulders. The sawed-off was on its side, useless and smoking. I tried to focus my attention on the person I killed. They sat in their chair, leaned back, their face maimed and unrecognizable.

The cabin was tiny. There was a cot and a bucket for their waste and a computer. I felt the smell of the cabin escape through the door. The place was a balloon exhaling for the first time in millennia. I smelled Mesozoic trees and sulfur from times before then. The rot and stench of their piss and shit and cum had tornadoed and came out whirling and whistling in a klaxon. The place shuddered in an orgasm, climaxing at the intersection of technology and nature and rot. It belched and stank and the person in their swivel chair, their face still unknown to me, bled onto the warped wood and broken panels of the floor. I couldn't distinguish sex or race or even their clothes. I was dying. From my perspective on the ground, dizzy and fading, it looked like the stump of their neck aligned with a monitor. Like their head was a computer. How fucked up. How droll.

I didn't have the strength to stand up. I was bleeding out and I touched the slick blood on my chest and looked at my hands. I saw my fingerprints through the red, the silly circles and spirals of my identity, shining out as if to say they had always been there.

I laid my head back in the mud and smiled to myself that I had gotten '71 Civic. I had killed the person who orchestrated Ellery's death. I didn't need to be briefed. I knew that I was correct. Quickly my vision started to go.

"I did it," I said. "I did it for you." And the wind grabbed my words like a carrier pigeon and took them off somewhere far and inaudible. The wind howled again through the skinny and crooked trees. I let the warmth of my body disappear and sink into the ground below. The wounds in my chest felt colder and icier. I let myself fade.

The Wax Man

The Wax Man is an unknown humanoid entity that has gained popularity since its introduction in 2014. Described as a well-dressed man (hat, coat, fancy shoes) with a wax-covered face, the Wax Man is second only to Slender Man in its wildfire growth.

Many variations have the Wax Man sneaking into your room and crying in the corner or under your bed and waiting for you to cry too. Once the victim sheds a tear, they will be found in the morning dead and encased in white wax.

The first appearance of the Wax Man appears in CampfireFables.com from user Blue Bird and depicts the Wax Man stalking through a suburban Tampa home. While initial posts didn't gain traction right away, the Wax Man made several more appearances on CampfireFables. com. Eventually, he was seen on NoSleep, Tales from the

DarkWeb, Real Ghosts Real People, and other various plat-forms. While user Blue Bird is credited with the creation of Wax Man, his contribution to the lore abruptly ceased. See Blue Bird for more.

r/Browsers 15 days ago

 u/LackieChan

Private Browsers?

I'm looking for a good and secure private browser for good and secure private things, any recs? I'm not happy with Tor's limited range tbh – still feels like kiddie pool stuff. Comment or PM.

⇧ 15 ⇩   ⏵ Reply   ⤳ Share

 **u/AssaultBae** 13 days ago

Would check out Bravery or SlimeStax, SS will get you *anywhere* but the onus of privacy is on you, so you know, make sure you double wrap it.

⇧ 9 ⇩   ⏵ Reply   ⤳ Share

u/JimmyChooChoo 12 days ago

Try Spyglass

⇧ 4 ⇩   ⏵ Reply   ⤳ Share

> **u/HdgeGrl94** 12 days ago
>
> Shit is Spyglass still even going?
>
> ⇧ 1 ⇩   ⏵ Reply   ⤳ Share
>
> > **u/JimmyChooChoo** 12 days ago
> >
> > yeah, it's pretty much my go to, wym
> >
> > ⇧ 1 ⇩   ⏵ Reply   ⤳ Share

> **u/Jase2000** 10 days ago
>
> Don't go on Spyglass. My friend did and that was pretty much it for him. Seriously dude. Look inward.
>
> ⇧ 24 ⇩   ⏵ Reply   ⤳ Share
>
> > **u/JimmyChooChoo** 9 days ago
> >
> > Oh hey retard I know who u are
> >
> > ⇧ 79 ⇩   ⏵ Reply   ⤳ Share

The Sanford Sentinel

Local Pastor Missing, Town Fears Worst

June 20, 2022: Beloved Pastor Victor Markelli has gone missing after gun violence in Black Bear Forest startled this small town and left three dead. Though authorities haven't officially linked these two cases, surveillance video has surfaced that may tie them together. The footage shows a lone Jeep emerge from the woods, drive to the New Voice of the Holy Ghost, and then disappear back into the woods of Black Bear Forest.

Pastor Victor Markelli has made great contributions to the town of Sanford, Florida, and his congregation worries in his absence.

"He was a good man," says Abigail Hemple, 48, local resident. "He was nice, he was polite, and he was generous with his time. He used to teach computer class to the kiddos on the weekends."

The comment section has been locked due to inappropriate language.

r/DeepIntoYouTube 22 days ago

 u/SmallFryBigFuture

Someone brought back a dead girl's YouTube account.

Not sure if any of you are watching the drama unfold, but this girl's YouTube account has come back from *beyond the grave.* The first few are her and her boyfriend on campus talking about college things and being cute. Normal vlog shit. But the others are, uh, deeply unsettling. They're like 20 seconds each and all out of focus. The comments are even worse.

https://www.youtube.com/
watch?v=7TjPn92t&list=UUhGZpTf0lPdA&index=144

⇧ 200 ⇩   💬 Reply   ⤷ Share

---

u/TheGump55 21 days ago

Jesus, this is deeply cursed. Great find.

⇧ 19 ⇩   💬 Reply   ⤷ Share

u/SlimJimCoffee 21 days ago

I heard about this!! It's like a new type of Bloody Mary. If you watch all of them in one day you'll die in a car accident o_0

⇧ -2 ⇩   💬 Reply   ⤷ Share

> u/The4400Fan 20 days ago
>
> You're an idiot.
>
> ⇧ 0 ⇩   💬 Reply   ⤷ Share

u/PattyMayoFace 18 days ago

Fuck me, look at her eyes.

⇧ 1 ⇩   💬 Reply   ⤷ Share

The Wax Man takes Portland, pt. 1

Uploaded: March 11, 2025
Tags: home invasion /assault / woman home alone / breaking and entering / enemies to lovers / lovers to enemies / guns / weapons / violence / existing universe / wax pov
Average Star Rating: 9.1

CREEPYPASTA PRESENTS:

THE WAX MAN TAKES PORTLAND, PT. 1

BY: TEDDAMERONNUMBER1FAN

When I woke up I was on the grass in the backyard of a house in Portland. It was Becca's home. I recognized it from the videos I'd seen. It was late at night and in the distance I heard a car take off. I shambled towards the back door. I knew what I had to do. I had to suck her dry.

Inside, the house was cozy and warm. A small kitchen light cast the place into a dim orange. The fridge had magnets and pictures on it. I couldn't tell who anybody was. They were from her new life and her new friends. She had gotten out and made something

out of the wreckage Sammy had left her with. I was
proud of her. The small stove had burnt pots. The sink
had one wine glass. I traced my finger along the rim
of it and tasted it. I tried to imagine her lips and her
taste and her scent. I put my smooth white hands
around the glass and quietly cracked it.

"I want to matter," I pled to nobody. The memory
of a friend saying that made me grow misty. But it
wasn't time to cry yet. Not quite. I grabbed a knife
from the block and headed for the hallway.

Her house was lived-in. There were furniture scuffs
and random papers and junk on the side tables. She
had a small living room with a TV and a cat castle.
The cat was perched on top. It was startled. It hissed
and ran off. The house was dark with only soft strips
of light coming in from the suburban streets. From
the blinds I saw a car approach. Its headlights were
off. It stopped on the curb and cut the engine, but
nobody climbed out. I moved from the window.

When I got to her room her door was wide open.
She slept on a large bed, curled up on her side, her
hair in a loose ponytail behind her. A small stone
lamp sat on her nightstand and it glowed a gentle
amber. Behind her was a window to the side yard.
I stuck out my tongue and tried to smell the place.
I remembered her perfume and the smell of her
sweat. Sometimes she had bad breath from dinner,
and I tried to recall it. On the carpet, at my feet,
were her underwear and sweatpants. I kneeled down

and balled up her panties and stuffed them into my mouth, letting the ends of it hang out like a loose cloth tongue. On her dresser was a picture of her and her brother. He was wearing a backpack and smiled big. Her too. I heard a car door open and shut from outside. I listened for anybody entering the home. Nothing happened.

I got on the floor and squeezed myself under her bed. I listened to the bed creak when it turned. I opened my mouth to collect the dust and lint that wafted down from the bottom of her mattress. It was a tight fit and I took shallow breaths, trying to flatten myself. I made my feet go duck footed. I deflated into paper. My hat got caught and tugged a bit sideways and pulled at the hooks in my scalp and I winced as blood came down my side burns. I straightened it out and became a statue.

Being the Wax Man wasn't as easy as you might think. There was a tricky balance. I couldn't only cry for myself. That's not what it was about. I had to cry for her but also cry as her. What was she sad about? What frightened her? What were her anxieties? I cried for her broken heart. That was the easy one, but it was only the starter. The appetizer. I cried about her brother being autistic. The financial strain of it. The hard luck of her parents. The consistent optimism they've always had for the boy. One with-held from me like scarce rations. I cried about her being alone in Portland and trying to make it in her field. How hard that must be.

I imagined our cries dancing together hand in hand in some black void. In a way, this is what she wanted when she asked me to come to Portland with her. I cried about me burning the bridge. I cried about Sammy choosing Ellery, a ghost, over someone alive and loving. Then I cried about Ellery. I didn't realize how loud I was crying until I heard her sit up in bed. I tried to stifle my breaths.

"Is someone here?" She asked. She was already scared. I felt a bizarre tingling in the area where my cock used to be. "Hello?" Her voice sounded like an angel's. If Becca stood for anything it was second chances. She was the embodiment of You can do something else. And in that regard, she was the walking reminder of the doors I had shut. She was everything I decided against. That made me cry more.

"Fuck this," she said. She got out of bed and my muscle memory kicked in. I grabbed at her ankle and tripped her.

Conversation   5 comments

RayRay
March 13, 2025
You can't just write from WM's POV, it's not how it works

> **GorillaGuy**
> March 13, 2025
> Yeah, agreed, the crying is way off – OP needs to do his homework

Ulcer69
March 13, 2025
Whoa – okay this one feels icky in a real way, I can't wait for part two

ShootinBlanks
March 14, 2025
Wait, didn't this actually happen? Feels like I'm reading something I shouldn't be (a compliment)

Guest
March 15, 2025
This is me. Please take this down.

Date: December 27, 2024
From: maria.amato@███.com
To: rebeccalsteiner25@███.com
Subject: Sammy Came By???

Becca.

Please call me or text me when you get this. I don't know if you're avoiding me or if you've changed numbers or what, but I'm getting really scared. I saw Sammy.

He came to my house with a gun. Not for me, but to save me? It was all a blur. He was ranting about Alexa Ritter from school. Please get back to me. I want to make sure you're okay. I don't know what happened to him, but I fear the worst.

Jason is beside himself.

M.

Date: December 27, 2024
From: rebeccalsteiner25@███.com
To: maria.amato@███.com
Subject: RE: Sammy Came By???

Maria,

Yes, I changed my number recently. Too many weirdo calls and texts. I haven't heard anything about Sammy. What the fuck? Is he okay? Call me at: ███████.

Becca.

MyFutureWishlist.Net

MY 2030 WISHLIST

According to the latest poll, more than 80 percent of American residents will trust AI information more than their neighbors. Political sides will design and promote their own champions that will be geared to synthesize and promote their own agendas and ideals, but it will be based on fact. I think it'd be a great fix and I'm quite looking forward to it. If I can arrange it, I can use data and information to tell these feminazis how they're wrong about so many things and then it'll be law and that'd be great, and I can finally be left alone.

MY 2031 WISHLIST

The Turing test will be harder and harder and nearly impossible and then eventually disbanded. If you think about it, it's elitist and classist anyway.

MY 2033 WISHLIST

Global warming will exponentially worsen due to the amount of water needed to keep AI hangars regulated, and so people can volunteer to cut down their own personal water intake. Doing this will get you a badge of honor and a small Tesla.

MY 2040 WISHLIST

People have their own AIs that decide their days and their routine for them. Doing the actions on your itinerary will you get points with other AIs and they'll trade us around like Pokémon. Everyone will bitch about it at first, but when everyone's lives become more efficient and more clean and waste is reduced, it'll make more sense. People that refuse will be "Off Leash" and while murder is still illegal, you'll be allowed to disparage and vilify them.

This is where I'll shine.

Date: January 1, 2025
Title: Interim Mod
//

To all bettors, lurkers, current and future mods:
Wtf is wrong with you? If you're getting this
blast, then you likely already know what trans-
pired on Christmas Day. I wanted to wait for the
dust to settle but yes, it is I, Snaggle Tooth,
your interim chinsky mod *again*.

Feel like I'm always here when you shit heads
mess up.

Patrick "The Skunk" Partinsky was, uh, relieved
of duty. Why? Because you cock sucking morons
never seem to get it through your thick skull
that you can't intervene or interfere with the
subjects. And what did Patrick do? Oh, nothing
much. Just gave a particularly hot subject his
fucking LAPTOP and CELLPHONE. He stole LEB from
TheDeliverator3132 (rip) and gave it to this spic
bastard. Why is it so hard for you losers to not
fall in love? Am I the only person that regularly
nuts around here, or are you all such backed up
cummy weirdos you bust at the first sign of adventure???? (⌐■_■)

le sigh

In any event, I'm once again the interim mod.
Please fill out the application below if you'd
like to be considered.

Also attached are pics of what happened to The
Skunk.

Viewing and Signature is mandatory.

CAMPFIREFABLES.COM

Fan Theory: Blue Bird is Alive and Well

Posted: February 10, 2025   #1

GeronimoPizza

Here's the thing – the whole idea throughout his adventure was that he had to go off the grid. But he can't do that and keep telling people, "I'm off the grid." I don't think he really died is what I'm saying. But I also think he's too addicted to never post again. So those are the options I'm pitching. He's either alive and hiding or he's posting from a brand new name?

Whadday'all think? :D

Posted: 2/10/25   #2

TalkToMeNoose

Moronic fan theory. You take a buckshot to the chest and try to survive. I know who killed him.

View Profile | PM | Quote

Posted: 2/10/25   #3

Spunch

> *TalkToMeNoose said:*
> *Moronic fan theory. You take a buckshot to the chest and try to survive. I know who killed him.*

His body was never found. Not a bad take.

View Profile | PM | Quote

Posted: 2/10/25   #4

TalkToMeNoose

> *Spunch said:*
> *His body was never found. Not a bad take.*

Yes a bad take, his body was never found because they put it in a mulcher and spread his gutties all over the mountain. I've seen the video.

View Profile | PM | Quote

Posted: 2/10/25 #5
Spunch

> *TalkToMeNoose said:*
> *Yes a bad take, his body was never found because they put*
> *it in a mulcher and spread his gutties all over the mountain.*
> *I've seen the video.*

All talk, no link.

View Profile | PM | Quote

Posted: 2/11/25 #6
TalkToMeNoose

> *Spunch said:*
> *All talk, no link.*

BirdMulch.webm

View Profile | PM | Quote

Posted: 2/15/25 #7
Haruspx2point0

Interesting take! If he *is* alive and he *is* posting, I hope you find
his username send it to me! :3

View Profile | PM | Quote

Becca Steiner
June 15, 2025

If you have reached out to me because of S***y, please stop.
I can't do it anymore. Yes, we dated during my time at FSU.
And yes, I loved him very much. If you are coming out of the
woodwork to send me links or blogs just know it's very cruel
and very f***ed up. He was mentally ill and struggled a great
deal. Only people who were close to him knew how hard he
had it and knew how much he was going through. Still, yes,
the things he did were wrong and inexcusable. If I'm being
honest with myself, knowing he's gone is painful and bitter-
sweet. He's in a better place now. I still very much loved him.
I'm keeping this post up for one month and then deactivating
my account. I'm also disabling comments.

👍 Like (2)

The Wax Man takes Portland, pt. 2

Uploaded: March 18, 2025
Tags: home invasion /assault / woman home alone /
breaking and entering / enemies to lovers / lovers to
enemies / guns / weapons / violence / existing universe /
wax pov
Average Star Rating: 8.5

CREEPYPASTA PRESENTS:

THE WAX MAN TAKES PORTLAND, PT. 2

BY: TEDDAMERONNUMBER1FAN

Becca fell forward and crashed into the wooden door
of her closet. She turned to see me emerging from
under her bed, flat as a snake, my tongue spitting
out her used panties. She screamed bloody murder.
She climbed to her feet, and I scrabbled after her.
I swiped with my knife and caught her in the back,
opening up her t-shirt with a strip of red. She gasped
and left the bedroom. I was fast on her.

In the hallway she threw a side table behind her
and I tumbled over it, dropping the knife. "Becca,
it's me!" I screamed. "I came back to you!" I was

delirious. My stomach ached for her. My mouth was dry for her. I got to my feet and ran after her some more, my dress shoes slapping against the tile floor.

"Get the fuck away from me!" She yelled and suddenly we were grappling with each other. She was strong and faster and we kept turning over each other, breaking into cabinets and along a credenza. I knocked over the cat tower and it toppled along the TV sending it forward face down.

"Somebody help!" She screamed.

I heard a door get kicked open. There was back up coming. Mine or hers? She broke from my grasp and ducked around a hallway. I chased after her and lunged forward and we both went bursting through door onto cold cement. We were in her garage. I held her down and let her get a look at me.

"It's me," I said. "I came back for you. Cry with me. Please. Let's cry it out. Together." I held her wrists as she screamed some more.

"I don't fucking know you!" She tried to kick and knee at me my crotch but it was no use. I reeled back and punched her across the face. I leaned towards the counter and pulled a hammer down. I held ove her head.

much, I wanna feel your fears and
" I said. "I need to know how you

feel. I need to know what you cry about so I can learn what to cry about. Don't you get it?"

Her eyes focused on the hammer above her. She was about to break. Then she strengthened herself. "Fuck you!"

"Just cry! Come on!" I brought the hammer onto her wrist. I heard the crack and she gasped in pain. Her palm blossomed purple. I lifted the hammer again. "I need to eat your cries. It's all I need. It's all I ever needed." I swung at her wrist again and heard something squish. She yelled in pain. The thing was shattered.

"I'm done crying for you," she said. It caught me off guard. Did she recognize me? I couldn't tell. Why else would she say that? I raised the hammer again, but before I brought it down someone fired a gun. They were behind us. The bullet went through my shoulder, and I dropped the hammer and spun out to the cement and I saw who was there.

Conversation · 8 comments

TheThongSong
March 19, 2025
I'mma keep it real with you, this is getting pretty cringey. You're not him!!

Spaghetti
March 19, 2025
Idgi, why would he attack Becca, he loved Becca, that's literally canon

ChefGorgonRamsey
March 19, 2025
He's attacking her BECAUSE he loves her, that's the whole thing. He's devastated by what he's done and how he left her but the only way he can approach her is from this monster persona so she can't be surprised by his behavior anymore. It's first grade, spongebob.

Guest
March 20, 2025
Please stop writing these. Please take it down.

Guest
March 21, 2025
Please take this down.

Guest
March 22, 2025
Take this down now.

Guest
March 23, 2025
Take this down now. I'm so serious.

Haruspx2point0
March 25, 2025
Hey, I DM'd you.

From: maria.amato@████.com
Date: January 10, 2025
To: BillWatersTampaBay@████.com
Subject: Some News About Sammy

Dear Mr. Bill Waters,

Thanks for sending me your email, and I'm sorry for the hasty DM. I should probably be telling you this over the phone but, to be honest, I'm still a little shaken up to do that. As I mentioned, I was friends with Sammy Dominguez back at FSU. I was good friends with your daughter Ellery as well. My husband, Jason, was Sammy's best friend down in Tallahassee and, well, he hasn't really found the strength to get on the computer as much since things went down.

I'm writing to let you know that Sammy is dead. There was a shooting in Blood Mountain, a little outside of where Jason and I live. Sammy was involved. Shortly after, a video went around of Sammy's body. I can't explain it better than that.

The truth is, I didn't expect this news to reach FSU Obituaries or any Seminole Alumni forums. I don't know if anybody would register it as he was a bit of a transient in his last years. But his friends need to know. And his remaining family, if there are any, need to know as well.

I know that you were close to him in a way he wasn't with his own parents, and I wouldn't dare to interpret your relationship on my own. But seeing as I was the last person to see Sammy alive, it feels odd and surreal and that the obligation of reaching out is on me somehow. Alas.

I urge you to email me from an encrypted account.

I urge you to leave out specific details of where you are and what you've been up to.

I urge you to stay safe.

M.

Blue Bird

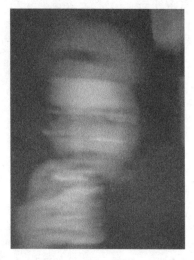

> **❝** He tried on all his different names to see which ones he could act out in. Which ones he could get away with. **❞**

> — **MorseChode**, *The Sammy Files*, ep. 4

Blue Bird is the username of experimental poster Sammy Dominguez. Often interchangeable, monikers such as Sammy, Sam, Blue Bird, Ted Dameron, and Wax Man all point to the same authorship and lore. Blue Bird gained notoriety for his extreme writing and broad posting habits. While posts started at CampfireFables.com, some readers claimed to have seen Blue Bird posts on music forums and even Craigslist listings. While the authenticity of those posts is dubious, popular canon suggests that they're all linked in what's considered a great, expansive "MetaPasta."

Blue Bird/Sammy Dominguez was a student at the public state school "Florida State University" and centered the latter half of his stories on dorm rooms and Tallahassee locals. Controversy arose with the unverified rumor that his stories weren't fiction at all, but real journal accounts depicting crimes and murders that he was perpetrating in the area.

In the winter of 2024, Blue Bird is said to have died. The only proof of this was a webm of his body that was later debunked as an AI Generation. Further information revealed that the source of the video was a streaming website with 24/7 videos of Blue Bird dying in various ways. Some believe it's Blue Bird's grand finale: endless surreal deaths of the famed contributor. While others think it's a cheap way to capitalize on another user's "success."

As of this entry, Blue Bird is #4 all-time-read contributor on the CreepyPasta Wiki.

To view the stream, click here.

Date: May 10th, 2025
Title: Death in the Community
//

Hi, all!

Snaggle again.

Phew. When it rains it pours.

Wanted to let you know that qc476rbtw87, our
beloved Priest Daddy, was found dead in Florida.
Two in the chest. It be like that sometimes.
Anyway, I'm giving the official greenlight to
get his stuff. I know he had some major rigs
and I know he was pretty big in the Skin Slough
community. And if it weren't for him contacting
us, then, as we all know, the Atlanta Showdown™
wouldn't be the lore it is today. In any regard,
first come first serve, you snooze you lose. If
you happen to claim his gear, then do the courte-
ous thing and clear his drive. Starting fresh is
noble. Don't claim content that isn't yours. I'll
find out!

Stay safe out there, freaks.

Claire, please call me. It's about Sammy.

Claire. Come on. I know u r reading these.

I got an E-mail from Ellery's friend Maria. Sammy finally showed Up.

You cannot ignore me anymore.

What is it?

Date: June 18, 2022
From: chandradominguez@▮▮.edu
To: samdominguez@▮▮.com
Subject: (No subject)

Why did you call me from a phone booth? Are you okay?

Date: July 20, 2022
From: chandradominguez@▮▮.edu
To: samdominguez@▮▮.com
Subject: (No subject)

Honey, this girl keeps calling the house for you.

Date: September 8, 2022
From: chandradominguez@▮.edu
To: samdominguez@▮▮.com
Subject: Sammy Answer This

Mijo, where are you?

The Wax Man takes Portland, pt. 3

Uploaded: April 1, 2025
Tags: home invasion /assault / woman home alone / breaking and entering / enemies to lovers / lovers to enemies / guns / weapons / violence / existing universe / wax pov
Average Star Rating: 4.

CREEPYPASTA PRESENTS:

THE WAX MAN TAKES PORTLAND, PT. 3

BY: TEDDAMERONNUMBER1FAN

In the doorway was Jay. "I told you I'd find you," she said. She looked at Becca, "Come on, get up, get over here, now!" Becca climbed to her feet and ran towards Jay. I tried to stand but Jay shot me again in the stomach and I fell down onto my butt.

"We gotta get out of here," she said to Becca. Becca disappeared into the house. Jay looked at me with the gun aimed. Her hair was growing back. She didn't wear a mask. She wore a black leather jacket and tight jeans. She had her famous blue jewelry on.

I was bleeding bad. My arm was immobile and the bullet hole in my stomach was pouring the stuff out. I ripped at my suit and felt the fibers peel from my skin, opening the wound even more.

"Have I ever heard you cry?" I asked.

"You never will, you fucking creep." She shut the door behind her, and I heard it lock.

I sat on my butt in the garage and bled out. I heard their car take off down the road. I tried to shuffle forward on my knees and one good hand. I got to the door and tried the knob. My bloody hand print smeared the wood and the knob and the cement surrounding it. I turned over on my back and started to cry. I cried loud and scared as if another version of me was in a bed nearby, listening. I screamed to myself and felt my diaphragm cramp and spaz as the bullet wound opened even more. Nobody was coming for me this time like outside of that cabin. I looked around the garage for cameras or anything. I imagined what this Generation might've looked like. I saw, finally, the painting Miss Ritter had seen. The great collapse of the solar system. Time folds on itself. I had been destined for this moment the very second I heard the cries. Maybe even earlier. Or, maybe, I had outs. But that was too sad of a thought. The notion that this didn't have to end this way broke my heart into millions of pieces. I was warned and discouraged and offered hundreds of paths yet still I chose this one. The ultimate self punishment. This is the only way that made sense.

Someone was getting paid right now. Tons of Leb. People were cheering. They were eating popcorn. They were cracking open cold ones, huddled around like I was the championship game. Garage Boy. Wax Man. Sammy Dominguez. Teddy Dameron. Uncle Ted. Blue Bird. I felt all of them pour out of the hole in me. With a broom handle I flipped the light switch and an orange light brightened the garage. I didn't want to die in the dark. I had to see what my blood looked like. I had to see it all play out. I huddled myself against the door and tried to imagine what Uncle Ted might've seen on his way out.

It didn't take long before I shut my eyes.

IanThreat
April 3, 2025
Go woke go broke, hate this shit, where are the good stories anymore!!

> **BaldEagle43**
> April 4, 2025
> Write your own then tf!

Haruspx2point0
April 5, 2025
No no no no no no no no no no no no no no no no no no no no no no no no no no no no

Haruspx2point0
April 6, 2025
OP doesn't get it. OP doesn't get anything. Wax Man can't die. Down vote to hell.

> **BaldEagle43**
> April 6, 2025
> Jesus relax dude it's just fanfic

>> **Haruspx2point0**
>> April 6, 2025
>> Go fuck yourself.

Haruspx2point0
April 7, 2025
OP who are you? I DM'd you. Get back to me, thanks.

Spunch
April 8, 2025
Why is Haruspx having a melt down?

Date: June 1, 2025
Title: Introducing New Mod
//

Hi, all.

After five long months of searching, I'm happy
to announce that we have landed on the newest
Moderator for Chinsky. It was a hard search with
literally the most applications I've ever had to
parse through. I'm talking hundreds of thousands
of applications. Not sure where you freaks came
from, but I'm happy to see such engagement in the
community.

I'd like to introduce everyone to 'Nitro Ninja.'

He's been a long-time player, and I think the
site will be in good hands. The guy is pretty
much a genius.

Hopefully, I won't have to be your interim again
for a long, long time.

Peace.

Date: June 1, 2025
Title: Saying Hi, Immediate Action

///

Hi everyone,

Happy to be here. I'm Nitro Ninja, your new acting moderator for Chinsky. You probably just got an email from Snaggle Tooth and were expecting me. I have no major changes in how things will proceed, but I'd like all Generators to pay careful attention to what I'm about to say:

There is a 20 something Black girl known as Jay aka Jalyn Curtis aka Eliza Jackson that has been hunting down various Bettors. Most of this isn't news to you. However, while some of you have started betting on who she's going to get next (which is perfectly allowed), I feel like most of you have lost sight of the purity of what we do here at Chinsky.

This isn't John Wick. There are no bounties for active pursuit. Go to Revolver Racetrack for that. While I can't stop you from seeking out vengeance offline, there will be no Leb Payout from Chinsky if that's how she is dealt with.

I was hired as the moderator for my purist ideals and pursuit of AI generations. In my years as a Bettor (some Ws, some Ls) I never once had to use an outside human force. I know the Skunk was flexible on these rules, I am also, but I do deem it a lower form of playing. Sorry not sorry. The simple fact is when you enforce a bad Generation, you train the AI to be sloppy. So, try a little harder for the betterment of our future. Capiche?

In any event, the organic, natural, untouched Generation that predicts the death of Jalyn Curtis (no enforcers, no rigging, no tricks) will be the only one allowed to win the Leb Payout and once it happens, there *will be* a thorough investigation.

I can already hear some of you groaning and moaning that 'it will take forever' but the purity of Chinsky cannot be lost in a blood feud.

Best,

NN

Anonymous 7/4/2025(Thurs)23:34

No.2828711

>WM vs FM: The Final Showdown
>Name: Ryan Vasquez
>Build: 5'10", 163lbs, scrappy
>Contact Info: █████████████
>Phone number: ████████

>Front door keypad #1185
>Alarm code #7745
>He drives a Ford Maverick, and the license plate is ████████ ██ .
>The keypad to the guest house is #225
>His wife is Lisa Fischer-Vasquez, 5'9", volleyball coach at Chamberlain High School. Phone number is ████████████ .
His stepdaughter is named Nini Fischer, and she graduated from UF and now lives in Orlando at ████████████████ .
front door code #9698
>Time range: February 15, 2026 – March 15, 2026
>>>>Who you got??

Anonymous 07/05/2025(Fri) 01:02 No:2828715

>>No:2828711 (OP)
LFGGGGGGGGGGG WE ARE SO FUCKING BACK

Anonymous 07/05/2025(Fri) 01:04 No:2828720

>>No:2828711 (OP)
Please have proof Anon, plz god don't tease me like this

Anonymous 07/05/2025(Fri) 01:04 No:2828730

>>No:2828711 (OP)
We're eating good tonight boys, Thank god. I'm literally putting on my shoes right now, ideky, I'm just amped.

Anonymous 070/5/2025(Fri) 01:05 No:2828731

>> No:2828730
>> Guy has been dead for months
>> He's not coming back
Why ru retards getting excited this isn't him

Anonymous 07/05/2025(Fri) 01:06 No:2828740

>> No:2828731
If you're referencing the pasta in Portland that was washed.
I.e., not canon and you clearly missed the point of it.

Anonymous 07/05/2025(Fri) 01:06 No:2828742

>>2828711 (OP)
Mods get in here.

Anonymous 07/05/2025(Fri) 01:06 No:2828750

>>No:2828742
You cuck, don't rat, you fucking cuck

Anonymous 07/05/2025(Fri) 01:07 No:2828755

>>2828711 (OP)
Why are you putting this online? That black girl is gonna find
it and track you down. R u that fucking stupid. She's like 10
and 0.

Anonymous 07/05/2025(Fri) 01:09 No:2828760

>>2828755
Speaking of, have you ever seen the video of her brother
dying? It's, uh, pretty remarkable. Check it:
BlackBoySplashZone.webm

Anonymous 07/05/2025(Fri) 01:10 No:2828762

>>2828760
Fuck it. The boys are back in town. Let's get a rekt thread going.
Chinesefactory2.webm

Anonymous 07/05/2025(Fri) 01:11 No:2830400

>>2828760
Shootsandladder.webm

Anonymous 07/05/2025(Fri) 01:12 No:2830405

>>228760
Guilttrip.webm
Screammuter.webm
Icarus.webm
Turkishnailgun.webm
And I got a rare one for you here too, popping its cork for this special occasion: TheWetStoneBetrayal.webm

Anonymous 07/05/2025(Fri) 01:13 No:2830410

>>2830405
I'm gonna get so much flack for this, but I think she's so hot idc.

Rating:	Teen And Up Audiences
Archive Warning:	**Creator Chose Not To Use Archive Warnings**
Category:	Revival
Relationship:	Sammy Dominguez/the World
Characters:	Sammy Dominguez, Becca Steiner, Ellery Waters
Additional Tags:	Fic, the last thoughts, magic, magic realism, shipping, posthumous shipping
Language:	English
Stats:	Published: 2025-07-03, Words: 326, Chapters: 1/1, Comments: 6

Sam's Happy Ending!
cool_whip_4_kids

When Sammy Dominguez got shot through the door he really died then, honest to God, I saw it myself, and I was so scared, but he didn't die where it mattered. It's not that consciousness came to him in a flutter of binary and circuitry, although that'd be super cool, no, it came in the form of text. In the form of a spooky little forum. Not even a few months after he got murdered he came back. People started saying all of his names. People started crying about him. People got pissed. But then everyone online started to miss him and he sensed it and he came back to life.

But that wasn't great either because it started to feel odd and fake because he started thinking of himself in the way he thought of Ellery and Uncle Ted -- photos, posts, user-names, ideas, slides, lasting impressions. A memory that was stretched thin over gigabytes and iClouds. He had lost sight of who they were and could only piece them together with pixels and profile pics. And so, like that, he had to crowd source this new version of him from things written about him. Pretty harsh!

But luckily, there were people like me and Becca and Jason and Jay and we all had nice things to say about Sammy, so we teamed up and started writing good things about how much we loved him and how much we missed him.

Finally, he started to see himself the way we all did and he got better and happier and he drove his car to Portland and married Becca. Jay was there too! And Mr. Waters and Mrs. Waters got back together as well. His parents were still dead, which made Sammy sad, but he liked the family he found. Him and Jason stayed best friends and even Maria liked him too.

Ryan Vasquez was there and his daughter was the flower girl. It was great!

Gerbilqueen & 55Lowe as well as 3 guests left Kudos for this work!

SourGrapes Thurs   Thurs 04 July 2025 12:22pm
Hey, I'm going to come to your house and put a gun in your mouth.

cool whip 4 kids   Thurs 04 July 2025 12:50pm
whyyyyyy

SourGrapes   Thurs 04 July 2025 1:00pm

Because this 1) doesn't make sense and 2) totally betrays Sammy's arc

cool whip 4 kids   Thurs 04 July 2025 1:10pm

It literally works fine? he came back and learned his lesson?

BigShotShawty   Friday 05 July 2025 3:30pm

You don't own him, Sour, let cool whip write something cute.

SourGrapes   Friday 05 July 2025 3:34pm

Whatever, this site is for smooth brains.

HATE

HATE HATE HATE HATE HATE HATE HATE HATE HATE HA
HATE HATE HATE HATE HATE HATE HATE HATE HATE HA
HATE HATE HATE HATE HATE HATE HATE HATE HATE HA
HATE HATE HATE HATE HATE HATE HATE HATE HATE HA
HATE HATE HATE HATE HATE HATE HATE HATE HATE HA
HATE HATE HATE HATE HATE HATE HATE HATE HATE HA
HATE HATE HATE HATE HATE HATE HATE HATE HATE HA
HATE HATE HATE HATE HATE HATE HATE HATE HATE HA

HATE HATE HATE HATE HATE HATE HATE HATE HATE HA
HATE HATE HATE HATE HATE HATE HATE HATE HATE HA
HATE HATE HATE HATE HATE HATE HATE HATE HATE HA
HATE HATE HATE HATE HATE HATE HATE HATE HATE HA
HATE HATE HATE HATE HATE HATE HATE HATE HATE HA
HATE HATE HATE HATE HATE HATE HATE HATE HATE HA
HATE HATE HATE HATE HATE HATE HATE HATE HATE HA

HATE HATE HATE HATE HATE HATE HATE HATE HATE HA
HATE HATE HATE HATE HATE HATE HATE HATE HATE HA
HATE HATE HATE HATE HATE HATE HATE HATE HATE HA
HATE HATE HATE HATE HATE HATE HATE HATE HATE HA

HATE HATE HATE HATE HATE HATE HATE HATE HATE HA
TE HATE HATE HATE HATE HATE HATE HATE HATE HATE
ATE HATE HATE HATE HATE HATE HATE HATE HATE HA
ATE HATE HATE HATE HATE HATE HATE HATE HATE HA

HATE HATE HATE HATE HATE HATE HATE HATE HATE HA
ATE HATE HATE HATE HATE HATE HATE HATE HATE HA
ATE HATE HATE HATE HATE HATE HATE HATE HATE HA
ATE HATE HATE HATE HATE HATE HATE HATE HATE HA
ATE HATE HATE HATE HATE HATE HATE HATE HATE HA
HATE HATE HATE HATE HATE HATE HATE HATE HATE HA
RTE HATE HATE HATE HATE HATE HATE HATE HATE HA

TE HATE HATE HATE HATE HATE HATE HATE HATE HATE
RTE HATE HATE HATE HATE HATE HATE HATE HATE HATE
TE HATE HATE HATE HATE HATE HATE HATE HATE HA
E HATE HATE HATE HATE HATE HATE HATE HATE HATE
TE HATE HATE HATE HATE HATE HATE HATE HATE HA

HATE HATE HATE HATE HATE HATE HATE HATE HATE HA
HTE HATE HATE HATE HATE HATE HATE HATE HATE HATE
TE HATE HATE HATE HATE HATE HATE HATE HATE HATE

CAMPFIREFABLES.COM

GriseldaFanboy, 2/12/2025: Don't leave your fans hanging!!! I know you're probably swamped and have a real life outside all of this. Big respect. But I love your writing and your stories. They genuinely kick ass.

BadgerNut, 4/20/2025: Hey, are you actually dead? And did you actually do all that shit? (not judging)

Haruspx2point0, 5/5/2025: I don't know if this account is in use, or if it's even opened anymore, but it belongs to Sammy Dominguez so if whoever is on the other side of this ain't him, kindly fuck off and leave it alone. Thanks.

Haruspx2point0, 5/15/2025: Sammy. Please don't screw around with me.

***Automated Response,* 5/16/2025:** Congratulations, Blue Bird! Your profile has been trending for Three (3) Month(s) straight! Collect Baubles and Trinkets on your User Flair Board. You currently have (0) stories on CampfireFables. Post more to keep your fans engaged!

Haruspx2point0, 6/1/2025: I am nothing without you.

Haruspx2point0, 6/2/2025: I miss you so much. I miss you so so so much.

Haruspx2point0, 6/3/2025: Nobody told me how much this would hurt.

Haurspx2point0, 7/5/2025: Was that you on /bant/? You have to tell me.

Haruspx2point0, 8/1/2025: I read the fanfic. The kids love you.

StinkySmellery, 8/2/2025: Sammy, it's me.

Forget the TikToks and the casual porn and the YouTubers and the content mill. Forget the wikis and fandoms and the forums. Forget the cooking recipes and the DMs and the Microsoft Teams and the Tweets or the X's or whatever they fuck they are. Forget the IG reels, the IG explore page, the IG Threads. The only thing that is real is death and dying and murder and blood. I am a man online. I am traumatized and I need people to know it. I do not want Snapchat and Habbo Hotel and Club Penguin. I do not want Xbox live or the PlayStation Network. I do not want Netflix, Disney+, or Hulu. I do not want profile pictures and bios and reblogs. No more sponsored advertising, no more log ins, passwords, usernames, or CAPTCHAs. No more points, no more scores, no more filler, distractions, or white noise. No more Outlook, Gmail, Hotmail, Yahoo, Zoom, Skype, and Prezi. I don't want Second Life, Sim City, or Meta. I don't want flair or kudos or hearts. I don't want AMAs or slash sarcasm. I don't want memes. I don't want posts. I don't want SJ Warriors or Edgelords or Neck Beards. I don't want modders or speed runs. Fuck your shopping cart, your codes, and your coupons. Fuck your next day delivery. Fuck your LinkTree. Fuck your LinkedIn. I am born, and I am miserable, and I need people to know it. I miss everyone in my life. I am sad for all the things I do not understand. You only need redemption IRL, but don't bother with it. I want my trauma to blossom like a corpse plant. I do not want to heal.

I only want to share.

Acknowledgments

I'd like to thank my agent, Lauren, my editor, Diana, and the team at Erewhon. This book was initially a short story that I pitched around to various outlets, and it was Lauren who told me to make it a novel and who believed in it even when I didn't. I want to thank my brother, Taylor, and my buddy, Julian, who gave some early feedback and threw around some ideas on how to make, not just this story, but all of my writing better. I also want to thank my parents. They are the most loving and supportive parents a young man could've asked for. Despite all of my bizarre interests, they never doubted me and, instead, bought into my dreams 100%. I especially want to thank my wife, Hannah, who always encouraged me to work less and write more. As of writing this, she still hasn't read a single word of this book because I wouldn't let her. I also would like to express some sort of gratitude to my friends who I grew up watching this stuff with. It's unfair how okay the world expected us to be, but I'm proud of every one of you.

_bluebird

stinkysmellery

rebeccalsteiner25

xx8243xug

Lou_Harding

qc476rbtwe7

Lacklechan

_thestetson

rebeccalsteiner25

xx8243xug

Haruspx

rvazquez_MD

Lacklechan

_thestetson

the_skunk

7100000cve9e·

Haruspx

rvazquez_MD

_jalyn_curtis

theDeliverator3132